SURPRI Baby!

USA TODAY BESTSELLING AUTHORS
LEX MARTIN & LESLIE MCADAM

Surprise, Baby! © 2019 Lex Martin and Leslie McAdam

This adult contemporary romance is recommended for readers 18+ due to mature content.

Copy Editing by RJ Locksley
Proofreading by Jerica MacMillian, Keri Roth, and Amanda Maria
Cover Design by Najla Qamber Designs
Cover Photograph of Lela Hazary and Nate Peterson by Cory Stierley

March 2019 Paperback Edition
ISBN 978-0-9975139-3-6

ABOUT THE BOOK

There's a fine line between lust and hate.

I don't care that Drew Merritt spent the last year transforming himself from grungy slob to sexy playboy. With messy, dirty blond hair and gorgeous eyes, his looks aren't the problem.

His mouth is.

And the stupid things that come out of it.

But after an emergency strands us together, and he does his damnedest to take care of me...

Let's just say there's one thing we don't clash on.

And it doesn't involve talking.

I've despised Drew since I met him years ago. One weekend can't change us that much, can it?

Spoiler alert: It doesn't.

Except he left me a little keepsake.

And in nine months, I'll have a surprise for Portland's most notorious player.

～

SURPRISE, BABY! is a romantic comedy and a full-length standalone. Due to adult situations and sexual content, it's recommended for readers over the age of 18.

DEDICATION

To our husbands, for their endless love, inspiration, and support

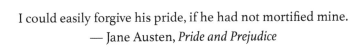

I could easily forgive his pride, if he had not mortified mine.
— Jane Austen, *Pride and Prejudice*

SURPRISE, Baby!

KENDALL

*O*ith one eye pinned on the naked guy in the plush white bed, I peel my lace panties off the lampshade.

This is a travesty.

Pink panties decorating expensive hotel décor should be reserved for truly epic evenings, but last night turned out to be a dud.

Lawrence is a nice guy. Handsome. A good conversationalist. Smart. On paper, we're the perfect match. We've gone on a few dates. Enjoyed a few dinners. Had a few laughs. He's a partner at Powell & O'Toole. He's affable and charming. Motivated and focused.

Too bad he couldn't find that spot between my legs even after a personal introduction.

My grandma Nonny always says a girl needs to take a car for a test drive before the purchase. Nonny knows what she's talking about.

Because despite how well Lawrence and I get along, despite how we're both career-minded with similar goals, when we got naked, everything fizzled faster than a soda past its expiration date. That's sad because I could really use some explosive bubbles.

Except every time he thrusts, he grunts like he's returning a volley at Wimbledon.

Shuddering at the memory, I slip on my skirt and blouse as I tiptoe around the room. As much as I'd like for Lawrence to wake up so we can have the awkward morning-after talk now and spare us an uncomfortable phone call later, I'm already running late. Judging by what he told me in his post-orgasmic state, he wants to do this again.

Me? Not so much.

I should've left last night, but I was so damn tired, my whole body ached, and that thousand-thread count felt amazing. Better than sex with Lawrence, sadly. I'll give him props, though, for splurging on the five-star hotel.

We'd had dinner at the beautiful bistro on the corner, including a fantastic bottle of wine. One thing led to another, and we ended up here. But my to-do list is too long to venture these dating waters with someone who doesn't rock my bedpost.

Is it too much to ask the universe for a boyfriend who can deliver stress-relieving orgasms and the occasional snuggle? I probably only need sex once a week and some mentally stimulating dinner conversation that doesn't revolve around my clients. Is that really an impossible request?

If I'm being completely honest with myself, no one has matched up to my ex. But now Bobby's happily married with a new wife and a new baby, living the suburban life *while* killing it in the NBA.

It shouldn't bother me.

But it does.

As if I need a reminder of what's on the agenda today—work, always work—my phone buzzes in my purse.

The screen blinks my assistant's name with a flurry of incoming messages.

If I were a normal person getting inundated by work texts at eight on a Saturday morning, this is where I'd curse like a sailor.

But I'm not a normal person.

I'm in public relations, so my job never stops. Ever. Because one of my clients is always releasing a new product or filming a new movie or getting in trouble. (*Sorry, ladies and gentlemen, my client did not mean to get head from his married neighbor on the side of the road! He swears rehab will help him walk the straight and narrow!*) And they pay me to clean up their messes, put the spit-shine on their latest pet projects, and make everyone believe they're gods and goddesses among the plebs.

I do a damn good job of it, if I do say so myself.

And while I love the adrenaline rush that comes with this gig, I'm starting to wonder how much more I can handle, which is not the thought I should be entertaining eight months into starting my own PR firm.

After I send a quick text to Lawrence—*Thanks for dinner! Hope you have a great weekend!*—I rush out of his hotel room while trying to hop into my designer heels, a rare indulgence from my old life. I have too many fires to put out today to worry about what I look like, unfortunately. Since it's almost Halloween, maybe the lobby will be too full of hungover zombie revelers for anyone to notice me. Thank God for my giant sunglasses. They're in my purse somewhere.

When I reach the elevator, I frantically push the button while I slip into my second Louboutin, but I can't seem to pull it on. So I lean my shoulder against the steel exterior for balance as I reach for my shoe.

Which is a mistake.

A big mistake.

Because I start to tilt and slide. Fast.

Fuuckkk.

"Whoa, Nelly."

Two strong arms come around my waist, and I'm so grateful I didn't face-plant on the carpet, I want to kiss whoever is holding me up.

My back is pressed against a hard chest, and I see the man's muscular physique like a giant shadow looming behind me in our reflection in the glossy steel of the elevator doors.

Hello, handsome.

From this angle I can't quite see his face, just his rugged jaw and a light brown five-o'clock shadow, but with a body like that, the rest of him has to be attractive. I have it bad for athletes, though lately I've been trying to stay away from them since my relationship with my ex went down in flames.

Suddenly, I regret flying out of that hotel room without making sure I'm completely presentable. I do a quick survey of myself in the shiny elevator exterior. My hair is in an off-center ponytail, and my face is free from makeup after giving it a quick scrub this morning, but at least my clothes are on straight. My white, silky top shows just the right amount of cleavage. It's still mostly tucked into my form-fitting skirt.

My heart pounds from nearly killing myself in my four-inch heels, but I'm smiling, almost laughing with relief because I didn't break my leg.

I'm about to turn around to thank my mystery man—because maybe something good will come from last night after all—when his phone blares "I'm Sexy and I Know It."

I pause, my face frozen, my brain flipping through an internal Rolodex of guys I'll never bone as that song rings like a harbinger of douchebaggery.

And then it comes to me.

No way.

I clench my eyes shut, willing my arch-nemesis to be somewhere else in Portland at this very moment and not right up against my ass and turning me on. Because if he's the one witnessing my walk of shame, I'll never live it down.

"Drew, if that is you about to cop a feel, I'm going to punch you in the throat."

His arms un-band from my waist, and I turn around so fast, I nearly trip again. Big hands steady me, and I slap him away.

He chuckles. "Hey, K-dawg. Fancy meeting you here."

Can he ever just call me by my fucking name? Is *Kendall* that difficult to say?

My nostrils flare when I finally see Drew Merritt face to face. And goddamn it, he's gracing me with one of his come-hither smiles, and it's all I can do to not knee him in the balls. Especially when I take him in. A snug T-shirt that showcases all of his recent efforts in the gym. Jeans that sculpt around his taut thighs. His hair disheveled in a way that makes his green eyes magnetic. Never mind that he towers over me in a manner that's both a little intimidating and arousing. *God, no.*

When did he get this hot? When I first met Drew more than two years ago, he was a slob, complete with baggy clothes, a beer belly, and a disgusting habit of getting shitfaced drunk at any and every occasion. He started losing weight shortly after our best friends started dating, but that's a far cry from this Instagram-model look he's rocking.

Drew comes from an absurdly wealthy family that founded the century-old MerrittCo, aka the famous Merritt Company Department Store chain, and is used to getting his way. Guys like him are the reason I have a job.

Because they always fuck up.

And Drew tends to crash and burn more than most.

I give him another once-over, expecting a wave of stale sex stench to waft my way, but I only catch a whiff of cigarettes and a hint of cologne.

When has Drew ever worn cologne? I want to laugh at the idea he tried to spiff himself up for whomever he screwed last night. *Ridiculous.* Drew never tries for anyone but himself. And just because he doesn't smell like an orgy doesn't mean one didn't happen.

I take a fortifying breath, ready to lay into him like I always do, because old habits die hard, when the door to the left of us opens, and out struts Lawrence.

Wrapped from the waist down in a sheet.

Headed my way.

What is he doing?

I have my answer when he pulls me into his arms and buries his face in my neck. "Hey, baby. Last night was *amazing.* Give me five minutes, and let's grab breakfast."

Drew's eyebrows hike up as he watches the guy I slept with last night—the one I need to break things off with—snuggle me. In the hall.

In front of fucking Drew Merritt.

What the holy hell have I done to earn this humiliation?

When I said I wanted a man to snuggle me, I meant in bed. In *private.* Not in front of this guy who's always hated me.

I clear my throat and peel Lawrence off me. I try to smile. "I'm so sorry, but I have a client emergency." Not a lie. Exactly.

He nods like he understands, and I nod back awkwardly. I turn toward the elevator and press the button manically. *Where is the fucking elevator?*

Lawrence finally seems to notice Drew and laughs. "Sorry, man. Just wanted to say bye to my girl."

Drew smirks at me over Lawrence's shoulder, and I roll my eyes. But he must see the desperation in my expression because he claps Lawrence on the back—hard—and then says the craziest thing.

"Sorry to steal her away, *man,* but KK here is the best publicist in the whole world, and I needed her input AS-AP or my life is gonna implode. Like"—he waves his hands in the air —"ka-pow!"

God, he's an idiot.

He is funny, though.

Then he shoots me this oddly sweet smile, and I almost smile back. Almost.

I press the button again. Drew and his nicknames. No one in my life has ever called me KK.

Lawrence's eyebrows pull tight. "Oh. You're her client?" He looks down at himself like he just realized he's not wearing anything but a white sheet. *Christ almighty, he's hairy. How did I not notice this before?* "Of course. I'll let you guys get to it."

He backs away toward his room with a sheepish grin. "I'll call you later, KK."

Drew snorts, and I wave, relieved as hell when the elevator doors open behind me.

I'm so elated to be making my escape, I don't even mind when Drew places his big bear paw on the small of my back and ushers me in or when he throws his arm over my shoulder and gives me a smug smile in our reflection once the doors close.

He wags his eyebrows. "So you did the dirty with Chewbacca?" He starts humming "Me So Horny," and I jab him in the ribs with my elbow.

"Why are you always an ass?" I ask under my breath.

Whatever. I refuse to be embarrassed because I had sex last night and I'm obviously hoofing it home the morning after. Drew's hooked up with half of Portland, which makes me wonder what he's doing here, strutting out of a hotel this early on a Saturday morning.

"Part of my charm, kitty cat." And then he surprises me for the second time this morning. "But I'm glad you didn't fall back there. I kinda like your face."

My head tilts. I don't think he's ever, and I mean *ever*, complimented me.

Are we...becoming friends? It would make sense that we'd finally be comfortable around each other since my bestie Evie is married to his BFF Josh. But Drew and I have always only clashed in the worst ways from the first moment we laid eyes on each other.

Extend the olive branch, Kendall. Be nice to him for once. He did save your ass this morning. Maybe he's finally growing out of that dickhead phase.

I'm about to thank him for being a somewhat decent human being and helping me upstairs when we walk out into the lobby, and one of the hotel staff comes bounding over.

He leans over and whispers to Drew, "How many panties did you get last night, D? I told Carlos you snagged at least two, but now I see you with this hot little angel, so maybe it's more?"

Yeah, now I want to punch him in the throat all over again. Especially when the helpful hotel employee, who's obviously one of Drew's "bros," points to the multi-colored lace hanging out of Drew's back pocket and asks me which pair is mine. At which point, a nearby mother shoots me a dirty look and ushers her three children away.

I clench my eyes shut, wishing I could channel some desperately needed Zen.

When will I ever learn that this guy is literally the last man on the planet I'll ever be friends with?

Because Drew Merritt is a PR nightmare.

Before I can say anything to him that I'll regret, I do what I always do.

I shoot him a glare and walk away.

2

DREW

*I*gnoring the shot of lust that spikes through me from her eat-shit-and-die scowl, I focus on not getting a big, fat boner in the middle of a hotel lobby.

Yeah, I'm a little fucked in the head. Why else would a woman's ire give me a hard-on?

But I'd need a whole room of shrinks to untangle my feelings for this girl.

I blow out a breath.

That was interesting.

Not the three pairs of thongs lodged in my jeans pocket. I call that phenomenon "Friday." But seeing Kendall Greer, the princess who's dissed me for years, in the sumptuous hall of the Huntington Hotel, early Saturday morning wearing a sexy short skirt—that incidentally showed off her fantastic toned legs—and fuck-me shoes...

Fancy meeting you here, Your Highness.

I thought she'd break an ankle upstairs, she was trying to escape so fast. Talk about dine and dash. While I didn't realize who I'd rescued from getting up close and personal with the carpet, I'll admit I stayed wrapped around her a beat longer once my brain fog cleared and I figured out it was her.

And boy, did she feel right in my arms.

Unless my eyes deceived me, Little Miss Priss had a booty call with Chewbacca, and judging by that post-coital interaction, it sucked. Especially since he seemed to have cranial rectosis— excuse me, shit-for-brains—if he couldn't keep Kendall in his suite for some morning nookie and room service mimosas. Clearly, if he were any good, he'd have kept her from doing a walk of shame that resembled a jailbreak.

Again, interesting. But I'm really not one to talk, given what happened to me last night.

Ever since Josh hooked up with Evie, I've had plenty of chances to bug the ever-living shit out of K-shizzle, but she's never given me such excellent material before. I'll have to think of ways to torture her about Fuzzball.

Now, downstairs, as I yawn by the bellhop stand and press a fist to my mouth, my eyes follow Kendall's pert ass as she sways out the hotel lobby doorway as if *ad hoc* sexual liaisons for her are totally cool. (How's that for big words? I went to college.)

Don't get me wrong, I'm for gender equality, and what's good for the gander is good for the goose and all that. Free love and whatnot. I'm just surprised.

Didn't think she had it in her.

With every step of hers, various forms of revenge on her booty call percolate in my brain. An image of him strung up by his thumbs while being waxed by several no-nonsense attendants strangely comforts me.

God, are those the shoes with the flash of red on the bottom? *Fuck, yes.*

Kendall's so practiced in acting just right that she exits with flair, hair swinging and petite body wiggling. She smiles and waves at the doorman in livery, then slides into her Lyft as if she has another date in ten minutes.

Leaving me in a puddle of wuss.

I can't help but stand and vacantly gaze at the foyer where she just left. What am I searching for, a shimmering after-image of her remaining mid-air? *She left, asshole.*

The truth is I always do this whenever she's around. Look for her. Watch where she went. I don't know why, and it's messed up, because she thinks I'm pond scum. Admittedly, I don't have a great track record around this woman. But every time I see her, it affects me. Like a hit from a Tesla coil.

Zap.

Right between the eyes.

Other places too.

I'm not sorry. I'm a guy, and I can't help but notice Kendall and her flouncy auburn hair and banging body, but she's been so untouchable I don't even try. You'd think I'd be sated judging by the thongs in my pocket, but you'd be wrong.

Way wrong.

"So, Drew. How many?"

Narrowing my eyes at Pete the bellhop, I cock my head to the side and shake it while my heart shrinks. The one time Little Miss Priss deigns to talk to me in a downright chummy tone, and these ass wipes have to ruin it.

I open my mouth to smart off to him, but I can't. Pete and his crew have seen some of my finer moments and gotten me out of more than one scrape. Still, I'm as irritated as a hungry, hissing opossum—if opossums wore yesterday's jeans—who can't get to his cat food.

But since Kendall has disappeared, I force a smile, turn to Pete, and lean my elbow on the concierge counter, my hair falling into my eyes. Carlos and Horace crowd behind him, backed by suitcase after suitcase of designer luggage. To the right, sleepy early-morning travelers check out. The lobby has elegantly placed gourds and pumpkins on counters and tables in preparation for Halloween.

In some ways, the Huntington Hotel has become my second home, which I admit is pathetic. If you knew my relatives, though, you'd understand. Ever since I discovered condoms and pseudonyms I've been coming here, in more ways than one.

But he asked a question. I'm not so stoked about what happened upstairs—I couldn't get anywhere, to be honest—but I have a reputation to uphold—and a room to put on my tab. Holding up the lacy things and dangling them just out of his reach, I say, "Three. The twins and their friend."

While they all grin knowingly, an Army Ranger-looking dude halts his journey through the lobby like he's yanked the e-brake on a manual transmission car. Nasty prickles run down my spine. I hope he's no one special.

But Fate thinks my life is her own personal—and very entertaining—reality show.

With the pissed expression on the Hulk's granite-chiseled face, I'd rather have a few blocks between us.

No such luck.

He's ten feet away.

He points. "What twins? What *friend*? Where did you get that La Perla?"

Uh-oh.

I guess filmy turquoise three-hundred-and-forty-dollar underwear is easy to spot if you know what you're looking for.

Carlos and Horace each grab a Louis Vuitton bag and exit, stage left. As the adrenaline levels spike in my body, I size up army dude.

The deep bass of his voice makes his crew cut and beefy arms—which are about as big as my legs—even more intimidating.

While I've spent the last year or two getting my health under control and I'm proud of my new physique, I'm calculating the odds of being able to take him on solo, since Pete has also faded into the background.

Slim to none.

Chances of me being ground into hops and made into an IPA at the Deschutes Brewery next door?

Seven to two.

Shit.

Yes, I know. I really shouldn't answer army dude's question. I should turn, walk away, and meet Josh for breakfast.

But since I'm an idiot, tired as fuck from last night, and don't know how to save my own hide, I say, with blood pumping in my ears, "Upstairs."

The next few seconds would be comical if they didn't involve a chance of getting my spine yanked out my ass. As his face drops, I see the words get processed in his brain along with the other three pieces of information in there. *Yes, dumbfuck, I ended up with your girlfriend's panties last night.*

He speaks slowly, since he's a meathead. "I gave Sadie Vandenberg a pair like those."

Here's the sad truth. Nothing happened last night. Sadie, Dana, and Chelsea had a girls' night out, and I caught them at a club downtown. Actually, when I saw them, I was stoked, because I thought Chelsea Buchanan might want to design a collection for my company, but they were too far gone to talk business. We ended up at the hotel with three bottles of Cristal and a game of truth or dare. They picked dare, which is why I have their delicates. But they were too drunk to touch.

I stayed until they passed out, made sure they were safe, dozed off around four a.m., and came to about five minutes before I saw Kendall.

Kendall.

Focus, dude. *Do you really want to get your ass kicked before breakfast?*

I don't respond, faking nonchalance, but his eyes harden and he continues, "And she texted me a picture of the Buchanan twins sitting on your lap last night at Club Styx."

With a situation like this, there's only one thing to do.

I yawn, scratch my belly, and zero in on this guy's face turning from pink to red to purple.

"Later, Pete. Guys." I lift my chin toward the bellhops, spin on my heels, and take off running like Usain Bolt across the marble-floored lobby and out into the cold, misty morning.

Feet thunder behind me.

Fuck.

3

DREW

"I'd sell a testicle for biscuits and gravy. I'm not kidding, either." Our waiter sets down our plates with an unnecessary flourish. He leaves, and I eye my breakfast with distaste. "Fucking diabetes."

I'm sitting with my best friend Josh at this Cajun joint just over the Burnside Bridge from downtown. Groups of all-nighters crowd the place, drinking Bloody Marys garnished with bacon and eating cheesy grits, fried catfish, and mac and cheese. Every day, Le Bistro Montage provides a central space to nurse more hangovers than anywhere else in Multnomah County, so I know about six people out of every ten, at least by sight.

I'm getting a lot of nods and people slapping my back, most of whom know my name, but I don't know theirs. *Good to see you, guy with the face.* My conversation with Josh is also punctuated by white-clad waiters calling out, "One oyster shooter!" to the kitchen. It smells like butter and foodgasms.

Josh shovels in his first bite of shrimp and grits, closes his eyes in satisfaction, opens them, and gives me a sympathetic grin. Fucker. "If it weren't for the fact that you know what it's like to be in a diabetic coma, I'd share this with you."

My body hurts with the memory. "This is true, my boy. This is true. Nothing like a few extra ketones in your blood to make you never wanna go there again. Still, I feel like a loser ordering an egg white omelet with spinach."

Gesturing at my mug with his fork, Josh adds, "And black coffee."

"Don't remind me." I almost gag looking at the slice of tomato. Two servings of biscuits and gravy get delivered to the couple next to us, and I stare at them, slack-eyed with longing.

The plates, not the couple.

Being responsible bites.

Not that I'm always responsible, but I can say I'm genuinely trying these days.

Josh catches the look on my face and bursts out laughing. "Better to suck it up with a few vegetables than the alternative. I'm glad to have you around even with your sour attitude."

"Yeah." What he doesn't say, but I know he means, is that it was damn scary. For both of us. I check my sugars, then grab the hot sauce in an attempt to salvage my breakfast.

If you haven't met him, my best friend Joshua Aden Cartwright is basically Clark Kent, but his superpower involves his dick and the internet. Not that I look at his dick often.

Let me start over.

Josh is the brother I never had. I grew up with him, we got each other in trouble in school—okay, it was mostly *me* getting *him* in trouble—and now he's a successful architect with a beautiful wife, Evie. Josh and his better half have a hit TV show, but he became internet-famous for taking me up on a dare to show his schlong to a woman. Josh being Josh, i.e. fastidious, he ended up designing whole cityscapes based on his junk. You'd have to see it to believe it.

Not that I check it out.

Anywho, he's given all that up, and now he's on the straight and narrow. Although judging by his famous dick pics that still float around cyberspace, he's more girthy than narrow.

And that's TMI even for me.

Moving along.

Should I talk to Josh about seeing Kendall?

Nah. As much as I want to, I'd have to mention her doing the walk of shame, and that doesn't seem like something she'd want getting out.

Besides, he's an old married man now and his wife would tell the Kenster. Some things aren't meant to be shared. I'm not used to keeping shit from Josh, though, so I tell him about every other part of the past twelve hours or so.

"So what happened after Robocop caught you with lingerie that wasn't rightfully yours?"

"I earned those knickers fair and square." He raises an eyebrow, and I continue. "I had the element of surprise on my side. Or maybe it's that I'm fifty pounds lighter. I'm fleet-footed. These days, people mistake me for a gazelle."

Josh gives me the stink-eye and sips his coffee. "You forget I've seen you on the treadmill."

I ignore his dis. "He chased me for about a block, but gave up fast, so I circled back and got in the Maserati and took off."

"Let me get this straight. You had a chance at *three women* last night, but didn't get laid."

Given how drunk they were, getting laid wasn't an option.

Frankly, all thoughts of those girls are crowded out by Kendall looking so damn feisty and hot, trying to put herself back together after doing the nasty with that tool.

She could do way better. I bet he doesn't even own a razor.

I'm not sure why I care.

"I don't wanna answer that," I mutter. "I'm too old for this shit, but it keeps happening to me."

He tugs his glasses down his nose and stares at me over the

rims. "You stay out all night, but don't have a good time, don't have any meaningful relationships, and almost get your ass kicked before the sun is fully in the sky. Maybe you need to reconsider your life choices."

Ouch.

This is the kind of judgment I get on the reg from my family. But coming from Josh, it's different, and even though it hurts, he's right.

I'm not one to navel-gaze, but mornings like this are unsustainable.

Hell, *my life* is unsustainable. Just giving a rundown of the bartenders I know by first name would take hours. Still, I've made some major progress.

I open my arms wide, bring them in, and point both index fingers down like a rapper at my mediocre meal. "If this doesn't say our little Drew is growing up, I'm not sure what does."

"If you judge your life by an omelet, you're even more of an asshole than I thought."

"Aww, thanks for the compliment," I coo.

But it's not just the food in my life that's changed. I've thrown out alcohol altogether. Getting so blackout drunk I lost a few days of my life made me get serious. I've been sober for several months, but Josh is the only one who knows.

Even last night, I drank cran-and-soda, not vodka cran, and left the champagne to the ladies.

Although it wasn't as much fun as it normally is.

Dammit. Maybe I am getting old. I'm pushing thirty, and as much as Josh and Evie's doe-eyes make me ill, I'll admit I'm jealous. None of the three girls last night had girlfriend potential—especially since one has a boyfriend.

And the one this morning? *What a pain in my dick.* I get enough shit from my family, I don't need her.

I have no idea why Evie insists Kendall was so much fun

growing up. That Debbie Downer's got a stick so high up her ass, it's lodged in her brain. She's constantly telling me to fuck off or arguing for the sake of arguing. If I say her dress is white, she'll say it's cream. *Eye roll.*

Since she's never given me a chance—and maybe I haven't deserved it—we've gone together like Vaseline and sandpaper.

All that attitude comes in an astonishingly beautiful package, though. Have you seen those tits? Fuck. She's tiny, but they're nicely proportioned. High and perky.

I bet they're totally suckable—

"So." Josh swallows. "I have a proposition for you."

I adjust myself slightly in my seat. "Sorry, dude, but my heart belongs to my Bee."

My phone pings, and it's a text from Frankie, my assistant who works on Saturdays. Not sure what I did to deserve her, but I'm keeping her. I text an okay for the purchase order and turn back to Josh.

He sets down his fork. "Do you have plans for Thanksgiving?"

"Show up at your parents' shindig uninvited, like always." I put my elbows on the table, lace my fingers together, and place my chin on my hands, batting my eyelashes at him.

"What do you think about going up to the new cabin? The renovations will be done by then."

Huh? "On Mount Hood? Sure. Just you?"

He lifts an eyebrow. "No. Thanksgiving is for family. I wanted to do something for Evie, make it extra-special, so I figured we'd bring her dad and invite Kendall, and you could hang with us from Thursday to Sunday. That way I can get Evie away from the city to relax. You know how driven my wife is."

I am not excited.

I'll do anything for Josh. He's everything I want to be—

admired, loved, responsible. Well, except for the proclivity to show off his dick.

But four days stuck with his father-in-law and angry Tinkerbell while Josh fucks his wife? *No, thanks.*

Let's see. Since I've known Kendall, she's yelled at me, lectured me, ignored me, talked over my head, talked down to me, and made sure that there was no chance in hell I'd ever be able to touch her.

Kendall's like a gorgeous IRS auditor—she's out to prove me wrong, but the words that come out of her mouth make me hard. I can't help but smart off to her, which makes smoke billow from her ears and her fists clench before she stomps off.

While I cackle.

And hide my chub.

I can only imagine how Thanksgiving will go down. Josh and Evie in newlywed heaven. Their dog Chauncey scratching his ass by the fireplace. Evie's dad watching football. And Kendall slicing off my balls with whatever cutlery she finds in the cabin.

I smile. "Sure, dude. Anything you want."

And as he tells me about the appliances he installed and all the views of the great Oregon wilderness, I plot my escape.

4

KENDALL

*S*itting in my car outside of my parents' house, I tap out another message to my best friend.

Kendall: What about lunch on Thursday?

Evie: Can't. Josh and I have to sand the kitchen cabinets. Maybe brunch on Saturday?

Kendall: I'm meeting a client. :(How about drinks on Sunday?

Evie: Josh and I are prepping for the show the following week and having dinner with his parents. WTF! I'm never going to see you at this rate!

I sigh. It seems like Evie and I talked more when she was a law student. On the East Coast.

This isn't all on her. Yes, married life has changed our dynamic, but my schedule is jam-packed too. I just wish I could unload on her in person with a big glass of wine while we veg out in our PJs. That's the only way to lament the shit show that is my love life. In person. With a pint of Chunky Monkey and the kind of sympathy only Evie can give me.

As much as I'd like to unload it via text, the fact it not only involves a hairy hookup with Lawrence but also that weird interaction with Drew gives me pause.

Because Evie isn't *just* Evie any longer.

She's Evie-*plus*-Josh.

And Josh comes with an annoying six-foot-something accessory named Drew.

Who you're still thinking about more than twenty-four hours later.

I scowl at the thought. Stupid Drew and his stupid abs.

Another text interrupts my pity party.

Evie: OH! I almost forgot! What about Thanksgiving? Wanna come up to the cabin with us? We could spend four whole days together!

My lips tilt up in a grin.

Until she texts again.

Evie: Um. One more thing about that...

Twenty minutes later, I'm still debating what to do as I watch my mother bustle around her kitchen, stopping to stir her mysterious vat of whatever's fermenting on the counter. She has her "Sunday Funday" apron on over her ankle-length, flowy periwinkle blue skirt. Even though she's too young to be a Baby Boomer, you'd never know it based on her clothing choices.

"Do you want to try my newest batch of kombucha?" she asks cheerily after dropping the bomb that she and my dad already have plans for Thanksgiving.

Ignoring her question—because homemade kombucha is where I draw the line in my attempt to be healthy—I press my thumb into my temple. "So you don't care if I spend that weekend with Evie and Josh?"

And Drew.

Holy fudge nuggets, no.

Unless we can pretend it's *Survivor,* and I can boot him out of the cabin.

When I heard his bellhop bro yesterday morning ask about the undies, any appreciation I had toward Drew for helping me with the Lawrence situation evaporated faster than my sixty-second quick-dry nail polish.

One good thing came from last night, though. I called it quits with Lawrence. We had The Talk and wished each other well. All very adult-like and respectful.

But it's irritating I find my thoughts drawn more to seeing Drew in the hallway than mourning the death of a relationship with Lawrence.

Evie-plus-Josh swear Drew's a changed man.

You mean, he won't get so stinking drunk, he schedules a hookup in the middle of dinner and then tells me about it? Like he did the first time we met?

Evie thought she was setting us up on a blind date that night. Yeah, he didn't get the memo.

The Drew I saw yesterday morning had a handful of women's lacy underwear dangling from his back pocket like notches on a bedpost.

Sure. Drew's different.

I snort to myself.

Mom shakes her head and waves a wooden stirring spoon in the air. "Your father and I were thinking of going on a retreat anyway. Your sister and Noah have plans with his family, so..." She shrugs. "It seemed like a good time to go."

Something about the tone of her voice makes me pause with a spoon halfway to my mouth to watch her closer. Is she blushing? My mother, the queen of inappropriate questions and awkward non-sequiturs?

I push my tomato soup away from me at her kitchen table. "What kind of retreat?" Who goes on a retreat over Thanksgiving?

The flush in her cheeks rises.

Maybe I don't want to know the answer, but before I can retract my question, she giggles.

"It's this wonderful tantric sex retreat my friend says your father and I will love. It'll be four days of reconnecting." She lowers her voice. "You know how I've been taking all that yoga? I'm *really* flexible now."

I shudder.

My instinct is to run and hide before she can divulge anything else, but my dad strolls in and smacks my mom on the ass. She waves him aside, but her eyes are bright and her expression soft.

Man, these two never stop. I'm grateful, though, that they have a good relationship.

"Hey, pumpkin. Nice to see you." He ambles over and kisses the top of my head.

"Hey, Dad." I smile up at him. "How are you feeling?"

His health has been improving over the last several years, since he had that scare when I was in high school. After that, my parents got into a huge fitness kick and turned around their sedentary lifestyle with proper nutrition and exercise, but I haven't seen him in a few weeks, and my old fears creep up on me.

"Did your mother tell you? My cholesterol is at an all-time low. She put me on this herbal concoction, and I've never felt better." He lifts his sleeve and flexes his bicep. I chuckle.

My mom mumbles something to him I can't quite hear, and he wiggles his eyebrows at her. I look away, not needing to see my parents flirting.

Since my dad recovered from his heart attack, my parents can't keep their hands off each other. As scary as that period was, it gave them a new lease on life, so even though they embarrass the hell out of me when they break out the touchy-feelies, I'm really happy for them.

People would be so lucky to have a relationship like Karen and Thomas Greer.

They downsized our big suburban house and now have a quaint two-bedroom overflowing with my mother's art projects and my dad's woodworking, but without that huge mortgage hanging over their heads, they've never been more content.

Staying nearby for college seemed like the prudent thing to do while he recovered. I figured one of his kids needed to look out for him. Although my overachieving big sister now works as the artistic director for the Portland Ballet, at the time she had just graduated from Juilliard and was dancing for the New York City Ballet, which had always been her dream. While she has a decent relationship with our parents, Brooke's priority is herself, and it probably never crossed her mind to come home to help Dad recuperate.

The benefit of going to school nearby meant I didn't rack up too much debt, which I'd kept low through my early twenties. Well, until I started my own PR firm with one of my best friends from college. I've done my best to keep start-up costs down, but it's been a challenge.

Being my own boss is worth it, though. At least that's what I tell myself, because after five years at my old job, I needed a change, and I wanted to call the shots.

Besides, everyone else I know was suddenly being promoted or getting married or having babies, and I wanted something for me. Something I could nurture and love and watch flourish.

Just because I don't want kids for a few more years doesn't mean I'm worthless, Bobby.

Not that I started my own firm to prove something to my ex.

My dad settles into the chair across from me. "How's work? I saw you at that press conference for Howard LaRoe. You looked fantastic. So poised." He winks at me, and my heart fills with his approval. After a moment, he reaches for his cup of green tea and frowns. "But he looked shifty."

"Tell me about it." I sigh and shake my head. "I keep telling him he needs to stop fidgeting."

Dad unfolds *The Oregonian*, because he's old-school and likes the feel of newsprint in his hands.

After taking a few sips of my tea, I circle back to what's bothering me. "So I guess I'll spend Thanksgiving with Josh and Evie?"

I'm still perplexed. What happened to us always spending the holidays together as a family? My parents drilled that into me when I was a kid. Brooke might blow us off from time to time, but I'll always opt to hang with Team Greer.

My mother reaches across the kitchen table to pat my hand. "Sounds wonderful! This is working out better than I expected. Who all will be there again? Evie and her dad?"

I nod, trying not to feel glum. I'll have a good time with Evie, and her dad is like a surrogate father to me. Except... "And Drew is coming. Josh's best friend."

Maybe Josh's cabin is huge, and I can sequester myself in one end of it from time to time. Because committing a homicide over the holidays is frowned upon.

"Which one is Drew? Did I meet him at Evie's wedding back in February?"

"He was the best man. The one acting like a dumb frat boy."

He spent half the evening getting trashed and the other half trying to toss M&Ms down my cleavage. I spent most of the night wanting to punch him in the face for being an idiot and the rest wanting to smack myself for thinking he looked hot in that tux.

"The one with those really big green eyes and thick lashes?" I frown because I don't like the excitement in her voice. "Oh, he is *so* handsome. Thomas"—she nudges my dad's shoulder —"isn't Drew handsome?"

She only thinks that because she and my father left before Drew started dirty dancing with two bridesmaids.

Dad mutters yes even though he's not listening.

Mom chatters on, and I automatically tune out as I tend to do whenever Drew becomes the topic of any conversation, but then she giggles again. "You know, he watched you all night. I think that boy likes you."

I snort, caught completely off guard. "Mom, number one, Drew Merritt hates me. Otherwise, he wouldn't try to annoy me to death every chance he has. Two, he's not a boy, he's almost thirty, but you'd never know it because he acts like a horny teenager." He wouldn't know what discretion meant if it hopped up and bit him on the ass. The publicist in me cringes when I think back to all of the ways he's made an ass of himself or his friends over the last few years. "And three, when we're in the same room, I want to stab him with an ice pick."

He thought he was God's gift to women *before* he got in shape. I'm even more annoyed with him now that he has abs and is genuinely sexy. Yes, he has a gorgeous face, and yes, that flirty smile could take down a whole sorority house of women at ten paces, but he's as unpredictable as Kanye West at an awards show and flakier than a pie crust.

I chalk up my fleeting attraction to him at the wedding as

shock from seeing him in something other than ratty T-shirts and jeans.

But the attraction shriveled up and died when I overheard those two bridesmaids giggling about their after-wedding late-night plans with Drew.

My mother sighs and pats my hand again. "I'm not saying you have to marry him and have his babies, but maybe he'd be fun for a romp."

I nearly aspirate my tea. Did my mom...did she just tell me to hook up with Drew "Demerit" Merritt?

Whereas most people who pull the kind of shit he does end up with a felony count and a "no ragrets" tattoo, he gets splashed on celebrity websites and tagged with a cute nickname. Just the thought of all the crap he's gotten away with since I met him is enough to make my eye twitch.

She motions toward my face. "Are you still having those migraines?"

I blink slowly, trying to make sense of my mother's train of thought.

"Yes. Probably from too much caffeine." It's best not to mention my seventy-hour work week, or that her damn buck-wheat pillow nearly incapacitated me. I was so sore after sleeping on it, I couldn't turn my head left for three days.

"I've read that a good orgasm helps with headaches." Her voice drops to a conspiratorial whisper. "Maybe Drew could help with that." I choke down the rest of my tea, and I get another hand pat while I try to keep my brain from exploding thanks to her outlandish suggestion. "Plus, I bet a well-to-do guy like that would wine and dine you. Not a bad way to spend an evening or two."

Unwelcome images flash in my head of Drew in the Hunt-ington Hotel hallway, looming over me, making me shiver. The weight of his arm around my shoulder.

Suddenly, I can imagine Drew's ripped body above me. All those muscles bulging with tension and dripping with sweat. His big emerald eyes searching mine. That killer smile aimed at me.

But then he'd open his mouth and undoubtedly ruin everything.

And that seals the deal.

I shake my head, willing those unbidden thoughts to disappear. Because I'd rather shave off my eyebrows than let him take me out, and I don't ever plan to be so hard up for money that I need someone like him to "wine and dine me."

Turning to my dad, I wait for him to interject since my mother apparently is fine with pimping me out, but he's five pages deep in his newspaper and not coming up for a breath.

"Let me put it this way." I tap on the table, rattling the mug in front of me. "It would have to be a cold day in hell for me to consider going out with Drew Merritt."

5

DREW

*A*s I reflect upon my life, two truths stand out. I am forever, irretrievably in love with my Bee to the extent that I will do anything she asks without question, and I can't seem to stop finding myself in the most challenging predicaments.

Like now.

I'm clinging to a maple like a stripper on a pole, but I'm being showered with dead leaves instead of dollar bills.

Because it's Tuesday, so naturally I'm up a tree.

The rough bark scuffs my palms as I reach around the trunk, my Vans-clad feet balancing on the thickest branch I can find. Rain clouds threaten overhead, and my heart pounds in my throat from the exertion of scaling this thing. I look down to the ground below. It would hurt if I fell.

The wind blasts the leaves at the end of the street and spins them around. This tree wobbles.

I'm not gonna fall. I can do this, no problem. Just a bit farther.

Below me, my Bumble Bee—my maternal grandmother Beatrice—calls, "Almost. You've almost got it." She's bundled up in a lavender tracksuit she wears with flair no one else can pull off.

"Meow," says the bottlebrush-tailed jerk, piteously shivering two inches from my fingers.

I hate cats, I think as I take a deep breath and lunge, grabbing the little bugger by the scruff of his neck and shoving him under my gray T-shirt. As I pause to breathe out a sigh of relief from a successful mission, the tree limb I'm standing on makes a dubious-sounding crack.

Shit.

Zipping up my North Face jacket to my chin with the kitten tucked inside my clothes, I make my way back down the tree, my jeans straining against my thighs. For some reason, the cat ceases to struggle as I climb down, curling his tiny body against my torso, his cold paws pressed on my skin. Maybe he can sense that he's made a dumb move and is now on his way to safety so his best plan is to shut up and hold on.

I know that feeling.

A few more feet down, and I swing from the lowest branch and land on the strip of dead grass in front of my Bee's modest 1930's cottage. Dusting off my hands, I extract the scraggly feline and hand him to my white-haired grandmother, whose eyes light up like she's twelve.

"You got him! Here, here, little guy." With a sure hand, she cuddles the now-wriggling gray cat and heads into her house. "I thought we were going to have to call the fire department."

"No need. You've got me to handle it." I wipe my brow and follow her up the three stairs edged with potted yellow and orange chrysanthemums that lead into her warm brick home. Once inside, she sets the little monster on her linoleum kitchen floor. He hisses at her, his back arched and tail fluffed, with a mohawk of hair going down his back like a tiny Stegosaurus. "Ungrateful bastard," I mutter. "You were nicer to me."

"Language, Andrew."

I shove my hands in my pockets and lean against the kitchen counter. "Sorry, Bumble."

There are only two people authorized to chastise me at will —my Bee and Josh.

I blow off everyone else who gets all Judgy McJudgerson. Which means someone like Kendall makes my inner dickwad come out to fight—not that she's been around since I saw her at the hotel. But based on how often she's starred in my dirty dreams these last few weeks, it's like I've seen her daily.

And since Josh called this morning and said due to weather our four days at the cabin are now five—we need to leave tomorrow afternoon to beat the snowstorm—I've been dreading this trip even more.

With a smile and a nod, my Bee accepts my apology, and sets down a bowl of water, clucking at the animal. The cat drinks, its little pink tongue darting down into the dish.

With its white feet and big tiger eyes, it's almost cute.

But still, I hate cats. Haughty, standoffish. Cats judge you.

Like K-noodle.

I wonder if Kendall likes cats. Or do they drive her crazy?

Why am I thinking so much about that little redhead?

Unzipping my jacket, I lay it on the kitchen counter. My grandmother stares at my chest and gestures at my T-shirt. "What does that say?"

"Nothing," I say sheepishly and cross my arms over my pecs.

"That doesn't look like nothing."

"It's my company." I'm not letting her see the logo emblazoned across my shirt. I've managed to keep it away from her for this long, I'm not changing that now.

She laughs and reaches down to the cat, who recoils and spits at her. "Nothing you could do would shock me these days."

"When did you get the feline?" I ask, needing to change the subject. "You didn't have him a week ago."

My petite grandmother fills up a kettle with water and sets it on the stove, flicking on the gas with a click. "Oh, he's not mine. In fact, I'm not even sure he's a he. His mother gave birth in the neighbor's basement a few weeks ago and took off, leaving him alone."

Is it weird that I sympathize with a cat?

Then what Bee says hits me, and I grimace and point a finger at her. "You had me come over and risk my life climbing up that tree to save a cat that's *not even yours*?"

"It was barely ten feet up. I knew you could do it." She pats my cheek. "Have a cookie."

My stomach growls, but it's all too easy to distract me. "You know I can't."

"You're so skinny now, I keep thinking I need to feed you. I'll make you a turkey sandwich instead." She turns and rummages in the fridge.

"Thanks." Speaking of activities that are hazardous to my health... "Bee?"

"Uh-huh."

"You wouldn't want to come with me to Josh's place on Mount Hood for the weekend, would you?"

She shakes her head and slips piles of turkey onto whole grain bread. "No, thank you, dear. I have my standing holiday date at Rose City Acres."

I don't remember the last time my family had any meal together, let alone a Thanksgiving dinner. I'm the only one who visits Bee, who has nothing but scathing words for the rest of our family. Me and her against the Merritts.

"Evie's dad will be there. You could talk with him."

Her hand migrates to her hip. "You know that I will be

perfectly happy playing pinochle with Tyrone, Sylvia, and John —happier than dealing with your parents—"

"Hate to break it to you, but Tyrone wants to get in your pants."

Slicing the sandwich in half, she arranges it on a plate. "Andrew, don't change the subject. Why do you need your grandmother as a wingman when you're supposed to be having fun in a mountain cabin?"

I kick at the floor. The kitten swats at my shoelace, and I pick him up. He's so tiny, he fits in the palm of my hand and curls up immediately, purring. "There's a girl coming who's a PITA."

"Flatbread?"

"Pain in the ass." She opens her mouth, and I hold my free hand up. "Yes, I know. Language."

She stifles a smile, pulls back her kitchen chair, and gestures at it. "Sit down, eat, and tell me about your girl trouble this time."

I settle in the wooden chair, dumping the kitten in my lap. When I attempt to shoo him down to the floor, he won't budge. I resign myself to him loitering on my body, and I ignore my Bee's question.

My phone buzzes with a text from my mother.

Andrew. I need to talk to you. Last chance to do the right thing and decline your inheritance.

She's exasperating. I text back, *It's not up to me. And you need to learn to trust me.*

Her response comes back fast. *You've never proven yourself to be trustworthy. And now this? It's a shame.*

I'm tempted to throw my phone, but I just stick it back in my pocket.

Pouring both of us a mug of tea, my grandma sits across from me, giving the kitten an appreciative glance. "I think that cat's adopted you."

"I need a pet like I need an STD," I grumble. Before she can open her mouth, I continue, "That is, I don't."

And thank God I've never had one.

To clarify, I mean both: a pet *or* VD. One "benefit" from all the visits to the doctor lately is I know I'm clean, from my dick to my diabetes, and I'm gonna keep it that way.

I'm glad to leave Bee with this animal, though. Maybe it will give her something to do. Although he seems to be stuck on me, unfortunately.

The kitten licks his paws—oblivious to my distaste—yawns, and rearranges himself on my lap.

Bee sips her chamomile and eyes me over the edge of her "World's Best Grandma" mug I gave her when I was eight. "It would do you well to have someone to look after."

With my mouth wrapped around my sandwich, I say, "I've got you to look after."

"Yes, but I don't count. I'm independent." She gestures at the cat with her elbow. "Maybe this kitten is like having a woman in your life. You never knew you needed one, but shazam, she appears out of nowhere, you save her, and it changes your life."

I raise an eyebrow. *Shazam?* Not sure where my gran learns words like that.

She holds up her hands and shrugs. "You know I'm right. Anyway, tell me about this girl who has you ass over teakettle."

"Bumble! Language."

Chuckling, she settles in to listen.

How do I tell my grandma that when I met Kendall I was drunk off my ass and scheduling a blowjob? Or the time I threw up on her fancy shoes? Or when I showed up to Evie's set so stoned they had to halt production?

And let's not talk about how wasted I got at Josh and Evie's wedding.

I'm not exactly the beacon of good decision-making.

Because at the wedding, I'd known I was diabetic. I'd lost weight and started to get in shape, which meant less pizza and junk food, but I still partied like a fiend on a bender.

No wonder Kendall thinks I'm an idiot.

I eye my Bee. "I haven't been on my best behavior around her."

"Umm-hmm."

"She seems to catch me—" I pause and correct myself. "Up until last winter, I was always drunk when I saw her. So what came out of my mouth was a bunch of crap. Plus, she's just so much fun to tease."

"So you get under her skin?"

I nod.

"And she gets under yours?"

I nod again.

"And you like it," she says with a little snicker.

I sit back and drink my tea. "Much to my surprise."

6

KENDALL

*S*hivering, I snuggle into my wraparound sweater and tap the thermostat, reluctantly turning up the temperature even though I shouldn't hours before we vacate for a long weekend. I'm not looking forward to getting this month's heating bill for the office, but I'm an icicle, and I'm probably also a shitty boss if I let my employees freeze their holiday balls off before Thanksgiving.

Thick snow from one of Portland's rare snowstorms lashes my office window, and for the tenth time today, I wish I could head home after work and sink into a hot bath, but I promised Evie I'd be on the road this afternoon since traffic will be hellish. Judging by the dark clouds descending over the city, that might not be early enough.

Tristan knocks on my door as he ducks into my office. His dark brown hair dips into his eyes, and he shoots me a crooked grin. I toss an eggplant stress ball at his head.

"I'm never going to finish this press release if you keep interrupting me."

His warm laugh washes over me, and I give him a mock admonishing glare as I settle back at my desk. My partner is a beautiful man, and he fills out a suit like nobody's business. Unfortunately, I've never had that kind of spark with him, so he's been relegated to my man candy folder, which I get to appreciate every day. I still count that as a win.

Tristan and I met in college, and while we used to work at competing firms, we've always commiserated over wanting to start our own company. After too many vodka martinis last year, we decided to go for it and started Greer and Laszlow PR. Even though I can almost count the number of nights off I've had since we started our company on one hand, I feel blessed to be working with one of my best friends.

"Did you just throw a phallus at me?" He snickers at my stress ball of choice. "I'm telling the boss you're sexually harassing me."

I roll my eyes. "You are the boss, moron. And as your partner-in-crime at our fine establishment, I suggest you stop talking to me so I can get everything done before our long weekend." My stomach flips over at the thought of not being able to get into the office for four whole days, but Evie said the cabin has high-speed internet, so I can work remotely. "Go bug Jess. It'll make her day."

My new intern Jessica has a crush on Tristan, and I give him endless shit about it.

"She's busy fawning over one of your clients."

"What client? I'm not expecting anyone." Did I forget I have an appointment?

Feminine laughter echoes down our hall, and I jog out of my office, only to come to a screeching halt when my eyes land on Drew and his...kitten?

What. Is. He. Doing. Here?

Mr. Frat Boy gives me a million dollar smile that makes little heart eyes pop out of Jessica's head. "Kenster. We gotta hit the road if we wanna miss the snowstorm."

I'm so stunned to see him standing in my office, I open my mouth, but nothing comes out.

Tristan chuckles next to me. "Yeah, *Kenster*." Under his breath, he whispers, "You didn't tell me you were seeing anyone."

"Because I'm not." I elbow him in the ribs as I migrate to the receptionist desk that my intern is staffing.

Drew gives me the once-over, from my heels, up my legs that are far too bare in this fitted skirt, pausing over my cleavage, and finally back up to my face.

He clears his throat. "I hope you have some warmer clothes for the weekend."

Jessica audibly sighs as she stares at Drew, and I take a moment to appreciate the fact that he does, in fact, look nice in a button-up dress shirt, a vintage-looking leather jacket that probably costs more than my rent, dark distressed jeans, and boots. He's usually sporting old hoodies with questionable stains and profane T-shirts, giving the metaphorical finger to his fashionable roots, so him *not* looking like a homeless gamer is unexpected. Him looking like a lost Abercrombie model cradling a cute fur ball is even more perplexing.

"Drew, what are you doing here? And why do you have a kitten?" If he's trying to prank me, I'm going to toss his balls in a sling.

His eyebrows furrow. "Josh asked me to pick you up. Said the weather looked too bad for your car to handle."

"And Evie didn't mention this why?"

He gives me his patented Drew Merritt shrug. "Josh said you were fine with this. He thought you'd be safer with me. He and Evie are picking up her dad or they would've swung by to get you." When I growl, he holds up the kitten to my face and talks in a baby voice, "Don't shoot the messenger meow!"

The cat is indeed adorable, but there is a good reason I'm

always two minutes from having a brain aneurysm around this man.

He pauses with the cat in the air, seeming to suddenly notice Tristan.

It feels wrong to allow the different parts of my life to collide like this. But as incongruous as it seems to have Drew in my office, it would be rude not to introduce everyone.

"Drew, this is my partner, Tristan. Tristan, this is..." *My penance for sins committed in this life.* "Drew."

Demerit lowers the kitten, his expression going blank before he gives Tristan a nod. I barely contain a huff of disappointment. *Don't go overboard trying to be friendly to my business partner or anything.*

Ignoring whatever weirdness is going on between Drew and Tristan, I stalk back to my desk and pull up my cell to find a message from Evie, one she sent an hour ago that I somehow missed when I was ass-deep in press releases.

Josh is worried about the weather. Don't kill me, but he's sending Drew to pick you up. You said you had all of your luggage in your car, right?

Drew clears his throat from my doorway, but I ignore him.

"Why do men always think women can't handle driving in bad weather?" I mutter to myself as I shove my phone back into my purse.

He laughs. "Is that a trick question?" When I don't say anything, he rubs his jaw. "KK, the roads are getting bad. I think Evie would feel better with us traveling together. You can drive the Rover if you need to prove your womanly automotive skills. You can always—"

"Shut up. If you say something about me working your gearshift, I'm going to shove it up your ass."

He howls with laughter and tucks the little ball of fluff to his chest. I'm beyond annoyed that my first thought is how this would make a great pic for #HotGuysWithCats on Instagram.

Get your shit together, Kendall.

"Fine. I need five minutes."

I settle at my desk, skim the press release once more, and email it to my client before I look at Drew again.

A part of me—a *big* part—wants to call off this trip. But if I bail, I'll miss the one chance I have to spend time with Evie, and we haven't hung out in ages. Between her show and my schedule, I'm not sure when we'll get another opportunity like this.

I pop two Advil and glare at Drew. "Are you going to annoy me for the entire two-hour drive?"

He bats his ridiculously long eyelashes. "It's possible."

Jesus, help me.

As I grab my keys, my phone pings with a text from Jessica.

OMG. You're friends with DREW MERRITT?! And you're spending the weekend with him?!

I direct Drew to sit on the chair in front of my desk. "I'll be right back."

Once I have my intern sequestered in her cubicle, I motion to her. "Say it with me, Jessica. What happens in this office..."

She nods. "What happens in this office is confidential." Then she adds in a whisper, "I swear I won't tell anyone you're BFFs with Drew Merritt, but whoa, he's so hot. He's even more beautiful than—"

"I'm not best friends with Drew. Forget it." I pinch the bridge of my nose. "Listen, the point is you cannot go around talking to your buddies about this or gossiping about what happens in our office, which includes whoever I socialize with. Agreed? Remember that part of your job is maintaining our clients' privacy and knowing when it's appropriate to divulge newsworthy aspects."

I hate being a hardass, but I need my employees to have

discretion due to the confidential information that filters through my office. Anyway, she knows I hate when she fawns all over celebrities and socialites.

She zips her lips, and I try to take a deep breath to fortify myself for the rest of the weekend.

A two-hour car ride can't be that bad.

7

KENDALL

A two-hour car ride *can* be that bad, especially when it turns into a four-hour drive. The snow is insane, the roads are slippery as hell, and our visibility is zero.

Drew's kitten, Shazam, is content as can be, though. He doesn't seem worried that we're one hairpin turn from driving off the mountain or into a tree and is busy kneading Drew's thighs and purring like he's a yummy biscuit.

I will concede that Drew smells really good. Like leather and some kind of citrus body wash or cologne. He took off his jacket and rolled up his sleeves, so I have an eyeful of forearm porn flexing in my peripheral vision that's damn distracting.

Surreptitiously, I study his handsome profile and the casual way his hand is draped over the steering wheel while he pets Shazam with the other. By all outward appearances, he doesn't seem worried that we're obviously lost. He's been humming to his satellite radio for the entire drive, a lot of 80s tunes that would make me laugh except I've been fighting a headache.

In all the times we've hung out together because of our best friends, I've never spent so much time with Drew alone. Something about his close proximity makes me feel like a compass that's rotating frenetically in a magnetic field.

I press a hand to my stomach. *Must be the long car ride making me feel so unsettled.*

I'm tempted to ask why he's dressed up, but I'm too freaked out by the fact that we're likely lost in the middle of a snowstorm to make casual conversation.

"We should be there already," I point out. Again. "Are you sure your GPS is right?"

A computer voice fills the cab. "Your destination is on the left in two hundred feet."

That's what it said five minutes ago.

I shiver in my seat. How is he not cold? "Can we turn up the heat? If I'm going to die today, I might as well be warm."

He chuckles and reaches over to squeeze my hand. "I'm not gonna let anything happen to you."

"Now I know we're definitely going to die. You're never this nice to me."

"'Tis the holiday season. Best time of the year. Why wouldn't I be nice?"

Grinning, he gives me another squeeze and goes back to petting his cat. I'm oddly touched he brought the kitten after his grandmother asked him to pet sit.

"Swear to God, I can never tell if you're flirting with me or fucking with me." I don't mean to say those words out loud, but it's not like I can get them back once I've muttered them.

The laugh that rumbles through him makes me smile, but I rein it in. No need to let him know I think he's entertaining. Not that he said anything funny. Honestly, I don't even know why I'm amused right now.

"Why can't it be both?" He lifts an eyebrow playfully, and I snort.

"Okay, Casanova, eyes on the road before we get wrapped around a tree. Because if we end up dead, I'm going to kill you."

I dig through my purse to check the signal on my phone. *Zero bars.*

"Why does the GPS work, but I don't have reception?"

"Sorry, babe. I've got no idea how these things work."

"Drew, I'm going to be honest. I'm freaking out. We don't have cell phone service to call for help, and it seems like we're driving around in circles on this mountain. I'd feel better if we could reach Evie and Josh."

I hold up my phone to the roof, carefully waving it from one end of the passenger seat to the other and pray I get a signal.

"Don't fret so much, princess," he says calmly. "At least we have four hundred and sixty radio stations." He taps on his console and Mariah Carey's "All I Want for Christmas" blares through the speakers. "So tell me, have you been naughty or nice this year? Imma bet naughty. If you've been nice, don't tell me and ruin the fantasy." Glancing at me, he gives me a little wink.

I blink, confused about the way my heart skitters in my chest.

Fantasy? He fantasizes about me? I pause, hand up in the air with my cell, to wonder if this is merely his way to redirect me so I don't go DEFCON 1 about being lost. Because there's no way Drew has ever thought twice about me. Mostly because I'm not the kind of girl to drop to my knees within ten seconds of meeting him.

Drew is all about the easy lay. Everyone knows this about him. He doesn't woo women, buy them flowers, or plan romantic dates. He's never struck out because he never tries. Because he doesn't have to.

For some unknown reason—like that force field in the Bermuda Triangle that's doomed many a plane—women trip over themselves to give it up to this guy. I've watched it happen with my own eyes—perfectly intelligent women going giggly in his presence before they offer themselves up as his dessert *du jour*.

Which is why I vowed long ago never to be one of his quick and dirty fucks.

I mean, I imagine they'd be dirty since this is Drew we're talking about.

Not that I think about Drew having sex. Much.

"You have arrived," the GPS system announces as we turn into a driveway.

"Omigod, Drew. You got us here, and we didn't die."

Thick evergreens tower over the narrow road, so the snow isn't bad, but when the forest opens up near the cabin, a frosty blanket covers everything. Drew pulls to a stop about ten yards from the house.

"I don't think we can get any closer."

"Whoa. It's beautiful. Like a Hans Christian Andersen fairy tale." I press my nose to the window and then wipe away the fog with my elbow.

The picturesque log cabin is nestled at the top of a ridge. I roll down the window and breathe in the crisp forest scent.

"Josh's new cabin looks pretty sweet. His parents have a cool pad up here somewhere too."

Excitement rushes through me. "I haven't made snow angels since I was a kid, but I'd love to flop on that snow and make one."

"KK, you'd freeze to death and ruin your boots."

Before we hit the road, I changed into jeans, a long-sleeve T-shirt that I paired with my wraparound burgundy sweater, and leather boots. I should be wearing hiking boots, but they're at the bottom of my bag in the back.

"Maybe, but it'd be worth it." I smile at him, and he grins back.

As we're busy smiling at each other like idiots, the realization that we're the first ones to arrive strikes me, and my anxiety kicks back in.

"Where is everyone? Shouldn't Evie and Josh be here? They left before us." Our car is the only one here, and there are no other tire tracks. The charming cabin in front of us is dark. His smile fades, and he turns to study the house. "Shouldn't there be other cars? Shouldn't the lights be on? Unless there's another way to get to the house."

He nods slowly. "Yeah. Maybe there's another road on the other side? Or they got stuck in traffic or stopped to get groceries. I'm sure they'll be here soon. They won't care if we wait inside for them."

"Do you have a key to get in?"

"Um."

After a beat, I laugh. I can't help it. "Okay, crazy man. I know you've done wilder things than break us into a house, but you have my approval to put all of your ninja skills to use and get us in there. Because I'm pretty sure we'll freeze if we stay in your Rover."

"I did break into a sorority house once. Well, I had permission. Kinda."

He trails off, and I let him. "Save your sexual exploits for another time because we both know that would take too long." I check my phone again. Still no signal. Drew doesn't have one either. "Maybe we can jimmy one of the windows, like along the back. Maybe there's one that wasn't locked. My parents always forget to lock all of their windows."

"Good plan." He hands me Shazam. "Hold him for a sec." He climbs out of the car and trudges through the snow until he opens my door, turns around, and pats his back. "Climb on."

"You want me to ride piggyback while I hold your kitten?"

"Yes. You guard my cat. I keep you dry and happy. Win-win. And we can figure out how to break in together. Unless you want me to commit this misdemeanor by myself." He grins at me over his shoulder. "Come on. Live life on the edge."

After a minute, I nudge his shoulder.

"You're very persuasive when you want to be." His smile widens. This is obviously not news to him. "Fine, but don't drop me, and if I get too heavy, let me know."

"I can handle you, tiger." He pats his back. "Let's rock this."

I've lost my mind. Clearly.

I wrap Shazam in my sweater so he's snuggled against my chest, and then I knot the tie at my waist before I tug on a thicker jacket, leaving it open so I don't suffocate Drew's kitten.

His little nose peeks up, and his purring grows louder. Guess he's okay.

Cautiously, I scoot out and wrap my arms around Drew's broad shoulders. Holy crap, he's muscly. And then he helps me wrap my thighs around his narrow waist.

When he straightens to his full height and hoists me up higher, I yelp, because dang, he's tall, and being pressed up close to his body is intense.

"Hang on."

He doesn't need to tell me twice. As he plods through the knee-high snow, I cling to him, praying we don't break our necks.

Except...Drew feels really sturdy beneath me. Solid. Plus, he has a good hold on my thighs with those big hands.

After a few minutes, I start to relax. If I weren't so uptight, this probably would be fun.

We make our way to the front of the house, but of course that door is locked. Since I'm up pretty high, we pause along the side of the house to check the different windows.

We're slogging through a particularly heavy mound of snow when a blast of wind blows my hair around my face and into his.

"Sorry. I should've tied my hair back before we started this trek."

"No worries. I'm good." He pauses. "Hey. Look."

I follow to where he's pointing.

A narrow window is cracked open along the side of the house. "Yay! Maybe you should take Shazam, and then you can give me a boost up there."

He gives me a look over his shoulder. "No way. I'll do it."

"You're not going to fit through that window. Your shoulders will never make it. I'm not sure you'll be able to even if you turn sideways. Let me do it. I'm fun-sized. Then you can go back to the front, and I'll let you in." I poke him. "You just told me to live life on the edge. How much more on the edge can I get than breaking and entering?"

After a long pause, he pats my thigh. "Just be careful. If you get up there and can't make it over, we'll figure out something else. It's not worth you getting hurt."

A flutter of butterflies hits my stomach. Either I'm oddly touched by Drew's thoughtfulness or the adrenaline is kicking in from the semi-crime I'm about to commit. Though I'm sure Josh won't care that I'm going to scale my way into his house.

I slide down Drew's big body and miss his heat as soon as we separate.

When we get into position, I help him tuck the kitten to his chest the way Shazam was snuggled to mine. Drew sniffs his fur, and his lips tug up. "He smells like you."

I stare up at him, pausing to appreciate how good he looks like this. Ruddy-cheeked from exertion and the cold. Eyes bright and attentive. Dirty-blond hair disheveled and wind-blown.

He's beautiful.

And when he smiles at me like that, I feel it all the way down to my boots.

As I think about the past few years, I realize he's not the same guy I met at that restaurant, the one I wanted to stab with my steak knife.

A thought crystallizes in my mind.

If we didn't have the history we have, I'd be totally into him.

I cough and turn to face the house. "Let's do this."

8

DREW

*K*endall inhales deeply and braces her arms against the snow-covered sill, preparing to scramble to the upper window. She glances over her shoulder at me. "I'm ready. Hoist me up?" Her teeth chatter so much I want to kiss her to make them stop—a thought I've had more than once in the past hour.

Correction, *hours*.

Okay, I've been obsessed with kissing her for days. And by days I mean months.

I pause, examining the puffs of warmth she exhales in the crisp mountain air from her fresh, pouty lips. My shortness of breath isn't from the altitude, but the bright look on Kendall's face. Downright friendly, if not...*inviting*?

Something changed on the drive. Despite the chilly surroundings, her expression is no longer Ice Princess of the Oregon Realm. At least, I'm not sensing that she's imminently going to duct tape my balls to my leg—which was previously the undercurrent of every interaction we've had since Josh and Evie got together. Instead, her attitude is softer. More open.

It takes me an embarrassing amount of time to answer her, and I end up just saying, "Yes, ma'am."

Before Spider Girl moves up the rounded wood sides of the log cabin, I extract the kitten from my shirt and set him on a ledge so I don't squish him. The mini-monster lets loose a pathetic, tiny meow. I rub under his chin as he picks up his paws gingerly, not liking the frost. "Just hang on a sec, Shazmeister. We'll get you curled by the fire and purring in no time."

"Let's get all of us curled by the fire," Kendall says, her inscrutable eyes on mine, and I nod.

Wonder if I could get her to purr, too.

Down, boy, I tell myself. *We've just moved from her hating your guts, to tentatively getting along. No need to jinx it, no matter how much you're attracted to her.*

Moving behind her, my hands linger on her small waist. I grin and murmur into her ear, "I'm full service. Pack mule. Personal slingshot. Whatever bodily services you need."

Best come-on words ever, I'm sure, but Kendall's forcing me to be creative. If I used my standard "Hey, girl, let's fuck" line, I'm sure Kendall's response would involve a garrote—or at least pain in two or three of my body parts.

Weirdly, I like the idea of her touching my body parts, even with pain.

Kendall looks over her shoulder and grins, her nose as red as a cranberry. "I'm sorry you had to carry me. I'm a total oaf."

I pause before responding, because when I carried her all I could think about was how those lean thighs needed to straddle my front. Preferably while I raided her smart mouth with my tongue. Since I was fantasizing, I imagined her wearing absolutely nothing as I thrust into her.

So, yeah, she's not an oaf. At all. But she doesn't need to know my X-rated thoughts. I'll stick to being transportation.

I adjust myself and take a step back to survey her. "You weigh about the same as Shaz." She blushes as snowflakes gather on her eyelashes. "Let's continue this conversation inside. As my cousin Sven would say, it's fooking cold."

A peal of laughter escapes her. "You don't have a cousin Sven."

"True. Get in the crack, woman. You, me, and this beast need to defrost, pronto." With my hands under Kendall's arms and her foot on my thigh, I push her skyward as she scrambles up the side of the house.

It doesn't get much better than this. A front-row view of Kendall Greer's juicy rear end as she gooses her way into the open window. She wedges her head and torso inside, but then gets stuck, balancing on the window like the world's sexiest teeter-totter, with her legs kicking and seeking purchase on any surface below her.

Dude, be a gentleman. "Need some help?"

"I can't believe I'm saying this, but will you give my ass a shove? Just a little more, and I'll be in." Her voice comes out muffled. "And don't get any ideas."

"Too late," I call.

Boy, is it ever too late.

I carefully place both of my hands on her pert boo-tay, cradle it for a moment because *reasons*, and aid her skyward.

Oh, God. I need to go to church now—that's a thought I've never had—since her ass is holy. I've checked it out plenty, but getting to touch? It's perfection. Toned, springy, soft, round. She's so full of beautiful butt I don't know what to do with myself.

Hot. Damn.

Her legs disappear in the house, one and then the other, and I hear a thump on the ground. Her face appears in the darkened window. "I'll let you in," she yells, and points toward the front door. I scoop up Shazzy and make my way through the drifts and snowfall up to the front porch. There's no way we're going anywhere for a while. Not until the storm stops and the roads are plowed.

I know what I want to plow.

Dammit, dude. Stop.

When I get to the entrance, I stomp the snow off my boots, and Kendall opens the door, greeting me. My heart races, but it's not from trudging through the icy terrain. It's from the sight of her poised in the doorway, with her flushed face and wild tendrils of hair.

Seeing her in this moment reminds me of the first time I looked up at the night sky and saw ten million stars shining back at me.

Overwhelmed. Unworthy.

Like my heart might break its way through my chest.

"Hi," she says breathlessly, her chin tilted up to me as I face her. We're just inches apart, breathing together. Suspended in the winter air with no one but us in the silence that hushes the mountain.

Her eyes have flecks of gold in them.

"Hi," I whisper.

She stands awkwardly for a moment, then says, "Come in, come in. This place is incredible." I peer over her shoulder at the shadowy house, then look behind me where the snow is getting vicious. Priorities. I don't want to have to shovel out the car to get clean clothes.

"Let me get our things. You take the cat." I hand her the kitten and turn around, trudging back to the Rover. Eventually, I haul in her luggage and mine, plus a box of diabetic-friendly provisions made by my Bee and about half of a pet store for Shaz. By the time I'm done, my jeans are soaked from the weather.

When I step inside, leaving my boots in the entry, I survey the room.

Goddamn. Josh is an architect with stellar taste, but this place is spectacular. The last light of the day showcases the great room with a huge stone fireplace stocked with half a cord of wood, comfortable leather couches and bookcases, and an open kitchen on the side. With tall ceilings and exposed beams, this place is a magical log cabin that's had a trip of ayahuasca and some Reiki to balance its energy. Wide-open windows face out into the woods, where snow falls like a layer of gauze.

But we're standing in the dark. And it's not much warmer inside than out. "Something wrong with the lights?" I ask.

"I tried. None of the switches work. Is there a security system that we need to worry about?"

I pause. *Is there?* I'm regretting tuning out last night when my best friend blabbed on about this place. But then I remember.

"Josh turned it off remotely so we wouldn't have to worry about the code if we beat him up here." I glance around. "Is the electricity knocked out from the storm?"

She wraps her arms around herself. "I don't know. Maybe a circuit is tripped?"

"Damn. I can check." *I have no idea how to untrip a circuit.* I inspect the heater, like I could tell anything from the thermostat. Flipping the switch does nothing. While Kendall shivers in the middle of the living room, I enter the top-of-the-line kitchen and start poking around. The sink works, but either the hot water isn't working, or it's taking way too long to heat up. The stove clicks and clicks, but I think I can light it with a match. "Thank God," I mutter. "We have water, and I think we can cook, but no electricity."

Her expression is a few notches down from panic. "No electricity means no Wi-Fi. No cell service either."

I size her up and give her my most soothing smile because her teeth are still chattering. "I think the first thing you need is something warm to drink and a roaring fire." Before she reacts, I find matches in a kitchen drawer, fill up the first pan I find in a cabinet with water, hoping that there's tea or cocoa stashed somewhere, light the burner, and place my makeshift kettle on the stove. Rifling through the cupboard, I find some hot cider packets and tea and hold them up for her. "As your barista, I can take your order."

Relief registers in her eyes, and her shoulders loosen. "Tea would be amazing, thank you."

"One steaming cup of tea, coming up." Finding dishes, I insert teabags in mugs for us and set down a bowl of water for Shazam, who laps it up.

As the tea water heats, the room gets dimmer and dimmer. The sun doesn't last long this time of year, and since trees shade this cabin—oh, and there's a storm raging—it's even darker than usual. "I'll start a fire, then see if I can find some flashlights or candles."

She nods, wringing her hands and shoving them under her armpits. "I'll help."

"Nah. I gotcha." Before she can say anything, I pick her up and deposit her on a cushion by the fireplace. "You need to defrost, my little icicle." I snag a Pendleton blanket with a bison pattern and drape it over her shoulders.

"Thanks," she says and gives me a small smile. She slides her knees inside her sweater like she's at a slumber party and hugs her legs to herself.

My gaze softens. "I'll warm you up. Just a sec." Kneeling down on the hearth, I examine the fireplace like I know what I'm doing. While every house I've lived in has had fireplaces, either they ignite with a switch, or someone else builds the fire.

I have no idea what I'm doing.

"Do you know how to light a fire?"

"Let's find out. After all," I grunt, "man tame wilderness. Man bring fire."

And man would like to not asphyxiate, so I reach into the fireplace to open the flue. See, I *do* know things.

While the cabin is stocked with plenty of logs, I need something smaller to use as tinder, and there's no newspaper or firestarter. On a bookshelf, I locate a stack of *National Geographic* magazines and start ripping out the pages—articles about the sex life of ducks, mysteries of the Serengeti, our evolving brains. Part of me wants to read more about ducks with big corkscrew wangs, but other things are more important right now.

Kendall chides me in mock shock. "Those could be collector's items!"

"I'll replace them. Right now we need fuel." I crumple up the pages, set them in the fireplace, and then lay a bunch of logs on top. A scavenging trip to a utility closet reveals lighter fluid and a few flashlights. I return with everything, strike a match, and set the whole pile of wood and paper on fire.

Thank God I don't burn down the house.

After a moment, the magazine articles crinkle, consumed by the licking flames, and the logs start to catch. I look back at Kendall, grinning with my accomplishment.

With the burgeoning warmth from the fire, her legs emerge from where they were tucked inside her shirt, and she relaxes. Shazzy pads over and sits next to her, like a Sphinx. A self-cleaning Sphinx. She pets him and says to me, "Maybe you are a mountain man."

"I'm full of hidden talents." Or at least not the nitwit she thinks I am.

"Uh-huh. That's it."

The rattling of the pan on the stove alerts me that the water is boiling, so I grab her mug and make tea. When I return, she clasps the hot drink with reverence and sniffs it gratefully.

"Thank you." Her pretty, slim fingers wrap around the cup. If she could step inside it, I think she would. My eyes catch hers, and she gives me a huge smile. Then she goes to take a drink, but her eyes widen, noticing the state of my clothes. "You're all wet. You need to get those pants off now."

I smirk. "You want me that badly, huh?"

She rolls her eyes with a laugh. "You know what I mean. Go change so you don't freeze."

Picking up my duffel, I take off to find my bedroom, but I only locate one, total. Perplexed, I go back, open the few doors in the hallway, but they either lead outside, to a bathroom, or to the garage.

There must be more to this place. Maybe there's another cottage. Throwing my bag in the lone bedroom, I undress, pull on black track pants, a long-sleeve T-shirt, and dry socks, hanging my wet clothes in the shower. Now that I'm comfortable and have a moment to think, all the stress of driving up here on the slick roads floods me, and my body sags in exhaustion. I sit on the bed.

What. The. Hell?

And what *the what*? Why doesn't the electricity work? Why isn't everyone else here? How long is this storm going to last? Can I shovel us out and get us back soon? Where were Josh and Evie thinking we'd all sleep if there's only one bedroom?

That said, it's a sexy bedroom, with mirrors, a huge king-size bed, and a now-dimming view of the trees.

I decide to make the best of what's going on here. And with Kendall in the other room, her claws retracted, the best is pretty freaking good.

When I reenter the living room, Kendall's moved to the couch. She's curled on some cushions, stroking the cat behind his ears while she sips her tea. The fireplace thankfully puts out some heat. Kendall's eyes widen at the track pants slung low on my hips and the shirt clinging to my waist. I grin to myself, but she doesn't comment. Instead, she muses, "I wonder whether Josh and Evie are going to make it."

"They will. Josh has four-wheel drive." I plunk down on the couch beside her, stretching my arms along the back of the couch—and behind her back—finally taking a load off. The only light now is coming from the fireplace. I toy with a lock of her hair. "You feeling better?"

A smile stretches her lips as she turns toward me. "Yes, thank you." She tilts her head. Her face is flushed, and her eyes sparkle from the fire.

I squeeze her shoulder. "My pleasure." I open my mouth to say more, and she does the same thing. I shrug and gesture at her. "You first."

"Just," she says quietly, picking her words and saying them into the mug. "Thanks for getting us here in one piece." She looks up and again, her startling clear eyes cause a chain reaction behind my ribcage. I watch her lips as her words come out haltingly. "I appreciate you looking out for me. Especially after the history we've had."

"Not a problem. I kinda like looking out for you." The admission rushes out before I can stop it.

Her cheeks redden, and the flustered expression on her face makes me want to plant a kiss on her furrowed brow.

After a stretch of silence, she blows out a breath. "Look, you seem different, and I'm worried that I've maybe misjudged you."

"So do I get a second chance?"

She shrugs. "You're obviously trying here, so I want to as well." She studies her mug again. "So yeah, thanks for not leaving me on the side of the road, or, you know, in your trunk or a ditch."

We both laugh.

"Glad to be marginally competent," I say. "Well, now that we're here, want something to eat?"

She glances over my shoulder at the kitchen. "I can't imagine there's more than stale crackers and condiments."

"No, ma'am. We are hooked up." I rise and gesture to the box of goodies I brought in with our luggage. "My grandma wanted to make sure your friendly neighborhood diabetic could eat at Thanksgiving dinner, so I've got everything from green beans with almonds to sugar-free pumpkin pie. Let me make you a plate. And then we need to talk about our sleeping situation."

9

KENDALL

W *hat did he say? Sleeping arrangements and what?*

"You're diabetic?" The health nut in me is triggered, and all I can think about is the myriad ways he's abused his body since I've known him.

When he nods with a somber expression on his face, it starts to make sense. "That's why you got in shape."

"Yup." He pats his now taut belly. "Certainly not because I enjoy Brussels sprouts." He sets a giant cardboard box next to the coffee table and returns to his seat on the couch next to me.

"Oh, Drew. All that partying..." I bite off the reprimand. He doesn't need a lecture. His face makes it clear he knows he behaved like a dumbass. And it's obvious he's trying to recover. I attempt to redirect my tone before he takes this the wrong way. "Are you okay? Did something happen?"

Something *had* to have happened. Drew is the world's biggest party animal. For him to get in shape to the degree he has means whatever went down was scary.

Now that I think about it, I can't remember seeing him drunk recently. Josh and Evie's wedding maybe? Around the time Tristan and I started our PR firm.

Drew winces and rubs his hand along his jaw. "Yeah. Three days in a diabetic coma has a way of making you see the light."

I gasp. "Jesus, Drew. When?" How did I not know about this?

"Early March. A few days after Josh and Evie's wedding. One minute I was downing the best mojito north of the Rio Grande, and the next I was face down in my own puke. Or so I was told. All I remember is waking up with fifty wires taped to my body, a godawful taste in my mouth, and a nurse named Ronnie jamming a tube up my dick." He laughs ruefully. "There's nothing like the indignity of pissing in a bag. I'm lucky to be alive, I guess. Trying to look on the bright side. You know, *not* dying."

"That sounds terrifying." To my dismay, my eyes fill with tears, and I blink them back.

I try to tuck that emotion behind feeling indignant no one told me Drew was in a fucking coma.

But why would they have? You've only professed your hatred for this man since the moment you met.

His brows lift under that blond mop of hair that's now hanging in his eyes. He sweeps it back with his palm.

"Aww, Kenster, I'm okay now." He grabs my hand to comfort me. With his other hand, he pets Shazam, who's returned to his lap and is now kneading his stomach.

I scoot back because this is getting weird. I've known Drew for two and a half years, and this road trip is the first time we've ever talked about anything serious. And then I find out he had this major trauma that reminds me so much of what my family went through when my dad got sick that I need a minute to collect myself.

"Sorry. Um. I...Uh..." *Very eloquent, Kendall. Are you sure you own a public relations firm?* Clearing my throat, I shake my head. "I'm sorry you were sick and went through so much." I motion toward him. "But you must be doing well now because look at you. You're an Instagram phenom with razor-sharp abs." And some very enthusiastic fangirls online. His inbox is probably a porn hub all on its own.

He chuckles. "Why, KK, have you been checking out my posts?"

"I'm in PR. I look at everyone's posts." So I might've sought out his specifically a time or two since I ran into him at the hotel, but I'll never admit it.

In fact, I looked at Drew's Instagram right after I scoped out my ex and his perfect little wife and their perfect little baby and wished I wasn't still hurt that he'd moved on to the next woman like a G6 heading down the runway after we broke up. It made me wonder if he'd been seeing her when he was with me.

God, that's depressing. Where's the wine when I need it?

I glance at Drew and realize I couldn't enjoy a glass now even if I had one. It would be rude to imbibe in front of Drew when he's trying to straighten out.

Listen to me. Here I am obsessing about my love life when this guy's dealing with sobriety and diabetes.

"Drew, let's dig into those snacks. Aren't you worried about your blood sugar level? We drove for hours, and then you ran around the property with me hanging off your back."

"Right. Food." He snaps his fingers. "What time is it?"

I pull out my phone that still has zero bars. "Six." In the last few minutes, the long shadows of evening have melted into twilight, giving the great room an ethereal glow.

He pauses, a frown on his face. "I'm not sure how Evie planned the meals. Don't want her to go nuclear if we tank Thanksgiving."

The Drew I know would've kicked his feet up on this coffee table and gorged himself on whatever was around, giving all of two fucks if anyone was inconvenienced.

Drew 2.0 is...sweet. And dare I say thoughtful? I like this new side to him. More than I care to admit.

Now it makes sense why he seems like a new person. Because he almost dropped dead from partying like a rock star. Talk about a come-to-Jesus moment.

"Drew, we're stuck on the side of a mountain in the middle of a snowstorm. If your sugars get out of whack, you're hours away from medical attention. I think that trumps Evie's plans. As her best friend, I absolve you from any worry over that."

"So if I ruin Thanksgiving, I get to hide behind your skirt, so to speak? Because I got a good look at what you got going on back there today when you were hopping through the window like a sexy cat burglar, and I don't think it'd be a hardship."

A wicked grin spreads across his face. *Ah.* So post-coma Drew is still a perv.

I shake my head, unable to keep my own smile at bay.

"Don't think I didn't know you were copping a feel when I asked for help. You might be reformed, but you're still a menace, huh? Good to know."

He leans close, so close that I can smell his cologne. "Don't pretend you didn't like it."

His green eyes go dark as his words settle over me.

I open my mouth, but the pithy comeback gets lodged in my throat when his full lips tilt in a flirty smile. *What is happening here?*

"Meow-ow-ow!" Shazam hops up between us and swipes at a dangling piece of my hair.

Startled, I jump back, my heart skittering in my chest.

"You crazy cat." I pick him up and tuck him against my neck. "Where's the love?"

Drew shakes his head with mock disgust in his eyes. "Cock-blocked by a pussy. There's a first."

I laugh. "Here I was thinking you were such a charmer."

"Oh, I am. Don't worry. I'm saving the big guns for later."

That's what I'm worried about.

Drew sits next to me on the floor in front of the low coffee table, and between us, candles flicker gently against the darkness that's descended across the living room, our faces illuminated by the banked fire.

It's terribly romantic.

I don't know how I feel about this. One minute, I find myself giving in to Drew's natural charisma, but the next, the voice of reason is screaming, *This is Demerit! He once told you you'd be pretty if you unjammed the rod up your ass.*

Shaking my head, I try to focus on the fact that he's trying, and I'm a big believer in supporting someone trying to change. That made all the difference in my dad's life during his health crisis, and it looks like it might in Drew's life too.

Once Drew's done laying out a few different dishes his grandmother made and a Ziploc bag of fresh veggies, he reaches into the big box and pulls out a bottle of wine.

"Pinot's your favorite, right?"

With a nod, I frown. "But you can't drink, can you? I wouldn't feel right enjoying a glass if you can't."

"I wasn't going to have any. This is for you. Though, technically, yes, I could have a glass if I wanted. I'd just need to check my sugars first."

As much as I'd love a glass right now, I'm still wary.

He motions toward the bottle. "Have some if you'd like. I don't even drink wine. It won't make me struggle with sobriety or anything like that. Now if you were offering me a shot of vodka with a line of blow, I might have a hard time."

He means it as a joke, but that's a level of partying I've never known or wanted to know. Sure, I've smoked a little pot—with my parents, no less. Crazy, I know, but this is Oregon where it's legal. But cocaine?

Drew must see the concern all over my face, and he sighs. "I haven't done coke or anything like it since I landed in the hospital. I used it as an example so you could see your glass of wine is no biggie." He gives me one of those somber smiles I'm getting used to, laced with regret. It makes me feel like a jerk for being a downer.

He leans closer. "Wanna hear a little secret?" I nod, wanting to change the tone of discussion. "I brought the wine for you. As a way to wave the white flag."

Smiling, I reach for a baby carrot. "What do you mean?"

"I've been trying to think of a way to apologize to you for all the shitty things I've said to you over the years, and I know you and Evie like the vino. So I bought you a case. Then I thought that seemed extreme—like, hey, your resident fuck-up brought you a case of booze—so I only brought a bottle this weekend." He chuckles. "But if you like it, I have more I can bring you."

"Oh, Drew." *What am I going to do with you?* Over the years, he's made me so nuts, I didn't think strangling him with my bare hands was completely out of the question. "That was very thoughtful. Thank you. When you put it like that, I'd love a glass, but you have to swear to me it won't be weird for you if I do."

The last thing I want to do when he's being so sweet is turn down his gift.

"Scout's honor." He holds up three fingers as he gets up and trots into the kitchen. After a few minutes of clanging about, he returns with an opener and a glass.

When he pours it a minute later, I ask, "Were you even a Boy Scout?"

"Yes." He nods slowly. "With Josh. Until I got kicked out."

We laugh, our voices cutting through the quiet of the room.

After he hands me the glass, I sniff the dark liquid, and it smells delicious. After a few sips, I grin. "This is the best wine I've ever had. Thank you."

"You're not just saying that? Because if you really like it, I gotta give props to my sommelier because I know shit about wine. My wine knowledge is limited to the 'How merlot do you go' meme."

"I love it." Boy, do I. It's the perfect pinot with hints of cherry and blackberry, my favorite combination. I actually don't know a lot about wine except what I like—nothing too sweet or too dry. Evie used to buy it by the box with the pour spout, so I wouldn't say it has to be pricey for me to enjoy, though judging by the label on this one, Drew spared no expense.

"I'm sure I would've loved whatever you brought me."

Although the wine goes to my head quickly since I haven't eaten much yet, it's helping me relax despite the mountain of work I should be doing right now and emails I can't check and messages I probably have.

"So what do you say about the truce? Do I get that second chance for real?" He hands me a plate of fancy cheeses and crackers and then settles in to slice an apple, which makes me wonder if he picked those up to complement the vintage.

Licking my lips, I nod. "I'd like to start over with you."

A huge grin stretches across his face, and his body straightens like a weight has been lifted from his shoulders.

As though maybe my words have helped him.

I return his smile.

Truthfully, I'm tired of this weird animosity between us. I know it bothers our friends. How great would it be to get along with Drew? To be *in* on his jokes instead of the butt of them.

He did tell some mean ones about me.

My eye twitches again.

He clears his throat, and his gaze grows more intense. "I appreciate a do-over more than you know. I'm not in AA, but I understand the make-amends thing. I didn't just want to apologize with a bottle of wine. I wanted to say it, too. For real. With words, I mean. God, I'm shitty at this." As he looks away, his laugh is rueful and self-conscious, an emotion I've never seen from him before.

But then his eyes are back on mine. "Kendall, I am truly sorry about how abysmally I've behaved toward you, starting the first time we met." He shakes his head and lowers his voice. "I barely remember that night at the restaurant, but the bits and pieces that come back to me are pretty horrendous. I was out of control, and I'm sorry I was such an asshole to you."

I swallow past the strange rush of emotion. "I appreciate the apology." I laugh awkwardly. "Yeah, it was a bad first impression."

"Quite possibly the worst ever."

"A hall-of-famer. I should make you a plaque."

We're both laughing now, and Drew winks conspiratorially. "I guess every friendship has a story to tell when it starts, right?" He clears his throat again as he places the apple slices next to the crackers. "So does this mean we can be friends?"

That gives me pause. Because forgiveness and friendship are different things, right?

I guess I *am* having a hard time letting go of the past.

He bought you a big-ass box of wine and wants to be friends. He gave you a real apology. Be like Elsa, Kendall. Let it the fuck go.

I swirl my wine and watch the color reflect against the glass. "I like Drew 2.0, so yes, we can be friends."

"Can we be friends who kiss?" He gives me a cheeky grin, and I shake my head, laughing.

And then I think I surprise us both with my next words.

"Let me think about it."

What the hell is that about? I look down at my almost empty glass of wine. It has to be the alcohol talking.

Although...the thought of kissing Drew right now does things to me. Because kissing this man would lead to other activities.

It flashes in my mind. What sex with him would be like. The way his broad shoulders would hover over me, and how he'd thrust, hard, and those lips—God, those lips. They'd be everywhere. On my neck, sucking and whispering filthy things. Because Drew is a dirty, dirty boy.

"You okay, KK? Do you want me to turn down the fire?" He motions toward my face. "You look a little flushed."

"I think I'm finally warming up." I pull off my jacket and smile when he holds up the bottle of wine.

"Another glass? We can save the rest for tomorrow."

I wave it on. Now that I'm starting to unwind, I realize how uptight I've been about work. The fact I can't do a damn thing right now is liberating, and I want to take full advantage of that before I have to return to the grind.

We eat and chat and watch Shazam chase his tail. When we finish, we lean back against the couch, side by side. I'm sleepy, so I lean my head against his shoulder, and he reaches over and plays with a strand of my hair.

"Drew, should we be worried about Josh and Evie? I hope they're not stuck on the road somewhere."

"Nah. Maybe they couldn't make it up the mountain, so they turned around and they're boning like bunnies at home."

"They do like to bone." I love Evie, but I'm a little jealous of her sex life.

Drew snorts. "Tell me about it. Once I crashed at their place and had to listen to them do the dirty all night."

"Have you noticed how they eye fuck each other whenever they're in the same room?"

His chest rumbles with laughter. "Did I ever tell you I caught them in the act in my closet once when I had a party?"

"Dang. Those crazy kids."

Talking about my best friend reminds me that I probably won't be spending any time with Evie if she and Josh did head back to Portland. A strange melancholy spreads through me.

With a sigh, I shiver. The fire has died down, and it's getting cold again. I can see my breath.

Drew wraps an arm around my shoulder, and I snuggle closer, and whisper, "I like this friends thing we have going on."

Yeah, maybe I'm lonely and cold and Drew is here, making me laugh. Helping me forget my state of singlehood.

"Me too. You smell good. Way better than any of my guy friends."

"You smell good too." So good, I'd like to lick him. Closing my eyes, I smile. "I had fun today, and I really didn't expect to."

Now that the wine has worked its way through me, I have a whole-body buzz that makes everything feel warm and fuzzy, like I could float away.

"Back at ya." After a minute, he tugs my hair. "Maybe we should talk about where you want to sleep."

"Hmm?"

"There's only one bedroom, but there's no fireplace in there. So you can sleep in there or in here on the couch, and I'll take whatever you don't want. It's warmer here, but you can have the bedroom if you want more privacy."

"That's crazy. How does this place only have one bedroom?"

"Not sure. I was thinking maybe there's another cabin in the back, although in this weather, I don't wanna trek out there to find it."

I crack open my eyes again and look toward the window, but it's solid black out there, with the exception of the snow that's built up along the bottom that looks at least knee-deep thanks to the wind.

"You're sure this is the right place?" I glance at the beautifully decorated living room, suddenly panicked.

He gestures around. "It's ultra-Josh. He always puts in Wolf appliances and big windows and shelves like this. He spent forty-five minutes telling me about the cantilevered-vaulted-cornerstone-something-or-other architecture of the place. It's his."

Drew seems convinced. But it's not like we have any other options if he's wrong.

"What do you want to do?" Sitting up, I tilt my head to look at him, and sheesh, we're close. His blond hair is dipping over his eyes in a flirty way that makes my breath come faster.

"What do *I* want to do?"

Smiling, I nudge him with my elbow. "About sleeping."

"Oh, I thought you just meant generally speaking." My nipples tighten when his eyes lower to my lips. "Because right now I'd like to revisit my proposition about being friends who kiss."

The pulse between my thighs cheers me on, and I tap my chin with my finger, pretending to think about it. "Do you think you could do a demonstration for me? So we could test out this theory? How would this be different than just hooking up?"

Teasing him is fun, but his flirty grin makes that pulse beat faster. "Oh, it would be very different." He dips his head to my neck and runs his lips up to my ear, erupting goosebumps across my skin. "Hookups are a one-and-done. But us? We wouldn't let the fucking get in the way of this BFF thing we have going on. We could be an FWF. Friends who fuck."

Swallowing, I try to ignore the immediate shock of lust that spears through my veins.

Hooking up with Drew is a terrible idea.

The worst.

Something I promised myself I'd never do.

Except he's different now.

This isn't the same Drew.

This is post-coma Drew who carries you on his back and makes you tea and tucks blankets around your shoulders.

His lips trail once more over the delicate area behind my ear, making it hard to think.

Why would this be so bad?

The more I mull over his words, the more I like the idea.

Because friends who fuck don't get in the way of work engagements or long hours at the office. Friends who fuck don't pressure you to put your career on the back burner. Friends who fuck don't get upset when the only thing you have time for is the fucking.

My breath comes out a pant, and I fist his T-shirt, but then his hands scoop under my thighs and lift me onto his lap so I'm straddling him where he's thick and hard under his flimsy track pants.

But as he leans up for my mouth, I pull away. "Can we keep the FWF status quiet? Just between us? I don't want to have to explain what we're doing to anyone."

"We can do this any way you want. As long as you come hard and often."

I grind myself against his sizable erection. "I like this plan."

When his lips touch mine, I groan, but when our tongues slide together, an electric spark shoots through me.

And I can't wait to detonate.

10

DREW

*K*issing a hot-blooded Kendall activates every single nerve receptor in my body. Kendall dry humping me is eyes-rolling-back-in-my-head good. Combine the two and I may not survive this night.

When I waved the white flag-slash-red wine of truce, I honestly had no ulterior motive. I just wanted to press reset on our relationship and see what would happen if we hadn't started off with me being a drunk asshole and her being a stuck-up snob. I'd hoped for neutrality, or at best, "well-wishing" in *The Simpsons* sense—that she didn't wish me any *specific* harm.

This, though? Test driving this weird *we used to annoy each other and now we're really getting along and let's see what it's like to be naked* thing?

Yes, please. Give me more.

Have I ever imagined a moment like this? Affirmative. Did I think it would happen? Negatory, Batman.

With a groan, I wrap my arms around her slim form to kiss the hell out of her. Although I taste the sweet-sour red wine on her tongue, she seems in control. Cogent. I clutch her pert ass as she rides me over my pants, her jeans causing friction that makes me throb. I deepen the kiss until both of us are panting, and we break apart.

"Wow," she whispers, her eyes hazy and half-lidded.

"Yeah," I whisper back. And before she can say something else, I press my lips to hers again, and she invites me in with her tongue. I take my time, paying attention to her breath coming faster, the way her skin heats up, her long, languid slides down my very happy dick.

At a horse race, there's the moment at the start when the gate falls and the horses are off. No hesitation, they just tear down the track, kicking up dust and aiming for the finish line as fast as possible.

I'll be delicate here. Let's just say—hypothetically speaking of course—in the past, if I were a horse in a sexual race, I would have been the fastest one down the course.

I don't want to do that tonight for so many reasons, and they all go back to the simple fact that Kendall deserves better. I'm taking it as a personal challenge to discover every single way I can get Kendall to moan.

But it's more than physical attraction. Over the course of the day, I feel like I finally see her without all the bullshit that convoluted our relationship—mainly me and my drunken stupidity.

And I realize I like what I see. Sure, she's gorgeous. That's not what's making me treat her with care.

The difference is that she appreciates the boring, adult changes I've made, which hits a deep, foreign place inside me.

Most of my "friends" give me a hard time about my new healthy lifestyle—*Drew, how come you're not drinking? Want a hit? Why are you leaving early? Where's your belly, dude? Are you a body Nazi now?*

Those comments from the bros get old fast. But I hadn't realized how few people understood how serious my shit was.

Kendall actually sympathizing about my health puts her in a rarefied minority consisting of her, Josh, and Bee. No one else cares. Not even my family.

So when I kiss her, I'm really not kissing a friend who I want to fuck. That offer was me throwing out a Hail Mary because I didn't think she'd actually go for me. Instead, I'm kissing a girl who sees me for more than I am, and I'm hoping I can treat her right.

At least I'm giving her the new and better me, and it's honest. I'm not hiding anything, and she knows all the gory details of pre-coma Drew. Now's my chance to prove I've changed for the better.

As my lips make their way down her neck and my fingers glide along the tense muscles of her back, I murmur, "You are wound up like a Slinky, Kendall Jackson."

She pulls back and pouts, although her body is still grinding on me, slow and languid and delicious. "My last name's Greer."

I tilt my head, put my finger on her lips shushing her, and give her my most serious expression. "I know."

She bursts out laughing. "Oh, Kendall Jackson *wine*. Your bottle is so much better. And I'm not that tipsy. I promise."

"Good," I say quietly, and reach between us to unbutton her jeans. "Pants off, woman."

Climbing off my lap and standing, she smiles and kicks off her boots. She reaches for my waistband, and I shake my head no. While I could shuck off my clothes, I'm not going to. I want to be the last horse in this race—one that could take all night for all I care.

I unzip her pants, and she shimmies them down, leaving her wearing a shirt, socks, and teeny tiny panties.

Dead. I'm dead.

She shivers, and I quickly throw another log on the fire. When she climbs back on me and our lips join again, now she's so much softer, closer, with only flimsy fabric separating her scorching center and my erection. This time, we both groan. If I don't stop this, I'm going to end up coming in my pants like a teenager.

While she moves, Kendall whispers in my ear. Her lips feel delicate, her words exquisite, her voice on the edge of satisfaction. "Drew, you have a really nice cock."

"Why, thank you. My cock likes you too." As the snow falls outside, and the fire roars within, I pull back, my hands gripping her thighs while she kisses my neck. "Here's what I think. If I tell a stressed out workaholic to relax, she won't relax."

"She's stubborn that way," Kendall admits against the stubble of my jaw.

"I'm wondering something, though."

"What?"

"If I tell that workaholic I'm not stopping until she comes so hard she forgets her name and only screams mine, I'd bet she just might do that."

Kendall's sharp intake of breath synchronizes with her eyes widening. She pauses on the down-grind and grins, a wide-open, no-holds-barred grin that makes me melt inside. "I'd like to see you try."

I rub over the soft cloth of her undies as she lifts up from my hard-on. "Try not, sweetheart. Do or do not."

She giggles and then lets out a sigh. "I can't believe you're quoting Yoda while you're getting in my pants."

"No better time," I mutter, and I gently increase the pressure on her, massaging the parts I know will make her purr.

Thankfully the other beast who purrs is leaving us alone, curled up by the fire.

I keep going, and Kendall's breath changes. I can tell by the way she's moving her hips that she likes this, but she's not letting herself go. This woman needs an orgasm the way a cabin needs a fireplace—it's simply wrong without one, and preferably, multiple.

"You're stunningly beautiful," I tell her. "Wanna make you come. Want more here?"

Nodding, she bites her lips and wriggles in my lap, finally abandoning her guardedness and showing me how much she's enjoying my hand both with the way she's losing focus and the way she's soaked the fabric.

"How about here?"

I get a firmer, more vehement nod.

"What about here?" I ask, and with my hand on her back, I flip her onto the couch as she squeals in delight. The back couch cushion supports her head, and both of her toned legs sprawl to the ground. I kneel on the ground between her thighs and scooch her lingerie to the side, exposing a neat auburn landing strip. The rest of her is smooth and baby-soft, a discovery that makes my cock thump in my track pants when I take a long lick on her most intimate part.

Yumm.

"Oh my God," she gasps. "M-m-more."

My tongue laps at her clit as my fingers stroke inside her, knocking against her G-spot. Her thighs squeeze around my face, and I'm almost coming myself, I love it so much. But I'm focusing on her and what will please her. What will make her shatter in blissful agony.

I keep going and going with my mouth, as she writhes on the couch, her head slashing back and forth.

It feels extra dirty since we're both basically clothed.

And I suppose we could get caught.

"Don't stop." She's holding herself still now, but her fingers claw at the couch cushions. "Drew Merritt, I want you inside me. Right fucking now."

I know better than to remember what Kendall says during sex. I know not to bring this up at any other time.

But dammit if it won't star in my dreams for the rest of my existence.

Naughty Kendall with my head between her legs, demanding that I fuck her?

This might be the highlight of my life.

With my face and my fingers, I lavish her with undivided attention until she throws her head back, her body goes rigid, and she quivers on my tongue. I keep going as she crests the wave of her O, getting off on the way her body quakes. Then I slow, letting her pulse on my face, as she comes back down.

When she revives herself, she asks breathlessly, "Can we do that again?"

I nod into the space between her legs, kissing the inside of her thigh, then giving it a tiny bite. "I can arrange that."

"Awesome." Glancing up at her, I notice her eyes have changed to bright and glossy and satiated. I stand up, my pants not hiding what my dick's thinking. She reaches toward me while she gets to her feet. "I think it's my turn to—"

Grabbing her hands, I hold them together firmly. "No. You first. Again."

"But I want to—"

I pause and inhale, still clasping her wrists and now catching her pretty eyes. "We both know my track record is abysmal. The longest intimate relationship I've ever had is with my hand. Left one, mostly. I'm way out of my league with you, and I have no idea what I'm getting myself into. I've never had a FWF. But if I mess this up tonight, I'll never forgive myself."

I must've said the right things because her eyes soften, and she gives me a vulnerable smile.

One she's never given me before.

And it makes me feel like a goddamn king.

"Okay," she whispers. "We'll do this your way."

I go to kiss her, but pause to whip off my shirt and wipe my face with it.

Her grin turns knowing as she drags a finger down my front. "This is not first edition Drew."

Flexing my bicep, I say, "First edition Drew has been discontinued. We have a new model in stock."

"I like the new model. It comes with extra features." She rubs my stiff cock. "I don't think we're doing much sleeping tonight."

"Fine by me. This might be the best Thanksgiving ever." I tug on her hand to lead her to the bedroom, and my voice comes out husky. "How would you like a cordial invitation to sit on my face?"

11

KENDALL

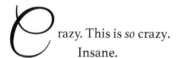razy. This is *so* crazy.
Insane.

Probably the nuttiest thing I've done since high school.

And fucking amazing! my sex-deprived inner nerd chants, not caring that I'm hooking up with literally the last man on the face of the planet I ever thought I'd bone. *And there'd better be full-on boning,* she warns me.

I'm buzzed enough to be able to lock away most of my reservations about sleeping with Drew, yet sober enough to know the freak-outs will commence tomorrow. And there will be freak-outs. But not now.

Because right now, Drew and I are sprawled across the king-sized bed like we own the joint. We stopped mauling each other for a full minute to light a few candles, and vanilla and lavender scent the air and mingle with his citrusy cologne.

Between the warm hue of the candles and the faint streak of moonlight from the bay window, I can make out the wispy, white puffs of my breath, but I can't bring myself to care about how cold it is. Between the two glasses of wine and the first orgasm I had on the couch, I feel like a car with its engine revving.

I'm still wearing my long-sleeved T-shirt and wool socks. And underwear if you count them since they're still dangling off my ankle. Sexy, right? Not exactly how I'd choose to seduce a new lover, but Drew doesn't seem to require any seduction whatsoever. He's ready to go.

Happily, I note the temperature has done nothing to tame Drew's thick erection.

From my perch on top of his face, I have the best view of his six-pack abs that lead down to those flimsy track pants and his own personal Mount Hood jacking up between his legs.

Why is he still wearing pants?

I lose my train of thought when his tongue does something magical under the hood, and my body tightens, a guttural moan bellowing from my throat.

"Oh, God. Do that again." I reach back to grip a chunk of his hair like he's a stallion who might buck me off.

He grunts in agreement, and when he swirls his tongue again, I arch my back, my shoulders almost hitting the headboard, as his hands clasp my hips.

"C'me back here." His words get muffled against me, but I nod even though he can't see me.

Those hands smooth up and down my thighs like I'm something delectable as he laves my slit, not caring that I might suffocate him.

Let me say that Drew is *very* thorough.

And really fucking dirty.

I like it. A whole lot.

Pretty sure I could ask him to lick my—

I squeak when a wet finger presses against that very spot.

He chuckles and takes a big bite of my left butt cheek, sending a shiver so strong down my back that I tumble forward and nearly get my eye poked out by his pocket rocket.

Panting, I laugh and feel his abs shake against me, as he

joins me, our sudden burst of amusement echoing in the room.

"Sorry, princess." He rubs my ass reverently. "Didn't mean to topple you over."

"S'okay," I mumble, trying to catch my breath as I appreciate being eye-level with his sizeable erection, which I reach for and lick slowly through the thin fabric.

"Nuh-uh. Appetizer first, then the main course." He bats my hand away, and I laugh again and rest my face against his warm body.

"When did you become such a slave driver? Yeesh. I thought you'd be on board to sixty-nine."

"We'll get there. Hold your horses."

Oh, I have every intention of holding the horse.

Keeping my knees pressed against his head like ear warmers, I strip off my shirt and bra and then lean back down to press my face to his lean stomach. The contrast in temperature—the chill of the air and his hot body—makes my nipples tighten to almost painful points.

Like a cat in heat, I rub my torso against those steely abs, the sprinkling of his rough hair abrading my sensitive skin in the best kind of way. He must like the motion because his dick jerks hard against my face.

"Oh, fuck." The need in his voice makes me do it again. "Your tits feel amazing. Can I come on them later?"

I'm finding that I like Drew's lack of filter when we're naked.

Smiling, I shake my head. "Jury's out, Mr. Merritt. You still need to ace your oral exam."

Will I let him do such a naughty thing?

Probably.

Who am I kidding? Yes, I will. Maybe not right this moment, but perhaps later this weekend, I'll let him ice my Pillsbury muffins.

Now that we've broken the seal, I will let Drew Merritt

debauch the hell out of me. Come Monday morning at the office, I'll be the most relaxed PR executive in the entire city of Portland.

Enthusiastic about my plan, I swivel my hips in his face, and it's his turn to moan.

But my victory in this sex game is short lived.

Drew's thick finger skates over my back nine like he's about to dive in, and I take a big breath, squirmy because while I like the idea of ass play, my ex was always too rough with me there, so I never let him get too far. Plus, call me crazy, but that seems more intimate than something I'd do the first time I hook up with someone.

Shut up, Kendall. Buzzed KK wants the kink. Besides, you're already gleefully kneeling over the man's mouth, like a crouching tiger waiting for his hidden dragon.

Drew kisses my inner thigh and licks between my legs, lapping me up like his favorite ice cream before he pushes two thick fingers into my pussy.

My eyes nearly roll back in my head.

I nuzzle against the sexy treasure trail that dips into his track pants, so high on endorphins, I could levitate.

Everything feels so good that when he rubs me *back there* again, a throaty moan bursts out of me.

And then he's pressing harder.

Dipping into that tight ring of muscles.

In and out.

Joining the rhythm of his other two fingers and that talented tongue.

And *ohhhhh myyyy Godddd.*

I shriek when I come, bowing over Drew so hard, I'm pretty sure I slobber all over his pretty abs.

Because damn. This is some next-level orgasm action.

A-plus on the oral, Mr. Merritt. A-fucking-plus.

~

Drowsy, I collapse on the bed. My eyes are screwed shut, and I curl into a ball, nearly comatose with pleasure.

A blanket wraps around me, and I sigh and burrow deeper. The sound of running water cuts through the quiet, and a few minutes later, a big body sidles up against me.

Instinctively, I turn toward Drew and paste my body to his. Strong arms come around me, and he presses a kiss to my forehead.

And he holds me.

Aww, Drew is a snuggler. Who knew?

A few minutes pass, and my bones feel like they've melted away.

"You broke me," I whisper against his chest as I rub my hand up against those perfect pecs.

I'm so exhausted, part of me wants to sleep until the new year, but the other part is dragging up my sleepy ass to seal the deal.

Because who knows how things will change in the morning? What seems like a good idea now might not then, and I've already come this far. If nothing else, I'll have one amazing night.

And while Drew is making no move to push me to reciprocate the O-town magic that nearly knocked me unconscious, I'd like to return the sexual karma.

Decision made, I slide my thigh over his and snake a hand down his stomach before I can change my mind.

But I'm surprised when his hand covers mine, stopping it before I reach my destination, his deep voice rumbling through me. "KK, we don't have to do this."

Should I be offended that the guy who never says no to hookups isn't barreling out of the gates right now? That he's...

telling me to stop? What happened to the man who wanted to ravish me until dawn?

Pushing up on my other arm, I look down at him through my cascade of wild, tangled hair.

I don't know what I expect to see on his face, but it's not the softness in his eyes or the thoughtful tilt of his brow.

My heart knocks against my ribs.

Swallowing what I want to say—because I've been to the rodeo one too many times to know that this horizontal tango we're doing means nothing more than a fun night—I paste a smile on my face. "I thought you wanted—"

"Fuck, yes, I want. But not if you're too tired."

Well, damn. Drew 2.0 skirts around all my defenses like a freaking ninja.

"I'm not too tired." But I don't make a move because he's already hit the brakes, and I won't throw myself at him.

Which turns out to be an unnecessary concern because the words are barely out of my mouth when I'm flipped onto my back, and my enthusiastic lover is back with a grin.

He settles his deliciously hard body between my thighs so quickly, we both laugh.

"Hi." His emerald eyes are dark but so playful.

"Hi, back."

His nose grazes mine softly, his minty breath whispering against my face. He must've brushed his teeth a few minutes ago.

Thoughtful Drew is almost more than I can take in one helping.

But I want to try.

I lick his bottom lip, and his eyes darken to inky black orbs.

Game on.

"Tell me if anything's too much," he grits out.

I don't have time to make sense of what he's saying before he thrusts a hand into my hair and plants a tantalizing kiss on me.

Our tongues slide together in a way that revs me up all over again, and when he yanks my hair back to hold me down to nibble and bite and suck on my neck, my breath stalls out completely.

And then he's caressing my breasts like they're God's gift to mankind. When I try to run my hands over his back, he grabs both of my wrists and holds them over my head with one enormous paw while he continues worshipping my body.

I almost can't keep up. He's playful and domineering? Sign me up for more.

Arching up, I give myself over to his attention. To the wide sweep of his warm tongue. To the sharp stings of his teeth. To the tight fit of him between my thighs.

My clit is pounding all over again, and I bring my legs up to push off his track pants with my feet.

Because they must come off. Now.

Before I die of lust.

"Condom. Hurry."

My throat is hoarse from screaming both times I came. I can't even scrounge up the energy to be embarrassed.

He lifts off me briefly and then he's back, his magnificent nude form kneeling in front of me, the hard lines of his muscles cut in relief by shadow. I might have dated an NBA athlete before, but my ex's lanky frame has nothing on Drew's broad shoulders and elegant lines.

His damp hair sticks to his face as we watch each other.

I'm splayed out before him. Legs spread. Hands above my head. Chest heaving. Sweat building on my skin despite the cold.

His arm flexes as he pumps his thick shaft.

Truly, it's a beautiful cock. Proud and beckoning when he releases it.

He tosses the condom, and it lands on my slick stomach.

A smile lifts my lips as I reach for it. I tear it open with my teeth while my other hand wraps around him. Or at least I try to. Drew's a big boy. All Magnum XL, baby.

It feels weird to want to say a prayer of thanks right now, but I'm tempted to.

Suddenly, I get the fuss about this guy. Why all the girls fall to their knees to service him. But I shut down that line of thinking before I talk myself out of this. I don't want to feel like a notch on his bedpost, and if I let myself delve into that thought any longer, I'll freak myself out.

Right now, in this moment, I want to focus on the guy I've come to know on this trip. The one who worships my body. The one who indeed treats me like a princess. Not Portland's most eligible bachelor.

"Hey. You okay?" His voice makes me look up, and the smile he sends me reaches deep into my chest. *This guy.* The guy on this trip. Drew 2.0. He's the one I want. Not whoever he was in the past.

I nod slowly and swallow, my blood humming in my veins.

Refocusing on my task at hand, I run my thumb over his wide head, spreading the precum. His chin lowers, his eyes glued to what I'm doing between us.

"Do you want my mouth on you first?" I wouldn't say blowjobs are my favorite thing to do, but I've also never had a man with this kind of equipment before. I'd like to offer one, especially after he went down on me like a starving man served steak.

"Nope." He takes his dick out of my hand and taps it against my pussy, sending a shiver down my spine. "Wanna fuck you into next week."

Another fuse in my body ignites.

"You're in luck because I'm gonna let you."

We're both grinning like idiots as I spread the condom over

his thickness, wondering how his incredible body would feel inside me bare.

Bad, bad Kendall. Don't go there. It's not like Drew wants to be your boyfriend. Stop thinking crazy.

When I'm done, he falls over me, one arm holding him up over my head, the other working himself into me.

He wedges his thick head in, and it's hot and magnificent. Downright electrifying.

I wriggle beneath him. Squirm to get closer. To make him move, but he pulls out, earning a gasp from me.

His lips turn up because the man knows he's driving me insane.

"Drew," I whisper as I lean up to ghost my lips over his. "Did I ever tell you that I'm really flexible?"

I can basically wrap both legs behind my neck. Thank you, advanced yoga classes.

When his eyes meet mine, I sling my leg over his shoulder and throw the other over his back and pull him down. With his erection trapped between us, I grind up against him as I kiss my way across his stubbly chin and suck on his earlobe. Lick his neck. Bite his shoulder. Taste his skin.

"KK, you're killing me."

A throaty groan rumbles out of him as his hips pull back to make enough room to nudge his cock at my entrance again, and this time he finally pushes his way into me.

It's a *tight* fit.

But after a few back-and-forths and several grunts from both of us, he's fully seated. My eyes roll back in my head because he's really freaking big.

Even though I've already come twice, a few slow thrusts later, I'm right there again, the sensation building when he tells me how he can't get enough of me. How he loves fucking me with his tongue. How he loves my sweet cunt.

Our breaths turn to pants, and when he leans back to thrust harder, the sight of him tunneling in and out of me, stretching me to the brink, pushes me over the edge.

My whole body clamps around him. I'm either having the best orgasm of my life or a seizure.

It goes on and on, waves of pleasure with that twinge of pain as he hammers into me in earnest now, but I love it.

"Kendall." He's hoarse too. Raspy and tight, like he's hanging by a thread. "Jesus, fuck. You feel so good. How do you feel this good?" There's wonder in his voice. Wonder and raw need.

Our bodies smack together as he swells impossibly thicker, every muscle tensing when he comes with a shout.

He throbs inside me, prolonging the surges of electricity sparking through my core, and I am wrecked. A wasteland of flesh and tissue. Bone and marrow.

My legs slide off his body, limp and sated.

With a grunt, he collapses on top of me like he just ran a marathon, our sweat-slicked limbs fitting together with a strange familiarity as though we've been doing this for years, not as first-time lovers or friends with benefits.

Although my eyes are closed, I recognize the soft touch used to tuck hair behind my ear. The gentle kiss to my forehead. The care he takes to disengage his body from mine.

No, definitely not friends with benefits.

In a daze, I realize I'm probably too out of it to make sense of what we're doing. To see how this changes things.

A few minutes later when I'm snuggled deep under the blankets with a warm, naked Drew spooning me from behind, I decide I'm too drunk with ecstasy to worry about all the lines we've crossed tonight.

Because maybe this doesn't change anything.

Maybe this is no big deal.

12

DREW

*I*n the snow-hushed morning, Kendall's quiet snore breaks the silence. It might be the cutest thing I've ever heard, since the unrefined noise evaporates her untouchable vibe.

Although after last night, I know for sure she's touchable. *Goddamn* is she touchable.

My hand cups her perky tit as her hair lies over me and drapes in a curtain on the white pillow. We're still naked, and my dick knows it. Any other time of year, or in any place with indoor heat, after our activities last night, we'd be sweaty and sticky. But we're not. It's just her warm skin next to mine.

Since no electricity means it's fucking cold inside, we're tucked far enough under the covers to need a Saint Bernard to rescue us. Our noses and the tops of our heads poke out of the layers of six blankets piled on us.

The dark gray clouds outside the expansive, uncovered windows tell me the storm hasn't cleared. I cradle Kendall in my arms, listening to her breathe, pleased as fuck I know a few of her secrets now—like, she's kinky, she snores, and she maybe cares about me, at least a little bit.

If I was into her before, I'm *way* into her now, and I don't mean just the sex—although incidentally it was, as they say on ESPN, the Greatest Of All Time.

Calling it "GOAT" sex seems wrong, though.

That thought makes me chuckle, and I still my body, holding my breath so I don't disturb her dainty snoring.

What I mean is it's now downright physically impossible to keep me away from her, clothed or unclothed. If we're gonna be friends who fuck, I'm gonna do my damnedest to set up multiple opportunities to do both after we escape the white fluffy stuff outside. At the same time, a voice inside me tells me to chill. Keep this casual.

But as I watch her, I'm thinking casual, but monogamous, since there's no way I'm sharing this girl with another asshole.

As Kendall sleeps, she appears younger, more carefree. Those faint stress lines that show up on her forehead have vanished and her gorgeous face doesn't have that drawn look it's had for months now. That's what an orgasm or three accomplishes. I could study the pretty, pacified expression on her face all morning, letting her snooze away whatever shit she's got going on down in the flatlands. Good thing there's nothing else for us to do up here in the sticks.

She mumbles something incoherent, then wriggles closer against me and my woody dick.

Guess that's what happens when you're staying in the forest.

As I give myself some room so I'm not poking her in the ass —there's a thought to make me harder—my balls suffer the most excruciating pain, like a half-dozen needles poking into my man garden. *Ow.* I yelp, reach down, and extricate a tiny, fuzzy kitten stretching his limbs.

"Shaz," I hiss, holding him up by my face. "Keep your paws —and your claws—to yourself. Package is off-limits to you. One pussy allowed down there, and it's not you."

The feline's only response is to yawn and rub his head against my jaw. *Damn cat.* I adjust my balls.

As the surprise pain subsides, and Shazam settles in at the top of my pillow, I can't help but mess with Ms. Snorey Pants. I find myself tucking Kendall's hair behind her ear, then bringing forward a tendril under her nose like a mustache. Tracing her arm. Touching her fingers. I know I should let her sleep but—

She stretches and opens her eyes. Blinks. Turns toward me. And stiffens.

A PowerPoint presentation of emotions flits across her face so fast I can't catalog them all. Comfort, confusion, a silent *oh, my God, what the hell did we do last night*, and then—goddammit—fear or resignation.

No.

Before she can open her mouth to say anything that kills my vibe, I roll her to her back, settling my hips between her legs, and give her a gentle kiss. I suck on her lower lip, then invite her tongue into my mouth.

I'd gotten up earlier and brushed, but I give no fucks about her morning breath. After some initial hesitation, she reaches a hand to my neck and pulls me to her tight.

When I've thoroughly kissed her good morning, I pause and gaze into her sky-blue eyes while I hold her hand, propping myself up by my elbow. "No freak-outs," I whisper. "I've already survived an attack on my balls by the deadly claws of that beast"—I gesture at Shazzy—"so I'll thank you to be sure to handle them with care. I'll also thank you to handle them as soon as possible."

Sleepy little crinkles form at the edges of her eyes as a smile peeks out. "Last night was, um—"

"It was." I begin sucking my way along the bare skin of her neck as she arches her back, giving me her breasts, making my dick throb. "How are you feeling this morning?"

The nails of her free hand rake through my hair. "The best I've felt in months." She wraps her legs around my waist, letting me position my cock up against her center, so tantalizingly close that I'm wondering how many condoms I brought. At this rate we're gonna run out before the storm ends.

I pull her hand to my lips and press an open-mouthed kiss on it. Then I ask in a low voice, "Wanna do it again?"

Goosebumps pop up along her arm, and I let go of her hand. She nods, capturing my face in her palms, pulling me toward her head.

Coming up even with her face again, I give her another kiss, letting my hips dance with hers down below the covers, rubbing her in a spot that makes us both sigh. "You're gorgeous in the morning." Her lips part, and her pupils grow larger. My hand skims her curves, headed between her legs. When I get there, she moans, and I feel her wetness gathering already. I murmur in her ear, "And you snore. My video of you sleeping already has eight thousand views on YouTube."

"You did *what?*" she shrieks, now trying to get out from under me. Her arms flail about, and she scrambles for her phone.

Holding her wrists over her head gently, I pin her to the bed. "Easy, killer. I'm kidding. We have no internet, remember?"

She shoves my bicep with her shoulder. "Don't scare me like that!"

I let her go. "I'd never do anything like that to you. There's no way in hell I'd ever share anything intimate about you." My eyes lock with hers. "I'm serious. I'm not sharing you."

"Good."

"I mean, if you want to make a video, I'm down."

Daggers come out of her eyes before she rolls them. "Uh, no."

It's so easy to rile her.

"Don't say no that fast. I need spank bank material when we get back to Portland."

"Oh my God, you didn't just say that."

But I can tell she's not upset, since she's trying to hide her grin.

Better go for it, though. "I won't need spank bank material if you hang with me when we're back in town. We need to stay in touch, KFC. No one has to know if you don't want them to," I say with a shrug.

Nibbling her lip, she studies me. "On two conditions." She pulls me to her and pivots us over so I'm on my back and she's straddling me.

Hell, yes. I like this position.

"What are they?"

Needless to say, she'll get whatever she asks.

As Kendall talks, she tugs the covers up to her shoulders and starts kissing her way down my chest. "One—not a soul knows about us when we get back into civilization."

Everything in me wants to balk at the idea I can't be open about this. It's bothered me a little since she brought it up last night, but I respond before I can jam my foot in my big mouth.

"Done."

"And two—you do that magical thing with your tongue again before we leave." As I nod, she scoots all the way down my legs, then leans so her mouth envelops my cock. I'd stopped her last night, but there are only so many times I can hold off. Now is not one.

I fight to keep my eyes open to catch every incredible moment of Kendall giving me head.

"This is quite possibly the best morning in the history of my life," I grunt, enjoying the feel of her warm mouth hitting all the sensitive spots on my erection. Sucking, tracing the veins, swirling her tongue. One hand bracing her up while the other jacks me.

Words tumble out of me with no filter. I tell her that she's beautiful, that I want to fuck her mouth so deep, that I'll do anything for her, anything. I call her baby, princess, goddess. I need to make her scream because she's making me feel so good.

Finally, with great restraint before this goes too far, I yank my hips back. "Not that way."

With her mouth glossy, she grins and waves over the condom.

I toss one on my belly—three remaining—and this time she rolls it down my length, climbing on my hard cock. Now this is a view I'll never tire of. Her milky skin. Those tits curving out. Her ribs and toned stomach. Head tilted back, red hair flying everywhere, blue eyes locking with me as she rubs her clit.

Riding me until we both come. Hard.

I must say, morning nookie with Kendall is not to be missed.

By evening on Friday night, we sit by the fire, the remains of our weird, diabetes-friendly leftover Thanksgiving dinner on plates all around us. *Thank God for matches and the gas stove.* Bee sent squash soup, green bean casserole, low-carb rolls, and low-sodium ham, which were all delicious. Even the second time around. Good thing she packed for a crowd, because we would've starved otherwise. The giant snowbank on the porch kept the food well preserved.

Since temperatures stayed well below freezing, we didn't want to sit way over at the dining room table, so the rug before the fire served as our space for breakfast, lunch, dinner, a Monopoly game, lots of card games, and the inspired use of two condoms. (I learned that she likes it doggy-style. So do I. Also

Go-Fish led to me fucking her against a tapestry on the wall. It happens.)

"I can't believe it snowed for two whole days," Kendall says, taking a sip of her hot tea and stroking the cat wedged against her thigh. "This storm is huge. Probably worse here on the mountain. I can't imagine it's this bad back home."

While she is a tiny person, Kendall currently resembles the Stay Puft Marshmallow man, wearing two pairs of sweatpants, her down jacket, and several pairs of socks, including one pair of mine. Whenever she shivers, I know it's time to stoke the fire.

"I'll shovel us out first thing tomorrow." Throwing on another log, I pull her into my lap, dislodging Shazam, who meows indignantly. "Sorry, dude," I mutter, and scratch the top of his head. With KK's back to my front, we both gaze at the flames in the fireplace. I wrap my arms around her.

"It's weird to be stranded. No internet. No phone. No TV. I'm not used to being disconnected." She leans her head against my cheek. "It's a good thing every once in a while," she muses, and I nod. "I have to say, this weekend has not turned out at all like I thought. I'm bummed about not seeing Evie, but taking a break from work is probably healthy. No clients. No crisis." She turns in my lap. "And I learned that you're kinda fun."

"You make me blush."

When I lean up to kiss her, she puts a finger on my lips. "I hate to say it, but I'm even grateful for your diabetes, because without it we'd be eating scary condiments. I never thought sugar-free pumpkin pie would taste good, let alone be an amazing breakfast. Twice."

"No kidding. I'm grateful too."

Now she lets in the kiss, and she tastes of comfort. When we break apart, she surveys the soaring cabin living room in the flickering light and focuses back on me. "It's weird to spend

Thanksgiving away. I kind of miss, you know, the turkey. The food coma."

"Be sure to overeat next year."

Her eyes lower. "I miss my family. We have this cheesy tradition."

My arms tighten around her. "Tell me."

"My parents are total hippies. They make goo-goo eyes at each other all the time. While I'm good with it now, it really embarrassed me as a kid."

"There are worse things your parents can do," I mutter.

"I know." Her eyes are sincere, although I haven't told her anything about my family. Once again, she seems to read between the lines.

She continues, "So anyway, every Thanksgiving, we had to go around the table, me and my sister and grandparents or whoever was there, and list things we were grateful for that year."

"That's adorable." I'd spend an afternoon in a Speedo making snow angels, even if it turned me into a Drewsicle, if it meant my family could have a meaningful conversation.

"Well, I was thinking. I mean, we've spent two days under these crazy conditions with three feet of snow outside, so we can't even open the door—"

"And the part you're grateful for is?"

"For this weekend. For being forced to unplug from work for longer than the drive through Vista Ridge Tunnel. For your grandmother's pie." Her eyes dip down, her cheeks turning a rosy hue. "And for you looking out for me."

I like looking out for you.

For the tenth time today, I remind myself that Kendall signed up to be friends with bennies, and if I launch into wanting to be her real-life boyfriend and not just her fuck buddy, there's a very real possibility she might laugh in my face. Or worse, say no. The fear is real.

"Everyone needs a break from business." Having her in my lap means my happy dick takes notice, ready for another round. Not sure where my recent stamina came from, but I'm not questioning it. Maybe this little redhead has always driven me nuts, and now she's literally driving my nuts.

"So what are you grateful for, Drew?"

"That session in the tub." I'd boiled water like a good frontiersman, added it to the frigid tub, and we'd cleaned off and warmed up, in more ways than one.

She gives me a shove. "What?" I protest. "It was a good use of the last condom." Damn. Why didn't I bring more? *Because hooking up with Kendall never crossed my mind as a legit possibility.* "Either we're gonna have to get creative, or I'm gonna have to shovel us out in the dark so we can get to a store."

Her laugh makes everything better. It's musical, gentle, and so sexy. "I'm up for being creative."

"Apparently I am too," I say, thrusting up my hips so she can't mistake my meaning. Resting both forearms on her shoulders, I examine her lively, lusty eyes. "Honestly? The thing I'm most grateful for this year is that you gave me a chance."

"Oh." She exhales. Gentle kisses turn into deeper ones. I climb to my feet with her legs hooked around my waist and her arms looping my neck.

"Should we call this position 'the sloth'?" I ask. "I'm pretty sure if we just adjusted some clothes I could carry you around all day on my dick and not get tired."

"I'd like to see you try, Andrew."

I pause. I like hearing my full name from Kendall. A lot.

Walking into the bedroom, I set her down on the bed and light candles to add to the one we had burning since the house got dark. "I've got a sexy sloth in my bed. What should I do with her?" I figure some mutual masturbation might be fun, but her next words make my heart beat faster.

"There are ways we can do this...without a condom." She pauses to curl a strand of hair around her finger. "I'm pretty sure I saw some lube next to your toothbrush."

We both know she doesn't need lube for regular P in V sex.

All the blood rushes from my face to my now fully-hard dick. "You're serious?"

"I'm nervous, though. You're kinda girthy—"

"True—"

"But we can try. If you want."

Oh, I fucking want.

13

KENDALL

*W*hat happens on Mount Hood, stays on Mount Hood.

It's been my mantra this whole trip, more so now as I consider what I just offered Drew. Judging by the wicked smile spreading on his face, he's into it.

I'm not embarrassed. I'm not.

The heat crawling up my neck belies the fact that part of me, in fact, wants to hide behind the giant dresser across the room for offering up this kind of sex, but I'm a modern woman, right? If I want to do that, I shouldn't feel ashamed. Men ask for anal all the time without batting an eye.

We've already had the safe sex talk. I know he's clean. He gets checked all the time because of his health issues, and I'm on the pill, but it has a lower dose of hormones, which is the reason I've offered the backdoor instead of the main entrance tonight. I use this prescription mostly to regulate my periods since my old pill gave me migraines.

Plus, I'm a little sore anyway. I've never had this much sex in my life. Drew is insatiable, and when I'm around him like this, I am too apparently.

But going without a condom gives me pause. Beyond the intimacy of what we're about to do, beyond the act itself, going bareback is something I've never considered with a lover.

Though I can't deny I'm curious. Feeling all of Drew like that? A shiver races through me.

He drops onto me like a playful puppy and kisses my neck. "Whatever you want, Ken Doll. We do or don't do whatever you want. You're in control."

I nod, relief loosening my chest. The biggest shocker this week is how much Drew puts me at ease. It's the only reason we've come this far, to me offering myself up on a buffet like this, which I never do. I can't even blame alcohol because I finished the wine yesterday.

He strips me out of the ten layers of clothes I'm wearing, and I recline back on the bed to watch as he reaches behind his head to yank off his long-sleeved fleece and T-shirt.

And then it's just Drew kneeling between my bare legs. Mischievous, disheveled, golden Drew beaming that devilish grin beneath his two-day old stubble. His blond hair sits askew on his head, shooting every which way, teasing me with glimpses of those mesmerizing green eyes.

I feel like a skier racing across a mountain, trying to dodge an avalanche. It's exhilarating and dangerous. A thrill ride.

What happens on Mount Hood, stays on Mount Hood.

Shaking off the voice of reason that says I'm taking things too far tonight, I smile and drag my hand across his abs. I watch my fingers dip in the valley of those washboard muscles. Across his smooth, taut skin that I know smells like citrus. Through the trail of light hair that arrows down into his denim.

He pulls a blanket over his shoulders as I flick open his jeans. Our eyes connect as he shuffles out of the rest of his clothes. When he pounces on me, I squeal with laughter. Like a jerk, he digs his fingers into my ribs where I'm really ticklish. I hate it, but I also kinda love it.

And then we're a naked tangle of limbs and bites and moans. With his hand shoved in my hair and his tongue in my mouth, he wedges himself between my thighs and thrusts against my slick core.

Our mutual groans fill the quiet room.

"You're already wet." His deep voice sends chills down my arms, and my nipples pebble against him.

He feels amazing. Thick and hard as he tunnels his bare cock through my folds. He leans back on his knees to watch.

With the blanket draped around him, the shadows cut hard across his body, but I can see what he's doing and the way his hips move between my legs. How his muscular thighs strain. How his stomach muscles clench.

I reach down to press him harder against me, and his head drops back for a second before he's on me again, his body fitted to mine like we were made from interlocking puzzle parts.

"Really want to fuck you like this," he whispers against my lips.

Bare. No condom.

The insanity is not what he says, but that I want to let him.

"Just...put it in to get it wet," I mumble against his mouth. "Then we'll go back to our plan." He pauses to look at me, his nose pressed to mine. I shrug. "I want to feel you like this." He's already fucked me ten ways to Sunday. I might as well get the deluxe package.

His eyes darken as a low growl sounds in his chest. "Just for a minute?"

"Just for a minute."

Seconds, really.

My head bobbles on my shoulders as I nod.

Because yes.

Yes, I want to do this.

Yes, I want to feel him this way.

He doesn't need more convincing. His hips part from mine as he positions himself at my entrance, his blunt head thick and hot against my skin.

With just his tip, he moves in and out, back and forth until I'm going out of my mind.

"Drew. Stop screwing around."

He chuckles, but his laughter stops the second he shoves himself all the way in. His groan reverberates through my entire body.

"Fuck, fuck, fuck, KK. You feel so good. Your tight little pussy wants to swallow me whole."

I'm gasping, dying to feel him move inside me. I forget I'm sore. That we've already boned like sex addicts for the last two days. All I can think is that I want him now. More. Harder.

I wrap my legs around him and swivel my hips, sending him deeper.

And then he's moving. Our bodies slam together almost violently, his push to my pull, and the tightness between my thighs intensifies as he reaches behind me to push in a slick finger all the while pumping his hips against me.

A full-body shiver makes me moan and arch back.

"Don't come yet, baby. Wait."

Another finger joins the first, and I almost fly apart.

I shake my head. "I can't wait."

"You can. You're gonna come with my cock in your beautiful little ass, and it's gonna feel like fucking nirvana."

Oh God.

I could pretend I don't like his crass words, that I'm offended or put off, but my body knows the truth. My body knows I'm a hair trigger away from disintegrating underneath him.

Just when I think I can't take anymore, he slides out of me

and flips me around so I'm crouched on all fours. I groan from the loss, but my heart ratchets up because I know what's coming. I'm apprehensive, but so turned on I feel like I might melt into the bed.

I hear the snap of a bottle, and then his fingers are back there again, this time cold from the lube. Probing. Rubbing. Sinking in deep and making me cry out from how good it feels.

"That's it. Take it, KK."

Two wet fingers tunnel into me, but this angle is more intense, and my elbows give out. My head lands on the pillow.

His other hand rubs my left cheek almost reverently before he parts me and presses his cock back there.

"Push back on me, okay? We'll go slow."

It takes a few tries because he's enormous. It's a snug fit, but when he finally wedges in, the pressure is intense, and everything inside of me locks up.

Who thought this was a good idea?

I'm, what, five and a half feet tall? Drew's well over six and built like a wide receiver. In what universe do his parts fit in my trunk?

My eyes well from the intensity, and I claw at the bedding, but I can't speak. Words don't materialize on my lips to throw on the brakes, but he must sense how uncomfortable I am because his big body immediately freezes.

"Relax, baby. Everything's okay. Say the word and we stop."

His soft words immediately loosen the tension in my shoulders, and I try to breathe through it because I don't want to stop. I want to try this with someone I trust, and for some reason, I trust Drew to handle me with care in a way I haven't with other men.

His hand smooths back my hair. And he just holds me to him as he lowers us to the bed on our sides, my back to his chest. We stay like that while I adjust to his size.

He kisses my shoulder. My neck. Drags his beautiful lips across my jaw. Tilts my face up so he can kiss me. He's so tall, he's practically wrapped around me from behind.

Sweet, gentle Drew touches me in a whole different way than the guy who fucked me up against the wall yesterday.

So when he asks me again if I want to stop, I shake my head.

Because in this moment, I know he won't hurt me. He won't push me beyond what I can bear.

More tears spring to my eyes, but not because it hurts. I can't explain the warmth I have for him right now. I just know we've transcended something in our relationship tonight, though I'm afraid to think of what that might mean.

Those talented fingers reach between my legs, and he rubs me until the tears subside.

Until the frenzy builds and the heat roars back.

Until I'm shaking in his arms and bucking back on him.

"That's it, babe. Oh fuck." He's moving in me, and I bury my face in the pillow and arch back because it's intense again, but now it feels right. It feels good.

Beyond good.

Amazing in an *oh-my-God-how-have-I-never-done-this-before?* way.

I'm flying again, coming apart in a litany of 'pleases' and 'yesses' and 'right there, don't stop.'

When the pressure explodes, my whole body clenches in waves of light and pleasure that have me screaming and flailing and shuddering so hard, my jaw aches.

Like our bodies are timed fireworks, he comes a second later, his arm banding around my stomach to hold me to him as a guttural groan vibrates from his body through mine.

Huffing into the quiet room and trying to catch my breath, I wait for Drew to crack a joke, because he always cracks jokes during sex.

But he doesn't.

I wince when he pulls back and separates our bodies. The loss is almost as intense as the intrusion for some reason.

Curling into a ball, I wait for the sensations to subside because everything is too much. The blood still racing through my veins. The sheets scratching my skin. The suffocating silence of the room.

Behind me, Drew clears his throat. "You okay, Kendall? I didn't hurt you, did I?"

"I'm fine," I whisper, feeling more off kilter when he says my full name.

There's no laughter as we clean up and get ready for bed.

No stupid quips about what we just did. No teasing or the easy banter I've come to love with Drew this week.

I want to ask a thousand questions about what this means and what will happen when we get back to Portland, but I don't.

Even when he pulls me to his chest under the covers and snuggles me close, as I blink in the darkness, I know something's changed.

I just don't know what.

The purring wakes me from a dead sleep.

Shazam is kneading my hair and trying to balance on my head.

I stretch, groaning from ten thousand aches, my body sore from that sexual decathlon I attempted over the last three nights.

Turning, I find that I'm alone in bed.

"Drew?"

The house is silent except for the kitten trying to eat my ear.

Shivering, I quickly toss on some clothes and shuffle into the living room, but it's empty.

A panic hits me hard that I'm alone. A fear that somehow Drew has ditched me, and I'm here all by myself. But the sound of ice being scraped across pavement has me running to the giant picture window at the front of the house.

Drew is knee-deep in snow as he shovels it off the driveway and tries to dig out the Rover.

I roll my eyes at myself. Of course he didn't ditch me. He knows full well that if he did, and I ever tracked him down, he'd be a dead man. I'd drive away from that massacre with his balls hanging on my rearview mirror.

I snicker to myself and head for the stove to make some coffee. It's just a sad can of Folgers that we found in the back of the cabinet, but it's keeping a caffeine withdrawal headache at bay.

Now that the sun is up, I'm thinking I overreacted last night. No way was everything as awkward between me and Drew as I imagined it. He still cuddled me until I fell asleep like the previous two nights.

Stop projecting on people, Kendall. Just because I was freaking out doesn't mean Drew was too.

After I bundle up in my jacket and throw on my boots, I pour two cups of coffee and head out to help him with the driveway.

I slip and slide my way over to his SUV. The sun is out and my boots slosh through thick puddles of sludge and slush.

When he sees me, he stills, and the smile on my face freezes when I see his cautious expression.

Shit.

Maybe I wasn't imagining anything last night.

Maybe he's freaking out too.

Maybe he's back to being Drew "one and done" Merritt and what happened here didn't mean anything to him.

I'm about to hand him his cup of coffee when a bullhorn blasts, scaring the crap out of me. As coffee goes everywhere, all over my arms and chest and jeans, someone shouts, "This is the police. Put your hands up! You're under arrest!"

Right.

Because as I'm being shoved face first into the mud and snow by Mount Hood's finest, I find out this isn't Josh and Evie's cabin.

I'm being arrested for breaking and entering.

And felony grand theft.

I might need to kill Drew after all.

14

DREW

Whenever I'm arrested, I play a fun game where I compare police stations.

Since my left ass cheek has fallen asleep in this rock-hard Mount Hood chair, I'm inclined to dock points in my mental tally.

For comparison, as far as police departments go, you can't get any better than the downtown Portland station. The magazine selection's killer, they serve decent coffee, and the cushy waiting room lined with framed local landscape photos feels almost cozy—at least for a place that's attached to a jail.

My parents funded the Portland police chief's campaign, as well as his four predecessors, so whenever circumstances align such that he has to talk to me, we go through the same charade, I mean routine.

He invites me into his expansive corner office.

I stare at the photos, commendations, and certificates on the wall behind his back, including the one arm-in-arm with my father.

The chief gets this pained look in his eye and calls me son.

I lower my eyes and endure a lecture, hoping that I don't look high.

He warns me that there better not be a next time.

I apologize, smile, and assure him I've sworn off throwing parties with drunk, naked women shrieking through the Pearl neighborhood.

He pretends he believes me and clicks some keys on his bottom-of-the-line state-issued computer.

I shake his hand, pay the fine, and remind my parents to pledge an increased donation to his next campaign.

Wash, rinse, and repeat.

Now that I actually *have* sworn off throwing parties in the Pearl district with drunk, naked women—and become attached to one redhead in particular—I have to deal with this bullshit.

Unfortunately, I'm not in Portland.

I grind my teeth, waiting for my lawyer to arrive at this podunk sheriff's station. Since we're two counties over from home, I know no one here, but the deputies have all heard of my family. And apparently me, too. Damn gossip columns.

They seemed to think my connections with the Portland police meant I'm an entitled asshole. Perhaps. But that flipped the switch on their *Live PD* behavior. While I sat freezing my ass off in the back seat of the squad car, I caught derisive laughter up front about the future of the nearest Merritt Department Store. It's pretty clear they're determined to make an example of me since they're doing everything by the book, like I'm some escaped fugitive.

So far I've talked with Good Cop and Bad Cop, who both seem to think they owe it to the public to ensure justice will be served. Even if we didn't think we were committing a crime.

For fuck's sake.

Although I'm still handcuffed, I tap my fingers on the metal table in the sparsely-furnished interrogation room. No magazines, coffee, or avuncular police chief in sight. Just me, three chairs, and the table.

It smells like birthday cake in here, which makes me think this room isn't used for many interrogations. Uniformed deputies saunter up and down the hall, with walkie-talkies squawking indecipherable babble. Windows line one side of the room, and I read the bulletin boards across the hall. "Sign up for our email newsletter!" "Follow us on Pinterest." "Consider a career in law enforcement."

This whole scenario makes me ill.

All I can think about is Kendall.

Shoving the wooden government chair back, I rise and pace the small room, swallowing hard, the metal cuffs biting into my wrists.

How is she? Where is she? Are they treating her well? How can I keep the PR princess from getting sullied by my shitty reputation? What can I do to make this better?

Because there's no way I'm leaving her alone after this weekend. I don't know what sorcery she has up her sleeve, but besides being the coolest chick I've ever met, the sex between us is mind-altering. Body-altering. So incredible I could barely breathe, much less speak last night.

I think back on the tremble in her lip as she offered up her gorgeous ass. The gleam in her eyes showing me she wanted it too. The intimacy of being bare with her—something I've never done with anyone. How she came so hard, *I* saw stars. The way we were so close, nothing could come between us.

But something did.

Burned in my brain is the hurt expression Kendall tossed my way as she was escorted into the black and white car back at the cabin. Eyes wide but brows tight, her chin shaking. Betrayed. Then she lowered her head and clambered into the backseat.

Convinced that I somehow knew we were doing something wrong.

The worst part about this whole shit storm is how it confirms to Kendall that I'm exactly the kind of douchebag she thought I was—the selfish asshole who parties it up, leaving a trail of chaos behind him, and damn the consequences.

I flinch as a door slams somewhere in the building.

No matter what, I've fucked this up big time. All that headway I made with her this weekend, connecting about her high-stress job and my health recovery. How cute she looked curled up by the fire petting my cat. All those moments—God, those delicious moments with her, naked or not, up in that cabin —taken away.

Still pacing, I drag my palms down my thighs, trying to keep calm. I have to fix this. If only I could talk to her, assure her that I'll take all the responsibility and pay any restitution I need to. I'll keep her out of this entirely. Somehow. Yes, I know she's a public relations expert and is probably squaring her shoulders and capably answering questions. But I still want to clear her name.

Then I want to take her out to dinner.

But I haven't seen her since Good Cop hauled her off in a different squad car, since they're clearly keeping us sequestered for questioning. I can only assume she's somewhere in this building, but I have no way of finding that out right now. The overly-officious deputies confiscated everything from my phone to my Rover and even locked up Shazam—clawing and spitting —in a cage. Shaz managed to scratch Bad Cop. I couldn't help but give my ornery cat a silent *atta boy*. Hope he's got kitten kibble and a soft bed.

I slump down in my seat and scratch the scruff on my jaw as I wait.

It's almost worse that we didn't do anything wrong. Because

while I can repeat, "We didn't do it," over and over again, no one here believes us. Squirming in my seat, I try to figure out how to prove I didn't break into and enter a house I, uh, broke into and entered. Just not on purpose.

Worse, even if I'm eventually believed, we still have our reputations to be concerned about. No matter what anyone says, it isn't a good thing to be arrested anywhere. People tend to associate being arrested with doing something wrong. People tend to be right in thinking that way. At least in my case. Usually. And while I could give two fat fucks about my rep, I want to make sure that Kendall's stays pristine.

Finally, after I get up and travel around the room for the three hundredth time, Tim Bryan, my attorney, walks in wearing a suit and carrying a laptop and briefcase. He's a handsome and aristocratic man, with close-cropped dark hair and an unlined face. I'm sure a few more years of representing me will turn his hair prematurely gray and give him wrinkles. I shake his hand, which is difficult in cuffs.

"You look like shit, Drew," he says without preamble.

An involuntary snort leaves me. "No kidding. I've been here for hours. What time is it?" Being without my phone adds to my anxiety.

"Almost midnight." While I certainly pay him enough to show up at this time on a Saturday three hours away from Portland, I'm still glad he came as fast as he could.

The most pressing question on my brain bursts out first. "Is Kendall Greer okay?"

"I'm sure she is. I'll check on her after I work things out with the arresting officer. I wanted to talk to you first."

"Did you post bail?"

"It's in process. For you and Miss Greer, as you instructed. I also called Mr. Cartwright and told him what I knew. He was worried sick about you. He's been trying to call for days."

"Thanks." I hadn't realized that as much as we were worried about Josh and Evie, they might have been worried about us.

I can't wait to get this whole thing straightened out and move on with life. And I can't help but hope I see Kendall after this weekend. I'm dreaming of hanging out in more than two rooms. Eating food other than Turkey Day leftovers. Having luxuries like, oh, electricity. Seeing her naked again.

If she still talks to me, that is.

"Drew, can you repeat what you told me on the phone? I want to make sure I've got the story straight."

I tell him everything from Josh inviting us to the cabin to making do until the white fluffy stuff stopped so I could dig our way out.

In our case, "making do" involved a lot of sexual activity, but he doesn't need to know that. I'll stick to the pertinent facts about our alleged trespassing.

He sighs. "I get it."

"Why are the police wasting their time on us?"

"One of the neighbors called the police after they saw smoke in the chimney. They knew the owners were out of town and had been asked to keep an eye on the place." He shuffles through some papers. "The cops couldn't come until the storm passed and the roads cleared, but when they approached the house, they ran your plates." He looks up and eyes me meaningfully.

"And they saw my record."

"Yep."

"Goddamn it. But I swear I thought the place was Josh's."

"While I was on my way here, my associate researched public records and made phone calls. She emailed me this report." He opens up his laptop. "You are charged with breaking and entering into private property located at 1141 NE County Road 246, which you say belongs to your friend Josh Cartwright.

Unfortunately, that address is owned by a Matilda and Jerry Haim. The real property owned by the Cartwright Family Trust is located at 1411 NW County Road 246." Tim eyes me over the top of the computer.

My stomach drops. "Fuck."

"It appears that you were a digit off and on the—"

"Wrong fucking side of the mountain." I shake my head in disbelief, then get up and resume pacing. "I'd never been to Josh's cabin before. He just got it. I assumed I was in the right place because he spent time renovating, and this place seemed like his style... Dammit."

"The good news is that I'm confident you had no criminal intent. You did not believe you were breaking into the property of another—"

"Well, I did—"

"Without consent, Drew." Tim gives me a hard look. "You believed you had implied consent from your friend, correct?"

"True." I stop and stare at him, hope finally taking root inside me. "So you think you can get those charges dismissed?"

"I already—yes, here it is"—he clicks on his laptop—"have a statement from Mr. Cartwright." Tim turns around his computer so I can read Josh's affidavit. "His corroboration, along with your testimony and what I assume Miss Greer will say, will go a long way."

"Thank fuck." I sit down again and sigh. "So when can we leave? We need to get Kendall out, too."

"Yes, I know. But there is the felony charge of grand theft."

A flash of irritation rises up my spine. I heard this before, but had no idea what they were talking about. Yes, we went into the cabin, but I didn't take anything other than old *National Geographic* magazines and a few matches. "What do they think I took?"

"Wine."

That wasn't what I was expecting. "What?"

"The Haims are concerned that you drank through their collection of rare French wine, and then the police found empty wine bottles in the bins outside. Nice bottles."

"We didn't drink any of their wine. I brought *one* bottle for Kendall. I don't drink at all these days." I'm so pissed I start laughing. "If they're worried I took advantage of their hospitality, the least they could do is have fresh towels and turn-down service. Oh, and indoor heat."

"Drew. I believe if you talk to them and tell them what happened, they won't press charges."

Waving my hand as best as I can, I say, "Show them in. I'll pay for any damage they claim. Not that we caused any. Hell, I'll pay for housekeeping service for a year, an improved security system, and a case of Haut-Médoc, plus a copy of every single *National Geographic* that's ever been printed. They can even borrow my parents' cabin in Vail, if they want."

He gives me a grin. "I'll go get them."

An hour and a large sum of money later, I've convinced the owners that we were not hooligans trying to destroy their property, but had mistaken their abode for our friend's and got stranded in a snowstorm.

In other words, the truth.

They agree not to press charges, and we are free to go. The sheriff gives me back my cat. The arresting deputy almost looks like I told him he's not getting a Christmas bonus this year.

But where is Kendall?

Tim's been so busy negotiating at my side, he hasn't broken away to talk to her. And after hours spent with him and my accusers, by the time I'm finally released, I'm informed that Miss Greer's older sister picked her up and she's on her way home.

Without talking to me.

Fuck.

When the deputy returns my phone it has no charge, but the second I get my car out of impound hours later, I plug it in and call Kendall.

No response.

I text her all of my apologies and explanations.

Then I drive home in the early dawn, worried it's not enough.

15

KENDALL

*W*hen I close my eyes, I can almost pretend I'm back at the cabin instead of waiting for my sister to bail me out.

Back with Drew in our cozy hideaway.

Before I was utterly humiliated and the cops took my damn mugshot.

I want to believe this was all a big mistake. That Drew didn't steal a three-thousand-dollar bottle of wine from the cabin's cellar for shits and giggles and pretend he bought it for me.

Because if that's a lie, what other lines did he feed me?

I don't know how you fake what we shared, but if it was all a façade, he's downright maniacal.

Everything in me hopes and prays I know the real Drew. That he's not the asshat this clusterfuck seems to suggest he is. That he's different now. That getting arrested had more to do with his record and the police not listening to our side of the story than our behavior. I hope this is some horribly stupid misunderstanding that I'll laugh about some day.

Just not right now.

How many times have I been on the other end of this situation? The PR pro who tells my clients to keep their act together and not break down? To put on a brave face. Now that I'm here, now that *I'm* the one with the arrest and potential felony, I'm seeing how callous I've been. How terribly out of touch. With my *entire* career on the line, I'm fucking terrified that everything I've worked so hard to achieve is about to go up in flames.

My jaw tightens as I will myself not to cry. Not here, a few feet away from the two receptionists who've been gossiping about me all night, yukking it up in a stage whisper I hear loud and clear.

"In my day, you had to buy the cow before you got the milk..."

"The deputy found used condoms all over that beautiful cabin..."

"And he comes from such a good family too. You'd think his momma would've taught him not to mess with trash like that..."

Harsh, ladies. Harsh.

I'm surprised they don't print out that *Game of Thrones* meme of Cersei Lannister doing her walk of shame and staple it to my forehead.

I don't need a mirror to know I have coffee stains on my clothes, mascara under my eyes, and mud in my hair. If I were my own publicist, I'd tell jailbird Kendall to buck up, ask to go to the bathroom so she can wash her face, and act like this isn't a big deal. Because this will all be straightened out soon and won't everyone get a chuckle out of it then.

But I'm scared shitless this whole situation *is* a big deal. That I'll lose clients if word gets out.

And I can't afford to lose clients. Not if I expect to make rent and payroll next month.

The odds are I'm in deep crap right now professionally because nothing involving Drew is ever covert or inconspicuous.

He's constantly in the society blogs, even after he started to clean up his act.

Tristan is going to kill me for this, if he isn't already plotting my death for being MIA for the last three days.

The chair across from me scrapes the floor, and I look up to see my older and very pissed-off sister.

"Brookey, you came. Did you bail me out?" I jump up and try to hug her but she shrugs me off.

"You smell like ass. I have your paperwork. Let's go."

The smart decision would've been to call Evie to bail me out, but when the cops frisked me—yes, I got the VIP treatment—the deputy pulled my cell phone out of my pocket, and it slipped into a big puddle of water.

God help me, but the only number I could remember off the top of my head was my sister's.

Clearly, Brooke isn't thrilled to be my "one call from jail."

"I'll pay you back whatever it cost you, I swear." Just maybe not this month, but I don't add that detail. If I give up my gym membership and my dental plan, though, I can get the money to her in a few months. "I'm so sorry you had to drive all this way."

Her nostrils flare. "You owe me. I had to leave Noah's promotion party early."

Underneath her wool coat, she's wearing a sleek, sparkly cocktail dress. Her hair and makeup are flawless, like the prima ballerina she's always been. Far too overdressed to be standing in the middle of this police station, hours from home, at nearly midnight on a Saturday.

"I'll babysit for free for the next month."

She scoffs. "Noah says you're not allowed to babysit Janie anymore. He's pissed about tonight."

My heart sinks like a boulder in my stomach. I love my niece with my whole heart and soul. When I opened the PR firm, I decided I was fine putting a family on hold for another four or five years because I have Janie to spoil.

I open my mouth to argue, but Brooke stomps out of the room.

Although I shouldn't be surprised by her attitude, I'm in desperate need of some TLC, so her cold shoulder feels like a pulverizing blow. But what's one more crushing disappointment today?

I poke my head out of the holding room, afraid I'm not really supposed to be leaving, but no one seems to care that I'm out and about.

My sister blazes through the front doors so fast, I'm half afraid she's going to leave me. Frantically, I look around, expecting to see Drew, but the police station is almost empty. Just a few deputies strolling about and one of those lovely ladies who's been trashing me all night.

With a resigned breath, I turn toward the main desk. The snarky receptionist watches me with an arched, unplucked eyebrow as she takes out a tray that has my still-damp cell phone, plus my laptop and purse. No idea where my luggage or clothes are, but when the deputy asked me what I left at the cabin, I begged him to get my laptop since they had retrieved my purse when they arrested us.

FML, I've been arrested.

It's still sinking in. Like I'm on the *Titanic*, watching the icy waters rise.

Really, Kendall. Dramatic much?

As I gather my belongings, I clear my throat. "Do you know —" I pause to glance around before lowering my voice. "Do you know if Drew Merritt is still being held?"

She gives me a blank stare.

Okay.

"Is he still here? Could you give him a message for me?"

"No."

A cold prickle of awareness washes over me.

Drew already left.

Without talking to me.

What the actual hell?

The car honk outside the station makes me flinch. Through the double doors of the station, my sister glares at me from her Mercedes SUV before she backs out of the parking spot. Snow shoots out from her tires.

Shit.

I race through the double doors, slipping and sliding along the walkway. When I get the passenger door open, I'm genuinely afraid she might leave my ass here as some kind of tough-love lesson.

But I've already learned one lesson tonight.

And that's never to trust Drew Merritt again.

16

KENDALL

*W*ith a groan, I press two fingers into my left eye to make it stop twitching.

"You sure you're okay?" Tristan is in war room mode as he stalks across his living room and places a steaming hot mocha venti latte in front of me.

"I'll be fine. Again, I'm so sorry, Tris."

"Shut up. Who saved my ass senior year when I wouldn't leave the house after Rhonda broke up with me? My favorite little redhead. I'll always have your back."

Gratefulness washes over me. "Thanks, bud. You're the best."

"I know," he says smugly while holding out his fist. I laugh and jab back. "You wanna stay another night? I might have some clothes you can wear tomorrow."

Want to know the icing on my shit cake? I can't go home since I'm locked out because I left my keys in my luggage back on Mount Hood. Fortunately, when Brooke drove me over here at three this morning, Tristan just ushered me in with a hug, handed me a big plate of game-day snacks, and offered his guest room. Thank God because my sister told me in no uncertain terms that I was not staying with her. So much for sisterly love.

I take a big sip of the latte and sigh with relief. "Which ex-girlfriend are we talking about? Shauna had really great taste, and if she left one of her dresses behind, I'm totally going to take you up on that offer. And thank you, because the locksmith can't come until tomorrow."

We've been putting out client fires all day, but in the few minutes we spend guzzling down coffee, I reload *Gary the Gossip*, Portland's homegrown gossip website, on my laptop as surreptitiously as possible. Not because I want to keep anything from my partner, but because I'm utterly mortified our PR firm might go up in flames at the flick of a mouse.

Tris motions toward my computer. "It's been quiet. I just checked five minutes ago. You're going to be fine." His confidence soothes my beleaguered soul. He lowers his voice even though we're the only ones here. "Don't forget I have that intern who's supposed to give me a heads up whenever either of us or our clients are in their headlines. God knows I pay her enough."

Any other day, I'd tease him about his mysterious connection at Gary's and inquire whether this mystery woman is someone he knows on a personal level that involves horizontal moves and Marvin Gaye tunes, but I can't dredge up the energy. Without my cell phone, I've been scrambling to piece together everything that happened while I was gone, and it's been exhausting.

One of my NBA players, Kyle Lumeer, separated from his wife, and despite the contentious split, he's been frantic to maintain a united front with his ex for the sake of his children. Fortunately, when Kyle couldn't reach me, he talked to Tristan, who easily took control of the situation. But we still have press releases to write and umpteen gossip mongers to quell.

In contrast, my mayoral candidate, Howard LaRoe, has been pissy that I haven't been at his beck and call, and he left me a nasty message on my work voicemail. How quickly he forgets all of the times I've helped him when he was in a jam.

Despite the work chaos, what's making me mental is not being able to check my personal messages until I get a new cell phone.

Given how busy Tristan and I are trying to catch up on work from the holiday, I give up any hope of getting that errand done before the weekend is up.

But I wonder. Did Drew call me? Text me? Or just ditch me on the mountain with nary a word after we screwed for three days straight?

Although in the moment, nothing we did felt wrong. Two consenting adults hooked up and had fun. But now I feel used, like I gave something away I can't get back.

The whole thing leaves me disconcerted in a way I'm not used to.

It's enough to make me call my parents.

Fortunately, they're blissfully ignorant of my crime spree this Thanksgiving, although they tell me Evie checked in with them to make sure I'd gotten back home.

I'm bummed they didn't get her number when she called, but at least I know she's not trapped on Mount Hood.

And as much as my sister pisses me off, Brooke kept her promise and didn't blab to our parents about bailing me out of jail.

My stomach tightens when I let myself think about what happened.

I don't know what I'll tell Evie about this week. Admitting I boned Drew within an inch of our lives only to get blown off by him at the police station is a level of shame I'm not sure how to deal with.

It shouldn't feel worse than the first time I saw Bobby with his wife, but it does.

Maybe I just need a day or two to process everything.

By Monday morning, that eye twitch is an evil migraine I can't seem to shake no matter how many Advil I down.

Because at the back of my mind, one word keeps flashing, usurping my obsession with whether or not I'll find messages from Drew when I get my new phone later today. And that word gets louder and louder as the day progresses.

Felony.

Felony!

FELONY!

So when Jessica sticks her head in the doorway of my office to announce that "some attorney is on line two," I nearly hop out of my shoes.

With my heart in my throat, I nod and pick up the phone. As I'm about to punch the blinking light, I look up to see my overly interested intern is still there.

"Thanks, Jess. Can you close the door, please?"

Tristan and I haven't told her anything aside from the fact that I was out of cell phone range this weekend, but it's obvious she knows something's up.

I'm so nauseated when I answer, I pull over the trash can in case I hurl the granola bar I ate for breakfast.

My attorney's gruff voice bellows in my ear. "Good news, Kendall. The charges have been dropped."

Holy shit!

I open my mouth but nothing comes out the first time.

"Are you sure?"

He chuckles, and I'm so buoyed with relief, I barely hear the rest of what he says except for the last part about sending me the bill.

After I hang up, I collapse on my desk in a heap of tired girl.

A few minutes later, a quiet knock has me looking up, and Tristan's concerned face pokes in. "Just wanted to make sure you didn't jump out a window." He closes the door behind him and slides into the chair across from my desk.

"I am officially free and clear. Charges have been dropped."

"Damn. I was looking forward to buying you a black and white striped jumper for Christmas."

I roll my eyes, but then we stare at each other and laugh.

"Who says I don't live dangerously?"

He nods agreeably. "Breaking and entering is absolutely bucket list material."

"I know, right?"

In the comfortable silence that follows, my mind goes back to the cabin. To the cozy fireplace and the guy who kept me warm. Did Drew have anything to do with the charges being dropped? Maybe I don't need to be raging at him. Maybe he's a good guy after all.

Despite the hour-long lecture my sister gave me about hooking up with Drew—because of course she reads the gossip columns—I don't want to be mad at him.

Like he's reading my mind, Tristan's eyebrows jiggle up and down. "So Drew Merritt, huh?"

I stiffen and then try to look casual. "What do you mean?" I haven't told Tris *everything* about the holiday weekend. No need to overshare.

He points to my neck. "That hickey is just now fading."

I gasp and wrap a hand around myself. "Are you serious?"

"Ha, sucka. Got ya!"

Reaching over my desk, I smack him on the shoulder. "Not a word about this. Not. A. Word."

After his laughter dies and my blush fades, he clears his throat. "Just be careful with that guy, okay? If he hurts you, I'm not sure I can afford the caliber of attorney I'm gonna need for the ass-kicking I'll lay on him."

I'm wondering if my professional reputation can afford to spend more time with Drew anyway.

Maybe what happened between us is meant to stay on Mount Hood after all.

17

DREW

"Cyber Monday's been bonkers so far," Frankie announces as she struts into my office, shoves a printout in my hand, and taps it with a short black-polished nail. "Even better than Black Friday. Speaking of which, why were you completely MIA? I called you sixteen times."

Her X-ray glare gives me the impression she knew I was naked, getting it on all weekend, although I haven't told her a damned thing.

"Sorry," I mutter, minimizing my browser and leaning back in my desk chair. "Shit happens."

"I'm only glad whatever you were doing didn't make the news. But look at this. *Look at this*!" She raps the paper in my hands again. "Sales are up four hundred percent over last year. And we're trending on the front page of Instagram!"

Calling up apps on her iPad, she illustrates that, yes indeed, our hashtag pops up everywhere.

My eyes pass over the sheet she hands me without comprehending any of the numbers. I founded this little company to stick it to my old-school, department-store-founding relatives. I know shit about business, so I basically hire people and sign checks. They can figure out all the details.

While we've been stumbling along for a couple of years, in the past week we've sold a gazillion shirts, causing my workers at the screenprint stations to work overtime in the adjacent warehouse. I'm sure they could use the extra money this season along with their holiday bonuses. My entire manufacturing facility smells like ink and machines and fabric and excitement.

I should be ecstatic. I should be hitting refresh on my computer screen every five minutes to review the latest figures. I should be picturing all the kids who are going to get new, comfy clothes.

But instead of paying attention to our meteoric climb, I'm Googling, "How many texts can you send her before you're officially declared a stalker and are arrested (again)?"

"If you go by her house and she's not there, what is the maximum number of hours it's okay to sit in your car staring at the front door?"

"Is it a good idea to go to her job with roses and/or a kitten if she might hate your guts?"

"Is it creepy to sniff your clothes that still smell like her?"

And similar queries.

Full disclosure: I may have forgotten to launder the T-shirt she slept in, and I may have taken a whiff of it. Once. Maybe twice. Don't judge. She smelled fucking amazing.

I stare blankly at my hands.

Frankie waves her palm in front of my face, silver rings on every finger. "Hel-lo. Captain. What the hell? Where is Drew? Earth. To Drew."

Every business has a person who runs the place for real. For me, that's Francesca Delarosa, a five-ten, raven-haired, tattooed badass with an iPad in her hand and a can-do attitude. She's passionate about making sure we're environmentally friendly on every level as well as profitable and high-quality. In short, she makes Martha Stewart look like a slacker.

I hire well.

While Frankie has been known to order me lunch, organize my appointments, and—at least in the past—call an Uber when I show up to work drunk and/or high, I don't tell her much about my private life. And I know next to nothing about hers. We don't have that kind of closeness. That said, I'm sure she could chart my life on *Gary the Gossip.*

It's weird. Frankie is my right hand at work, and yet I told Kendall more about my life in three days than I've told Frankie in three years.

I might have issues.

"Long weekend." I lift my feet off the desk and put them on the floor. Shazam bats my shoelace. I glance up at Frankie. "That's awesome, though," I say lamely.

Her hand flies to her hip, and she gives me a stare that would make a prize Portland rose wither to the ground.

"That's *awesome,*" she repeats, with the same nonexistent level of enthusiasm I displayed. "Awesome? Jeez, try to muster some emotion. Your lifestyle brand is everywhere. You got some of the hottest celebs wearing the T-shirt. And you're making tons of money for charity. Why are you not jumping up and down?"

I open my mouth to think of an excuse, but the office door opens, letting in the buzz and clack of the screen printing machines. Josh stalks in, saving me from an inquisition I'm not ready for.

But apparently he has one of his own planned.

He shakes both his head and his finger at me. "Dude. Loser. What the hell?" Then he realizes Frankie is in the room, straightens, and turns to her, lifting his chin. "Hey."

"Hey, Josh," she says, then gives me a gesture like, *You and I are going to talk.* She swishes out in her ripped jeans and heavy belt to crack skulls or whatever she does to make this place run, closing the door behind her.

"Hey, man," I say, and stand up from my messy desk to give Josh a man-hug. "Missed you last weekend."

"Missed you last weekend?" Josh's voice is so loud, I'm glad the warehouse is going at full volume to drown him out. "That's all you can say?"

I cringe.

"I invite you to my cabin, and you don't show up. No one's seen or heard from you or Kendall in days. Evie freaked out thinking you guys ended up in a ditch. And then I get a call from your lawyer that you've been arrested." I'm wondering if steam is going to erupt from his ears. "You're lucky I didn't send out the National Guard."

I shiver and return to my seat, pointing to the open chair across from me. "Thank fuck. I've had enough of our men and women in uniform." He doesn't laugh. "Sorry, man. Didn't mean to worry you guys. Just, you know, add this to my long list of fuck-ups."

A sympathetic expression passes over his face as he sits down too. "What happened?"

Briefly, while I reach down and scratch behind the cat's ears, I tell Josh the safe-for-public parts. How Kendall and I got lost. Got stuck. Couldn't go anywhere. Broke in. Found out it was the wrong address. *Yadda, yadda, yadda.*

When I trail off, he says, "And..."

"And what?"

Now his eyes resemble Frankie's, turning into X-rays. Unlike her, he knows every single damn thing about me. He lowers his voice. "You're snowbound with a pretty girl you've secretly lusted after for years—"

"Have not—"

"And I know you never travel without at least six condoms."

"Only four."

He grins.

Putting Shazam on the desk to swat the detritus, I shove my hands in my jean pockets. "Shit."

Josh's Cheshire cat smile now stretches all the way across his face. "I'll drive," he offers. "You can buy me lunch. You'd better start singing your story."

We end up at a fucking salad place, and after checking my sugars, I eat a fucking salad. As I lift a forkful of cucumber to my mouth, wishing it was a burrito, I say, "Yeah. Kendall. Who'd have thought?"

Setting down his roast beef sandwich, he starts counting on his fingers. "Uh, me. Evie. Your gran."

I stare at him, blinking. "Seriously?"

He chuckles. "Seriously. You guys are like two cats in a confined space. You were either going to hiss at each other and spar with your claws out until one of you killed the other, or cuddle."

A quick drink of water saves me from choking on a lettuce leaf. "Cuddle. *Dude.* No way."

Pressing his lips together, he just looks at me.

With a sigh, I admit, "Okay, yeah. There was some cuddling. But what is happening to me?" My voice quiets down. "I haven't talked to her since Saturday, and it's driving me crazy. She won't return my texts. I went by her apartment, and she wasn't there. She's not returning my phone calls. I'm turning into someone who scares me."

"You've scared me for years, so what's good for the goose is good for the gand—"

"Has Evie talked to Kendall?"

"No. Guess they're playing phone tag. She managed to get in touch with Kendall's parents, who said she got home safely, but they haven't had a chance to catch up. Ken's parents didn't seem to know much beyond you guys getting stuck in the snow, though, so you're in luck there. At least her dad doesn't want to track you down with a shotgun."

He chuckles, but this time I'm the one who can't find humor in the joke.

I'm too fixated on the fact I haven't seen this woman since she got thrown into the snow by the cops after a three-day fuck-fest that rocked my world.

Kendall might not want to talk to me, but I'll lose my mind if I don't explain, face to face, what happened back on the mountain.

"I'm gonna swing by Kendall's work later. I have to talk to her." I finish off the last bite of my salad, wishing it clogged my arteries.

Josh wipes his fingers on a napkin. "Can I ask something?"

"You just did."

He arches an eyebrow at my stupid joke. I make a gesture like, *Go on.* Leaning forward on the table, he asks, "Why do you care so much? Why don't you wait for her to get back to you? What if she doesn't want to talk to you for some reason, like, oh, you got her arrested?"

I consider my thoughts, which is new for me. "That's more than one question."

"So answer them all."

Scuffing my feet on the linoleum floor, I mutter, "I like her. We had a really good time, and it surprised me. She was different than she's been before. I got a glimpse of the cool girl who's friends with Evie, not the... I don't even want to use the word I used to call her anymore. Let's just say she was cool."

"She was cool," Josh repeats. "That's it?"

"No," I admit. "I want to see more of her. And dude. Not sayin' what happened. But it was hot."

He smirks.

"But here's the crappy part. She asked to keep what happened up there quiet. No one should ever know." Twisting the salt and pepper shakers, I continue, "Well, I suppose you don't count."

"Thanks."

"Frankly, it sucks to keep any of this—whatever is or was going on between us—a secret. I mean, I know I'm, well..." I wave my hands around, indicating all of the nonsense that has been my life up till now. "But I'm not crazy about her being ashamed to be with me in civilian life. And that's what she said *before* she spent time in the pokey. We almost got this thing off the ground only to crash and burn. And it's not like we even had a thing. It's a friends-with-benefits thing. Not a relationship thing. As is obvious—"

Now I'm babbling.

And I shouldn't be saying anything about this except I'm losing my shit and need to talk to someone.

Josh's eyes brim with light, and he presses his right fist to his heart. "Fucking proud of you, D-man. I think if you don't watch it, you'll find yourself with a ring on your finger."

My heart palpitations are audible. "Uh, no. Not ready for that."

"Uh-huh. Yeah. So friends with bennies?"

"Yes."

"That's not gonna get you in any trouble, I'm sure." We pay the bill and go back to my office, where I play with the cat and continue Googling everything wrong with my life.

Five hours later I'm ensconced in my car across the street from the front door of Kendall's office debating whether or not I should go in. It's not like I can hide—my Maserati is bright red and cost a hundred thousand dollars. Even in the constant northwest drizzle, I stand out.

Shazam nestles on my lap, having insisted on coming with

me. I pick up my phone for the umpteenth time to text Kendall, then set it back down.

I don't want to bug her at work or make a scene, although I'm pretty good at that. Our agreement was to keep it on the DL when we got back to town. I'll honor it.

But damn if I don't want more.

Fiddling with my phone, I resist Googling the definition of "Friends who fuck."

Friends who fuck, my ass.

Ha.

Well, it was *her ass*.

And now I'm thinking about last weekend, remembering all the sexy times. If I don't watch it, I'll be greeting her with a flag-pole sticking out of my pants.

Finally, at seven thirty-eight p.m., after I have to pee, am hungry, and have a yowling cat, the door to Kendall's office opens. I place my finger on my door handle, ready to spring into action, when I realize she's not alone.

That guy at her office has his arm around her shoulders. Their heads are bent toward each other. And they're ducking and laughing as they run to his car. Together.

My brain stumbles while I blink away the red haze heating my eyes. My thoughts resemble torn pieces of paper in the wind, fragments of ideas that don't make sense.

They... she... him... she was just with me.

And now she's with him?

No wonder she's ignoring me.

I start my engine and burn rubber as I accelerate, hoping to drive faster than my thoughts.

Or the disappointment in my gut.

18

KENDALL

*W*ith a swipe of my hand, I shove the cellophane wrapping and boxes into the trash and stare at my new pearly white iPhone, which arrived an hour ago by courier.

I'd hauled my tired ass to the Apple Store after work yesterday only to find it closed early due to a water main that burst.

I almost cried.

But that's been my luck lately.

I'm still seething over losing my old one in the puddle last weekend. The replacement cost is a huge expense I hadn't budgeted for, but I can't go any longer without a cell. It's only Tuesday afternoon, and being hamstrung like this makes me crazed.

Two hours later, I'm still messing with passwords and codes and trying to upload all of my apps while researching how to retrieve the files I need.

When Tristan swings by with a press release he wants me to proof, I drop my head on my desk.

"How goes the tech battle? Any luck getting your contacts loaded?"

I keep my forehead planted on the hard counter and tilt my head back and forth. "I'm the genius who didn't back up to the cloud. I had an older-model phone that I could never sync up with my laptop for some reason."

"Oh, shit."

I'd wanted to get a new cell that worked properly but sank all of my money into our new firm. Into decent office furniture and a small kitchen so our staff had somewhere to eat. Small amenities so working long hours wouldn't be a drudgery.

Sitting up, I shove my hair out of my face. "Even better, there's no way to retrieve the messages or texts I missed since my old phone broke. *And* I had to pay full price for this shiny marvel since the old phone was damaged, and I couldn't trade it in for a discount."

"Aww, boo." He sinks into the chair across from me.

"I know, right?" I mock cry into my hands, but I really do feel like crying. But I've learned my lesson and everything now is synced and ready for the apocalypse.

"If it makes you feel any better, I think we've managed to keep the roof from blowing off this place even without the mighty Kendall Greer plugged in twenty-four seven to all of her clients and ten million social media accounts."

"You joke now, but if there had been a major crisis, you wouldn't be so damn cheery. And I'll be sure to return the Little Miss Sunshine routine when this happens to you."

"Forsooth."

"Shut up, nerd."

We chuckle, but my laughter fades when I return my attention to my phone. I run my finger over the glossy glass. "Can I ask you a question? I need a guy's perspective."

"Hmm. This sounds serious." I glance behind him to the

open door, and he reaches back and gives it a shove so it slams closed. He waves at himself. "Bring it. I'll even put on my thinking cap."

I snicker at my best bud, so appreciative to have this wonderful guy to work with every day, but when I consider what I need to ask, I groan. "I can't retrieve my messages, so I have no way of knowing *who* might have called or texted me." I give him a meaningful look because I'm obviously not talking about clients anymore.

"Are you sure you can't upload that stuff?"

"Nope. You have to have the old phone to migrate everything. Trust me. I just spent the last hour Googling the problem and messing with my phone. It's not happening."

"So we have no way of knowing whether Alcatraz called."

I laugh at Tristan's nickname for Drew. "Right. And I don't have his contact info to text him, so if I want to send a casual 'Hey, I'm not locked up in the state pen, thanks for asking' kind of message, I have to go through Evie to collect his digits." Rubbing my forehead, I moan to myself, unable to shake off this tortured, twisted sensation in my chest. "Honestly, though, he's probably the reason the charges were dropped, so I shouldn't be so snarky."

His eyebrows lift slowly. "And we're not telling your BFF about this why?"

My lips twist. He knows me too well. I'd usually beeline to Evie to dish. At least regarding the big picture. "It's not that I'm *not* telling her. Exactly."

"Uh-huh."

"It's complicated."

"Because it's about the party boy, the one you swore off eons ago."

I cringe. "Something like that. Ugh, Tris, I'm so conflicted. On one hand, before the cops came down on us like we were

Bonnie and Clyde, we'd had an amazing weekend. He was nothing like the guy I first met. He was sweet and thoughtful and really attentive." Yes, Drew gave me lots of special, naked attention. My face heats from the images flashing through my brain.

It's Tristan's turn to snicker. "And he obviously rang your bell. Many times."

I sigh, unable to help the wistfulness in my expression. "He's a magical bell-ringer."

"Waving his magic wand." Tris jumps up, thrusts his hips, and pretends to spank someone.

"Oh, dear God. Never do that again." I'm laughing so hard, tears form in my eyes. Tristan puts on a super serious front to people who don't know him, but once you get past that, he's a jokester and the biggest sweetheart. He always knows what to say to make me feel better, which is why we make such perfect business partners and best friends.

He settles back into his seat. "I still got the moves. Just saying."

"You totally do, Ace Ventura."

He motions to me. "My guess is the guy probably called or texted you, especially if you think he was responsible for getting the charges dropped. If the weekend went as well for him as it did for you, then he'd want to check on you at the very least."

"But why did he leave the police station without talking to me?"

He rubs his chin slowly. "Are you sure he left?"

I stare at him a moment. "I mean, I can't say with one hundred percent certainty, but that's the impression I got from the receptionist. Plus, the prima ballerina had her knickers in a knot and was going to leave me behind if I didn't book it out of there, so I didn't have time to ask anyone else."

He rolls his eyes. "You should've called me. I would've bailed your sad little ass out of jail."

"I would've if I could've remembered your number!"

"I'm so hurt right now." He sniffles and wipes pretend tears. "Here I thought I was your male equivalent of Evie."

"You are. You *so* are. And I've learned my lesson—I'm going to commit your number to memory so the next time I commit a felony, you can rescue me instead of my scary sister."

Tapping my phone, he directs us back to my internal crisis. "Call Evie. Ask for everyone's digits since you have a new phone. Her dad's. Josh's. Drew's. Those are all numbers you had, right?"

I nod slowly. "I feel bad not telling her what happened, though."

"You mean all the nookie you got this weekend?"

"I guess I'm embarrassed because Drew and I have had *epic* arguments over the years, and Evie's been front and center for most of them. But she and I haven't really talked much about sex since she and Josh got serious. It's not like she wants to share what goes down in their relationship."

He laughs. "Can't say I blame the girl given how they started out."

Tristan is one of the few people who knows about Josh's naughty blog, which is what initially brought him and Evie together.

"But yeah, I'm not wild about sharing that Drew and I hooked up."

"Judging what you just said about her and Josh, I'm sure she'll understand if you keep it under wraps while you figure out what's going on with you and the party boy. Evie's solid. Then bite the bullet and give Drew a call. You've waited a respectable amount of time since this weekend, so he's not going to think you're planning the perfect wedding. Mention your phone was DOA but you wanted to let him know you got home and ask if he's why the charges got dropped."

That all sounds reasonable. Relief finally settles over me. "You're good at this."

"I am."

"Why don't you have a girlfriend again?"

"Can't tie down this beast, babe." He blows on his knuckles like a jackass.

"I'm so glad I'm not attracted to you."

He rolls his eyes again. "It's not my fault you kiss like a crazy chameleon."

I gasp and toss his dumb press release at him. "I do not."

Tris and I kissed once in college on a dare, started laughing in the middle of it, and swore to never do it again. And now we're besties through and through.

He dusts off the piece of paper and places it on my desk. "Stop deflecting. Call Casanova, and then let's grab something to eat before I waste away."

After he walks out, I stare at his empty seat for a few minutes trying to work up the courage to call Evie and then Drew.

For some reason, I'm scared to do it, which means I must really like the guy because I'm never this nervous about anything.

God help me. I have a crush on Drew Merritt.

After hunting high and low, I finally find Evie's number in one of my old planners at the bottom of my desk drawer.

"KENDALL!" Her shriek makes me pull the phone away from my head.

"Are you okay? Because you sound like you're being murdered."

"There's water everywhere." She curses and then curses some more. "The new property we just closed on flooded from all of the melting snow. I'm standing in a lake of ice-cold water in the freaking kitchen."

"Oh, man. That sucks." I check the time, internally groaning at the idea of squeezing in one more thing today, but there's no way I'm going to leave my best friend hanging if she needs help. "If you give me a few hours, I can head over and give you a hand with the cleanup."

"I knew there was a reason you were my best friend."

"I'm your best friend because I gave you tampons in junior high when you were too embarrassed to ask your dad to get them."

She laughs, and I smile at the impromptu trip down memory lane. "Don't remind me. My dad still shudders if you bring up anything dealing with Aunt Flo."

"Give me the address to the property, and I'll get there as soon as I can. Just promise me there'll be no cameras." She and Josh flip houses for her TV show, and I refuse to sweat while being filmed.

"That's okay. I know you're slammed. Josh should be here soon, and he already called in an agency to handle the major cleanup because he wants to make sure we don't get mold, but thank you so much." She pauses a moment. "Ken, I feel terrible about what happened last week. That you got stuck up on the mountain without electricity or heat!"

So Drew must've told Josh *something*.

That knot in my stomach tightens.

"It's fine. I'm okay. I'll give you all the gory details the next time I see you."

Because I can't do it right now. I can't make sense of it myself much less explain what went down with Drew.

We agree to grab lunch as soon as she's able to get a handle on life, and when we start to get off the phone, I remember why I called in the first place.

"Wait. I need one more thing." I keep it simple and tell her my phone died—while listening to my heart beat in my ears. *Seriously, why am I so nervous about this guy?* "When you get a chance, can you email me everyone's phone number?" I rattle off all of the names, hoping I sound casual enough when I include Drew's.

"Sure! I should be able to do that tonight or tomorrow."

I feel guilty that I don't tell her more, but I promise myself to come clean about everything when we grab lunch.

Except one day turns into two.

By Friday morning, not only has Drew not called or texted, but Evie never sent me the phone numbers, and she hasn't texted back about hanging out. I'd bug her about it if I didn't know how busy she is right now.

Plus, I might be chickening out.

Because what the hell? I bone this guy all Thanksgiving like I'm a sex addict and he doesn't call?

The cautious part of me says Drew played me. That he isn't calling because he's on to the next best thing.

And as I click on *Gary the Gossip's* blog to make sure my clients aren't being scandalized, I freeze when I see a photo of Drew at a party.

Last night.

With a drink in hand.

Surrounded by three gorgeous, scantily-clad girls hanging off him like barnacles on a ship.

That twisted, gut-wrenching sensation returns with a vengeance, stinging my eyes with tears.

So much for Drew 2.0.

He's back to being Drew-you're-dead-to-me.

19

KENDALL

I nudge the glossy bag over until it's perfectly aligned with the ten in front of it. Presentation is everything in this business.

With a contented sigh, I step back and admire the bright labels and cheery bows adorning each package.

"Our donors are going to love these." Howard LaRoe's campaign manager Marshall gives me a wide smile. "This was a great idea, Kendall."

"The best part is how the products tie into his speech." I don't usually get into this level of detail, but Howard is one of my highest-profile clients, and I didn't want to trust this to my staff. So I spent the last two weeks researching items made in Oregon to promote Howard's buy-local philosophy, which will hopefully garner him extra face time on tonight's news.

Howard's image has needed a boost, and extending my attention to these gift bags from my typical focus on his press kits has been fun. Although Howard might be a pain in the ass sometimes, I love his platform, so I'm willing to go the extra mile. I don't even mind that Howard will take the credit for my ideas.

The ballroom doors open and donors stream in. In the background, a quartet plays holiday music softly. An enormous Christmas tree sits in the corner where guests place gifts they're donating to families in need. Although my gift bags might be getting the attention tonight, the fact that we'll donate so many presents to children who might not otherwise get something this winter is the best part of my evening.

An image of Drew sitting by the fire at the cabin a few weeks ago comes to mind. I wonder how he'll spend the holidays.

When it was just the two of us wrapped around each other over Thanksgiving, I'd wondered if we might see where things took our relationship afterward and even thought about getting him a present for Christmas, which is in a few days.

That's when I get hit so hard by a wave of melancholy, I have to brace my arm against the pillar next to me.

I never did speak to him. To talk or tell him off or tell him I miss his face.

Evie's had all kinds of problems with her new property, and between that and being somewhat of a newlywed, we've barely spoken in the last two weeks since her kitchen flooded.

Which means I haven't had a chance to broach the subject of Drew again, not that I've wanted to. Much.

But yeah. I miss that douchebag more than I care to admit.

I might have a serious case of the stupids. Because one minute, I want to sock him in the face for being an asshole and the next I'd do anything to strip him naked just to cuddle.

Sure, the feminist in me has been riding my ass to call him and bitch his ass out for going MIA. But sometimes—especially after what we shared over Thanksgiving—a woman wants to know she's important. That what she shared with a man was significant enough for him to pick up the damn phone and call her.

Apparently I wasn't.

A waiter stops by with some hors d'oeuvres and waves a

platter of golden crab rangoon in front of me. I rarely eat anything fried, much less at a client's event, but for some reason, I want to devour everything in front of me.

Marshall must sense my hunger because he motions toward the server. "Please enjoy the food, Kendall. I know Howard's been a slave driver lately, so the least I can do is feed you."

I press my hands to my suit skirt, needing a minute so I don't dive face first into the finger food. The smell of my lunch this afternoon almost made me hurl, so I've been reluctant to eat anything because I could not miss Howard's event tonight. I'd chalked it up to nerves and stress and downed a ginger ale instead of what I'd brought from home.

Needless to say, I'm ravenous as I place crispy nuggets of deliciousness on my plate. I catch the scent of bacon and my head swivels toward it like a dog in search of a bone.

But as I'm driving home two hours later and the crab rangoon, fried shrimp, bacon wraps, and egg salad with tapenade are shooting out of my mouth—while I lean out of my car on the side of the road—I know I shouldn't have deviated so far from my typical eating habits.

The next day isn't much better, and I groan into the phone as I catch up Tristan with the details from last night's fundraiser.

"You hurled your cookies on the street?"

"On the corner of Burnside and Third. Everyone at Voodoo Donuts saw it. Hopefully I drove away before anyone broke out the camera phones."

"Yikes. Well, next time give me a heads up, and we can sell tickets to your late night showing of the *Exorcist*." We both laugh, and I reach for a granola bar. "I think we should charge LaRoe more for giving you food poisoning."

With a shrug, I tear the wrapper. "I wasn't feeling great yesterday afternoon, so it probably wasn't the food at the hotel."

"You might have a stomach bug." He pauses. "Or maybe you're pregnant."

We've joked about one of us having kids a few times over the years, always laughing off the idea that either of us was ready to settle down like that.

Except right now, I'm not laughing. With the granola bar halfway to my mouth, I'm petrified like one of those people in Pompeii when they got axed by that volcano.

When I don't fill in the silence, because I'm too busy internally screaming *WHAT THE FUCK?* Tristan clears his throat. "Honey, are you pregnant?"

"Oh, shit."

I drop the granola bar and phone and reach for my laptop.

After I type in the wrong password three times, it finally unlocks, and I pull up iCal. Like a zombie, I reach for my cell. "Tris?"

My hands are shaking as I do the math.

"You want me to come over?" His deep voice is the only thing tethering me to this couch.

"Yes, please."

By the time he rings my doorbell, I'm frantic.

I throw my arms in the air as he walks into my apartment. "I can't be pregnant. No one gets nauseated this early in a pregnancy. Just because I missed my period and I've been a little queasy doesn't mean I've got a bun in the oven."

Maybe I have cancer or a brain tumor or irritable bowel syndrome. I know because I Googled the symptoms.

"I would've gotten you some pregnancy tests, but I have no clue what kind to get."

I pause. "You mean none of the girls you've banged have had a pregnancy scare? *Ever?*"

Tristan shakes his head.

"You've banged a lot of girls."

"I wrap it up. Always."

"We did too!" I pause as all of the dirty, naked things I did with Drew come rushing back to me. "Except for that last night. Goddammit. What was I thinking?"

A chuckle escapes him. "I have a pretty good idea what you were thinking."

"Now is not the time to be funny." I start pacing back and forth in front of my coffee table. "We ran out of condoms." A sound of disbelief bursts from his mouth. "What?"

He rolls his eyes as his jaw tightens. "Some guys are looking for an excuse to not use condoms, or they let them slide off in the middle of the act. I hear bastards at the gym brag about that all the time."

I blink and blink again. "So the whole 'we used the last one' line could've been bullshit? He was just trying to get his jollies?"

The hysteria in my voice has him pulling me to his chest. "Before I go after him with a rusty saw blade, let's get some confirmation about the stork sighting, okay?"

I don't remember getting in his car or driving to the pharmacy, but once we're there, Tristan takes my hand and pulls me down row after row of medical supplies until we get to the pregnancy tests.

We pick out several different kinds and grab a giant container of Gatorade and head to the counter. I'm getting out my credit card when I notice the magazine next to the register.

"Portland's sexiest bachelors." I scoff because those guys are always such assholes when you meet them in person.

But then I see who's on the cover, and for the second time in two days, I lean over and puke.

I stare at the four positive tests lining my bedside table and start to cry. Now that Tristan went home, I let it all out until I'm hiccupping into my hands.

Tris assured me everything would be fine, that he'd help me with whatever I needed no matter where things ended up with Drew. And even though it's reassuring to have his support, I still feel like the sky is falling.

After the tears subside, I consider calling my mom, but she'll be delighted to be a grandmother regardless of the fact that the baby's daddy is probably out fucking cocktail waitresses two at a time this weekend. I can see him now, sitting in a bar with that damn magazine, pointing to his photo, and scheduling blowjobs into next year.

And even though my sister's been through pregnancy, she'll be as sympathetic as a dishrag.

So when Evie texts and tells me to come over tonight so we can catch up, I immediately tell her yes.

Because I could really use my best friend right now.

It doesn't matter that my face is puffy and that I feel like death. I just need to cry on her shoulder. Surely she'll know how to advise me on how to talk to Drew about this.

And that makes me cry more.

When I envisioned my life and having a family, it came in a certain order. Build up my career. Save for a rainy day. Buy a house. Date and marry a great guy. Fuck like bunnies for a few years, maybe travel, and then start a family.

It did *not* include getting knocked up by Portland's most infamous bachelor.

I look around at my small bedroom, wishing I hadn't sold my condo to start my business. At least then I'd have some liquidity. Because I'm pretty sure I have a gazillion-dollar deductible on my health insurance and giving birth is expensive.

Babies are expensive.

Doctor's appointments are expensive.

I know because I've been Googling the hell out of everything baby-related today.

When I pull up to Evie and Josh's house an hour later, I don't care that I must look like a car ran over me. They can deal with me looking disheveled and maybe slightly psychotic.

My hair is knotted on top of my head, but pieces are hanging in my face. I'm rocking some hiking boots and the yoga pants I slept in. At least I changed my shirt because I didn't want to smell like vomit, and I mustered the last bit of energy I had to brush my teeth and wash my face.

When I ring their doorbell, I paste a smile on my face.

Which promptly slides off the moment Drew answers the door.

20

DREW

*I*nstead of the Uber Eats delivery of Taste of India, I open Josh's door to a startled redhead drowning in oversize clothes. My brain halts, and my body falters. I blink.

What is Kendall doing here?

Too many days have passed since I've seen her—too many weeks, really—and I don't know what to say.

I don't know what to do either, so I just rub my hands through my hair as my hungry eyes take her in. But I can't bring myself to confront her about where she's been or why I never heard back from her. Not here, not now. And I definitely can't look her in the eyes, since she might see the rawness in mine.

Rather than scrutinize her expression, I focus my gaze everywhere else as she stands in the industrial-chic hall. Her slim legs in yoga pants. Her tendrils of messy-sexy hair. Her narrow shoulders that seem more hunched since I last saw her. Despite my immediate concern, I'm elated to see her. Fuck chicken tikka masala and vindaloo fish curry.

I want Kendall.

I've missed her. So fucking much.

My chest tightens, and I'm about ready to throw my arms

open to her before I remember she's not talking to me. No, she very deliberately blew me off. Plus, she's seeing someone else.

She must hate me for the shit that went down on our last day. Why else wouldn't she have responded to at least one of my thirty million texts and calls?

"Hey," I say hoarsely as I do a double take.

Red rings her sky-blue eyes, and there's a presence behind them I've never seen before. Noticing the puffiness in her face and the splotches on her cheeks, I subdue a growl. *Who hurt her?*

A burst of protective anger pulses through me.

But she isn't mine, I remind myself.

She's not my problem.

I swallow hard.

She frowns, and her brows knit together. "Is Evie home?"

Without a word, I hold the door open for her, but before Kendall takes three steps in, Evie bounds over, her dark brown hair pulled back in a ponytail and her gray eyes lit with friendliness. She gives Kendall a huge hug.

Like I want to do. I've never had my body and heart ache the way they do right now.

"Kendall! So good to see you!"

"Hey, girl. Missed you," Kendall says, her voice sounding scratchy.

Evie's face falls as she sizes up her best friend. "Oh my God, what's wrong? Come in."

Evie ushers in Kendall and takes her over to the dining area. Josh kicks back in the middle of the room on his black leather couch drinking sparkling water, looking all smarty-pants in his typical dark-rimmed glasses. I make a beeline for my asshole best friend.

Okay, the fact that he's drinking sparkling water instead of a beer in solidarity with me means he's not a total asshole. He's not off the hook, though, because I'm suspicious this meeting was planned by him, if not Evie too. I shoot laser eyes at him over Kendall's head as I walk his way.

While Josh and Evie live in a restored farmhouse, they kept Josh's old open-plan loft and stay here from time to time because it's so convenient and features a view of the sparkling, misty city. Since he's an architect, it's stunning to photograph, but there's no privacy. So instead of being able to shut a door and rip into him, he and I have a silent discussion, which involves me widening my eyes and trying to communicate with my face without the women seeing.

Me: What the hell, dude? Why the fuck didn't you tell me she was coming over? Or for that matter, that you'd buzzed her in? Here I was expecting saag aloo...

I'm positive he understands all of the above from my pointed glare, but I only get a shrug and a wide-eyed, innocent stare back from my ex-best friend.

Him: Whaaa? I know nothing.

I plop down on the couch across from him and gesture with my ear to the women.

He holds up his hands over his head, framing a halo.

This silent argument would go on for another hour, but the doorbell rings and Josh buzzes in Uber Eats. The real Uber Eats this time.

I get up again and open the door for the delivery dude, but all I want is to talk to Kendall, but I don't know how to do it with everyone here.

Even though I think Evie and Josh want us to talk.

Irony at its finest.

Ten minutes later, we sit without speaking at the dining table surrounded by takeout boxes of fragrant Indian food. Kendall swears she's not hungry, and her expression makes no one want to push it. There's food on my plate, but I move it around, none of it making its way to my mouth.

"So." Josh clears his throat, spears a samosa, and grins in a wicked way that means he's getting me back for, like, everything I've ever done to him. At least the time I pantsed him in eighth grade and when I shaved his eyebrow on winter break in college. And, oh yeah, that time I replaced the cream in his Oreos with toothpaste. "We're graced by the presence of Portland's most eligible bachelor. Bow down to Andrew, everyone. Can we get your autograph?"

"Fuck off," I mutter. "Let's not forget you've had the honors, too."

"I'm old news. You're the hottest thing around now," he says cheekily.

I'm wondering if I can murder Josh with chutney or maybe yogurt sauce. Some sort of water torture with condiments instead? I can MacGyver it. I lean back, giving up pretending to eat. Josh notices, but he's used to all my food issues by now.

"It's all they could talk about on set," Evie says. "The producer wants to get you on the show."

"No can do, Mrs. Cartwright," I say stiffly. "I will have to formally decline the invitation."

With a sniffle, Kendall toys with her fork. Her voice sounds brittle, and her expression hardens. "Why not? Milk it. Give the gossip bloggers something new to say."

The stilted tone of her voice makes me wonder. *Is something new posted?*

Not that I care what anyone says about me.

I do care, however, what Kendall thinks of me. "I guarantee you in a few days, no one will remember who was on that dumb magazine."

"You have to admit it's flattering," says Evie.

Shaking my head, I toss my napkin on my plate. "It's a bull-shit title. It means nothing."

"But what about that picture of you the other night with two girls on your knees? Did that mean nothing?" The edge in Kendall's voice pierces right through my heart.

My response is immediate. "I haven't been anywhere. I haven't been out in weeks. I work. I work out. I go home." *And Google self-help questions*, I don't add. "If anything's circulating the internet, it's old."

Kendall doesn't look convinced. Especially with Josh's next words.

"So what about the new sex tape?" He breaks off a piece of naan, fully conscious of the bomb of glittery dicks he's just thrown down in the room.

I splutter. "Sex tape? What sex tape?" I've been a monk since the cabin. Before Kendall, I wouldn't care what showed up on the internet. Now, though, I'm panicked something incriminating from my past decided to make its public debut. Especially when I catch a glimpse of Kendall's wounded expression. I'm about ready to kill my best friend for real this time. "What the fuck are you talking about?"

"Got ya." His smile is way too toothy.

"Mother. Fucker," I growl, then open my mouth to say more but am interrupted by Evie, who must have a sixth sense I'm about to disembowel her husband with whatever I can find in their apartment.

"Oh, crap, Ken. I forgot to send you all of our phone numbers. I totally spaced. I'm so sorry!"

I swivel my head between her and Kendall, curious why she doesn't have that already. "Numbers?"

Kendall stares at me long and hard before she responds. "When the cops threw me face down into the snow, my phone landed in a puddle, and I lost everything on it. All my data and contacts. And I had to get a new cell."

After I note she's still a little salty over getting arrested, the more significant realization flashes over my head like a Vegas Strip neon sign.

My jaw drops, and I sit forward, white-knuckling the dining table. "Did you get any of my texts?"

Slowly, she shakes her head. "No." Her eyebrow arches. "Did you send any?"

The tone of her voice suggests she doesn't think I did.

"Only enough times for you to get a restraining order." I half-choke out a laugh. "All this time—"

Relief, hot and swift, blasts through me.

But Kendall doesn't look convinced.

In fact, she looks pissed.

And if she thinks I didn't try to contact her after that weekend we shared, of course she'd be pissed.

Not to forget that minor detail of getting her arrested.

"Swear to God, KK." I hold up a hand. "I called, I texted, I would've sent fucking smoke signals."

She crosses her arms over her chest. "I got a new phone three days later."

We stare at each other. The implication is clear. If I called so many times, why weren't there any after that time frame?

Should I confess to waiting outside her office and seeing her with that guy?

My stomach revolts as I contemplate having this conversation in front of Josh and Evie.

"And I didn't hear from you *after those three days* why?"

"For reasons," I say, wanting to get her the fuck out of here right now. "Reasons I will gladly share with you if we could talk just the two of us."

I glance at Josh. He's the stupid cat who ate the canary. Okay, fine. I'm glad he orchestrated this. But I really need to talk to Kendall *alone*.

Evie catches her husband's eye. "While I think Josh and I

could make you guys miserable for the entire evening, why don't you two go. Ken, I'll call you later."

Kendall's eyes narrow on me like she's not quite sure what to believe.

"I solemnly swear on Shazam that I am not bullshitting you. I have legitimate info to discuss that will shed light on"—I wave between us—"this situation. Now get your lovely ass up and come with me."

Grabbing her hand, I tug her up from her seat and lean down to whisper in her ear, "Give me a chance to explain."

After the longest minute of my entire life, she nods and heads over to Evie to hug her. I wave to Josh and shepherd Kendall to my car, my heart pounding in my throat.

Why am I so nervous?

Maybe because I care.

For once in my fucking life, I care—what this woman thinks, how she feels, that I've clearly hurt her feelings.

As we step out of Josh's building into the Portland drizzle, I extend my fingers to hold her hand and then pull back. I've lost the right to do that. But I have to do *something* to make amends.

"I'm sorry," I blurt out, stopping in front of her in the middle of the sidewalk. I pull her into an overhang so she's not getting dripped on. She shivers, and I take off my jacket and wrap it around her.

While she accepts my jacket with a grateful, "Thanks," she still won't look at me. She bites her lip, her eyes anywhere but on mine. "What are you sorry for?"

"A lengthy list. Feel free to add suggestions. In fact, it might just be easier to name what I'm not sorry for."

Dammit. She doesn't smile.

Here goes everything. "I'm sorry for fucking up," I say, hoping she can feel my sincerity. "I'm sorry the police hurt you. I'm sorry you had to spend time in a cell by yourself. I'm sorry you had no communication. I'm sorry for getting the address wrong." I chuckle and run my hand through my hair. "Do you know what happened? I was off by a digit and a cardinal direction."

She blows out her cheeks and releases, then cocks her head to the side, slowly blinking. "What?"

"Northeast instead of Northwest. The address. I typed it in wrong in the GPS."

Kendall closes her eyes and rubs the middle of her forehead. "Seriously?"

My hands cover her shoulders, and she finally gazes up at me.

"Seriously. Oh, and I fucked up on the digits, too. Got them transposed."

I kick the ground. She doesn't say anything further. I take that as my cue to keep going.

"I'm so sorry that the police came." As my voice gets lower, aware of passing pedestrians, I cross my arms. "I'm sorry they separated us. That no one let me talk to you when we got arrested. That by the time my fucking attorney got to you, you were already gone. I'm sorry your phone broke. And I'm sorry for whatever made you cry on the way here." I pause. "But I'm not fucking sorry about spending the weekend with you."

A faint smile registers on her lips, but then it's gone.

But I'll take it. I know this girl and I have a connection, and damn if I'm not going to prove it to her.

With a deep breath, I say, "Let me take you home." I pull her to my car before she can respond. "I can send someone to bring your car to you if you give me your keys. That okay? Just...I want to spend some time with you."

I open the door and wait for her to decide.

"Before I get in your car, I need to know about those photos." Her tone is accusing, and it stings. "I mean, up on the mountain, whatever we had? That was one thing. We were stranded, and we had a good time. But we're back here for two minutes and your party pics are posted everywhere. You might say those images aren't recent, but given your track record, I'm afraid if I believe you, I'm being a fool. And like it or not, you deserve your reputation."

Ouch. But true.

"I know it's hard to believe, but I'm still sober and boringly low-glycemic. I'd tell you if I weren't. I respect the hell out of you, Kendall. I have no reason to lie about that. You know me. I let it all hang out." I grab her hand, knowing there's a good chance she might knee me in the balls, and look her in the eyes. "I've been a shithead in the past, but this is the real me. The guy you hung out with at the cabin."

She studies my expression.

"You swear? You promise me I'm not going to regret believing you?"

I hold up my hand. "I solemnly swear on my nutsack. And you know I love my nuts."

A laugh bursts out of her, and I smile back and tug her to me until she's nestled close and my arms are wrapped around her.

After a minute, she whispers, "You got the charges dropped? You're why I'm no longer a felon?"

I smile against her hair. "Maybe. I'm not opposed to playing with handcuffs under different circumstances."

She leans into me, giving me a quick squeeze. I reluctantly let her go and usher her into my car.

We pass a few quiet blocks. No radio. No cat in our laps. Just the thrum of my engine and the slick water on the streets.

Finally, I pipe up. "I really did send you all those messages, Ken. Here's an example." I mimic holding up my phone. "Beep. 'KK, this is Drew. I'm so fucking sorry, blah, blah, blah, for landing you in jail. Call me.'"

She narrows her eyes at me, but a smile is pulling at her lips.

"Beep. 'KK. I know you're probably still pissed, but please know I got them to drop the charges. You'd left before my lawyer sprang us out. Call me.'" I take a breath. "Beep. 'KK. Baby, please give me a call when you get this. I'm kinda going out of my mind.'"

Then I remember the other guy, and I go quiet. I was so busy begging for forgiveness, I'd forgotten about that asshole.

"What's wrong?"

I ignore her question. "Turn here?"

Her face hardens as she turns in her seat to face me. "What is it, Drew?"

Fuck it. I yank the steering wheel and pull us over to the side of the road. "I was honest with you. Now it's your turn. Who's that guy you're seeing?"

"What guy?" She looks genuinely confused. "What are you talking about?"

"I went to talk to you at your work the Monday after we got back, and you were leaving with that guy."

One long pause later, she tilts her head.

"*Tristan*?" She couldn't be more amused. "You met him. He's my male version of Evie. Totally just a friend."

Some old-school Biz Markie *Just a Friend* rings in my ears.

"You guys looked closer than business partners. Chummy." I feel like an idiot for not recognizing him, but I was too busy seething to think clearly.

"No." She smirks. "He doesn't do it for me."

But I do. *I do really hard, if memory serves me.*

"Drew Merritt, are you jealous?"

It's my turn to roll my eyes, but then she tugs on my shirt, and when I catch the smile on her face, I can't keep the truth from her.

"Yes." I scrub my face, horrified I'm admitting this. "It was sending me off the deep end." And since I've already come this far. "You wanted to know why I hadn't called you once you got your phone replaced? I'm not proud of this, but it's because—"

"—because you saw me with Tristan."

I nod, and she grabs my hand.

The cage around my heart opens. "You mean—"

"So we've not talked because—"

"Yeah. Every possible thing that could go wrong did."

"Good Lord." She chokes out a laugh. "We're a hot mess."

I could be the starting pitcher of the *Bad News Bears* of romance.

"Right?" I throw the car into gear, feeling lighter, and head to her apartment.

As we drive along, I update her on Shazam. "He misses you."

"He does?"

"Yep. Every night, he says, 'Where is K-Bear?' Of course he can only say meow, but I get the drift. He's getting bigger. Pretty soon I'm gonna have to take him to a vet and get his balls chopped off. His days of carousing late at night and cruising for the ladies are just about over."

Like someone else I know. Namely me.

"He needs to be fixed already?"

"Yep. From baby to full-grown in a few short weeks."

When I pull up to her curb, new awkwardness settles in my chest. Is she going to invite me in? Everything in my body wants me to come up with her, but she's not been overly friendly.

Without making a move to open the door, she sits and looks at her hands. Clears her throat.

"There's one more thing I need to talk to you about."

Shit. I thought we'd hashed out everything.

Why am I nervous all of a sudden?

That's when I notice she's pale.

And trembling.

The concern I had for her when I first opened the door at Josh's submerses me all over again.

She picks at her lip. "I need to tell you something, but I have a request."

"Anything."

"Don't walk me up. I need—I can't—I'm so damn tired, it's making me nauseated," she mumbles. "And I still need some time to process this by myself."

This woman drives me out of my fucking mind. I want nothing more than to spend the night. Find out what's going on inside. Hold her again.

"Kinda freaking out here, Ken. What is it?"

"Promise me."

"I promise."

"So...speaking of Shazam no longer being a baby and life changes and growing up..." She takes a deep breath. Swallows. "I guess there's no easy way to say this, but ..." Her voice drops to a whisper. "Surprise. I'm pregnant. And it's yours."

I blink.

A baby? Wait. Am I hearing things?

No, based on the expression on Kendall's face, I'm not imagining anything.

With a lurch, my gut revolts, and I'm dizzy.

I open my mouth to say something, but she holds her hand up. "I know we need to talk more, but I don't have the energy to do it now." She opens the car door and gets out. Leaning back in, she says, "Let's talk later. In a few days or something. Just—" She presses a hand to her stomach. "I can't right now."

Nodding mutely, I stare like a fool as she walks out of my life. Again.

21

DREW

*Y*ou know how it goes. You think you've cleared up every piece of psychic baggage between you and the girl you like. You're feeling all right, hoping you're gonna end the night with a cuddle or some nakey time. Hell, maybe even schedule an actual first date.

Then you find out your seed's gonna walk the earth.

Kendall slams my car door shut, and my brain struggles to process what she just said.

"Pregnant?" I whisper out loud—by myself in my car—trying out the word on my tongue to see how it feels.

For the record, the word feels as foreign as that wall of feminine hygiene products at the grocery store.

I don't make a habit of talking to myself, that's for Gollum, and the fact that it's not bothering me right now says something. Like, *my life just became a fucking mess.*

A bigger mess than normal.

Portland rain smacks my windshield, and the wipers slash back and forth. My engine idles in park. I don't move a muscle. I can't, because I'm torn. I want to run after her, bang on her door, and demand that we discuss the grenade she just threw.

The only thing stopping me is my word—oh, and the tiny detail that she doesn't want to process this shock with me tonight. Sure, we can talk about it later. But since what she's processing definitely involves me, her reluctance to share packs an even bigger wallop to the gut than finding out I knocked her up.

Doesn't she trust me? Does she think I wouldn't support her? Does she not know I care?

God, I *do* care. Having Kendall so close tonight activated everything I've been moping about for the past few weeks—the loss of her sparkly personality, her intoxicating scent, her incredible body. The sound of her voice and the silky feel of her hair.

I've missed her. After spending years fighting with her, then getting together, then a stupid misunderstanding—I thought we were finally in the clear.

Nope. Apparently not.

The loud honk of a horn startles me into taking my foot off the brake and putting the car in gear. I drive in the darkness lit up by holiday lights everywhere. It's the season of good cheer and togetherness. Of family.

Well, not my family. They're cretins, except my gran.

Fuck. How the hell am *I* supposed to have a family?

I want to call Josh, but it's getting late, and if I know him, he wouldn't want to be disturbed right now since he's probably engaging in naked acrobatics with Evie. While this is important enough to bug him, maybe I just need some time to think.

Dammit. Dammit all to hell.

I'm going to be a father.

Somehow my car ends up on Interstate 5 going south. As I listen to the swish of water under my tires and squint into the glare of headlights on the other side of the freeway, my thoughts enter a Zen zone. I cross vast swaths of Oregon, but it's too dark to see more than billboards and the occasional building lined with holiday lights.

Stopping in Salem to get gas, I notice that I never turned on the radio. I've been driving in silence the entire time, which tells me I'm so preoccupied, I'm lucky I'm wearing clothes and have my wallet. While the attendant fills the tank—it's illegal in Oregon to pump your own gas—I numbly go inside the convenience store looking for something. Anything.

Of course the first thing I see is a yellow "Baby on Board" warning sign to hang in the back window of your car, like a beacon to all. Worried about my insulin levels, I buy snacks from a cashier in a Santa hat and head out. As I get in the driver's seat, a liquor store across the street catches my eye with its yellow sign lit up, calling me to come and forget all this shit in my brain.

Jaeger. Captain. Jack. My old friends.

Fuck.

I need to get out of here. I peel out of the gas station and get back on the road.

Hours later, bleary-eyed, I head back home. I haven't figured out anything except I miss Kendall and I feel like someone ran over my life with a bulldozer. As the gray-pink dawn lightens the sky, I go to the only place where I know I can deal with life. I pull up at Josh's apartment, park, and ring his loft from the lobby. After hitting the button several times, I get his slurred, sleepy answer. "Hello?"

"Josh-man. I need you, bud. Please."

He buzzes me in. When he opens the door in his underwear and no glasses, his yawn turns to a horror-struck gape as he gives me a once-over. "You look like shit."

"Thanks." I'm sure my eyes are red and have bags under them. My hair stands on end like a bedraggled porcupine, and I'm wearing yesterday's clothes. "Can we talk?"

"Yup. Need breakfast?"

I nod.

Rubbing his hands through his hair, he glances back inside in the general direction of his sleeping wife. "Give me five to get dressed and let Evie know where I'm going, and then you can tell me what happened to you."

I have a soft spot for greasy spoon diners, the kind that are open twenty-four hours a day with menus that read like a food bible and serve coffee immediately when you sit down. Josh and I go to an old favorite, left over from our days prowling the Portland night scene. It's been years since we've been here together.

We're both stubbled and yawning, wearing hoodies and half-asleep expressions. Although I'm strung out from pulling an all-nighter, I've never been more grateful for my best friend.

The waiter plunks down water glasses and coffee, and I glance up at Josh, suddenly feeling like I might lose it. I busy myself with the sugar packets to avoid his eyes.

"Can I guess?" he asks, after we order.

"Yes, it's Kendall," I mutter to the dark faux wood tabletop.

"I figured that. But what happened? You guys were going to talk. I'm guessing you didn't work everything out?"

Now that the sugar packets are in color order—what the fuck has gotten into me?—I trace the condensation on my water glass. "We talked. It was good—until it wasn't."

"Thanks. That's perfectly clear." Josh waits for me to say more.

"I almost drove to California last night. And back again."

Concern radiates from Josh's eyes as he peers at me over his glasses. "Drew. You're worrying me. What's going on?"

I slump back in my seat. "Remember that part where I told

you what happened over Thanksgiving between me and her wasn't for public consumption? That it was just between us?"

He nods.

The waiter sets down a bagel and cream cheese for Josh and scrambled egg whites for me. When I'm sure the waiter is out of earshot, I continue. "In a few months, like about nine months, it will be glaringly obvious what happened between me and Kendall Greer on that mountain."

His mouth drops open. "No."

"Yes."

"You're gonna be Kendall's baby daddy?" He sounds mystified, like I just decoded the secrets of the universe.

Slurping my coffee, I let out my breath. "I'm gonna be someone's parent. Fucked up, right? I mean, assuming she wants to keep it. I'll support whatever she wants to do obviously, but yeah, the idea of having a mini-me roaming the earth is fucking terrifying."

Saying it out loud makes it real. And everything I've been thinking all night comes out in a low, vehement whisper. "How can I be a father? I can barely keep my cat alive. I mean, sure, I can figure out which side to put a diaper on, but other than that, I have no clue. And what the fuck kind of parent am I going to be? It's not like I had a good role model. You lived it with me." Josh gives me a sympathetic look. "I barely saw my father growing up."

Now I'm building up some steam. "What's more fucked? She didn't want to talk to me last night. Just, 'buh-bye, I'll call ya later maybe.' I don't know what's worse, having her hate my guts for years or having her know me better and not trust me."

My best friend's at a loss for words. He raises his eyebrows and tears off a piece of his bagel. Finally, after he chews and swallows his bite, his voice lowers. "This is out of my wheelhouse, D-man. I could talk to Evie about it. See if she has any suggestions?"

"Thanks. No. I'm not sure where Kendall is with people knowing, but I'm guessing she'd like to tell Evie herself. Still, I don't want her to go through this all alone. *I* don't want to go through this alone. And it's driving me crazy that she wouldn't discuss it last night." I pause. "And it's almost Christmas."

"This sucks, dude."

After scooping up some eggs, I take a bite. "My head is fucked right now, Josh. This is one way of changing a relationship status to 'it's complicated.' I'm pretty sure I went through the stages of grief on my drive. Denial, anger, bargaining, confusion, Happy, Dopey, Sleepy, Grumpy."

He chuckles. "At least you didn't lose your sense of humor."

I'm almost tearing at my hair. "Everything looks different now. I mean, our waiter? He's not that old, maybe in college, but the fact that he's younger than us and yet an adult makes me feel ancient. Is this what's going to happen when I'm a dad? I look at people as my potential kid instead of my peer?"

Gesturing at the waiter for a refill of coffee, Josh says, "Probably."

"Very soon, someone quite small is going to be relying on me, whether I want it to or not. Whether I can handle it or not."

"I think this is why they give you nine months to get used to the idea. You can't figure it all out at once."

I drop my voice to barely a whisper. "I'm scared shitless of screwing up a kid."

Or making one who turns out like me.

22

KENDALL

*B*ehind me, Evie trails like a helium balloon on a tether. I jerk one way, and she follows a split second later. It helps that I have a vice grip on her hand. But if I don't get something to eat, RIGHT NOW, I'm going to hurl all over these nice holiday shoppers.

For once, I don't mind the mad crush of humanity bumping into me on their way to retail bliss because I'm on a mission. Even if it means being at the mall on Christmas Eve.

"Girl, slow down before you run me into another elf."

"Sorry about that." I slow down to a brisk walk as I spot the sign.

I sigh with relief when I see the shop.

"Donuts?" Evie wrinkles her nose. "You want donuts?" She stares at me like I've sprouted blue horns. "Don't get me wrong —I love donuts. Those yummy balls of sweet dough are like crack, but I can't remember the last time I saw you eat them. Maybe in Mrs. Healey's class?"

That was high school.

Awkwardly, I shrug. Breaking the "I'm pregnant with Demer-

it's baby" thing to my best friend is proving harder than I antici-
pated, especially since the moment we arrived at the mall, my
stomach revolted and demanded food.

And yes, I'm back to calling him Demerit. In my head at
least. It gives me an emotional distance from the man who has
made me batshit crazy since the day I met him, and since I got
good and knocked up, I need some kind of footing. I tell myself
that if I don't have to depend on him, I'll be fine. It's when I
consider needing him for something important that I go into an
emotional tailspin.

Last night helped clear the air, and while a part of me is
clamoring to pick up where he and I left off, I'm scared.

I don't want to feel like I did when I got back from the cabin
and wondered why he didn't call me. Wondered if he was off
banging other girls like those gossip blog pics suggested.

Fuck that. I'll be friendly with Drew, and we'll talk about this
whole baby situation, but I know I'm on my own. It's better this
way. If I don't need him, he can't hurt me.

"This is going to sound weird," I mumble as we get in line.
I'm not sure how to start this conversation.

"Can't be weirder than Drew showing up on our doorstep at
sunrise." My eyes widen. "You responsible for that boy losing his
mind?" She gives me a pointed look.

I open my mouth but nothing comes out.

"Next!" The guy at the counter impatiently waves us forward.

The glass case of deliciousness makes my stomach rumble
with anticipation. As though my pea-sized child is chanting,
"GIMME! GIMME!" like a starving linebacker banging his fists
on the table.

Holy shit, I'm having a kid.

Sweat breaks out on my forehead. *I'm not prepared for this. I'm
supposed to be focused on my career and—*

"Lady!"

Startled, I jerk back, my heart racing. *Jeez-Louise, dude.* I want to tell him his snarky attitude is bad PR.

"I'd like two—wait, make that three—devil's food with chocolate icing, please." My arteries ache as I consider what I'm going to eat, but I swear to myself I'll have something with kale for dinner. Although that does not sound appetizing. *But come on, kid, you need to eat your greens.*

Pivoting to Evie, I motion for her. "What do you want?"

"You're not sharing your three donuts?"

"Negative. But this is my treat, so get your sugar on."

Once we get our bags of fried grease, we wade through the holiday crowd again until we find a table for two on the concourse. We have to stop twice because people want Evie's autograph. Ever since she got that do-it-yourself home repair show on *Bravo*, she's become a local celebrity.

If I weren't starving and about to gnaw off someone's thigh-bone, I would encourage her to ham it up.

The moment I'm off my feet, I hold up my finger. "I need to eat something before we talk." Reaching into my purse, I pull out some hand sanitizer, squirt it everywhere, and then grab the gorgeous chocolate pastry.

Come to mama.

The sweet, velvety dough melts in my mouth, and I moan. That's what I'm talking about.

After I've gobbled down the entire thing, I clear my throat. "I've been wanting one of these since I threw up in front of Voodoo's the other night." Strange but true.

"Oh my God. What happened? Did you drink too much?" She holds up a bottle of water to take a sip.

"Nope. I got too pregnant."

Water shoots out of her mouth and nose as she sputters.

She's wide eyed and choking while mouthing, *What?*

"Sorry, Eves." I smack her on the back a few times until she's able to breathe again. "Guess that was a bad time to tell you one of Drew's swimmers burrowed up my channel."

"*YOU SLEPT WITH DREW?*"

I freeze and cover my eyes with my hand since half of the mall heard my best friend's screech.

"Could you keep it down? I'm not sure your announcement reached Northern California."

"I'm sorry." She glances around. "Sorry."

When everyone who's eyeballing us has returned to their overcooked Panda Express, I reluctantly continue.

"What did you think happened when Drew and I got snowed in together at Mount Hood?" I'm seriously shocked that my best friend didn't guess what went down on Thanksgiving. Although we haven't had any heart-to-hearts recently, I thought she'd puzzle it out with her Spidey sense.

"After I learned you survived the trip with all of your extremities intact, I figured you guys argued nonstop until you prayed for deliverance."

I chuckle. "Close. We banged like bunnies until neither one of us could walk. But good guess. I thought we would kill each other too."

Evie's eyebrows are still under her bangs, the shock of my situation not wearing off one bit. "I started to wonder last night, though, if something *major* had happened." Her voice drops to a whisper. "Aside from getting arrested. But I didn't think you'd ever go that far since you've always loathed the guy." Her eyes crinkle with amusement. "Except you two were acting so weird with each other. It was like watching you both interact in an alternate universe, one where you reciprocated his feelings for you. I mean, why else would you care about Drew's extracurricular activities?"

And there it is. The one thing that would make me want to run for the hills—if Drew returned to his old life.

He said those were old photos. That he's been a hermit.

Ignoring the way my stomach pitches at the mention of Drew's old partying ways, I reach for my water.

And then pause.

"What do you mean 'reciprocated his feelings for me'?"

She snorts. "The way you guys used to fight like rabid badgers? I figured it was something akin to the way little boys tease girls, just more insane because, well, it's Drew."

I stare at her in disbelief.

Have I been missing some huge piece of the puzzle all this time and Drew's been interested in me? Or is it that he always gets what he wants and found me a challenge?

"Please tell me how this happened," Evie begs.

How do I explain what transpired between Drew and me when I don't even understand it? "Maybe I should start at the beginning."

She nods comically. "Girl, I want every gory detail. Like how you went from hating him with a religious zeal to—"

"Bumping uglies?"

"Yes. That." She shoves a chunk of donut in her mouth without losing eye contact, like she's watching a riveting movie.

"Let me begin by saying this is all your fault. Had you not asked Drew to pick me up from work to drive me to the cabin, he never could've taken me to the wrong house where we got snowed in for days with a limited number of condoms."

Briefly, I consider that conversation with Tristan yesterday morning, about douchebags not wanting to wear condoms and letting them slide off, and dismiss it outright. Drew's not the kind of guy who ever wanted to get saddled with a kid. I'm the one who wanted it in the V without a condom "just for a minute." I should punch myself in the face for suggesting it and then punch him for agreeing with me.

Evie hops up and down in her seat. "I take full responsibility for the ensuing nakedness. Now spill."

So I dive in. How he picked me up from work. The drive up there. How we bonded by the fireplace and snuggled Shazam. How Drew seemed like a genuinely different person from the one I met a few years ago. And then, of course, the *many* orgasms he gave me, courtesy of his big dick and talented mouth. Though I don't go into details about the nakedness. Just that he's gifted in the sex department.

But then I get to the arrest and jail and not hearing from him for days. My phone dying and miscommunication galore. And how Tristan figured out why I was hurling chunks all over Portland.

It's so good to talk about it with her, I'm almost buoyant with relief.

When I'm done, her mouth is a rounded O.

"You're having Drew's baby."

"This is what I'm saying."

"And that's why you looked like a ghost last night."

"Also correct."

"He really didn't call you all that time after you guys got back from the cabin?"

"He thought I was fucking Tristan." I snort, the idea so outlandish. Except then I see the question in Evie's eyes. "I have *never* gone there with him. Ever. I know you joke that we've done the dirty before, but Tris and I are just buds."

I pick at my last donut and wait for her to process everything.

Finally, she tilts her head, the gentleness in her voice belying the intensity of her questions. "What are you going to do? About the pregnancy?"

"I guess I want to keep it." Hearing myself say those words makes everything feel real. It's fucking terrifying. "This"—I place my hand on my belly—"this feels like one in a million." I lower my voice to a whisper. "We used condoms. Lots of condoms. Until the last time when we ran out. So, uh, we went backdoor."

It takes her a moment to understand what I mean.

"I've only done that with Josh, but he's built like a baseball bat, so we can't do it often."

She giggles, and it feels like we're back in college and chatting about boys. How I wish life were that simple again.

I cover my eyes a moment as I head into major overshare territory. "In the moment, I was like, hey"—I wave my hand —"who needs lube? Stick it in the pussy palace first. It was like two seconds of unprotected dick-in-vag sex until we got to the main event. But that's all it took."

"That's all it took."

I nod.

"So that's why Drew came over this morning. How did he take the news last night?"

Blowing out a breath, I shake my head. "He didn't freak. But we had so many other issues to work out before I could tell him that by the time I dropped the baby bomb, I was too exhausted to discuss it with him."

There's a long pause of silence. Evie folds her lips between her teeth.

"You think I should've talked to him more."

She shrugs. "I understand it from your position. I also get why he seemed overwhelmed this morning. You're both dealing with a lot. And I'm sure you want to know where he stands on...everything."

"Honestly, I'm prepared to go it alone if I need to." A cold sweat breaks out all over my body at the thought. "Yes, I need to talk to him." I take a deep breath. "I promise I'll talk to him. It's just...I'm afraid, okay?"

"Of Drew?"

"Of how tentative this feels. Drew being a responsible adult is a new thing. What if I rely on him, and he lets me down?"

Or reverts back to the number one bachelor of Portland.

Or decides to go on a bender.

Or bangs two flight attendants while snorting a line of coke.

The options are endless. He's a beautiful man with a bottomless bank account and a history of bad decisions. *And absolutely no history in anything more than being Down To Fuck.* I've never even seen him with the same girl twice in a row.

Sure, last night, before the baby news, he sounded like he wanted us to reconnect. Now? He might be on a one-way trip to Cabo at this very moment. Isn't that what playboys do? Go on vacation and Instagram it while the plebs toil?

"He did get you out of that felony situation."

I squint at my best friend. "He's also the reason I was arrested."

"Tomato, tomahto."

"I'm not saying I won't give him a chance, but we're talking about having a child." The more I talk about it, the more confident I am that I need to be smart about Drew. If those weeks after the cabin are any indication, I'm already in too deep with him. Add a baby to the mix, and I know I'll lose it if he hurts our kid because he reverts to his old ways.

"Promise me you'll give him a chance to gain your trust. Like you said, he has come *a long way* since you first met him."

It should say something that Evie, who has never been Drew's biggest fan, is advocating on his behalf.

I'm guessing she had a front-row seat to his recovery after he landed in the hospital last March. If Josh was there for him, Evie likely was there too.

I glance away, annoyed with myself for feeling jealous that I had no clue Drew was gravely ill, but my friends did.

Not that this would've changed anything, my inner voice reminds me. *Why would she have told you about Drew? All you've ever done is complain about him.*

My conscience twinges, reminding me how wrong I've been about Drew, because once I gave him an opportunity to redeem himself at the cabin, he came through with flying colors. And if I was that off base then, maybe I'm misjudging him again now.

Needing to change the subject, I give her a look. "You really had no idea Drew and I hooked up over Thanksgiving before last night? Didn't Drew tell Josh something? Those two gossip more than we do."

"Josh has been vague about what he knows. He kept telling me I needed to hang out with you." Evie thinks about it longer and frowns. "Damn it, he's been holding out on me!"

I laugh and get up, gather our trash, and hook my arm in Evie's. As we're making our way through the food court, her advice echoes in my mind.

Maybe she's right and I need to give Drew a chance to step up. If that's what he wants to do.

Thinking back to the cabin, I remember how much it seemed to mean to him that I recognized the changes he'd made in his life.

Ugh, I don't want to be the person who throws his past mistakes in his face.

Guilt swells in my chest at the idea of barricading him from the opportunity to be a part of this. That is, if he wants to be a part of the whole baby thing.

Shit, I really need to talk to him.

Clearing my throat, I squeeze Evie's arm. "I guess I could use your help with a Christmas gift. I have no idea what to get the guy who knocked me up."

She gives me a wide smile. "His birthday is in a few days too."

All the more reason to dial back my ball-busting ways when it comes to Drew, I suppose, and maybe extend a peace offering.

What do you get the guy who has everything? I mean, aside from a baby?

I'm roasting by my Bee's flickering fireplace, sweltering in an ugly Christmas sweater of an anatomically-correct reindeer—he's got shiny silver balls in the right places.

Shazam's nipping at my toes.

My Bumble Bee's playing Bing Crosby yuletide carols, and she's dressed up in one of her signature tracksuits. She unwrapped two from me earlier this evening. In return, she gave me a Teenage Mutant Ninja Turtles wallet, saying it was my favorite when I was little.

I may be almost thirty, but since she gave it to me, I'm using it. I've already transferred my driver's license and cards into it.

Bee bustles to the table set for two, her hands swallowed by huge oven mitts, cradling a covered casserole dish. Rising from her flowered armchair by the fire, I mosey into her tiny dining room and take an appreciative sniff. "Whatever you made is mouthwatering. Can I help?"

She tuts. "You sit down. Let an old woman have the pleasure of serving a perfectly cooked roast."

Ignoring her protest, I snag a warm dish of Brussels sprouts and mock mashed potatoes—really cauliflower—from the kitchen and haul them to the table. She's set it with our traditional décor—a tabletop Santa who drops his drawers when you pull his hand. She retrieves the last dish, sets it down with a flourish, and beams.

A pang of something fierce hits my solar plexus when my Bee settles across from me. At eighty-seven, she's going strong now, but how many more holidays do I have with her? Her eyes shine as she reaches over and holds my hand, squeezing mine with her surprisingly firm grip under thin, papery skin.

"Merry Christmas, Andrew."

"Merry Christmas."

As I sip sparkling water and she drinks cider, we serve ourselves and dig in. She tells me all about last week and the way she cleaned Tyrone's clock at bingo. While her meal is tasty and I love my Bumble Bee, I can't help but think this celebration feels incomplete. The table is missing a place—the one with the woman carrying my child.

What is K-dawg doing today? Will she spend the day with her family? What are they like?

They're the grandparents of my child, and I don't even know them. She doesn't know mine, either.

Oh God, my parents are going to be grandparents. How will I break the news to them?

And how is Kendall feeling? Does she have morning sickness? When is her first doctor's appointment?

Fuck it. After we finish eating, I'm texting Kendall. Enough with this time apart.

"Were you listening?" Bumble asks.

Busted. "What? Sorry, no."

"Is it your redhead? The one who's got your boxers in a bundle?"

I can't glare at my grandma, even though she deserves it for being so prescient. "Yes."

She grins like Shazam with a mouthful of feathers. He's crawled in my lap to sniff at the roast. "Do tell."

While it might be weird, my grandma has always been my confidante. Since the rest of my family is so judgy, her unconditional love and acceptance has gotten me through tough times. I know that no matter how hard I fuck up, my gran will hug me, scold me, give me a cookie, and help me through it.

I'll do anything for her, although she's too proud to accept money, instead choosing to live in the modest home she's owned her entire life. Over the years, I've tried to shelter her from some of the more sordid details of my life, but she's tough. I bet even this won't shock her.

"So, you know I've gotten into trouble a few times in my life..."

My gran humors me by adopting a serious expression to mask her dancing eyes. "I'm aware of it occurring once or twice."

Understatement of the millennia.

"Well, up on Mount Hood—" My cell phone interrupts my confession. I set down my napkin and furrow my brows. Who calls on Christmas? Is it KK? "Do you mind if I get that?"

"Not at all."

I leap across the room, dislodging Shazzy and cringing at what an obedient boy I am heeding Kendall's beck and call. Then I realize I don't care. I just want to talk with her.

The number isn't familiar, but I answer anyway. "This is Drew."

"Mr. Merritt. This is Pearl Collins." My parents' social secretary is calling me *on Christmas Day*. She rushes along before I have a chance to hang up on her. "The senior Mr. and Mrs. Merritt asked me to follow up on your response to the invitation for their New Year's Eve soirée. You would be most welcome to attend. Would you like to RSVP yes?"

Seriously?

Bumble can tell by my expression who's on the phone and rolls her eyes. I pace around the living room.

"Let me get this straight. My parents don't even give you Christmas off?"

"I'm pleased to be of assistance to your family, Mr. Merritt. Shall I put you down for attendance?"

"No," I spit out. "I have other things to do."

Pearl takes a sharp breath. "Very well, Mr. Merritt. Thank you. A happy Christmas to you."

While I can't get out of seeing my parents forever, a party with people who fake interest in me sounds as fun as knee surgery. Maybe I can put off an in-person visit until next year.

Or until Kendall is showing.

I gotta talk to her.

My fingers press the letters on my phone screen.

Hey, Ken Doll. Lay off the eggnog.

Then I add, *Miss you. Merry Christmas. We should talk.*

Three animated dots tell me she's typing.

Thanks. Happy holidays. I can come over later, if you want.

A sense of relief washes over me as I text her my address, realizing she's never seen my place. We know each other so well in some respects, but in others we're almost strangers.

Strangers who are going to have a kid together.

When I peer up, I realize my gran has been watching my every move with amusement as she chews her roast. Of course she knew exactly who called. And who I'm texting with urgency. She points to my phone with her knife. "I like this one. She keeps you on your toes."

"I know. Kendall's going to be doing that for the next eighteen years at least."

If I was in a laughing mood, my gran's face would be comical. She drops her fork with a clatter on the table. "What are you saying?"

"It's early, but we just found out Kendall is pregnant."

"With your child?"

Kendall and I might not have always gotten along, but if there's one thing I do know, it's that she would never lie about something like this.

"Yes. It's mine."

She purses her lips and picks up her utensil. "Well. This is *verrry* interesting."

I return to my seat across from her. "You're taking this rather well given that I impregnated a woman out of wedlock."

"Andrew, I served you Christmas dinner while you're wearing that sweater." She gestures generally at the reindeer's balls. "I can handle a little pregnancy."

"I don't know if I can though," I mutter.

"I've lived long enough to go through a few surprises like this. When I was a young woman, several of my friends were married, only to have a child seven months later. Spoiler alert, as you say: People have sex before marriage."

"I always knew you were a realist."

"Yes. I am. And realistically, I think you will learn to be a very good father," she says with a smile.

I'm glad she has some faith in me, because I don't.

When we're finished with dinner, I help her clean up at lightning speed, then race home to meet Kendall.

An hour later, after I've changed into sweats and a tee, my intercom buzzes. While I'm waiting for her to go up the elevator,

I pace until the doorbell rings. I bound to the door and open it to a flushed Kendall, bundled in a big winter coat.

A protective beast in my chest roars to life at the sight of her outside my home. I want to tug her inside by her cuffs and squeeze her so tight she squeals. I want to tell her everything I've been thinking since she told me the news. I want to get over this damned awkwardness with her.

I'm struck dumb at the sight of her, but I can't help my smile.

She shoves her hands in her pockets, then looks up and catches my eye. "Hey."

"Hey."

Stepping in, she shrugs out of her coat. I take it and stare at her, fascinated by the way she checks out my place, as if she's trying to figure me out by the décor—framed black and white landscape photography, sports memorabilia, and paintings of the Portland bridges. White lights outline the patio, and garlands hang inside, courtesy of my decorator.

Tapping her lip with her index finger, she walks around the living room slowly. "You don't live in a frat house."

"Not when my best friend's an architect. He wouldn't let me get away with that even if I wanted." For the record, I removed the neon beer signs a while ago. "Josh redid my house, made me buy real art and real furniture. And while it's a man cave, yeah, it's not gross."

Anymore.

Especially with the housekeeper.

"Want something to drink?" I continue.

Ignoring my question, she cocks her head, inspecting my shirt that says #phuckifino. "What's your shirt mean?"

God, there's so much we don't know about each other. Somehow we managed to spend days together without ever discussing my work. Perhaps she assumed I didn't need to do any work and lived on a trust fund.

I mean, that's accurate, but I'd be bored out of my skull if I didn't have something to do.

"That's my company, Detention. We make T-shirts and apparel, kind of like Tom's Shoes. One shirt goes to a child in need for every one we sell. But the ones for the kids don't have the logo."

I shouldn't be surprised she doesn't know this. An internet search only pulls up page after page of bad press, arrests, and the socialites I've partied with over the years.

She scrutinizes me a long moment and then waves her hands. "Why am I *just now* learning this? It's like you deliberately hide that you're a decent guy."

"Not that decent." *We've done a few indecent things together, K-shizzle.*

She sounds it out. "Hashtag phuck-if-I-no. 'Fuck if I know.' Ohmigod. This is the most Drew company I've ever heard of." Her light laughter fills the room, and I'm delighted to hear it. "The next time you're arrested, you should wear that in your mugshot. It would be great PR."

"Good idea, but I'm not planning on ever being arrested again," I call out, heading into the kitchen to get her some water. I guess that's what I said the time before last, though.

But now, I mean it. Because what kid wants their parent to get arrested? That's some trauma I'd like to spare my spawn.

Again, I'm rewarded with her laugh, and it loosens a knot around my gut. Returning, I hand her a glass and sit down next to her on the couch.

She smells irresistibly alluring. Her lustrous hair shines in the low light of my living room. Her legs are tucked under her, and I want to get my hands on them.

I can't say any of that. Instead, I ask, "How was your Christmas?"

"Good. Yours?"

"I just hung with my Bee. She's great. She got me this wallet."

When I reach for the side table, my shirt rides up and I sense Kendall's eyes on me. Maybe not. I hand the wallet to her. She frowns. "Why ninja turtles?"

"When I was a kid, I liked the show. Grandmas don't forget that stuff."

Her mouth slackens, and she blinks rapidly. "So you're gonna use that?"

"Yes. Absolutely."

For the first time in a while, I get a full-fledged Kendall grin. "You're really sweet to your grandma."

"Thanks." My heart beats a little faster. "Actually, I got you something." Crossing to a desk, I pull out a small box from a drawer. "Don't worry," I say, judging by the panicked look on her face. "It doesn't have a ninja or a turtle on it."

As she cups the box in her hands, her expression relaxes. "Can I open it?"

"Yep. It's Christmas."

She rips the paper and reveals a white box. A moment later, she pulls out a gold necklace with a snowflake charm, which dangles from her slim fingers. Carefully inspecting it, she murmurs, "It's beautiful."

"It reminded me of being stranded with you in the mountains." I catch the curious look on her face. "I didn't mean to assume anything. I just...I just wanted to get it for you."

During the few weeks we were apart, during a moment of weakness, I bought it, hoping we'd find a way to reconnect and I could surprise her.

"It's so delicate and gorgeous, Drew." She unclasps it and puts it on. The gold glows against her pale skin and red hair.

Her beaming smile sends a rush of satisfaction through me.

She leans over to her purse and pulls out a small wrapped package, which she sets in her lap. "I got you something too. I think the problem is...I don't know..." Exhaling, she stops, closes her eyes, and begins again, steeling herself. "I want to keep the baby. I don't know how you feel. You can be as involved as you want. I'm not going to pressure you into anything, but"—she reddens, clearly embarrassed that she's blurted too much—"I don't know how to navigate the changes that are going to happen."

A buffet of emotions flash in her eyes, and she braces herself as if I'm going to disappoint her, which makes me ache.

I never want to hurt this girl.

Letting out her breath, she asks, "What? Please tell me what you're thinking."

My face serious, I take both of her hands in mine and gaze into her blue eyes. "I want to help you with this pregnancy, KK. There's no way in hell you're going through this on your own, feeling alone. I want to go with you to the doctor. To every appointment. I'm going to do whatever I can to ensure you have everything you need."

She bursts out in a muffled sob and tugs her hands back, wiping her tears with the backs of her hands as she sniffles. "I'm not a crier, I swear. I'm just hormonal. I've been so scared of what's going to happen. And how you were going to take it."

Wrapping my arms around her, I nod. "I'm scared too. It's going to be weird for a while. But I'm here. I'm going to help you with this pregnancy."

With tears still streaking down her face, she shakes her head and blurts out, "I'm sorry I couldn't talk more about it the other night. I was exhausted from freaking out the whole day and then we had all that other stuff to work out. By the time we got to the bun in the oven, I thought I was going to pass out." Her whole body shivers, and I run my hand up and down her back. "I didn't mean to drop a bomb and ditch you in the foxhole."

I chuckle when I think about how I nearly drove to California. But I don't wanna make her feel any worse.

"I get it. You need to take care of yourself, especially now. And Kendall," I whisper against her hair, "I got you. You need something, I'm there, okay?"

She takes a deep breath. It sounds like a sigh of relief.

I reluctantly let her go when she sits back. Even though her face is mottled from tears, she's still the most beautiful woman I've ever laid eyes on.

Hesitantly, she hands me the package in her lap. It's a pair of yellow baby booties. "I didn't know if you would want these," she says. "But if you're going to be a dad…"

They both fit in the palm of my hand.

"Holy shit, we're going to be parents."

We both laugh nervously, but she's smiling, so I'm smiling.

Kendall stays for hours, although our conversation feels like minutes. I want to ask her to stay, to spend the night, but it's not right. Not tonight. We have a lot more getting to know each other to do if we're going to be parents. Even though my body and heart revolt from this decision, wanting her near, always.

When she goes to leave, she says, "I thought this would be really awkward, but I had the best time with you."

I hug her tight and kiss the top of her head. "I did too."

24

KENDALL

*S*urreal.

There's no other word to describe this feeling.

I'm having a baby with Drew. A child. A living, breathing entity who will depend on us for everything.

A breath catches in my throat at the thought.

"You look like you're having an existential crisis."

Tristan's deep voice makes me jerk.

He studies me across our conference table.

"You okay there, Mama?"

A small smile tilts my lips even though I scold him. "Shh. I'm not ready to share the news."

Even though we're the only ones in the office because everyone is taking vacation days this week, I don't want to get in the habit of unleashing my personal life here.

It's been three days since I saw Drew at his condo, but we've been texting and plan to meet up for lunch this weekend.

As a woman who crashed and burned in her last relationship because my ex had his own agenda that did not take into consideration what I wanted, I appreciate Drew's efforts to be my friend. He must sense I'm not ready to dive back into whatever we had at the cabin.

My chaotic brain registers this is too much, too fast. We just stopped wanting to kill each other last month. We need to drive in a lower gear for a while before I consider what else he and I might mean to each other aside from being parents to the nugget I'm gestating.

But hanging out with him was promising.

He genuinely seems to want to be a part of this pregnancy. He seems sincere in his concern and said all the right things to put me at ease until we were having fun and enjoying each other's company.

Old Drew never said the right thing. He basically had his foot sewn to his mouth twenty-four seven. Drew 2.0, however, is sensitive to my needs in a way I could never fathom.

I admit I like getting to know Drew like this—with training wheels instead of speeding down the highway on a motorcycle without a helmet. And I figure we've already seen each other at our worst. If he's serious about his health recovery and staying out of trouble, I figure we have a shot at being decent parents.

Last night he sent me stupid memes, texted me links to ridiculous baby names, and asked if it's too early to order our kid a Tesla.

For that last one, I have to admit I wasn't completely sure if he was joking or not, but I erred on the side of caution and told him Baby Merritt needs about ten thousand other things first.

Baby Merritt.

I sigh, delight and fear commingling in my stomach to form a wicked heartburn. But deep down, I'm excited, nearly jumping out of my skin sometimes when I realize what's happening.

Is this baby fever? I didn't even know I wanted a baby.

But I do want this baby. So much.

Even if I don't have a clue what I'm doing.

While I'm lost in thought, my finger circles the gold snowflake resting on my collarbone. I can't stop touching it.

The movement catches Tristan's attention, and he lifts a knowing eyebrow. "Christmas present?"

An eager grin spreads on my mouth. "Maybe."

"From your baby daddy?"

"*Maybe*."

He returns my smile. "I'm happy things are working out for you. I wasn't looking forward to kicking Drew's ass if he turned out to be a douche." He pats his trim abs. "Please thank him for the fruit basket. It was delicious."

"He sent that to me, dummy."

"The note was lovely too. Sorry I didn't see it until I'd ravaged all of the chocolate-covered pineapple."

I roll my eyes. "This is why we need better interns."

"LaRoe's numbers are up," he says, switching gears. "You killed it at his event last week. His campaign pay yet?"

"No, that cheapskate."

I wish I could be a hardass with Howard, but I need his campaign, perhaps as much as he needs our company. While we represent several national brands, I want to build my local roots. That was a major reason I started my own PR firm—to help companies and brands I grew up with and help them thrive. So the fact that the heart of LaRoe's campaign touts buying local means I can do that while building my relationships with those Portland companies.

After a moment, Tristan sighs. "We gonna make payroll this month without it?" He drums his fingers on the table, a rare expression of worry on his face.

"I know we have more overhead than we thought we would, but our dilemma is mostly a cashflow issue. We have the clients. We have the work. It's a matter of—"

His low chuckle cuts me off. "I understand the dilemma." He rubs his chin slowly with his thumb. "What about your boy?"

"What boy?"

He gives me a look. "You juggling more than one man right now?"

I toss a crumpled piece of paper at his head. "What are you talking about?"

"Just that Demerit has that killer T-shirt company. Wouldn't hurt to represent him. At least you know he'll pay his PR bills on time."

"No." I shake my head vehemently. "I'm not interested."

Tristan's expression morphs from teasing to incredulous in a nanosecond. "Why not? Why wouldn't you want to rep him? He's local and always in the headlines. Gossip mags love him. Why not work with someone who's naturally inclined to put himself out there? Isn't that easier than having to drag a wall-flower into the public eye?"

No. No. No.

I pause before I answer so I can calm down.

Holding out my hand, I count off. "One, it's breaking your cardinal rule and mixing business with pleasure." Ignoring his eye roll, I wave a second finger. "Two, I don't want to approach him for something he already has well in hand."

After Drew and I hung out on Christmas, I Googled his company and a shot of pride ran through me from head to toe when I realized how well it was doing. He doesn't need me for this at all.

"Third, I've seen how people glom on to him for things. They want his connections. They want to be in pics with the famous name. They want his booze." *They want his drugs or his dick.* I don't say that part. Though the thought of some chick coming on to him now makes me homicidal. "I won't be one of those people. I don't want his money."

Could Drew bail me out of my financial crisis? In a New York heartbeat. But I would never ask him to. Hell to the mother-fucking no. The idea of needing him for that makes me itchy all over. Besides, I haven't worked my ass off all these years to go to a man and beg for money.

Tristan's eyes soften, and he nods. "Sorry, boo. Didn't know it was like that for you." My brows furrow in confusion, and Tristan's lips tilt up. "I just thought you guys were having a kid. Didn't know you'd caught feelings."

I sit there a second and process his words.

Huh.

"I guess I...*really* like Drew."

His smile widens. "You think?"

A flush washes under my skin, and I laugh.

Tristan holds out his fist, and I jab him back. This is why we work so well. He gets me.

We're still all aglow with our BFF-ness when his cell phone lights up with a notification. And then another. And then another.

It doesn't stop. It's practically levitating off the table with alerts.

His concerned eyes meet mine for a second that seems to stretch out.

Neither of us have clients right now in the middle of a press conference or event.

His frown deepens as he swipes his phone and scrolls.

They always say that any press is good press. But as Tristan holds his phone up to me and I'm greeted with the sight of my own mugshot, I wonder if this is the death knell of our public relations firm.

Folding at my waist, I lean back against the wall of my office and take another wavering breath as I listen to Tristan pace.

"You still can't get hold of Drew?"

I shake my head.

"How the fuck did Gary get this story? I thought you said Demerit took care of everything?"

He doesn't wait for a response before he curses again.

Here's our conundrum. If we make a statement before touching base with Drew, we run the risk of contradicting whatever Drew might've told the press, and then we both look like idiots.

The phone rings again from the reception area, but thankfully stops after two rings.

Jessica runs in with a handful of yellow slips. She looks as harried as I feel, but I'm grateful she could come when Tristan called her two hours ago and asked her to handle the phones.

Tristan flips through the messages and growls, "Jess, why didn't you transfer Drew's call like I told you to?"

She winces. "Sorry. I'm so sorry. I tried to transfer him, but I kept disconnecting the call and then I thought it would be easier if I told you myself." She's as bad as Evie's old secretary, Penny. An awkward smile spreads on Jessica's face as she picks the slips from Tristan's fingers and waves them in the air. "So yeah. Drew called."

For fuck's sake, I can't deal with this today.

One very small voice warns me not to fire her since it's the holidays, but it's being drowned out by the desperate cry that wants today's craptastic adventure to end.

My cell has been lit up with calls from several different gossip blogs and celebrity shows. Tristan has been fielding them and wondered if we'd missed a call from Drew since my line might've been busy when he called.

I'm guessing it was. So he called my office. And then my intern hung up on him. Maybe more than once.

"Thanks, Jessica," I grit out. "You can go back to your desk. If Drew calls again, just come get me."

She smiles, relief on her face.

With one trembling hand, I hold the paper bag to my mouth again and take three more deep breaths before I hyperventilate and pass out. With the other, I scroll through my phone and reread the article that's going to destroy my life.

Portland's number one bachelor, Drew Merritt, arrested with PR executive Kendall Greer over Thanksgiving for breaking and entering —details emerging.

Gary's article has everything—how I crawled through a window to get into the cabin, how Drew and I holed up there during the snowstorm, the larceny charges, even quotes from an anonymous source that detailed the slew of used condoms that littered the trash can at the cabin.

I crumple up the bag. "It was that bitch at the front desk. I bet she's the one Gary quoted in his article."

But before I can finish venting, voices in the hall have me and Tristan whipping our heads around.

"Wait here. If it's the media, I'll handle it," Tristan says as he slips on his suit jacket.

A moment later, Drew's busting into my office with a very frazzled Jessica on his heels.

"Mr. Demerit's here!" she announces from over his shoulder.

Tristan chuckles, but I can't find the humor in her messing up the name of my...*friend*? Boyfriend? Baby daddy?

The second my eyes connect with Drew, he heads straight to me. One second I'm struggling to find the words to express how frustrated I am over this whole situation, and the next I'm wrapped in his arms with my feet dangling off the floor.

Well then.

My arms respond automatically, tightening around his neck. Glorious relief swells in my chest from his mere presence.

I breathe in his scent. Shower gel, expensive cologne and fine leather. Last month, I would've described it as the smell of rich boy, entitlement, and bad decisions. But as quickly as that harsh assessment enters my mind, it's brushed aside by the assertion that he's changed.

He's here.

"I'm sorry all this shit got out," he whispers in my ear. "Do you trust me?"

He sets me down on the floor.

I stare up at his brilliant green eyes that shimmer with an emotion I'm not sure I've seen before in this man. He threads his fingers through mine and squeezes.

Do I trust Drew?

The words come without a second thought.

"I do."

25

KENDALL

*T*ongue-tied, I stare at the pics on my laptop. *How did he...?*

I clear my throat. "When did you do this?"

Drew, Tristan, and I crowd around my laptop at the conference table. Twisting around to look at Drew over my shoulder, I almost laugh at how nonchalant he seems about the whole thing when he shrugs. "After you suggested it."

Tristan chuckles from my other side. "This was Kendall's idea? It's pretty brilliant."

Drew frowns at him, his jaw ticking. "She *is* brilliant."

"I can't take credit for this." I mean, I might've said something in passing, but this exceeds anything I had in mind.

"Sure you can." Drew squeezes my arm and drops into the chair next to me. "Call that fucker and let's see what he has to say about it. I might have a few more tricks up my sleeve in case he balks."

Tristan dials and puts it on speakerphone. "This is what we need. A united front. Makes it harder for Gary to twist our words around."

Like the beating wings of a bird, hope that I might be able to navigate this PR nightmare builds against my sternum.

I chew my lower lip, afraid to be too optimistic. I've seen the messages Jessica took—LaRoe is pissed and wants to cancel his account. Never mind that he owes our firm thousands of dollars.

No matter what happens with Gary, I might not be able to reassure Howard if he's afraid my tainted reputation will affect his mayoral run. But this is the best shot we have of salvaging my career and everything I've busted my ass to build.

As the phone rings, my heart hammers so hard, I feel it in my neck. Under the table, Drew takes my hand in his large one, and my breath steadies.

Shit. What if Gary's not in the office? It's a little after five on a Friday evening, so it's possible he's already taken off.

Fortunately, the slime ball answers, and Tristan tells Gary we're all on the conference call. Tris motions to Drew, who takes over.

"Hey, man. Did you get my email?" Drew pauses to give me a wicked smile. "The one with the new campaign photos for Detention, my T-shirt company?"

The room is silent as Gary considers Drew's words.

I can almost fill in the asshole's thought bubbles. It should be, *What the fuck is going on right now?*

Because Drew just emailed him a dozen "mugshots" of models in #phuckifino T-shirts, including photoshopped images of our actual mugshots so it appears as though we're part of the campaign.

"Yeah," Gary says cautiously. "I got it. And?"

"And you're not the least bit curious about how you managed to publish mockups of my campaign and not actual arrest photos? That's not important to you?"

"You gotta be kidding. You think for one minute anyone's going to buy that story?"

"Well, Gary, I have one very finicky attorney who thinks your liability insurance is gonna go through the roof when I sue you for libel, so yes, I happen to think people will believe me. Especially since my campaign is blowing up on Instagram right now."

I grab my phone and open Instagram. Drew's hashtag #phuckifino is trending, and the models he hired have all posted their pics and are getting thousands of likes. By the minute. *Whoa.*

Drew laughs, and it's not the one I've heard recently. It's the one he uses when he's around socialites and his drinking bros. "Do you actually think Kendall Greer, one of the most respected public relations executives in the city, was arrested on charges of larceny? You're losing your touch, man. Who shopped this story? Some underpaid assistant at some shithole police station who now has enough money to pay for her kids' Christmas presents because you paid her handsomely? I guess I'll give you points for philanthropy, but you get an F for your reporting skills."

Papers rustle on the other end of the line, and then it sounds muffled, like Gary covered the receiver while he yells at his minions.

When he comes back on, he sounds out of breath. "I have it on good authority you and Ms. Greer were arrested over Thanksgiving."

My heart stops. How do you defend against something that really happened?

Drew leans back in his seat, not breaking a sweat. "Prove it."

Oh, fuck. *Please know what you're doing, Drew.*

"Those photos prove everything," Gary argues.

"See, to me, they look like all the other pics in the campaign Kendall helped me craft. What you got were the mockups we created to make sure we got the flavor of the brand correct before we hired the models."

Silence.

"What? You think I had time to do this photoshoot today with all of these models—half of whom live on the other side of the country—after you published your article this afternoon? Sure. That seems reasonable." Drew chuckles. "But hey, if you need confirmation about any of this, I can send you the contact info of the police chief there who can confirm he has no record of our arrest."

More silence on the other end of the line.

"So Gary, I'll expect a full apology on your blog tomorrow, including the images I just sent, and we'll overlook this little snafu, or you'll be getting a call from my attorney bright and early on Monday. Oh, and if you want in on my parents' New Year's Eve bash—because I know you get year-long press passes to their events—Kendall had better come off looking like a goddamn angel, *capisce*? Awesome, bro. Thanks."

The second the call disconnects, I reach over and kiss Drew like my life depends on it.

26

KENDALL

*W*hen the elevator doors open to Drew's condo, we stumble out laughing. My hand is in his hair, his is up my skirt, and we've barely been able to pull our mouths off each other to get from my office to his condo.

Deep down, I realize there's no way to know how the truth of our arrest will play in light of Drew's demands to Gary. But the fact that Drew had this amazing plan at the ready and took over like a total PR pro today—for me, to come to *my* rescue—puts him in a whole new light. A *really* attractive light.

So even though I'm not a girl who wants a guy to rescue me, I have to admit it's an incredible feeling to know Drew has my back.

And my booty, apparently. I snicker as his hands squeeze my cheeks.

In fact, the relief of putting Gary in his place is so intense, I would fly away were it not for Drew's arms, which now hoist me up around his waist while he unlocks his door.

"Good thing there's only one other condo on this floor," he mumbles against my mouth. "Don't wanna show off your sexy ass to the whole world. We'd have to come up with another media campaign."

We both laugh harder as he kicks the door closed behind him and stomps over to his couch, where the world suddenly goes horizontal and all I can see is his handsome face hovering over me after a surprisingly soft landing.

Drew's hair is disheveled, and we're both out of breath.

His big hand travels along my hip possessively, stopping to stretch across my belly.

"I'm realizing I can't throw you around anymore," he says tenderly.

All of a sudden, I tense and wait for him to freak out about the baby. To tell me he isn't ready or doesn't want it.

But he doesn't, just gives me this look of affection, one that warms me all over.

"No, I guess not." I brush his hair out of his eyes as I shake off the flicker of uncertainty.

Internally, I admonish myself. I'm not sure why I default to this mode where I question Drew. He's been nothing but a standup guy since we started...whatever this is. Today should more than assure me he's not going to take off at the first sign of trouble.

Is that what I'm afraid of? Because Bobby bailed on me so easily, I think Drew will follow in his footsteps? Until this moment, I never realized how much my ex screwed with my head by breaking up with me so abruptly. One minute we were in sync, and the next—after he said he wanted kids as soon as possible and I threw on the brakes—he was gone. *And on to the next woman who would give him a baby.*

Ironic that I'm now doing the very thing that douchebag wanted but with another man.

But I don't want to think about that anymore. Especially not when I'm with Drew and he's looking at me like this.

Drew drags his thumb over my bottom lip. "You're so fucking beautiful, Kendall. I don't think I tell you that enough."

My eyes burn as my heart jackknifes in my chest.

I'm overwhelmed all over again, but not about my ex or work. I'm overwhelmed by the guy who saved my ass today.

Drew slides between my welcoming thighs, and I palm his stubbly chin.

"Thank you for today. For having everything ready to go. For doing all this work and knowing what to say and—"

He cuts me off with a kiss, moving closer until I can feel his heartbeat against mine.

"I would do anything for you," he whispers, trailing his lips against my jaw. My neck. The hollow of my throat.

Again with the sweet things. This guy kinda melts my heart.

He pushes onto his knees to strip off his leather jacket and kick off his shoes, then helps me sit up to shove off my coat and heels before he settles over me again.

"Is this okay?" Drew's deep voice in my ear makes goosebumps erupt across my skin.

I nod slowly, realizing I don't want to hold myself back with Drew. It's not fair that he receive the fallout from my old relationship.

Except I'm wondering...

Pushing him back carefully so I can see his face, I lay it out.

"What is this, Drew? What are we doing? Are we dating?" I feel like a royal moron asking these questions because I'm having his baby, for God's sake, but people have all kinds of arrangements these days. "I don't want to make any assumptions. Maybe you just want to help me through the pregnancy and then go our separate ways. Or you want to co-parent and not, you know, be in a relationship."

A pang of sadness washes through me at the thought, but I lift my chin and try to be rational about what a guy like Drew would really want. "This isn't the 1950s. You don't have to put a ring on it or anything. Not that I expect a ring or that kind of commitment," I rush to add.

With a groan, I fling my arm over my face.

Way to make things weird, Kendall.

A little voice pipes up in my head. *You're having his kid. All the more reason to know where you stand.*

Drew pries my arm off my face. And then I word vomit some more.

"I don't want you to do anything because you feel obligated or guilted into something. It's a modern day. We're not chained to outdated mores or pressure."

The corner of his mouth tugs up. "Are you done freaking out?"

"I don't know. Maybe?"

His smile deepens and hope blooms in my chest.

And then he dips down to drag his lips across mine. "So are you asking me if I want to date the beautiful, talented woman who's having my kid?" He peppers kisses along my jaw, picking up from where we were before I decided I needed some kind of clarification on our relationship. "Because that answer is yes."

He pauses to look me in the eyes. To study my face. To smooth his hand over my hair. "Let's see where this goes. Let's date like we would if you weren't pregnant." He pauses a beat. "Well, maybe not exactly as though you weren't pregnant." A wicked grin spreads on his face. "I probably can't fuck you as hard."

Heat creeps up my face as memories of all the ways we went at it on Mount Hood invade my mind. But it's the way he caresses my face that makes the doubt about starting a real relationship with him subside.

Drew is still on top of me, hard, thick and heavy, and my libido is pleading to shut the hell up and get to the sexy things already, but I can't throw caution to the wind. I need to think clearly.

Sitting up, I scoot out from under him because with Drew invading my space, I'm fifty shades of horny and all I want to do is strip naked.

Taking a deep breath, I realize what I want.

Instinct has always directed the big steps in my life. Deciding to stay close to home for college. Starting a business with my buddy from college. Not wanting to settle down and have kids with my ex.

This path with Drew? This feels right. Despite all of my reservations, moving forward with him seems like the right thing to do.

"Okay. Let's date."

"Okay?"

I nod, liking how reasonable everything he said sounds.

"As for the baby"—he pauses to squeeze my hand—"I'm on board to co-parent if, uh...if we decide things don't work between us."

I give him another nod, because, again, he's being so logical —and yet I can't deny I'll probably be devastated if we crash and burn. I have feelings for Drew *now*. Add eight more months of pregnancy, sex, and a baby, and if things end badly between us, it'll feel like a nuclear bomb went off in my life.

When I consider how, at our very core, we're so different, the odds are not in our favor. Drew is a recovering party animal with a penchant to love the one he's with. I'm a wine-with-dinner girl who prefers long-term commitments over hookups.

Clearing my throat, I rip off the Band-Aid because we'd might as well let it all out now. "So does dating mean monogamy to you? Because to me it does, and I'm not sure what you're used to in your relationships—"

"I don't have relationships. You know that. Or at least nothing that lasts longer than the pictures the next day."

My stomach starts to sink, but he tugs me closer. "Don't. I know what you're thinking. But before you jump to conclusions, what I mean to say is that, *up to this point*, I've not been in any kind of significant relationship. And fuck yes, this means monogamy. I'm not sharing you with Chewbacca."

When I realize he's talking about the morning he saw me sneaking out of Lawrence's hotel room, I laugh.

"God, that was a mistake of epic proportions." I glance up at Drew's handsome face, the one that looks a little pissed to be talking about another man. "But then I ran into this great guy in the elevator. And I haven't been with anyone else since. It's just been you."

His eyes soften. "Just me." He leans over me and places a feather-light kiss on my mouth. "I haven't been with anyone either."

"Really?" I don't mean to sound so surprised, but I guess I'm still having a hard time reconciling the claims he made last weekend that he's a hermit with the guy I've always known.

"It's been me and my left hand and some really hot memories of this beautiful woman who wrecked me on Mount Hood."

Aww.

"I know we're talking about you beating off, but that's really sweet."

"I'm a sweet guy." He bats his eyelashes, and I smile.

But then my lips twist, and I give him an angry stare. "Just for clarity's sake, I'm not into sharing my man either. I will cut a bitch and the motherfucker who cheats on me if it ever comes to that."

Whoa. Even talking about the possibility of cheating makes my blood boil. Are pregnancy hormones supposed to make me murderous? I've never been a particularly possessive person, but Drew brings out my crazy.

A growl rumbles in his chest as he pulls me onto his lap so I'm straddling him. "You're fucking hot when you're jealous, Ken." He shoves his hand into my hair, whips my head back, and kisses me like I'm the best dessert he's ever had. "And I may not always be the sharpest knife in the drawer, but I promise I'll be loyal." His hands tighten on my hips.

Between kisses, I gasp the question I've been mulling over for a while. "Drew, do you...get turned on...when we argue?"

"What do you think?" He thrusts against me, and I moan, my hormones instantly going on high alert.

I tilt my head. "We've always argued." I mean, not so much now, but our history before Mount Hood is one long series of blowups. His emerging smile gives me the answer before I can ask the question, but I say the words anyway. "Did you want to have sex with me before the cabin?"

"That would be a fuck yes."

"Since when?"

"Since always. I've always wanted you, Kendall."

Just like that, we can't get close enough. I push off his T-shirt. He yanks off mine, gets up long enough to take off his jeans and boxer briefs and then he's on me again. Pushing up my skirt and tugging down my underwear so that it's dangling off my ankle that I promptly wrap around his waist as he wedges himself between my legs.

"Do I need to grab a condom?" he mutters against my mouth.

"Your swimmers already got to the motherland and erected a flag, so that seems redundant. I mean, I can't get any *more* pregnant."

Drew throws his head back and laughs.

The sight of him—relaxed and happy, all of his muscles taut

as he leans over me with that boyish grin—increases my frenzy to connect with him.

Because I'm tired of talking. I'm tired of the 'what ifs' and the 'what have I done.' Drew says he's here for me. That we're in this together. And after the way he kicked Gary's ass on that conference call and said all of the right things tonight, that's the only evidence I need to try to make this relationship work.

After the intensity of everything that happened today and the weeks we've spent apart, I expect him to ravish me. To fuck me so hard, I can't walk straight tomorrow. But the minute our bare bodies are completely pressed together—chest to chest, belly to belly, thigh to thigh—he pauses to kiss me so slowly, every part of me aches from the most luscious sort of pain.

Because I feel cherished.

Pushing my hand into his hair, I yank him closer. I bite his throat. Lick his lips. Relish the sound of need that rumbles in his chest when I suck on his tongue.

We part briefly to stare at each other, our breaths charging the space between us.

Now, this moment, somehow changes everything.

We're no longer scratching an itch. We're something more. Something meaningful.

I nod, wanting what he has to give me.

Above me, he braces himself on his forearms as his hips move between mine, until his thick crown prods my entrance.

When he sinks into me, we both groan, and I cross my legs over his back and let myself appreciate every second it takes him to bury himself inside me. I'm stretched to the brink in the best way, and I claw at his back to get closer.

He nuzzles into my hair. "Fuck. You're like a goddamn vise. So good. Jesus, you feel good."

"Don't stop," I pant, needing to feel him. Wanting him to break me apart.

Little pulses of pleasure beat a steady rhythm between my thighs when he starts to move, and my eyes roll back in my head as my hips arch.

His couch thumps against the wall each time our bodies come together. The scent of his cologne and shampoo and clean sweat makes me hungrier to get closer.

Every single stroke inside me feels electric, and when he hikes my leg over his shoulder, I burst apart. My thighs quake, my vision seared by a white light, and when he thickens inside me and pulses his own release, I come again, tossing my head back and letting loose a scream that leaves my throat raw.

Sex with Drew is sublime.

In my wildest imagination, I never would've thought we'd be like this. That he'd make me intoxicated. Wild. Unbridled in a way I never knew I needed.

Slowly, he lowers my leg to his hip and rolls us to the side, somehow preventing us from rolling off the couch.

With a kiss, he says, "I'm thinking that was makeup sex, which, for the record, I've been wanting since I saw you at Josh's last weekend."

I smile, my lids so heavy I have to close my eyes. "Wanna do that again in the morning?"

He brushes a strand of hair away from my face and places another soft kiss to my forehead. "We really should make up for the last several weeks apart. Seeing how I missed the fuck outta my girlfriend."

I'm Drew's girlfriend. And we're having a baby.

A mere month ago, that scenario would've set my hair on fire, and I'd have run away screaming.

Instead, he carries me to his bedroom, and I fall asleep with that smile lingering on my lips.

27

DREW

I wake in my bed draped over Kendall like a duvet that's slipped to the side, my face tucked into her neck, arm tossed across her torso, and thigh hiked up between hers. My bicep twitches over her slim navel. Compared to me, she's so tiny I overwhelm her, though that just makes me want to hold her closer. Protect her.

A rough, scraping noise assaults my ear, but it's only Shazam cleaning himself while sprawled in the most uncouth position on my pillow. He's got no shame, the little bastard.

Other than my rescue cat and our breathing, though, it's silent.

Mist from the gray dawn edges up the windows of my quiet bedroom. As I snuggle into Kendall's warmth, basking in the comfort of her in my arms, my mind is at ease, which is a weird thing. I've spent so many manic years racing through my days, searching for the next distraction, that I've never really had a sense of calm. Ever. I've woken up hungover with regrets more days than I can count, and since I've been sober, I wake up not sure what I'm doing. But I never wake up happy where I am.

Except now.

212 | LEX MARTIN & LESLIE MCADAM

This morning, I can't help but settle into being content. I've got my Ken. We're on speaking terms. Hell, we're not just communicating, we're *dating*. We have non-Thanksgiving food, central heat, reliable electricity, and cell phones. There's no snow. And we're not in jail.

Best day ever.

Seems like all my best days are spent with her.

And nights. Like the way our bodies moved last night. The way she looked at me with trusting eyes. The way we connected.

In summary, I don't want to move from my bed, thank you very much.

An electrical current charges up my back and along my arms as I touch her and look at her, but my mind isn't racing ahead. I'm just taking in her peaceful face.

Honestly, I've never had a greater feeling of wellbeing.

I blink and scratch my balls. *Easy on the self-help books, asshole.* Lifting my head to scan the room, I curse.

Damn you, gray mist, for making me sound like a dipshit, even in my own head.

The pads of my fingers start tracing lazy circles on Kendall's velvety belly.

She stirs. Reaching down, she kisses the top of my head and toys with my hair. "Hey."

"Hey, back." I lurch up to kiss her—*God,* I love to kiss her—then go back to my Drew-is-a-blankie position partway down her torso, relishing the way her nails begin this soothing scratchy yummy thing in my hair.

I'm definitely not moving.

"How are you feeling?" I murmur into her side, and begin to massage her tits. Because tits. "Morning sickness?"

Settling her hand on her abdomen, she breathes in and out, scanning her insides. "Not yet."

"Has it been bad?"

"Like a tsunami of vomit." She pauses, and a shiver runs through her body. "That's not sexy. I'm sorry."

I pull back and put my finger under her chin so she has to catch my eyes. "KK. Never be sorry about how you feel. Oh, and newsflash. There's no way you could not be sexy." She shrugs, but can't help beaming. I keep talking. "I'll be honest. I'm responsible here. My baby batter's baking in your oven."

She snorts.

"I'm stepping up to help. I need you in my life. Even if it's just to kick my ass."

Scooting down so we're nose to nose, belly to belly, she kisses me. "I can do that. Kick your ass. Whenever you want, just say the word."

My voice turns husky. "You do it well, and it turns me the fuck on. Give me Kendall hashtag no filter any time."

Her hands trace my face. "It's funny. We went so long sniping at each other that it's taking some adjustment to reconcile how we used to be with how we are now."

I'm really liking how she says *we*. That deserves a big old sloppy kiss, and I indulge. After we break apart and are breathing hard, I say, "Agreed."

"What do you want to do today?" While her words are innocent, her hand is anything but, creeping down my abs toward my dick.

I'll happily let her have her way with me, but I want to take a gander at her. I roll to my back, lifting her up so she straddles me. Naked. Tits out. Nipples pointing. Long, red hair mussed like she's just been fucked. Sleepy, sultry eyes. Satiny skin. "On a day like today, I recommend hanging out and taking in the view from my apartment."

Her head turns toward the windows, her cute nose pointed up. "Your place is pretty cool."

My paws cover her boobs, and I squeeze. My dick jumps underneath her. "I mean this view."

A grin crosses her face, but it quickly morphs into a grimace. Her hand flies to her mouth, and she vaults off of me, sprints to the bathroom, and slams the door shut behind her.

I rise and pad after her, torn between wanting to give her privacy and making sure she knows she's got support. Tapping on the door, I call, "Kendall? You okay? I'm here if you need me."

A muffled voice tells me to go away.

Still doesn't change the fact that it's the best day ever.

"Hey. This is delicious." Kendall cocks her head to the side and uses her spoon to gesture at my homemade oatmeal *Chez Maison Merritt*.

I smirk. "Don't sound so surprised." Between the added crunch from nuts and granola, plus some strawberries, I make a decent breakfast, especially for those with poor tummies. Experience with hangovers comes in handy.

We've showered. KK's rocking my too-big #phuckifino T-shirt and gray sweatpants that engulf her toned legs.

My mind latches onto the fact that she's not wearing a bra or underwear under my baggy clothes. Another part of my anatomy sits up and takes notice, too.

But seeing her relaxed and happy and content? It's *everything*. My dick can wait.

At least until Kendall's fed.

She scoops up another bite and closes her eyes in enjoyment. "Breakfast is so good it almost makes up for the fact that I can't have coffee." With a sigh, she continues. "*Almost.* I don't mean to whine, but being without caffeine? My inner monster has zero chill."

I almost made a pot of coffee out of habit, but thought better. Instead, I dug out tea and made two cups of decaf in solidarity. "Whine all you want, babe. You're taking one for the team. Let me know what I can do to make you feel better."

With a sigh, she smiles and goes back to her bowl o'oats. "Thanks."

Score—Drew, 1.

Sipping my decaf tea, I sit back and take in downtown through my windows. "You know? We've never spent a normal day together. Not one. We've never even had a date."

With a twist of her lips, she considers this statement. "You're right. We've argued, and we've been stranded, but we've never had a regular day hanging out."

While I don't want to sound overeager, I ask, "Can we fix that? Today?"

Her lips tug up into a shy smile when she nods.

I try to be cool about this even though I'm psyched to be spending time with her. "We could do something crazy like spend the entire day together in civilization. I could shock you and take you out to lunch and a movie."

"I don't know," she says, fake doubt in her voice. "That's pretty wild."

My voice lowers to a whisper. "I bet I've never shown you this secret side of me. Sometimes, I run errands." I eye her meaningfully.

Mirroring my seriousness, she presses her palms to her cheeks in shock, *Home Alone*-style. "Holy shit! Who are you and what have you done with Drew?"

"Oh, I'm working on Drew 3.0." I stiffen. "*Shit*."

Setting down her mug, she pushes her eyebrows together and looks at me quizzically. "What's wrong?"

"I just remembered something."

"Which is?"

"Today's my birthday. The big three-oh. I really *am* Drew 3.0."

A wide smile takes over her entire face, making her delight visible. Her skin glows, and her eyes shine. She pushes away from the table and races into my lap, wrapping her arms around me and giving me a kiss. "Happy birthday!"

Having Kendall Greer in my lap, planting a big wet one on me, is the best birthday present I've ever received.

I go to kiss her back, but her expression turns mischievous, and she stifles a giggle.

With my mouth against hers, I ask, "What?" I kiss her more. Then she leans away.

She places one hand on each of my shoulders and gazes directly into my eyes. Her lips part. "I think you need Dirty Thirty sex for your birthday."

Schooling my features into being serious, I nod. "Yes. Very much so." Using my chin, keeping my eyes on hers, I indicate the remains of her breakfast behind her on the table. "How hungry are you?"

"Ravenous. But not for the last of this oatmeal." I don't need any further invitation and waste no time picking her up, wrapping her legs around my waist, and hauling her into my bedroom.

"I'm not sure why we bothered getting dressed," I say against her lips as her tongue seeks mine.

"For the fun of taking it off?" Her hands rip into my hair, and I groan in pleasure. Settling her on my bed, I flip her T-shirt up and over her head, and pull off her sweats.

"Damn. That got you naked too fast." I shake my head. "Never mind. There's no such thing as 'naked too fast.'"

My mouth begins to roam over her body, a deep rumble forming in my throat. My lips sucking her nipples as she gasps. Tongue licking down her torso. Teeth grazing her navel.

My fingers wend their way between her legs and part her, finding hot wetness.

Rubbing.

Caressing.

Enjoying how she responds to my touch.

Meanwhile, she reaches down to the hem of my shirt and tugs. I pause my exploration of her body to let it go flying across the room. Her hands travel over my shoulders, arms, chest. With legs spread wide, her hips reach for me, grinding, seeking purchase against my dick.

"Gotta taste your pussy, babe," I mutter, moving down her body to dip down between her legs, throwing her thighs over my shoulders. My tongue darts out, and I take a long lick up the entire expanse, smelling the clean soap from her shower this morning and the slight bite of her natural flavor.

Fuck. I'm so hard I'm pulsing, but I focus on her.

"Need to taste more than that," I continue. Pushing her knees backward toward her chest so her entire underside is exposed to me—thank you, K-doll's yoga instructor—I begin licking every part of her I can find. Her slick, swelling pussy. Her taint. And I go down to her ass and begin loving on the tiny puckered part. Circling it. Darting around it.

"Oh—fuck," she grunts. "I've never—"

Long strokes of my tongue interrupt her as she writhes. The fingers of my one hand enter her slick channel and stroke upward, aiming for that rough wall that I know brings pleasure, with my thumb insistent on her clit. Then I drift my other hand, coated in her arousal, lower, and press a finger into her asshole. And my face is everywhere—sucking, tasting, fucking wallowing in her.

Yeah, I'm dirty. I don't care. I want her to come on my face. I don't know how else to show her how I feel than to be no-holds-barred.

To show her I'm into her. In all the ways.

As I keep going, between my fingers and my tongue, I sense her muscles bunching up. Her breathing getting tighter. The folds of her soft skin plumping. Blood rushing to all her sensitive parts.

She's struggling to hang on, but I continue laving her with broad passes of my tongue. With the unrelenting rhythm of my fingers. Coaxing her closer and closer and closer.

Pretty damn fast, she comes, a cry of pleasure on her tongue, and her body trembling as waves pulsate through her.

But I keep going and don't give up until she wails out my name, and I can tell the orgasm is wrung out of her.

Then I get up on my knees and gaze at her.

"Holy fuck, Drew. It's *your* birthday, not mine."

I wink. "Exactly." Hooking my thumbs in the waistband of my pants, I shove them down, along with my boxer briefs, and free my erection. Before she can move, I'm over her, ready to thrust my dick into her tight, wet pussy. I brace myself above her with my hands on either side. Thinking quick, I grab a pillow, shove it under her ass for a better angle, and go in.

"Fuck, yes," I moan.

She holds me inside as we both throb.

I pause, joined with her.

Loving this.

Then I slide in and out slowly, groaning at the friction. The heat. The attachment of our bodies in the closest way possible.

She claws at me to move faster, and I comply.

From here, it's a fucking free-for-all. Literally. I let go, pistoning into her. She matches my moves, her blue eyes lust-driven and her hands clutching my ass.

I couldn't stop this motion—this emotion—the driving into her if I had to. I know I should go easier on her, but at this stage,

I can't. She doesn't want me to either, judging by how she's grabbing me and hanging on.

Can I get one more orgasm out of her?

Hauling her up, adjusting the angle again, I drag my hard cock along her walls, again and again, seeking her O.

Her eyes pop open wider when it's about to hit. She's going to come again.

"Come for me. Let me feel your beautiful cunt squeeze my dick. Milk it, babe," I growl.

I'm about to blow my load. I'm urgent. Needy.

But she's still first.

With a mewl, she releases again, her eyes closed and body oscillating. I hold my breath and jet, pumping myself into her as I hold her tight.

We collapse together, intimately bound, breathing as one.

Goddamn.

If I was into Kendall when she hated my guts, and fell for her up at the cabin, now that she's here in my bed—in my arms—in my life, there's no other way to say it. I'm a lucky sonofabitch. Scared shitless, but smart enough to know a good thing when it smacks me in the face.

I've gone through life being able to buy pretty much whatever I wanted. Cars, real estate, businesses? No problem. Nights out on the town? Easy.

The right partner? I'm in over my head. These tender feelings have been in short supply. They're new. Kendall makes me a beast in bed, a guard dog to anyone threatening her, and a lovesick fool—

Shit.

I'm not gonna label what I'm feeling. I just know she makes my heart expand. I can figure it out later.

Cuddling into her, I draw her to me, not caring how messy we are. That's what showers are for.

I just wanna be with her.

After zoning, she turns to me. "That was—wow."

My arm squeezes her middle, but as I replay the pleasant memory of what we just did, my gut sinks. "Fuck, KK. I'm sorry. I twisted you like a pretzel after I said I wouldn't get crazy."

I get a full, tongue-in-my-mouth kiss, along with a purr. To clarify, the purr's from Kendall, not Shaz. "I don't think it's that big a deal right now. I say we take advantage of the fact that, for the time being, I'm bendy."

"Still. Maybe we need to ask your gyno." I shift her to my side. "You haven't gone yet, have you? Can I go with you?"

Her expression makes my heart warm. "Yeah," she says quietly. "I'd like that."

"You sure? I mean, I'm gonna ask your doctor which sex positions are out. Might be awkward. Maybe you don't want me to come."

She gets a devilish gleam in her eyes. "Oh, I definitely want you to come."

I chuckle. "I love it when you innuendo." Speaking of... Sitting up and leaning over, I use my sexiest, lowest tone. "Ready to run some *errands*?" I whisper, and she laughs hard.

28

DREW

"I can't *believe* that ending!" Kendall says, as we burst out from the darkness of the Sellwood movie theater into the darkness of my birthday evening. She presses her hands to her cheeks, and I'm not sure if it's from the adrenaline rush of the past two hours or the cold, rainy air misting our faces.

I'm as pumped as she is. "Agreed! That boat-plane-motorcycle-helicopter-train chase was *insane*." I wrap my arm around her, and she snuggles into my side.

Where she belongs.

My light heart skips, elated from enjoying a strange day of *normal* with Kendall. After the morning at my house, we stopped by her place to pick up fresh clothes. She dressed, then, all nonchalant, snuck a package wrapped with "Happy Birthday" paper down from the top of a bookshelf. With a bite of her lip and a hopeful glint in her eyes, she handed it to me, secretly pleased that she'd planned ahead.

She said the cashmere sweater matches my eyes.

I put it on immediately, and I don't ever want to take it off. Unless, of course, she does the honors.

Now, outside, her eyes remain wide as she tightens her arm around my waist. Pieces of her hair fall into her face from the wind, and she brushes them away. "That last fight scene was badass. I've never seen anything like it."

"I've never seen anything like *you*," I say, chuckling and giving her a kiss on the top of her head. "I had no idea you got so into movies. It's pretty fucking adorable."

A flush warms her face. "I love them. I just never have the time to enjoy them anymore." A wistful look passes across her face and disappears. "Guess that's something I gave up when I started my own agency."

"Well, we're gonna have to go more often."

She reaches up, gives me a kiss, and slips her hand into mine. I stroll down a regular Portland street in the rain on a cold night, hand-in-hand with my girlfriend like I do this all the time. With effort, I keep from fixating on where our hands are joined.

Because it feels intimate. It says, *I claim you. We're together. You're mine. We're a team.*

I could get used to holding her hand.

When we return to my car, I reluctantly let go of it to open the door and let her in. As I'm circling around the trunk to my side, I pull out my phone, switching it to regular mode.

Beep, beep, beep, beep, beep...

Jesus, I have a lot of notifications.

Between hanging with KK and shutting it off for the movie, I've ignored my phone all day. Apparently now it's payback time, but rather than stand outside and freeze my nuts off, I hustle into the driver's seat, slam the door behind me, and stare at the screen.

Kendall's quizzical glance invites an explanation. I hold out my phone and let her take a look at the crazy. "Everyone messaged me. I bet for my birthday." We watch a video sent by

Josh and Evie where they're on set wishing me a "bitchin' birthday."

I snort. "What is this, 1987?"

Then my finger starts scrolling.

Ian: Hey man, I'm in town and wanted to stop by, but I ended up partying with Sam and just woke up. Next time I'll stay at your house. Have to catch a red eye back to NYC.

Frankie: Hope you have a good birthday, boss. Year end is gonna rock.

Ashton: D-bag! HBD. Need some blow?

Candy: I looked for your sexy ass at Club Citron last night and didn't see you. Are you coming with us tonight?

Steve: What are you doing for NYE? Come hang. Or is the party at your house?

Fernando: You having people over tonight or what? Ian said you might.

Mark: What's this I hear about a party at your house?

Bumble Bee: Happy birthday, Andrew. May your thirties be wonderful.

Dude, even my grandma texts.

"Fuck," I grumble, running my hands through my damp hair.

"What?"

"Somehow everyone thinks there's a party at my house." I raise my eyebrows and shake my head, letting out my breath in an exasperated gust. "Hang on, let me deal with them. Do you mind?" She shakes her head, and I mutter my responses as I type my texts back. "No party... Thanks... *Block this number*... Not going to the club... Sorry, busy... Don't come over... You heard wrong... Thanks, Bumble."

Kendall smooths her hands down her thighs, her expression pensive. "I don't want to be the kind of girlfriend who makes you change your plans or takes you away from all your friends."

Her use of the word *girlfriend* makes goosebumps rise on my skin. I'm adding it to *hand holding* as my new favorite thing. "They won't miss me. Some people can't take no for an answer."

She nods, picking at lint on her coat and staring ahead.

My finger traces her dainty chin. "Hey. I swore off these guys a while ago, but it's taking a while for the message to compute."

"I get it," she says, and her eyes soften.

When I pull up at her house, Kendall tilts her head to the side. "Wanna come up? We already had dinner, but maybe we can have dessert."

I point my thumbs at my chest. "Diabetic, remember."

"I'm talking about a different kind of dessert."

I can't get out of the car fast enough and spend the rest of the evening taking Kendall up on her offer.

Best. Birthday. Ever.

Two days later, on New Year's Eve, we return to the same historic theater in Sellwood, only this time, I punk Kendall. Instead of crashing a big, public party with champagne and half-friends like I'd led her to believe, we open the glass doors to the smell of fresh popcorn...and no other patrons. Since Josh did the remodel, he hooked me up with the owners, who let me rent out the place for two, since they'd planned to be closed for the night.

We're gonna spend the last hours of the year enjoying our way through a few of KK's favorite movies. Like *Pretty Woman*, which Evie told me she loves.

After we step in and take our seats, I watch the dawning recognition appear in Kendall's blue eyes. When the first movie starts and she realizes what I've done, she tackles me with a hug.

Worth it.

So is the fact that I get her all to myself tonight.

At midnight, when I envelop her in my arms for a thorough kiss, I'm certain this will be a very different and momentous year to come, and for the first time, I'm looking forward to my future.

Now, more than ever, I need to get my shit together.

For real this time.

Which means I can't put off the situation with my parental units any longer, so the following week, I bite the bullet.

When I pull into the circular driveway of my childhood home, I wish warm memories flooded me like they probably do for most people.

But there's nothing typical about my family.

Neat, clipped hedges frame the enormous brick manor estate. Since I do my best to avoid this place, every time I return it feels less and less familiar. I know my way around, for the most part, but everything's shifted and feels off. I've changed, it hasn't, and I'm only here today because I've been summoned from on high, and I have to be. My nod at adulting is I made an effort to be on time and I'm not wearing any shirts with cuss words. So there's that.

As I walk up to the front door, a rueful smile tugs at my lips. It's been a while, so I'm practically a stranger. Should I knock?

Nah. I never do.

Opening the door, I call, "Hel-lo. Anyone home?"

While the place is heated, it still feels unused and empty.

More for show than for living. No wonder I spent all my time at Josh's house as a kid.

Victoria, the housekeeper, comes bustling up. She seems almost apologetic. "Mister Andrew. Come, come. They're waiting for you in the garden room."

"Thanks."

I stroll inside whistling, my hands shoved in my pockets. We pass through four rooms until we arrive at my mom's office-slash-sitting room, where everyone's gathered.

"Andrew," my mom says in a flat voice, giving me the once-over. "So glad you could come."

She's anything but glad, given the last time we talked she screamed at me about being arrested after she saw the law firm bill that was accidentally sent to her. As well as the time before that when she told me the name of my company was a disgrace. And the time before that. At least, I know she screamed, but I don't remember why.

She's spent years fighting this trust transfer because she doesn't think I can handle it. In other words, it siphons funds from her monstrous fortune.

Sorry, Mom. I didn't ask for this.

Her eyes betray years of criticizing everything I've done, and her strangely smooth forehead from too much Botox is eerie. Mom's got one of those Barbara Bush-Nancy Reagan-Betsy Bloomingdale haircuts that's shaped into a perfectly coiffed helmet. Basically, she's in danger of being mistaken for a wax statue.

God forbid she wear anything comfy in her own home. Nope. Haute couture Chanel suit and perfect heels to greet her son. I dutifully peck her cheek, smelling her heady perfume, which reminds me of evenings she'd go out to parties with my father, leaving me with the nanny.

I *hate* how being around my parents makes me remember being eight.

My dad's stretched out behind her on the one piece of furniture she's conceded to him—a leather recliner.

"Drew. Nice to see you." He gets up to shake my hand with a gleam in his eyes, like a falcon zooming in on prey. In his world, showing off how big a man you are is paramount. More money, prettier wife, fanciest car, biggest yacht. It makes me want to vomit, which is why I spent most of my life in ratty old T-shirts, ripped jeans, and muddy sneakers. I've outgrown that stage and live my life for me, but that doesn't stop the tide of memories from returning whenever I come here.

And he thinks I don't deserve this either. Maybe I don't, but I'm gonna turn it into something that's worthwhile.

"Dad." I grip his hand like I'm going to arm wrestle him to the ground, and he almost looks impressed. Then he straightens his face and remembers he's pissed at me, too, since I'm getting a controlling share in the family business.

While my father's wearing a button-down shirt, chinos, and loafers, everyone else—the team of lawyers—is in a suit. Tim Bryan, the one who bailed me out, stands in the corner with his partner, an associate, and a notary.

I beam my biggest, fakest smile to the room, because I'm not letting them win. Any of them. "It's *fantastic* to see everyone. I hope you all had a *fabulous* holiday season." Then I mutter under my breath, "Let's get this over with."

After giving the lawyers a general chin lift, I settle my butt down on the nearest antique couch, kick up my feet on the expensive coffee table, and cross my arms over my chest. Because even though I've outgrown a lot of this, I'm still an asshole.

My mom stiffens.

I wished for so many years that she'd loosen up. Smile. Get a wrinkle. Pretend she loved—or hell, even liked—her kid. Pretend for one minute that I mattered to her.

But now I've given up hope she'll ever be human.

A younger guy pulls out a notary book and stamp. "May I see your driver's license, Andrew, to enter your information?"

I pull out my Teenage Mutant Ninja Turtle wallet and pass my license to him. So much for being an adult. My father's brows knit together.

"Like it?" I ask, waving my wallet. "Bumble gave it to me."

Tim's partner hands me a sheaf of papers. "These are trust transfer documents for you to review and sign. Trust transfer deeds, share certificates, a buy-sell agreement, shareholder agreement, and beneficiary designation."

Now that I'm thirty, a whole lotta shit kicks in with no strings attached and nothing making me beholden to my family.

Thank fuck.

Obviously, I'm damn grateful my paternal grandparents did this, and I'm planning to use the funds to expand the charitable arm of my own company while making MerrittCo more environmentally sustainable. But my mother's made no bones about her belief that I can't handle the money and will waste it, and my father thinks I'm taking it away from him, even though he has more cash than several small countries combined. While this could be a joyous occasion, it's more like signing up for the draft.

After I sign my name a dozen times, ink my thumbprint in the notary book, and receive a folder full of documents, the lawyers leave.

I stand, my thumbs hooked in my belt loop, rocking on my heels, staring at my parents.

"Now that you have your inheritance, Andrew," says my mother in her steeliest voice, "you better not foul it up with any of your mistakes." She hisses this last part. Gone is the veneer of social nicety now that it's just me and her and dear ol' Dad.

"Thanks for your vote of confidence." I force a smile and long to let it all out. Tell them my plans. Let them know what I've been doing lately. How I've been successful in business, because I don't think they believe my company had any chance.

But it would be a waste of breath.

They don't care.

With a leaden heart, I wave goodbye and zip out of there, not realizing until I'm home that I never told them they're going to be grandparents.

29

KENDALL

Covering the receiver of my office phone, I hurl into the trash can, but as soon as I expel the evil egg sandwich I had for breakfast, my stomach immediately settles. Thankfully that one didn't spurt out my nose too. Those are always so gross.

Tristan comes bounding into the room as I'm wiping my mouth. I balance the receiver on my shoulder and hold up a finger. He nods, taking the seat in front of my desk while I resume the call.

"Sorry for the interruption. Like I was saying, it won't be a problem to get you those mock-ups by Monday." I smile when my new client tells me how excited she is about the campaign I'm helping her craft.

When I hang up, Tristan's laughing at me. "Did you just vomit during that call?"

"So? She didn't hear me. I was multitasking."

"Where we at now, Wonder Woman?"

"At this rate, we might have to hire another rep by the end of the month."

We've gotten so much business from Drew's T-shirt campaign and Gary's retraction, Tristan and I have been slammed. LaRoe not only dropped his threats to fire us, he actually paid us.

Euphoria threatens to take over my face when I think of the video Drew posted, raving about how I came up with the idea for his campaign. Then he shared the new T-shirt he designed for me, which said #SavageAF emblazoned across the front.

I make a mental note to give my boyfriend some extra-kinky sex for all of those tags on Instagram. If I can stay awake that late.

I pause to mull it over.

I'm dating Drew Merritt. Seriously dating.

Still seems surreal.

Because he's actually a great boyfriend. Sends me flowers. Buys me lunch. Always makes sure I come first. Who would've thought?

"Kendall. You listening?"

"Sorry. What?"

Tristan points a finger at me. "You're making that face again."

"What face?" Reaching for my bottled water, I start to take a sip.

"The one you make when you're thinking about banging your dude."

I choke and water dribbles down my chin. After I clear my throat and wipe my face, I glare at Tristan. "I have no clue what you're talking about."

Although, yeah, I was thinking about sex.

Because even though Drew and I talk daily, and sometimes he spends the night, I've been so busy, and *soooo* tired, sometimes I don't have the energy after work to fuck his brains out. Even though I want to. The heart is willing, you know? But damn, I'm always exhausted.

In the last month since his birthday, I've spent the longest days of my life planted in this chair, trying to juggle all of the

232 | LEX MARTIN & LESLIE MCADAM

incoming business. While I can cover our overhead more easily, I didn't anticipate what getting so many new clients would mean. Although we hired two new associates, I also have to babysit their projects to make sure they're doing quality work. I won't always have to once they've settled in, but our jobs are high-profile, and we can't afford any mistakes as a fledgling company.

Tristan taps on his watch. "Don't you have a doctor's appointment today?"

"No, that's tomorrow."

He lifts his eyebrows.

I double-check my calendar. "Shit. I'm supposed to be there in twenty minutes. Why didn't you meddle sooner?"

A chuckle shakes his shoulders. "Get outta here. I'll hold down the fort for a few hours."

"I'll be back to meet with that new designer."

He shrugs. "I can do it."

Pausing to put on my jacket, I groan. "I hate not being here for things."

"I know. And that's one reason why I love you, but seriously, get to your appointment before Merritt kills me for working you overtime."

Annoyance prickles my spine. "Why would it matter how much I work?" Even as I say those words, I want to bite them back. Because Drew *has* noticed I don't leave the office sometimes until eight or nine at night. And he *might* have mentioned that he thinks I should get more rest.

Tristan gives me a look.

I return it.

Side note, I like that my best bud and I can speak without words, just twitchy eyes.

With a sigh, he gets up. "*I'm just saying* if my pregnant girl-friend was working so hard that she had to puke in the middle of a conference call and then resume it like nothing happened, I might *suggest* she not work so hard. If that makes me a chauvinist, so be it. But I call it caring."

My glare intensifies. "Drew won't tell me what to do. He knows better."

Tris pats me on the back. "You didn't hear anything I said, did you? Just take it easy, Mama. You're driving around your baby bean too."

Instinctively, I rub my belly. "Isn't it the size of a pea? Hell, I don't really know, but I guess that's what the ob-gyn appointment is for." Damn, why didn't I look this up when I was researching pregnancy?

"This your first appointment?"

"Yeah." Guilt for not checking in sooner with the doctor settles in my stomach, but I brush it away. There's nothing anyone can do in the first trimester if it's not a viable pregnancy for some reason. Or at least that's what Google told me.

I pause mid-stride to hope and pray my little bean or pea or whatever vegetable he or she is right now is fine and enjoying some R&R in my uterus.

So I've eaten well, hydrated so much I have to pee every fifteen minutes, and taken my vitamin with folic acid. Plus, I've tossed out any beauty product with BPA, phthalates, or sulfates. I already eat organic, non-GMO foods and do yoga every morning. I am a paragon of health. If I eat anymore greens, I'm going to crap a Christmas tree.

Besides, I can't help that I've been busy. The whole point of busting my ass now is so I can take some time off once the baby arrives.

Although the thought of taking maternity leave gives me hives. I have no idea how I'll be able to disconnect from this place for long.

But I'll cross that bridge when I get to it.

~

By the time I yank open the door to the doctor's office, I'm sweaty and slightly nauseated again, but this time I suspect it's from nerves. I don't know why the idea of this visit has made me anxious because I've never had an issue going to checkups before.

But visiting an ob-gyn, getting an ultrasound, getting a due date—that all makes this so real, I'm almost grateful there isn't anything in my stomach so I likely won't throw up again. At least, I don't think I will.

Slowly, I scan the waiting room. It's packed with women, and nestled between them is my boyfriend, doing his damnedest to not look awkward while two very pregnant ladies chat him up.

I fold my lips between my teeth so I don't laugh at how fast he jumps out of his seat and rushes toward me.

"Hey, babe." He kisses me soundly, and I nuzzle into him.

"Sorry I'm late, but I'm glad you made some friends." He rolls his eyes, but his cheeks turn pink as he rubs the back of his neck. And because I can't help it, I nudge his arm with a teasing grin on my face. "Want me to wait here while you get their numbers?"

"Shut up." He laughs and slings his arm around my shoulders.

I'm not surprised that the preggos here were flirting. Drew's sexy as hell and adorable. Though I'll probably never mention that last part to him.

I take a minute to check him out. Worn jeans that mold to his ass and thighs. A faded T-shirt that stretches across his broad chest. Dirty blond hair and a devil-may-care smile. Yup. Total lady-killer.

My guy. Here for our ob-gyn appointment.

My ovaries throb. And maybe one other part throbs too.

Shaking my head, I try to focus. Because it's really inappropriate to be turned on before I see the gynie.

Fortunately, the receptionist waves us toward the counter and hands me a stack of forms and asks for my co-pay.

But before I can reach into my purse and grab my wallet, Drew has already whipped out his Amex Black.

"What are you doing?" I'm wrestling with my coat and my purse and trying not to drop my forms and the clipboard.

"I got this." Drew gives me a quick kiss as he hands over his credit card.

"I can cover my co-pays."

"I'm sure you can, but I figure since you're carrying our little nugget and puking every ten minutes, the least I can do is cover this." He gives me a sexy grin and lowers his voice to a whisper. "Doesn't seem fair that I get hot sex and a hot girlfriend, and all you get is nonstop morning sickness and bloating."

I blink, my female indignation over wanting to cover my own expenses evaporating as quickly as it overcame me. Because he's making a lot of sense. But then I frown. "Do I look bloated?"

"Nope. You look perfect." He plants a smooch on my forehead, and I sigh at his sweet words. "You were complaining about it last weekend, and I remembered."

He remembers things about me.

Another Drew Merritt quality I wasn't expecting when we started this.

Thirty minutes later, after I'm weighed and asked to pee in a cup, I'm handed a paper gown, and Drew and I are ushered into an exam room.

When the door closes with a quiet click, Drew's eyebrow lifts. "Can I watch you change?"

"No. Turn around."

"I've seen it all already. Up close and personal. With

surround sound. In HD." He crosses his arms, like he's already made his case and thinks I'll fold.

"If I let you watch, I'll get turned on, and then my gynecologist *will be able to tell*."

I wait for that to sink in.

And then chuckle when his eyes dilate. "No, Drew. Seriously, no."

"Fine, but I'm asking the doctor all of my sex questions. I'm not folding you like an accordion if she says I can't." With a grunt, he turns around while I shed my clothes, don the horrid paper gown, and hop onto the table with stirrups.

"Okay, I'm all set."

He turns toward me and stares a long moment. "How often do you visit PornHub?"

"Drew," I warn.

"What? I'm not into that *Fifty Shades* shit, but I'd be willing to get pervy on that table."

Judging by the boner straining at his fly, I don't doubt it. But damn it, he makes me smile.

"Come here, Andrew, before we traumatize the doctor."

"Jesus, I like when you get stern and call me by my full name."

I reach over, yank him around to the other side of the exam table to hide his giant bulge.

"Is this the first time you've been to a gynecologist appointment?" I ask, almost afraid of his answer. Because this is Drew. I wouldn't put anything past him.

"I've never been within a hundred-foot radius of a place like this."

I'd laugh at the tone of his voice, but when he takes my hand, it's clammy, and I realize he's nervous too.

"Are you still up for meeting my parents this weekend?" They know I've been dating him, because I figured that would make the baby revelation easier to digest, but I haven't divulged much else.

"Absolutely." He's quiet a second. "Your dad's not gonna kill me, is he?"

"Not right away."

"Har, har. No, really."

"My parents aren't the 'go after you with a shotgun' type. If they don't like you, my mom will try to poison you with her homemade kombucha."

I turn to look at him, and his expression is blank.

"Kidding."

He rolls his eyes with a smile.

I've been waiting for him to mention when he plans to tell his parents, but he hasn't. I know they're not close, so I haven't pushed the issue even though it's starting to make me apprehensive. Except right now, I want to focus on the positive.

"Thanks for coming today. It means a lot to me," I say quietly. He doesn't have to be here. He doesn't have to support me this way. But I'm grateful he wants to.

Stalking around the table, he nudges his hips between my legs and tilts my head up.

"There's nothing—*nothing*—more important than this."

Does he mean me? The baby? Both?

My heart leaps in my chest from the way he looks at me and the whisper-soft kiss he grazes across my lips.

A knock at the door makes him jump back and return to my side, and I push down the paper gown so I don't flash my goods to the woman in the white coat entering the room.

"Hi, Kendall. I'm Dr. Michaels." She shakes my hand and then Drew's. "Is this Dad?"

I nod, my insides going all gooey at the expression on Drew's face. *He likes being called Dad.*

We chat for a few minutes while she reviews my chart, and

then calls in an assistant. "Since we're in the first trimester, we'll do a transvaginal ultrasound. Kendall, you think you're about eight weeks along?"

I'm about to agree when I realize I was at eight weeks *when I scheduled this appointment.*

I cringe. "Now that I think about it, it's probably closer to eleven at this point." Guilt for procrastinating this appointment blankets me, and I wonder if I'm already failing at this parental thing. "Am I a terrible person for waiting this long?" I'm nearly in the second trimester, for fuck's sake.

"Not at all." She studies my chart. "You said you were taking your prenatal vitamins and staying hydrated. Eating well. Avoiding alcohol and caffeine. Sounds like you're doing all the right things."

She gives me a reassuring smile and introduces the technician named Bella, who rolls a machine with a dark screen over to the doctor.

Dr. Michaels washes her hands, snaps on a pair of clear gloves, and grabs a slender wand off a tray. "We'll be using a transducer probe to conduct the ultrasound, which uses sound waves to create the picture."

She covers the wand with what appears to be a condom and then squirts a gel all over it.

I glance at Drew, and his expression makes me smirk. *Dirty boy.*

But his whole demeanor changes with the doctor's next words.

"Today, we should be able to hear the heartbeat, measure your baby, and determine the due date."

His eyes widen. "That's incredible. You can tell all of that from this one test?" But before the doctor responds, he asks, "This won't hurt Kendall, will it?"

"Not at all. She'll just feel a little pressure."

He squeezes my hand, relief all over his face.

That gooey feeling in my chest expands, and I swoon a little more.

Until the doctor motions toward me. "Mom, please lie back, get your feet up in the stirrups, and scoot your bottom toward the end of the table."

I swallow, hating how my heart suddenly pounds in my chest. I'm feeling a little lightheaded, but I take a few deep breaths to calm down.

As I lean back, I push down my gown so it doesn't ride up. And then I elevate my feet, embarrassed that I didn't shave my legs this morning.

But then there's Drew, leaning over me with that beautiful smile. Holding my hand. Kissing my forehead. Reassuring me.

My eyes sting, and I blink it back. Because I cannot cry simply because my boyfriend is here. That's crazy. That's not why I'm about to cry, is it?

Get a hold of yourself, Kendall.

The doctor begins her exam, explaining what she's doing as she inserts the wand. My toes curl over the stirrups.

The technician adjusts a knob on the ultrasound machine, and a wavy blob comes into view. And then she flips another switch, and the room is filled with a wild thumping sound.

Dr. Michaels turns toward the screen and smiles. "I'd like to introduce you to Baby Greer. And you're listening to his or her heartbeat. It's too early to tell the sex."

Now I can't help the tears in my eyes. They overflow, running down my cheeks.

It's like my heart. Overflowing. Overwhelmed in the best way.

The doctor points to the blob, my precious peanut, as the technician takes measurements on the computer that show up on our screen.

But then the doctor stills to squint at the image. Leaning closer to the monitor, she tilts it away from us and confers quietly with the technician, which spikes my anxiety.

"What? Is everything okay?" I ask, feeling like I might pass out or vomit again.

After the longest minute of my life, she swivels it back and makes a few adjustments on the screen. That blob waves and wobbles as the sound of the thumping increases.

The doctor turns to me with a smile. "Everything looks great. But I have a surprise for you. We're not listening to one heartbeat."

I frown, not understanding what she means.

She continues. "You're listening to *two* heartbeats. Congratulations, Mom and Dad. Looks like you're having twins."

And then, because I must have a flair for the dramatic, I lean over the table and throw up.

Hi, I'm Drew. Nice to finally meet you. I knocked up your daughter. My bad. But I'm stoked about being her baby daddy. You'll be seeing me around more often.

I wince. Pretty sure that's the exact wrong way to meet Kendall's parents.

As her car splashes through the rainy streets on our way to dinner, I rub my palms on my thighs and mentally rehearse a different approach.

Nice place you've got here. I'm the guy you warned your daughters about. And you were right. But enough about me. Congratulations! You're gonna be grandparents. To twins. Ta-da!

Yeah, no. That's not gonna work either.

Unease spins in my gut because I've never had to meet the parents before under *any* conditions, let alone presenting the fallout from our fuck-monkey activity.

Calling the twins fallout, though, is seriously trivializing how I feel about them. More like, *best thing to happen in my life.*

Next to Kendall.

Guess I'll use my old standby—wing it.

I've been doing that a lot lately.

When we listened to the muffled, rapid *thuh-thump, thuh-thump, thuh-thump* broadcast in the doctor's office a few days ago, the awesome weight of what that means hit me, and I had to use short words to process.

Kendall and I are going to be parents together, very soon, to not just one baby, but two.

To be clear, that's *babies*.

As in *plural*.

This means I am going to be a dad.

To TWO other beings.

Besides my cat.

And even though I still need to meet these babies, they've already stolen my heart. I keep pulling out the ultrasound pictures from my wallet—yeah, the Ninja Turtle one—and imagining hanging with them.

And beating up anyone who looks at them the wrong way.

I'll be honest. Before going to Kendall's appointment, since I can't see the changes in her body—not yet, at least—and I can't feel her nausea or fatigue, her being pregnant didn't feel real. More akin to something we talked about and might do someday that doesn't require real or immediate plans.

Like taking an air balloon ride over France or buying a parrot.

But seeing the grainy black and white images and hearing their heartbeats brought it home: we're gonna meet these little guys—or girls—soon.

Whether we're ready or not.

Do I need to put them on a waiting list for kindergarten already?

As I glance at KK steering her car, a pang of tenderness hits me, and I reach out and trace her jaw. She smiles against my palm, her eyes still on the road. I don't care if I'm being sappy.

She's precious cargo, and she's carrying precious cargo. It's my job to make sure she's safe and comfortable.

But beyond keeping Kendall physically safe, what does she want to do about our relationship? Does she want something more?

With me?

I'll have to talk to her about that soon. I stifle a chuckle. At least I know *something more* includes the green light on just about all the sex acts we could dream up per Dr. Michaels. That was a fun conversation.

If, hypothetically speaking, I were to bend Kendall over a couch before her belly gets too big—not a couch with a hard wooden side, but one with a blue upholstered edge—and have sexual intercourse at this angle (I demonstrated), *should I use an extra pillow here* (I demonstrated) *or will that get in the way?*

Not that I've thought about that specifically or anything.

If I give her—I mean if she were to have—too many orgasms, will she go into labor early?

Can the twins taste lube?

Do I have to tap out at a maximum number of inches of penetration or can she get the whole nine?

Okay, I may have exaggerated a tiny bit on that last one just to see how Dr. Michaels would react. The answers to all of the above were no. She told us all sex was on the table as long as it feels good.

That's my plan.

Feeling good on the table, on the bed, on the floor...

But I had to ask, *Is anal sex okay?*

Kendall stifled a laugh, because duh, anal is *more than okay.*

Anal made these tykes.

The doctor didn't blink at that last question either. "All sex is fine unless contraindicated, and you have no reason to limit it now. And in fact, Kendall's sex drive will likely increase in the second trimester."

She told us this while KK was wearing no panties and had her legs spread on that exam table.

And now I'm thinking about KK wearing no panties and her legs spread—

The hot woman in question interrupts my thoughts by stopping the car at a charming Portland bungalow landscaped with classic rhododendrons and roses that will be gorgeous come summer. She turns off the car. "You ready?"

"Of course," I say hoarsely. I clear my throat. "Totally."

I'll stick with 'nice to meet you' and a firm handshake.

We walk up the brick path, and Kendall's mother opens the door wearing a long, loose skirt and a fuzzy sweater. Her face has the same fine features as Kendall's, with a gentleness around her eyes showing she's spent a lot of time smiling. I like her immediately.

"Drew! So nice to finally meet you. I'm Karen Greer." She shakes my hand, her left one covering our clasped hands. The gesture feels warm and inviting. "So pleased you could join us tonight." When we step inside, the house welcomes us and smells like something wonderful for dinner.

"Nice to meet you too," I say, relieved my voice comes out strong. "Kendall's talked so much about you."

Her dad rises from his chair and strides toward us, a tall, slim man with a compassionate face, wearing a sweater and cords. Meanwhile, Karen turns and has some sort of psychic communication with Kendall in the foyer that consists of widening her eyes and gesturing toward me with her shoulder. Kendall's cheeks flush, and she shrugs.

I choose to ignore whatever is going on between them and focus on Mr. Greer.

He extends his hand, and I shake it. "Great to meet the man our daughter is dating. I'm Tom. Welcome."

"Thanks. She's pretty great."

I breathe out a sigh of relief.

Now to see how they handle the big news.

"Dinner's almost ready," Karen says. "Come in and make yourself comfortable."

Tom takes my coat and Kendall's. "Your endorsement's helped our girl tremendously. I hear business is booming, kiddo."

Kendall looks adorably uncomfortable at the praise. He puts our coats in a closet, gives her a hug, and leads us into the living room. KK and I share a couch while her parents take seats in cushy easy chairs. A fire flickers in the hearth to ward against the late winter chill. With framed photos of Kendall and presumably her sister, this room feels so much better than any part of my parents' house, I'm tempted to move in.

I address her father. "I'm glad the promo video worked well."

"Not only did it get her more business, it ended up being an excellent way to handle your incarceration," Karen says, as if this were no big deal.

Kendall's voice rises an octave. "Mom! What?"

I gulp. *Shit*. I'd forgotten about that.

Add "got your daughter arrested" to the list of uncomfortable topics for the first meeting with the parents.

Her mom's face remains neutral and her voice nonchalant. "Oh, we saw the article."

I turn to KK. "Your parents knew about that?"

"First I heard about it," she mutters.

"We use the internet, dear. I even have a Google alert set up for you."

"Oh my God." Kendall lifts her hand to her forehead and shakes her head, trying to hide.

"We found it to be an interesting article. Although since the retraction from the writer came so soon, we decided it wasn't real news and didn't call you about it."

"It really was all a big misunderstanding," I say. "Ken did nothing wrong. I made a mistake on the address, and we got snowed in."

Thankfully, her dad looks amused. "We figured there was some story behind it. There's no way our Kendall would need to do any breaking and entering."

I shake my head. "Definitely not."

"Maybe it will be something you can laugh about when you're older. I mean, I could tell you some stories from college—"

"Dad!"

"Sorry, pumpkin." Her dad doesn't look sorry at all.

Now I want to hear his stories.

Kendall lets out a sigh. "Actually, our trip to Mount Hood ended up being fun. Drew's gran sent up plenty of food and there was a fireplace, so we were comfortable. And it ended up being a mini-vacation. I couldn't work because we had no cell-phone service or electricity, and the roads weren't plowed so we couldn't go anywhere. It forced me to relax." Kendall's face reddens just a touch, and I can tell what she's thinking—that we spent that time *relaxing* in a very nekkid way.

"You didn't have electricity?" Her mom wrinkles her brow in concern, but I can't help but admire her. She's so different than my mom both in being an actual human who shows concern and not fighting her wrinkles with Botox. If Kendall grows up to be like her, I'll be a happy man.

Not that I'm getting ahead of myself at all.

I've been getting ahead of myself a lot recently.

"We had to rough it up there. But Drew came through." Her pat on my knee means everything.

What do her parents think about PDA? Because right now I want to kiss her. Instead, I just shrug. "We had to make do."

Karen's expression morphs into a smile. "While I was worried, all's well that ends well, I suppose." Then she clucks at Kendall. "Though you could stand to be snowed in again if it would give you more time to relax. You work such long hours, honey."

"I know, Mom, but I need to take advantage of this momentum. My business is finally taking off, and Tristan and I have busted our asses to—"

"And we're proud of that," her dad interrupts. "But don't forget to take care of your health."

"I know, Dad. I learned from your example. I eat right and exercise. Just because things are a little busy right now doesn't mean my life is always going to be that way..." I can tell what she's thinking. Her life is going to change drastically by summer.

"Still, pumpkin, we worry. I don't want you to have to suffer with those headaches anymore." Her dad turns to me. "After my heart attack, I had to prioritize what really mattered."

Karen nods. "It makes a difference. Honestly." She presses her lips together. "Doesn't Tristan see how hard you're working?"

"We're partners, Mom. I have to pull my weight."

I clench my teeth at Tristan's name and 'partners,' and my muscles tighten. No matter what Kendall says, I'm not sure I'll ever like the guy. It's hard to when he's the one spending twelve hours a day with my girlfriend. Is it wrong that I want to be the one she thinks of when she says 'partner'?

You *have a female assistant, douchewad. Is it possible you're being a hypocrite?*

I frown, feeling like a turd.

"Still, he should be looking out for you." Her mom tilts her head thoughtfully. "I always thought he had a thing for you, and you'd think he'd take better care of you—"

"Mom. *No*. We're *just* friends. We've always been friends."

"Close friends," I mutter, more irritated than I have a right to be.

Kendall whips her head to me and reaches out her hand to give mine a squeeze. "Drew, it's not like that. I promise."

A timer goes off in the kitchen, sparing me from spilling my guts and confessing that her relationship with Tristan is turning me into a lunatic.

"Ready to eat?" her mom asks. She gets up, but Kendall stays put.

"Um, can we hold off on dinner for a moment? I have something I need to talk to you about, and I'd rather not wait."

"Sure, honey." A puzzled look passes on Karen's face. She goes in the kitchen, turns off the timer, and returns.

Meanwhile, Kendall takes a few deep breaths.

"Want me to tell them?" I murmur in her ear.

She shakes her head no and leans forward in her seat. As she does so, PR Kendall emerges poised, in control, and unemotional.

Her parents gaze at her with expectant eyes.

"It's okay," I whisper, and reach out to squeeze her hand.

"I'm pregnant."

A sharp intake of breath.

A pause.

The words hang in the air like vapor trails from a plane for everyone to see.

And I can tell Kendall wants to take them back.

But then the room falls into uproar. Kendall's mom rises and gives her a fierce hug. "I can't believe it! I'm going to be a grandma again. Now Janie will have a cousin. I'm so happy! Congratulations!"

Her dad's eyes get misty, and he daubs them with his sleeve. "Never thought I'd see a grandchild again so soon.

Congratulations." He gives her a hug and reaches over to shake my hand.

"Actually, two grandchildren," Kendall says. "Twins." She digs in her purse and pulls out the ultrasound pictures.

While I adore those ultrasound pictures, the captions say Baby Greer A and Baby Greer B.

I want the photos to say Baby Merritt A and Baby Merritt B.

Caveman thinking at its best, I suppose. But I can't help wanting everyone to know they're mine. I'm proud as fuck.

The screech from her mom deafens us. "Twins? You're having twin babies? Now I know you didn't need that tantric sex retreat after all."

I burst out laughing. "Tantric sex retreat?"

"You don't wanna know," Kendall whispers, but she's got a smile on her face and relief in her eyes.

She told them. They didn't freak. In fact, they're excited.

My gut tightens when I think about my own parents.

I'd give anything to have them react like this. Because I know, without a doubt, that they won't be pleased.

Her mom finally lets go of Kendall, and sits down to examine the pictures. "When did you find out?"

"A little while ago. But I went to the doctor this week."

"Tell me everything! Where were you when you realized you were pregnant?"

"Tristan figured it out, actually."

Of course. I cross my arms in front of my chest, a hot spear of jealousy tearing through me.

Karen's eyes widen. "You mean Tristan knew. Before Drew? But"—she pauses to look at me and then back to her daughter—"Drew's the father, right?"

"Yes, Mom."

"Yeah. You telling him first doesn't bother me at all," I mutter, not able to rein in my mouth.

Kendall turns to me. "I'm sorry it happened that way, but it wasn't intentional. He just figured it out before me."

My words slip out before I can pull them back. "Because you see him more than me. He's not planning to name our kids too while he's at it, is he?"

I mean it as a joke, but it doesn't come out that way.

What the fuck is my problem?

"I don't understand why you're jealous of Tristan. He's *just* a friend." She must see something in my eyes because she threads her fingers through mine. "I swear." Kendall's expression is insistent and sincere, and the knot around my heart loosens just a little.

But not too much. Tristan's still on my shit list.

I rub my face with my other hand, all at once understanding how much is on the line here.

Ever since I heard and saw those babies, on the screen, pulsing with life, I realized that not only do I want a family, but I want *this* family. With Kendall.

If she'll have me.

"So does that mean you two are considering tying the knot?" her dad asks. "Drew, are you planning to marry my daughter?"

I freeze, my heart hammering in my goddamn throat.

Fuck. Why didn't I plan for him to ask this?

But before I can react, Karen tuts. "Don't pressure them, Tom. Let them handle one thing at a time."

Kendall clears her throat. "Exactly," she says quietly, her eyes darting away. "We're just talking about babies here. No one says we have to get married."

My body feels heavy all of a sudden.

Is marriage not in Kendall's vocabulary? Because when we were in the doctor's office, I almost dropped down on one knee and proposed to her right then and there. I thought of it when I handed the receptionist my credit card to pay for her visit and told myself if I married her, she'd get better health insurance with my company.

But I was lying to myself.

I want to marry her because I'm in love with her.

I want to marry her, and I knew it before the health insurance issue came up. I just want her. Babies or no babies, I'd want forever with her, and I've been a jackass to not see it sooner.

For years, she's been under my skin, and since we've drawn a truce, I can't get her out of my head. Nor do I want to.

This pregnancy has forced me to think about a lot of things. Like what I want in life and who I want to spend my life with.

Her. I want her.

She brings out the best in me. She makes me want to step up and be the dad I never had.

But moreover, she makes me want to be her lover. Her husband.

Fuck, I love her so much it hurts to think that she probably doesn't feel the same.

But I don't want to scare her away. So if keeping this relationship in dating mode will do that, I'm down.

Even if it kills me inside.

With a few more hugs on all sides, we head into the dining room and eat Karen and Tom's delicious meal. We talk about the babies and our jobs. Her parents want to know about mine, and I show them Detention's Instagram page.

Thankfully they laugh.

Karen asks, "When can we meet your parents, Drew?"

The thought of these kind people meeting my immediate family makes my skin crawl. "I don't know, but I'll have to set it up."

"We'd like that. And we'd like to have them over as well."

Like that will work.

"Sure," I say, trying not to wince. "I'll ask."

When we're in the car headed back to Kendall's apartment, I try to look for the silver lining today.

"Your parents took that really well. I shouldn't be surprised. They made someone like you."

"That's a nice thing to say."

"I mean it. They're awesome. Not like..." I trail off, not wanting to finish my sentence, but she picks up on my meaning.

"When are you going to tell your parents?" she asks softly.

I scrub my hands over my face. "I've called a few times, but they haven't been around, and I don't want to leave a voicemail message."

Her sigh kinda kills me. It feels like I'm disappointing her. And I hate that.

"I'd like to meet them," she whispers as she stares out the window.

"Yeah." I twist my watch. "I'll work on that."

A hot, sick feeling washes over me.

Shame.

And guilt.

Because as much as I want my family to be warm and welcoming to this incredible woman and our twins, I can't imagine any scenario where that's even a remote possibility.

She sits back in her seat. "Drew, I want to know you. I feel I've brought you into my world—you know all about me. You've been to my work, now you've met my parents. You've met my friends. But I don't know your life at all."

Her sad eyes stab me in the gut.

"Is that really how you feel?"

The silence says everything she doesn't.

"Fuck, Ken. I've let you in... I've let you in more than any person ever." I shake my head, wanting her to understand. "Look, my family isn't like yours. They're not going to pat me on the back or congratulate us." I'm at a loss for how to describe the emotional wasteland of the Merritt household. "But I don't give a shit what they think. You're the only thing that matters, and *you* know more about me, the real me, than anyone."

Because it's Portland, rain beats down on the car out of nowhere. But it feels portentous somehow, the steady drumbeat surrounding us reducing the scope of the world to this woman next to me. The one who doesn't seem to know what she means to me.

We're quiet for a long time, just the sound of the tires and windshield wipers and rain.

"I'm sorry," she whispers. "You're right. I guess I don't understand, but that's kind of my point. I *want* to understand." When we reach a light, she turns to the side, addressing the windshield. "This is still new. Even though we've been acquaintances for years, we still don't know a lot about each other. Maybe we need to figure out what our relationship means to each other."

"Maybe." I know I don't sound convinced.

I'd tell her what our relationship means to me in a heartbeat, but based on her quick dismissal of marriage earlier this evening, I'm so off base about her feelings, I'm not even on the map.

Cringing internally, I imagine how she'd react if I proposed. She'd turn me down like a bedspread. And I'd embarrass the hell out of her.

I don't want to pressure her into saying something she doesn't mean.

Or a relationship she doesn't want down deep.

Can't say I blame her. Why would she want to marry the Merritt family fuck-up?

31

DREW

I pause before entering Chez Pierre, a French restaurant where I'm meeting my parents for lunch, and stare at the Cartier jewelry store next door. While I've never had a reason to shop there before, the window display catches my eye, the pinpoint lighting making the diamonds sparkle like, uh, diamonds.

I'm a fucking poet, okay?

But no matter their brilliance, someone whose name starts with *Kendall* apparently doesn't want one from me.

I've spent the past week replaying our conversation with her parents, analyzing it from every angle, and trying to figure out if there are any chinks in her no-matrimony armor.

It seemed bigger than an offhand remark, which makes sense for someone as fiercely independent as Kendall. She genuinely does not want to marry anyone.

Especially not me.

I mean, that's cool. No big deal. We don't have to get married.

Doesn't mean I want another bastard to touch her.

I can be patient. Maybe she'll change her mind. Because the

alternative—her not being in my life—is too excruciating to contemplate.

Maybe my parents won't respond to my news in their typically caustic and soulless ways.

I look up at the sky. Without a sign of the apocalypse, I realize I should temper my expectations. I'm tempted to put off this conversation, but I promised Kendall I'd talk to them.

Deep down, I know I'm a fool for hoping they'll share in my excitement.

A shimmer from the storefront draws my attention back to rings, and just like that, my focus is clear. I'm doing this for Kendall and our babies, not for my parents. If they decide to be dicks, it's on them.

I smile at the thought of what the future might hold with Kendall. At the possibilities.

I might have to come back and pick out something in the size *humongo diamond* just in case I grow the balls to ask her.

When I step into the adjacent restaurant, a huge floral arrangement, a long polished brass and wood bar, and an expanse of black and white tile greet me. The place has been transported straight out of Paris, chock full of shit my mother likes. I'm hoping a Niçoise salad will soften her up.

Because what I have to say won't.

The host seats me at a table in the middle of the busy room, which bustles with patrons and servers. He hands me a wine list. I order a club soda from the guy who drops off the bread—not that any of us will touch it—and tap my fingers on the table.

A few minutes later, my parents arrive. I stand and kiss my mother's cheek, then shake my father's hand. He's in a business suit, and she's wearing a tweed skirt suit. Both of their expressions are wary. I suppose that's to be expected since I've never asked them to lunch before.

256 | LEX MARTIN & LESLIE MCADAM

After they order drinks, my father turns to me. "Well, how does it feel to be majority owner of the MerrittCo?"

"Great, actually. I've been looking into getting a new board of directors who will modernize our practices. I'd like to use US manufacturing and avoid FOC merchant ships."

Contrary to what my parents believe, I plan to make the most of the opportunity.

My mother sips her water. "Why would you want to do that?"

"It's a chance for us to be leaders. Consider how much of our shit is sent here using flags-of-convenience." That's a way for shipowners to register their merchant ships in Panama or Liberia, thereby using substandard regulations. Ever since Frankie told me about it, I've made sure none of Detention's products are transported that way.

My father exhales with an exasperated sigh. "The cost increase is going to be unsustainable."

"Human rights violations matter more than costs. So does environmental protection. It's the right thing to do."

My mother sniffs. "Really, Andrew. Do we need to discuss such things at the table?"

I should know better than to tell my parents what I really think. My father looks at me as if I have lobsters crawling out of my ears. "Your idealism is no way to run a business." His voice lowers. "You're going to run this company into the ground."

"No. I'm aiming for long-term sustainability. I want to make sure MerrittCo is rebuilt on sound footing. Like my T-shirt company—"

"Well, well, if it isn't Demerit." A familiar saucy voice wafting over my shoulder makes my gut churn.

I twist around.

This is bad.

I've been with the busty waitress in the biblical sense, but I don't remember her name. I internally shake my head. No matter what I do, I can't seem to get away from my past. *Fuck.*

And Kendall wonders why I don't want to introduce her to more of my friends.

Because they can list all of my drunken mistakes, point out the women I've hooked up with, and show her the commemorative pics.

No-fucking–thank you.

My mother shifts her soul-piercing stare slowly from the waitress to me and back again.

"Hey. Nice to see you," I choke out.

"It's been a while." The waitress reaches out and touches my sleeve, and I do my best not to jerk my hand back. Dammit. "Maybe we can *catch up* tonight if you have time."

"I'm pretty busy," I say. "Sorry."

Her face falls, and I don't mean to make her feel bad, but Kendall's the only one for me. If I could just establish a perimeter around us keeping the outside world and former hookups away, that would be great.

My parents and I order lunch. Thankfully, after the waitress leaves, we change the subject, and make chitchat, mostly about my mother's upcoming spring fashion show. When the food is set down, my mom asks, "Andrew, I suppose there was a reason you wanted to meet with us? Or did you merely intend to lecture us about your liberal causes?"

I'm not taking the bait.

"I wanted you to know I'm dating someone."

My mother rolls her eyes. "Who? The waitress?"

"No. I don't know who that is."

"Honestly, Andrew."

"I've changed. I have a new girlfriend, and it's serious."

She takes a delicate bite of her salad. "I'll believe that when I see it. If the magazines are to be believed, you go through women faster than—"

The waitress picks that moment to materialize at the table again. "How is everything?" she asks, bending over to give me a front row seat to her cleavage.

I cough, looking away.

"The baby potatoes are divine," my mom coos at her plate, smiling until she glances up and undoubtedly sees boobage.

"Wonderful." The waitress bats her eyes at me and drops her hand on my arm. "Hope to see you around, Drew." And to my horror, she slips a note under my glass, which I'm sure has her number on it.

For fuck's sake.

Clucking, my mom shakes her head. "Is this typical behavior, Andrew?"

"What?"

"That woman gave you her number and practically offered her *services*. But apparently you're dating someone. Why do I find it hard to believe you've changed?"

I open my mouth, but my father interrupts. "You're not ready to settle down."

"I've been making a lot of changes, and I have a great girl-friend. I think you guys should know that she's the one. Her name is Kendall."

My mother's face screws up like she's eaten a lemon. "Who are her parents?"

"They're wonderful people." Warm. Welcoming. The opposite of the vampires in front of me.

The look on my mother's face tells me that *nice people* isn't enough. They need to be listed on Forbes' Top 500.

"Have Pearl pencil in a brunch one weekend next month so we can meet her. If you're still dating then."

I don't miss the dis. "Sure. But you need to know something first."

Swallowing past the dry lump in my throat, I brace myself for impact.

Both of my parents set down their silverware and give me their full attention. I can tell by the expression on my mother's face that she's drawn the correct conclusion.

"Oh, Andrew. *No.*" One wrinkle between her eyes dares to make an appearance.

"No, what?" Maybe I'm wrong.

"You got that woman pregnant, didn't you?"

Of course she figured it out. There's really no other reason for me to have lunch with my parents. But maybe I can salvage this conversation.

"She's not 'that woman.' I'm in love with her." I'm so fucking crazy about Kendall, I can't see straight, and I don't give a shit my parents look like they're gonna flip out.

I clear my throat. "And, yes, she's going to have my children."
Two for now. Hopefully more later.

I rub my face, unprepared for the truth bombs my subconscious is laying out for me right now.

My mother laughs coldly, derision oozing from her. "Are you going to make her take a paternity test?"

"No. I trust her. We're serious."

You don't get more serious than having twins together.

"You're 'serious' about a woman? You have the nerve to say that ten minutes after you were propositioned by a waitress?" She stiffens like a starched napkin and snarls, "How could you be so careless?"

"Was this planned?" my father asks.

I shake my head. "No. But I think—"

"You never think. What about your inheritance? Now it's going to—" My mother is getting worked up.

I aim for a soothing voice, even though my insides are boiling over. "What better place for the money to go than my children? *Your grandchildren?*"

She rummages through her purse. Looking for meds. Smelling salts. A hand grenade to lob my way. "Children with someone we've never heard of. From some no-name family." She sniffs. "Andrew, we can trace our family tree all the way back to the Mayflower. Can this woman say the same thing about her lineage?"

Christ, she's a fucking snob. "Who cares where her family came from? Listen to yourselves." I crumple my napkin in a fist. "Kendall's the best thing that's ever happened to me."

"Hardly. She's likely some whore you found." Her eyes narrow. "You should demand she sign a prenup or pay her to terminate the pregnancy. Those are the only two viable options here."

That's it.

The screech from my chair as I stand makes every head in the restaurant turn toward us.

Like I give a shit. Let the whole world watch.

Facing my parents, I toss my napkin on the table. "I tried to include you in my life. In your grandchildren's lives. But you two are *assholes*. Maybe it's better if they never meet you after all."

My mother clutches her pearls. Good. Fuck her.

"I don't need your approval." I growl. "And Kendall doesn't deserve your hatred or snobbery. She's amazing. Don't ever say one more fucking thing about her."

Turning on my heel, I storm out.

When I get to my car, I slam the door and dial Kendall.

Before, I would have called Josh or my Bee. But I want her to be my someone.

While I need to protect her from my parents, she'll put this in perspective for me. Maybe she'll know how to smooth things over some day.

She should know how awful they are.

A deep male voice answers.

I look down at the phone to make sure I dialed the right number.

"Is Kendall there?" I ask.

"No, sorry, Drew. She's with a client. This is Tristan."

"Hey." Why the fuck did he pick up?

"Sorry, I meant to mute her phone and accidentally answered it."

Fuck. Him answering is *not* what I need today. There's a reason why this guy gets to me. She spends every waking hour with him. They work together—I get it. But I don't like it.

I let out my breath, feeling unreasonably deflated. "Okay. Just tell her I called."

Later, she texts me that she's working through dinner.

So when Ian messages, wanting to grab dinner, I agree. It's better than sitting alone in my condo, wishing I could hang with Kendall, who has better things to do than sort through my bullshit problems.

Ian and I meet in a bar. Of course, I don't drink, but that doesn't stop him from wanting to throw back a few.

I watch him, missing the way I used to drink to oblivion. Because I wish I could erase this entire day.

But I know I can't deal with life like that anymore. I have too much on the line.

"You really are a teetotaler now, huh?" he asks, while taking a slug of his gin and tonic. He's dressed in a Brooks Bros Oxford shirt, khakis, and loafers with no socks. Even though he's classic East Coast preppy, he's always hung with me, maybe because I was the bad boy he needed in his life.

But I'm not one anymore. I do my best to explain it to him, but he slaps me on the back.

"You don't have to be so gloomy about it, though," he says. "If you don't loosen up, you're gonna die of boredom."

"Fuck off. Just because I'm being responsible doesn't mean I'm boring." And I mean that. While it gets old when my 'friends' needle me, I know I'm stronger than that.

He raises his eyebrows like, *Wanna bet?*

Clearly, I need better friends.

"You could try supporting me," I point out. "Kendall's pregnant."

"For real?"

"Like I would joke about something like that?"

He clinks his glass to my club soda. "Well, congrats, Daddy-O. Now you've got a whole slew of things to be responsible about. You sure you don't want something stronger?" His whole face contorts in a grimace. "I'd be drowning myself in booze if I had to think about all the things that could go wrong with a pregnancy."

With the club soda halfway to my mouth, I freeze as the hairs on my arms stick straight up.

"What are you talking about?"

"Pregnancy is some scary shit. When my sister got knocked up, my brother-in-law lost his mind researching all of the things that can go wrong. You start reading on the internet, and I swear you begin feeling the symptoms. Even though you're a guy."

Just when I think I've got everything all figured out, now I have another set of things to worry about.

As he talks to me about pregnancy-induced hypertension, gestational diabetes, and all sorts of other shit that makes my balls crawl up into my body, I start to think if I make it through this pregnancy, I should get a medal.

And Kendall should receive the Nobel Prize.

32

KENDALL

FIVE AND A HALF MONTHS LATER

A moan wakes me.

It's low. Deep. Like someone is in pain.

That would be me.

My eyes spring open on a gasp when one of the twins kicks me again.

Jesus fu—

Drew storms into my bedroom. His hair is sticking straight up, and his clothes are rumpled.

"Ken, you okay?" He kneels by my side of the bed and brushes sweat off my forehead.

"Not really."

It's an honest answer. I'm not fucking okay.

Exhaustion lines Drew's face, and I stare up at him, frustrated that I feel so helpless right now. Frustrated that I can't roll over without first hoisting my belly with both hands.

"Sorry you're not feeling well, baby," he whispers, helping me to sit up.

Because I can't sit up on my own.

The indignity of pregnancy.

Being thirty-five weeks pregnant with twins is no joke. I

barely fit behind the steering wheel of my car when I have the seat cranked all the way back.

Drew hugs me to his broad chest, and my ribs squeeze painfully with emotion.

How can he be so sweet with me but sleep on the couch almost every night?

Sometimes he even goes home. He says my bed is too soft, and he can't fall asleep.

I want to call bullshit, but it's eight in the morning, and I'm so tired, I can barely move.

Heat stings my eyes. Not from the pain radiating from my pelvis, but from whatever is happening between me and Drew.

He kisses my temple. The bridge of my nose. My lips.

More tears fall.

This is also a dilemma. I can't watch a damn Hallmark commercial and not cry. Where have my nerves of steel gone? Why can't I handle life the way I used to?

"I have morning breath." I turn my face away, choked up by his careful touch and tender tone of voice.

"You know I don't care about that." Gently, his thumbs dab away the wetness on my cheeks. "Sorry this has been such a tough pregnancy, but you're almost at the finish line. Wish there was more I could do to help, though." His bear paw rubs a gentle circle over my belly. "What was it this time? Did they jab your kidney again?"

"My cervix. I swear one of them wants to break a foot through my uterus. It reminds me of *Aliens*." I chuckle and wipe my eyes. "Except instead of busting out of my chest, they crawl out of the hidey hole like little commandos going AWOL." I mean it as a joke, but he shudders, his eyes wide. "I'm kidding." Obviously. But he still looks a tad green.

After a moment, his left eyebrow hikes up. "Wanna kick me in the balls to make it even?"

I laugh because he's ridiculous, and I love him even though he makes me so nuts sometimes I could scream.

He smiles back at me, and I open my mouth to say something, to ask him what's going on, to ask him what's changed, when the front buzzer rings, jolting us apart.

Two minutes later, he strides in with a plate of fresh fruit, croissants, and orange juice, which he sets down next to me.

"From that bakery you like. They deliver."

"Thank you. That was thoughtful."

He ignores the compliment and tugs on a hoodie. "I have a meeting in half an hour. I gotta jet. Will you be okay?"

I nod, wondering if I'm making up things in my head. Drew treats me well. Really well. *Then why do I feel like something is missing? Like he doesn't want me* like that *anymore?*

"Do you have time to meet up for lunch later?" I ask hesitantly. I'll have to move around my whole schedule this afternoon, but I want to get to the bottom of this. We've been dancing around this issue long enough.

"Probably not. I'm scouting that second warehouse today. How about dinner?"

"I'm prepping the marketing materials for the new boutique on Nob Hill."

"What about dinner tomorrow?"

"Can't. Tristan and I have an event at Waterfront Park."

He runs his hands through his hair, looking suddenly annoyed. "Please tell me it's indoors and you won't be standing in the rain all evening."

"It's at that mansion. I'll be fine." If I'm being honest, the thought of having to do *anything* this week but sleep makes me want to crawl into the closet. But I'm about to take three months off for maternity leave, and I need to make sure everything's in order first.

He nods. "Okay, well, I guess I'll see you soon."

My shoulders deflate when I realize we're *this close* to having the twins, and I'm not sure when I'll see Drew.

"The shower," I blurt out. "It's Saturday. Don't forget."

A frown tugs at his brows. "I'd never forget that." He rubs the back of his neck. "Tell Tristan when you need a break and be sure to take it."

Leaning over, he kisses me briskly on the forehead and walks out.

As if I have to ask Tristan for permission. Please.

I sigh and listen to the front door close behind him.

We've had this argument before. He thinks I work too much. I think he can go fly a kite.

That's the easy argument.

The tough one? The one I can't bring myself to say out loud?

I want to ask why he won't sleep with me anymore.

But I'm afraid I already know the answer.

33

KENDALL

"*D*on't you think that's odd?" I whisper into the phone. "Don't you think this is more than a 'dry spell?'"

It pains me to have to discuss my sex life with Brooke, but she's gone through pregnancy before.

A long pause greets me on the other end before my sister says anything. "Mark and I didn't have sex after the first trimester. He told me he felt like a deviant fucking the mother of his children, especially once he could feel the baby move."

I'm locked in the bathroom like a weirdo, whispering to my sister when I should be getting ready for my baby shower.

As much as I hate to admit it, she's making a lot of sense.

"But everything went back to normal afterward?" I push my damp hair off my face and grip the towel around my torso. "Please tell me you boinked like bunnies after you had Janie."

"You mean while I was juggling diaper duty and midnight feedings and nipples that were sore from being gnawed on all day? Sure."

"You're supposed to give me a pep talk. Not make me want to throw myself off the ledge."

"I won't sugarcoat it, Kendall. You wanted the truth, and I gave you an honest answer. Drew probably doesn't see you as a sexual object right now, and I'm guessing it's unlikely he will for a while after you give birth. Let him jerk off. Who cares?"

I care. I miss that intimacy with him, and if I have to go the last four weeks of the pregnancy in this state of limbo, I'll go postal.

"Now, don't get upset." She pauses again. "But maybe he's waiting until the babies arrive to break up."

Dragonfire heartburn tears through my esophagus, making my eyes sting. Or maybe I'm already crying. It's hard to tell.

My sister rambles on like she's not drilling nails into my soul. "Did he ask you to move in?"

"Yes, a few months ago, but I told him no."

At the time I thought we needed to be a normal couple and ease into this, not merge our lives at lightning speed. I'm the first significant relationship he's had, and I wanted us to take our time. Which is why I told my parents I didn't want to get married —because I didn't want Drew to feel pressured.

Only we've both been so busy, it's been a challenge to do anything "normal" like date. Case in point—I barely saw him this week despite how much I wanted to have a heart-to-heart with him.

"Did that upset him? You turning him down?"

I bite my lip. "He seemed fine. Like it was no big deal."

She hums in my ear. "Maybe it's good that you kept your place. If this relationship doesn't work out, at least you won't be homeless."

My knees get wobbly, and I lean against the bathroom vanity. "I gotta go," I croak into the phone. "Don't say anything about this to anyone."

"I'll see you at the shower. I'm excited it's at Josh and Evie's! Do you think I can get them to donate to the ballet?"

I roll my eyes. "Bye."

The knock on the bathroom door makes me flinch, and I re-tuck my towel around my melon-sized boobs.

"Babe. You doing okay?" Drew's laidback voice instantly calms me. *That's not how someone who wants to break up talks to you, right?* "Can I help with anything? We need to leave in fifteen minutes."

"I'm okay." Mostly. "Could you grab me a ginger ale for the car?"

"Sure thing. Lemme know if you need help getting dressed."

I gaze at the locked door in the mirror until his footfalls tell me he's walked away.

I won't ask him for help getting dressed because I can't bear for him to see me like this. Sporting underwear ten times larger than I usually wear. Waddling around like a hot air balloon about to burst. Swollen everywhere and not in a sexy way.

Letting the towel drop, I stare long and hard at myself. At the road map of stretch marks. At the dark line that extends up my belly. At the fur lining my crotch because I can't reach my pelvis to shave.

Do I think birth is miraculous and amazing?

Absolutely.

But I've felt like shit for almost the entire pregnancy thanks to the extra hormones of having a second bun in the oven, so I've been pretty miserable.

Can I blame Drew for not being attracted to this?

Not at all.

I can't lie—what Brooke said has me reeling.

It's possible Drew feels responsible for getting me pregnant and is trying to be a good guy and just see me through it.

Which means he doesn't love me. Not like I love him.

And how can I not love him? He's been here for me every step of the way.

Except being a good boyfriend to the girl he's dating because she's knocked up doesn't mean he wants forever.

It means he's a responsible person. *Not* that he's in love.

He hasn't even introduced me to his parents or his friends. I don't need to ask Brooke her opinion to know she'd say I'm a case study for a *Cosmo* article: *How to tell if he's not that into you.*

Maybe that's why I've waited until the last possible moment to have this baby shower. Why I've devoted every spare second to my job.

Drew might fade out of my life once the babies arrive. Sure, he'll be in their lives, but that doesn't mean he wants me as a part of that equation.

Because my intuition tells me he's being cagey.

At the top of the list of what he's hiding is the very real possibility he doesn't want to be with me anymore.

And I'm not sure what to do about that.

34

KENDALL

*T*he drive to Josh and Evie's condo is quiet. Drew glances at me from time to time, but we don't say anything.

"You don't have to stay if you don't want to." I dig through my purse to grab a mint. "Evie thought a Jack and Jill shower would be cute, but I know guys are never into this sort of thing."

"I don't mind staying. There'll be cake, right?"

He's making a joke, and I force a smile.

He's trying. I can see it in his eyes. But *why* is he trying? Because he wants the mother of his children to be happy so his kids are healthy or because he wants me to be happy?

Drew can't even eat the cake. Damn it. Why didn't I think to get something sugar-free for him too?

"You okay? You've been sighing a lot lately."

Now is not the time to unleash the rant that's been developing in my head since I got off the phone with my sister. I nod and take a sip of my ginger ale. "Just tired."

That's the wrong thing to say because his jaw tightens, and he's quiet again. *He's probably still mad I worked so late this week.*

But then he taps on the steering wheel. "Don't forget that

after the shower, I'm hanging out with Ian. He's only staying with me another night, but then I'll be by your place to help you unpack the shower gifts."

Another one of his bros I haven't met.

I don't say anything, but what's there to say? 'I want to meet your friends, but you never offer?' That sounds desperate.

By the time we reach Josh's condo, all I want to do is crawl into bed and sleep for the next three days, but if we wait any longer to have this shower, my mother is going to go ballistic. She says I'm pushing my luck to wait until I'm almost thirty-six weeks.

Drew parks and then comes around the car to haul me out. Just as I'm standing upright on the street, one of the babies gives me a swift kick to my ribs.

"Fuck me sideways." I press my palm to my belly. Everything in my stomach tightens, and I screw my eyes shut.

"Oh, baby, you okay?" Drew pulls me against him, and I let him embrace me even after the pain in my side subsides.

"Yeah, sorry." I breathe him in. The crisp scent of his body wash. The warmth of his skin. His aftershave. The words are on the tip of my tongue. *I love you. And I want you to love me too.*

I take a step back. "Your kids are going to be soccer players."

His wide smile is so beautiful, it almost brings tears to my eyes. *How long has it been since he's smiled like that?*

"I don't care what they decide to do as long as they're happy and healthy."

I return that smile because my weird head issues are nothing compared to that goal—deliver two babies safe and sound.

He laces his fingers through mine, and for a second I wonder if I've been making an issue where one doesn't exist. I know Drew cares about me. Maybe he'll even love me some day. Granted, this is not how I'd choose to write my own love story, but life—real life—is not a Disney movie. I have the stretch marks to prove it.

We make our way up to Evie's condo, and Tristan opens the door.

"Hey, preggers." He pulls me into a side hug.

Drew gets that weird tic in his jaw.

I default into work mode anyway. "Did you get my email about the Larimer account? You'll need to call her for a one-on-one. I told her I was going on maternity leave, and—"

"Stop working, my little psycho. The job isn't going anywhere." Tristan makes a face at me, and I stick out my tongue.

"Whatever. You'll be crying when I'm not at the office to save your ass."

"Truth."

I turn to tell Drew a story about one of our clients, but he's not there. He's on the other side of the room talking to Josh.

Needing to blink quickly, I find myself getting choked up.

Why do I feel like he just ditched me?

There's no time to wallow, though, because my mom, dad, and Evie run up to me.

After hugging them all, I feel a little more centered. "Thank you so much for putting this together."

I finally get a good look at the decorations.

Delicate Chinese lanterns crisscross the ceiling. A buffet of food sprawls across the back of the room. Dozens of balloons sway above one of Josh's leather recliners.

"That's where the star of the party gets to sit and open all of her gifts," Evie explains as she waves toward a mountain of presents. "And don't worry. Josh says he'll personally recycle the balloons."

We all laugh.

"The girls did everything," my dad confesses. "I just got a head start on the shrimp cocktail."

"This is so beautiful." I'm overwhelmed in the best way. My sister waves at me from across the room, and I wave back. I might not have liked what she had to say on the phone this morning, but perhaps I needed to hear the truth.

She's talking to Drew's grandmother. Aww.

Music swells, and I turn to find a quartet playing *Somewhere Only We Know* in the corner.

"This is too much, guys."

I realize my friends are loaded, but I have a healthy appreciation for what things cost.

"Nonsense," Evie says. "We wanted your shower to be perfect, and every time we go to a cocktail party, you always say how much you love quartets."

"Thank you. This is amazing."

We're hugging it out when a gruff voice behind me makes me turn. "Hey, sunshine. Congratulations."

"Mr. Mills! I can't believe you're at a baby shower!" Evie's dad is like a surrogate father to me.

"I wouldn't miss it for anything." He pats me on the shoulder and motions toward my belly. "You've been busy!"

I chuckle. "Yup. It's hard work percolating my babies, I'll tell ya."

"Where's your man? I gotta give him the hairy eyeball for knocking you up."

I let out a loud bark of laughter, and he cracks a smile. Seriously, though, I know Evie's dad would want to go toe-to-toe with Drew if he ever did me wrong. I give the old guy another grateful hug and tell him to load up on the buffet.

"Hey, who's that over there?" I whisper to Evie.

Motioning toward the beautiful woman with long, black hair and tattoos talking to Drew, I try to tap down my jealousy.

It's obvious they're close. They're chatting with Josh and laughing.

"That's Drew's assistant Frankie. Haven't you met her yet?"

Negative. I have *not* met her. I've spoken to her on the phone a few times, but they were short conversations, and I've only been to his office on the weekends when there was a shell crew working.

That's who he spends all of his time with? She's gorgeous and edgy and confident. Thin. The way I used to be before I got pregnant and too bloated to walk without a waddle and cankles.

I look down at my pumpkin-colored shirt and want to hide under the table. Frustration overwhelms me. Frustration for hating that I'm the size of an economy car. Frustration over hating how I look. Because femininity is awesome and all that, and deep down, I want to embrace the power of my body to procreate, but I'm too close to tears to do it.

"Roh-roh." Evie leans closer to me. "What's going on?"

Taking a deep breath to calm down, I ask her what's really got a burr up my ass today. "Did Drew invite anyone other than his grandmother and assistant to the shower?"

One glance at her face tells me everything I need to know, and in this split second of communication, she understands what I mean by asking.

All of my friends are here. Both of my parents. My sister. My coworkers. Hell, even a few of my best clients showed up.

While my boyfriend invited *two* people.

Even though one of his friends is staying at Drew's this week. And my significant other is one of the most popular guys on Instagram. So *Portland Today* tells me.

And I don't even know if Drew has told his parents that we're dating, much less having twins.

"Josh is here!" Evie points out.

I scoff. "Nice save." Shaking my head, I grab her hand.

276 | LEX MARTIN & LESLIE MCADAM

"Whatever. It is what it is." See, I can be Zen. I'll show Drew how goddamn Zen I can be. "Let's baby-shower the fuck out of today."

Because I am done tiptoeing around this issue with him. We're having that conversation tonight, come hell or high water.

35

DREW

*A*s I take in Josh and Evie's extravagantly decorated home for this special occasion, I'm so fucking relieved the only people here are friends and family Kendall and I genuinely care about and would do anything for—Ken and the buns in her oven, Josh and Evie, my Bee, Frankie, and any and all of Kendall's peeps, since if she cares about them, I care about them.

The only thing that matters is that Kendall's happy.

I'm not sure she is, though.

She's smiling, but there's a heaviness in her eyes. Her grin ramps up when she talks with Evie or Evie's dad, but wanes with everyone else. And she's got a hand on the side of her belly most of the time, since one or both of our little buggers is being particularly kicky.

Part of me wants to go over and talk with her, but I think that's a bad idea. She needs space to enjoy the party without me hovering over her like a drone, even though being physically separate from her in the same room makes me lonely somehow.

Perhaps seeing everyone today is reminding me who's not here.

Of course my parents declined my invitation.

It's probably for the best. I wish they were different, that they'd be the kind of people who'd love this instead of only thinking of how my actions reflect on them.

But that's not gonna happen.

Frankly, I wish they were like Kendall's parents, who are #couplegoals. Seeing where she came from makes me want to shield her from ever experiencing the dysfunction of my family, though, so I didn't insist they come.

I'm even more grateful I don't have to deal with any of my asshole "friends." Our baby shower shouldn't be a welcome place for anyone I've ever gotten high with. While I've tried for months to stay away from my old crew, it's hard. A few won't go away—like Ian, who showed up in town yesterday and wanted to crash. Fine, dude, but no invite to this event. It's too special.

By spending time with Kendall, I've felt in my bones—not to mention my liver—how far I've come from the days of drowning my nights in alcohol. I used to not care, but now I cringe every time I see any of my old pictures. While my hashtags sell clothes, the online life is exhausting bullshit, and I pay as little attention to it as possible outside of business.

That's why I'm careful about not taking pictures with Kendall beyond that one post to credit her for our campaign. I've said nothing publicly about being a dad, and I'm not making any comments about being the designated driver for the rest of my life. People can believe whatever they want about me, because it only matters that the closest people around me know my real life.

Taking a sip of sparkling water, I tune back into Josh.

"Dude, I'm sorry," he says. "Your parents are twats."

"You know as well as I do there's no way to get them to be decent humans."

As much as I wish they would be.

Josh pushes his glasses up his nose. "You'd think that even if they didn't like the circumstances of the pregnancy, they'd still like the babies, though. Most people like babies."

"They're not most people."

"Dude," is all he says, but I know he gets it. That I could defend Kendall with all the breath in my lungs and my mother would still be harping about money and inheritance and shit I don't care about.

But I can think of no one better it can go to than my children.

My children, who I already love so much it makes my chest hurt.

Looking around, I can imagine a wedding with Kendall being just like this—only close friends, only mattering to us.

If she wanted to get married.

I haven't brought it up since she soundly turned down the idea at her parents' house, and given her immediate rejection of moving in with me, it feels like we're so precarious. She's uncomfortably pregnant. She spends all her time at work with Tristan—cue my jealousy—and apparently hasn't a clue how much I love her.

And I'm not sure I should tell her. If that's what she'd want to hear or if it would send her running in the opposite direction.

We have moments where everything feels good. When she's in my arms, smelling so sweet, feeling so right. Other times, though, she's distant and withdrawn, and I don't know what to do.

Is that pregnancy? Is she so uncomfortable physically right now and I'm misinterpreting it?

One thing is certain, I wish like hell I had some experience with a serious relationship. That I understood women better. How to say the right things to reassure her.

Because clearly I don't.

I glance over at her across the room as music from the quartet fills the air. Kendall has never looked more beautiful. She perches on her throne, hands cradling her belly, like a tiny red-headed queen surrounded by presents from her citizens.

My phone buzzes with a text from Ian. I'm glad his flight is early tomorrow morning. He reminds me too much of who I used to be. Who I'm not anymore. Who I don't want Kendall to ever see.

Gonna order pizza for me and the guys. You be back in time?

Nah, I respond. I want to stay here as long as I can.

"Thanks for doing this," I say to Josh. "You guys really went all out."

"It's not often our best friends are having a baby. Or two. I'm proud of you, D-bag. You've finally got your life in order. You gonna stop with the twins or try for more kids?"

The idea warms my heart, but I can't dream about that right now, because everything is unsettled with Kendall.

Also, let's just say the sex has died down. Blame that one on some unfortunate Google search results I conducted after hanging out with Ian. I internally shudder.

"Earth to Drew," Josh says, waving his hand in my face.

"Sorry. Yeah." My voice sounds creaky. "I want more kids. But let's get her *safely* through one pregnancy first."

Josh nods, a thoughtful look on his face.

"Ready to open presents?" Evie chirps from across the room.

Kendall's eyes widen, taking in the mountain of pastel-wrapped gifts around her. "Sure." But she doesn't sound convinced. Evie hands her the first present, and Kendall starts unwrapping.

A breast pump. Clothes too tiny for humans. Cribs. Car seats. Diapers. A baby monitor. Some pillow called My Breast Friend.

Jesus, I'm on a different planet with this baby gear. But I'll figure it out, I'm sure. About halfway through, I whisper in Kendall's ear. "How are you doing?" I can't help but kiss her forehead, my fingers cradling her face.

"Overwhelmed. The babies are kicking hard. Happy about this party, though."

"Can I get you anything to drink?"

"No, it makes me have to pee every five minutes."

I lean down and plunk a kiss on her lips, hoping it communicates what I can't. "Okay, babe. Let me know. I'll get you anything you want. Just say the word."

My phone buzzes in my pocket again. I fish it out and read Ian's text.

Sooooo a few more people showed up. That okay?

I frown and type, *How many people are we talking about?*

The animated dots tell me he's taking his time to respond. Or composing a novel. Or he doesn't know how to tell me shit's going down at my house so he keeps typing and deleting. As I wait, I'm getting grumpier and grumpier thinking my place is going to be trashed, and I'm about to just call him.

I don't want to distract everyone from the party, so I try to keep the phone off to the side, but dammit he's taking too long.

Kendall glances up at me, and her eyes narrow briefly. Then she straightens up and coos over the next package.

Finally his text comes through.

Party-sized. Sadie and the Buchanan twins are headed over. Right now there's just Fernando. Steve. Ashton. Their friends. Come back and celebrate. Bring your girl. We put in a last minute Elephant's Deli order for food. And just saying, the GoPuff App kicks ass. Got reinforcements on drink as well as a cigar for you, Daddy.

Don't call me Daddy, I text.

But I'm kinda loving that word.

I gaze down over my phone at the girl I love.

Hopefully when it's quiet tonight, I can get Kendall alone to tell her how much I miss being with her—even though she's sitting right here.

As soon as I kick everyone out of my condo.

36

KENDALL

*M*y mouth stretches open in the world's biggest yawn.

"Sorry," I say with a laugh as I cover my face with the back of my hand.

Evie shakes her head as she drives us to my apartment. "No worries, honey. You must be exhausted."

She glances in the rearview window where Josh and Drew are following behind us in an SUV loaded down with presents.

"Can I ask you something?"

I tilt my head as I wait to hear whatever is on her mind. I'm expecting gossip from this afternoon. Someone's engaged or got a promotion or broke up. Some tidbit of news I hadn't heard because I was knee deep in wrapping paper and hugs.

"Is everything okay with you and Drew?"

An imaginary bubble inside me deflates. *Of course Evie would notice.*

I've been in a mad dash to get everything ready at work for my maternity leave, and I haven't had much time to hang out with her, or anyone else for that matter, in the last few months.

But Evie and I have never needed a lot to catch up and be in sync.

Rubbing my lips together, I mull over how to answer.

Because on the surface, everything is fine.

On the surface, Drew and I are doing all the right things.

Underneath that serene water, though, are too many currents. Too many rough waters I'm not sure how to navigate.

"I don't really know."

And it pisses me off.

My resolution this morning to have a heart-to-heart tonight resonates in my mind. I need something to eat first, though, before I yack all over my heinous maternity shirt.

We pull up to my apartment, and as soon as Evie throws the car in park, she reaches for my hand.

"I can honestly say I never imagined I'd see Drew at his own baby shower. Or that he'd fall for my best friend. Whatever is going on, I really believe you'll work it out. From talking to Josh, I can tell you Drew is over the moon about the babies. He's so in love with them."

Yeah, but is he in love with me?

But I can't tell her what I've been quietly obsessing over these last few months because one of my kids gives me a swift jab.

"Holy *fuckkkk*." I reach down and press my hand to my stomach, which clenches so hard, I think I might pee my pants.

When I open my eyes, I see the concern on Evie's face.

"It's okay. I'm okay. Just a karate kick and some Braxton Hicks contractions. Nothing serious. My uterus isn't falling out or anything."

My door opens, and Drew sticks his head in. His brow is furrowed, the expression on his face so serious, it makes my heart ache.

He wouldn't be so concerned if he didn't really care about me, right?

I need to talk to him. I'm making myself mental, questioning his motives all the time. Wondering how he feels about me.

Drew is a good guy. He'll want to put me at ease. He'll want to talk.

I think.

Evie fills him in on the martial artists duking it out in my belly, and he rubs it sweetly.

"Poor baby." He leans closer and whispers to the basketball tenting my clothes, "Hey, guys. Take it easy on your momma. You're wearing her out."

I'm not sure why it happens now. Why tears fill my eyes at this moment instead of at the shower. Maybe it's hearing Drew say that word.

Momma. That will be me. I'm going to be a mother.

I smile at him, and he beams back at me. I lean forward and kiss him, not caring that my best friend is about twelve inches away and watching the show.

When he pulls back, he has that goofy grin. The one he only breaks out for me. "What was that for?"

"Just, you know, for being here."

"Of course."

I'm going to do it. Talk to him as soon as it's just the two of us. I know it'll feel good to voice all of my concerns. To hear what he's thinking. Then maybe we can move forward instead of wading through this weird limbo in our relationship.

He helps me out of the car and gets me settled on the couch in my apartment before heading outside to unload all of the gifts with Evie and Josh.

Fatigue hits me so hard, I curl up with a blanket and knock out before they make it back upstairs. I don't even wake up with them trampling in and out to drop off the gifts in the nursery.

~

When I finally open my eyes, it's dark outside.

"Drew?" I clear my throat. How long was I asleep?

Instead of Drew's voice, I'm surprised to hear Evie's. "Hey, honey."

She's nestled in the love seat next to me. Josh comes in from the kitchen.

"Hey. Where's Drew?" I yawn and look around, confused why Evie and Josh are still here.

"He said he had some errands to run but would be back soon."

My stomach sinks. Damn it. I really need to have that conversation with him. And I have to do it before these babies arrive.

Frustration claws at me, the kind that used to make me aim for Drew's jugular and ask questions later. While I don't want to be that person anymore, the one who judges him snidely, I can't ignore the sense that he's hiding something.

"On a Saturday night?" I reach for my phone. It's almost eight. "Seriously, what does he have to do *right now* that's so important?"

Evie looks at Josh, who shrugs. "He had some friends over at his place and wanted to get rid of them. He asked us to hang out here until he got back."

"How long ago did he leave?"

Josh runs his hands through his hair. "Few hours ago."

"He needed *a few hours* to get rid of people at his condo, which is fifteen minutes away."

To get rid of the friends he won't introduce me to.

Any sense of peace I'd had this afternoon when I got home from the shower evaporates.

In its place is doubt.

So much fucking doubt.

I'm thinking about those texts he was firing off when we were unwrapping presents that made him so secretive.

His beautiful assistant Frankie whom I've never met before today.

The fact that he stopped staying overnight or only crashes on my couch.

That we haven't had sex—hot, burn-up-the-sheets sex like I've been craving—in ages.

"Can you do me a favor? Can you guys drive me to his place?"

Josh's eyebrows pull together. "You sure you want to go there right now?"

I stare at him.

"Why would that be a problem?"

The potential answer makes my heart knock against my ribs.

Evie stands and slings her purse over her shoulder. "It's no problem. It's not like Drew's hiding anything. I mean, right?" She turns to Josh, who hasn't budged one inch. He's barely breathing.

All at once, he starts to talk. "Drew's not hiding anything. It's just late, and he was worried you'd overdone it today and needed to rest."

I stare at my best friend's husband and realize who I'm addressing. Drew's best friend since they were kids.

"Josh," I say slowly, "let me be as clear as possible. If you're covering for him right now, I swear to God..."

Evie takes my hand. "Josh isn't covering for anything. Right, babe?"

We both stare at him, and he clears his throat. "I promise, Kendall, there's nothing going on. Of course we'll drive you."

None of us speak on the way to Drew's. I'm too busy listening to my heart pound in my throat and cringing every time we hit a speed bump that makes my children tap-dance on my pelvis. My whole body has been aching since I woke up from that nap, but I feel like if I don't do this right now, I'll be missing some big piece of this puzzle.

Because I'm not crazy.

I know Drew has been keeping something from me.

When we step off the elevator, I can hear the music blasting from his condo.

Then again, the door is open and people are streaming in and out.

"Oh, shit." Josh places his hand on my arm. "Let me go in and find him. You guys stay here."

"Not a chance." I shrug him off and swallow the bile that threatens to push up the back of my throat.

Each step fills me with dread, like I'm part of a slow-motion train-wreck, but I have to know.

I waddle through the door but jerk to a stop the moment I cross the threshold.

People are everywhere.

Booze is everywhere.

Beautiful women.

Everywhere.

Two of them are half naked on my boyfriend's couch, gyrating on some guy while he sucks on their tits. Pretty sure that's a line of coke on the coffee table.

My hands tremble as I hold them over my belly that spasms. I clench my eyes shut and wait for the Braxton-Hicks contraction to stop.

Please, please don't let me find you with another woman, Drew. I swear right now, if you're cheating on me, I will never forgive you. We will be over from this moment on.

A cold trickle of sweat slides down my back, sending a chill through me. People are talking, but everything is muffled, like I'm underwater.

When I open my eyes, my heart is pounding so hard, it matches the bass beating through the speakers.

As I make my way through his condo, I cover my mouth with my palm to avoid a massive cloud of pot.

What the fuck, Drew? You promised me you'd changed.

Fear knots in my throat. Beats against my breast. Steals my breath.

Every worst case runs through my mind.

Drew drunk and passed out somewhere.

Overdosed on drugs or booze.

In bed with another woman.

I press my hand to my stomach where the babies kick and remind me that I have to be strong enough for them.

I come to a halt in the kitchen where dozens of containers litter the counters.

This has been catered.

Making me wonder if this party was planned and not some spur-of-the-moment thing.

Betrayal mixes with a hot, thick anger so blinding I could scream.

Is this what he's been up to when he leaves me at night? Partying with his friends? Fucking socialites? Lying to my face?

"Let's get out of here." Evie takes my hand, and I shake my head.

"I need to see this with my own eyes."

Even if it breaks my heart in a million fucking pieces.

People are staring at me. It's the pumpkin-colored shirt or maybe my cankles or my buffalo ass that waddles. But I feel it. How out of place I am right now. The women here haven't eaten in the last week. Everyone has perfect hair. Blindingly white teeth. Designer clothes. Or porn-perfect breasts.

Everyone is Instagram-worthy.

Everyone except me.

Maybe that's why he's never introduced me to his friends or his parents.

Maybe he's embarrassed about me.

Tears are streaming down my face by the time I step out onto the patio. I'm beyond the point of caring that my emotions are out of control.

Because *this* is my worst nightmare.

That Drew's still living his old life.

Behind my back.

I choke back a sob when I see him. Relieved that he's not lying in vomit somewhere. Pissed that he's shooting the shit like this is no big deal. Confused that he can be smiling while my heart is breaking.

He's leaning against the ledge of the patio, as casual as can be, laughing with some guys and a few women in slinky cocktail dresses. He has a drink in one hand and a cigar in the other.

"He's just talking to some friends," Evie says quietly in my ear.

She sounds relieved.

I would be too if the beautiful blonde with her cleavage on display in that itty-bitty dress, standing next to Drew, wasn't rubbing his arm.

He smiles down at her, and she says something back.

They laugh.

The woman's friend starts to tug her away, and for a split second, I think maybe I'm not watching the worst moment of my life go down in Technicolor.

But then the blonde moves in front of Drew and reaches for

his face, says something to him that makes him smile, and then kisses him.

"You goddamn asshole." As soon as the words are out of me, it happens.

My stomach clenches so hard, white dots spot my vision.

And my water breaks.

37

DREW

*W*hen I walk in to my condo, I'm greeted with a bong, a few cases of beer, and pizza boxes stacked on the coffee table. Trays of food cover the kitchen table like they're waiting for an army. The music's on, and about ten people are in my living room.

My inner balloon of happiness fizzles to the floor.

God, I've had enough of this shit for the rest of my life.

Guess this is what happens when I've been living like a monk for months. When I give an inch, they take a fucking football field.

I open my mouth to yell, "Everyone get the hell out of here," when I'm bowled over by Fernando, my tall, wiry hipster friend in a porkpie hat and pointy-toe shoes.

"I can't believe it! Big, bad Drew's gonna be a daddy." Fernando shakes my hand and slaps my back.

An unimpeded smile spreads on my face.

I'm gonna be a dad.

The reminder is so intense, I almost forget I'm pissed at Ian for throwing a party at my place.

"That's right," I say, focusing on his horn-rimmed glasses.

He's always a Red Bull energy drink about to explode, but I'll admit his enthusiasm is contagious.

"Is it true?" asks Mark, a friend from high school wearing a neat, button-down shirt and dark jeans. "Your choad nectar is incubating?"

"Fuck." I throw back my head and laugh. "Choad nectar? Seriously?" Someone shoves a glass of whiskey in my hand, and I reflexively take it.

He smirks and pulls his hands out like he's weighing choices. "Would you prefer high-fructose porn syrup? Daddy sauce? Dongwater?"

Okay, maybe I miss these guys sometimes.

In small doses.

Not at my house.

They make me laugh, though.

"I prefer to call the twins the best things that have ever happened to me."

Mark stares at me and blinks. "You serious, bro?"

"Abso-fucking-lutely." I can't help grinning like a dumbass.

"Twins. Holy shit." He cackles and pulls me into a bear hug. "That's awesome. So stoked for you, man!"

While I'm growing up, maybe my friends are too.

Ian, wearing preppy shorts and a polo shirt, hands me a cigar. Gripping it, I feel like a 1920s mobster, although I appreciate the tradition. Makes me feel even more like an expecting father. He turns off the music, waves to the others like a ringmaster, and clears his throat. "I have an announcement to make."

Everyone's eyes are on him, but I speak first. "I'm gonna be a dad!" I yell.

A shout goes up. The music volume increases. And I'm surrounded by friends who tell me how happy they are for me.

I'm happy for me, too.

And it's such a relief to tell everyone and experience their smiles, best wishes, and congratulations. The pats on the back and the hugs. The high-fives.

People who know me who don't act like my parents.

We shout over the music. We laugh and clink glasses.

It would be rude to kick everyone out now.

Four people I recognize from the clubs walk in, give me hugs, and drop off bottles of Jack and Coke. Then Dana and Chelsea Buchanan arrive, dressed to go out after this. I smile as I think about last time I saw them at the Huntington Hotel and consider how far I've come. And all the big things in my future.

The light lingers late on this warm summer evening, and I want to take advantage of it. Shazam races out of the bedroom like a hellcat, and I stick the cigar in my mouth, scoop him up, and head to my patio. Leaning against the railing, I set down the cat, who rubs his face against my calves. With Kendall napping, I bet she'll knock out for a few hours. Josh and Evie will make sure she's safe. I check my phone to see if there are any messages from her, but there aren't.

While the cigar stays in my hand, I don't want to light it, since they stink. I haven't sipped the drink either, but having it in my hand is a defense system. If I have a drink, I don't need one.

I like being tested like this and passing with flying colors.

A few people join me on the patio, then more, until it's getting crowded out here. Guess the entire party has moved outside. Shazzy curls up on a cushion in a last ray of sunshine and tucks himself in.

As the sun goes low, Ian wanders out. "I love your place."

"Glad you made yourself comfortable," I say sarcastically. He laughs and asks about work.

The volume inside rises. A few more people must have stepped in.

"Next time I come back, you're gonna have kids. Living beings. Mouths to feed. That's...overboard."

I nod. "I know. I can't wait, though. I didn't realize it, but I've always wanted—"

Mark opens the sliding glass door and comes out with a whiskey bottle. "Need a refill?"

I hold up my still-full glass. "I'm good."

He gestures at Shaz. "Where'd you get the cat?"

"It's a long story," I begin—but the door opens—the music louder—and this time Sadie comes out with the Buchanan twins. Sadie's wearing a summer dress and weaving a bit.

How much has she had?

How long have I been outside?

Sadie gives Mark a sloppy kiss, and Ian and I exchange amused looks behind their backs. When they finally disentangle themselves, I ask, "How long have you two been dating?"

"A few months. You haven't been out with us!" she complains, with a fake pout.

How come I never noticed how whiny she is?

"Been busy." I gesture with my cigar.

"I think you're gonna be a great dad," she says, nodding drunkenly. "I mean that. You're gonna be the best dad ever. Ever."

While tipsy praise means nothing, it still feels good to hear it. She pats my bicep and gives me a kiss on the cheek.

"You goddamn asshole!"

I pause, wondering who fucked up and how badly when I turn and see Kendall.

And realize she's screaming.

At me.

Everyone stills, parting around her.

She's standing in the doorway, pissed and gorgeous and very pregnant.

Based on her expression and the hurt look in her eyes, I know I'm the one who's fucked up. Badly.

Questions rush through my mind.

How did she get here? How late is it?

Oh, fuck, I've been here too long.

Is that why she's so upset?

"Ken—babe, what are you doing here? Sorry I'm running late—"

She doubles over in pain with a grunt. As I reach my arms out to steady her, she shrinks away from me like I'm a monster. That's when I notice fluid streaming down her legs. The puddle at her feet.

My gut clenches, and I feel lightheaded.

She's in labor.

She's not due for another four weeks. Wait, five? Shit, I can't remember. But she just went into labor.

The doctor said twins often arrive early, that they could be delivered safely around the thirty-fifth or thirty-sixth week. I scramble to do the math in my head, freaking the fuck out.

Automatically, I reach for her shoulders to steady her. "Let's get to the emergency room, KK."

"No," she cries, her arms thrashing, pushing me away. "Not you. I need Evie. Evie?" she calls, her voice shaky as tears stream down her face. Out of nowhere, Evie's at her side. "Can you take me to the hospital?"

Evie whispers to her and takes her hand.

I'm so fucking confused. Hurt Kendall seems to want nothing to do with me. Jesus, what is happening right now? She must be in so much pain to be crying. KK never cries.

I want to wrap her in my arms and carry her out of here, but she looks horrified.

By me.

Josh materializes by Kendall's other side to take her other arm.

He glances at me over his shoulder with a pained expression I don't understand.

Until I reenter my condo.

Goddamn it.

And then I'm fucking speechless.

What had been a party with a little pot and a dozen or so people is now packed. What was just a group of friends, pizza, and beer is now a den of debauchery.

I'm seeing what Kendall saw.

Naked women gyrating on Fernando to the thump of loud music.

Drugs.

Molly.

Coke.

So much pot it feels like my living room's been hotboxed.

Glasses, bottles, drinks, heat, sex.

I'm too stunned to do anything at first, I just push my way through the horde trying to figure out the best way to get everyone the hell out of here.

But then I notice my babies' ultrasound picture on the floor in the kitchen speared under the stiletto of someone I don't even know, and I snap.

What. The. Fuck?

Rage like I've never experienced before hammers my heart so hard, I might stroke out.

I'm absolutely fucking done.

Striding over to the stereo, I shut off the music, which makes everyone take notice. "Party's over! Get the fuck out. You have two minutes before I call the cops."

I stride over to Ian. "Get everyone out of my house, or I will personally remove your scrotum with a dull blade."

He cringes. "Dude—"

"You made this mess. Clean it up. My girlfriend's in labor.

She saw this shit and looked like I stabbed her in the heart. I can't imagine what she's thinking." I rub my face, feeling like the douchebag she always thought I was. There's so much momentum from my past that when all the dirty crap surfaces again, it's so much worse than when I was living this lifestyle. "Ian, you know I haven't been partying. I don't want my house trashed with drugs when I'm trying to get my shit together. If you were a halfway decent human being, you'd understand. I gotta go to the hospital. Don't be here when I get back."

He gives me a wide-eyed nod and starts shuttling people out the door. "Everyone out. We'll meet up at…"

I grab my keys, wallet, and phone, shove through people leaving, and race down my hallway to catch up with Kendall. Too impatient to take the elevator, I open the stairwell and practically leap down the whole flight.

But when I get downstairs, I realize she's gone.

A lump forms in my throat.

Fuck. *FUCK.*

Once I get to my car, I tear out, headed to the hospital, hoping I make it before she does.

The devastation on her face will haunt my nightmares for the rest of my life.

I need to talk to her.

Explain how this happened.

Tell her I love her.

Damn it.

How have I never told her I love her?

After breaking about ten traffic laws, I powerslide my car into the first parking spot I find, jump out, and sprint into the hospital, hoping I'm not too late.

For the birth. For our relationship.

For everything that's ever mattered to me.

38

KENDALL

*I*n between each soul-wrenching contraction, vicious thoughts slice through me.

Drew's partying.

With naked women.

And lines of coke.

And so much fucking booze.

"Are we almost there?" I whimper from the back seat of Evie's car.

"ETA is five minutes." She twists in the passenger seat to reach out and grab my hand while Josh swerves around a vehicle.

When I release her grip, I slump down deeper into the leather seats. I'm grateful they had a spare blanket to sit on because my legs are sopping wet.

Nothing like having your water break in front of the beautiful woman draped over your boyfriend.

And it wasn't a drizzle of liquid. No, it wasn't dainty like that. It was a Big Gulp releasing from my crotch like a dam broke. So much water that some drunk girl in Drew's condo stopped me on the way out to ask me if I'd peed my pants.

I lean over onto my side and curl up into a ball and ignore the tears leaking out of my eyes.

I realize I don't know exactly what I saw tonight. If Drew was truly macking on some girl. Or if that was just the appetizer. If I hadn't shown up right then, would that have gone farther?

Has it already?

My mind is reeling with questions and suspicions and betrayal.

All those times he left me in the middle of the night to sleep at his place.

Has he been seeing someone?

Has he been bullshitting me about how much he's changed?

Truly, I never thought he could lie to that degree, but what do I know? I just walked up and saw him kissing some woman. Maybe I'm a game to him.

And that's why he hasn't introduced me to his parents or friends.

I cry harder.

In this moment, I realize this is heartbreak. That nothing I've experienced with any man before has ever reached this level of intensity.

Of love.

And hate.

One thing is certain—nothing will ever be the same after tonight.

Josh clears his throat. "Kendall, I know that looked bad back there, but—"

"Shut up, Josh," I croak, my voice thick. "Have you been covering for him? Has he been cheating on me all this time and you've had his back?"

"Fuck, no, Kendall. Eagle Scout's honor."

He holds up three fingers like a moron.

Evie turns back to me. "He really is an Eagle Scout, you know."

I roll my eyes.

"Listen to me." Josh glances at me at a stop sign. "Drew loves you. He's so obsessed with you and the babies, I promise you —*on my life*—that he's not cheating on you. Yes, shit got out of hand at his condo, and you have every right to hand him his ass when you see him, but I know that man, he loves you with his heart and soul."

He loves me so damn much but he's never said it? He's never brought up marriage or what happens after the babies arrive. He's never told me he wants more.

Drew loves me? Yeah, right.

I'm done being a sucker.

As though to punctuate my misery, a teeth-clenching contraction tightens my whole body, and I gasp into the leather seat.

"Her contractions are six minutes apart," Evie whispers to Josh.

"It's okay. We're here."

The car lurches to a stop. Doors open and close. A nice nurse sticks her head in the back seat and introduces herself.

She's maneuvering me from the car to a wheelchair. I stand, only for a moment.

And my water breaks.

Again.

Seriously?

I cover my face. No one told me I'd have two waters break.

Along with my heart.

I'm the fucking moron here. All around.

"It's okay, Mom." The nurse rubs my back gently. "So you're having twins? Your friend tells me you're due soon. Looks like you're doing great. Twins almost always arrive a little early. Let's get you inside and comfortable."

She's wheeling me away, and I realize I don't have Drew anymore. I'm doing this by myself. All by myself.

I tell the nurse to stop and then reach for Evie. "Call Tristan. Tell him I'm here. He'll want to know."

Drew might not give a rat's ass, but Tristan will.

39

DREW

"Kendall Greer. I need to know what room Kendall Greer is in." I close my eyes, squeeze the bridge of my nose, and try to slow down my roaring pulse while the hospital intake employee behind the glass enclosure hunts and pecks the letters on the keyboard with aggravating slowness.

K-E-N-D—

If there wasn't plexiglass between us, I'd hop over the counter and type it myself. A riot of coughing starts behind me, and I wince. Full of the injured and sick, the ER is a wholly miserable place.

I gotta get to Kendall.

Come on, come on.

"There is no Kendall Greer in the Emergency Room. She's up in Maternity. Fourth floor."

I hit my forehead with the base of my hand. *You dumbfuck, Drew. You should know this. You took the prenatal class with her.*

But I'm so out of my element I forgot. Guess I figured since Kendall's water broke she'd be here.

"Thanks," I call, as I race out of the waiting room, then skid down the hall to the main lobby of the hospital.

After taking the world's slowest elevator to the fourth floor, I dash to the maternity reception area.

"One moment, please." The nurse smiles at me, holds up her finger, and continues talking on the phone. While she seems friendly enough, I don't have patience for this. I'm ready to violate any hospital regulation to get to my girlfriend.

I hope she's still my girlfriend.

God, that's a horrible thought.

But when I think about the look on her face and how she didn't want me to touch her... I can't imagine the shit going through her head right now.

Despite the chairs scattered around the room, my nerves force me to keep standing, and I start to pace. Back and forth, back and forth, memorizing the lines on the cold linoleum floor. Waiting for the nurse to finish her call.

Fuck it. I'm gonna roam the halls and find KK, with or without permission.

Railings line the wide hall, which has fluorescent lights overhead. I sprint down the corridor, look at the last name on the board outside a room, sprint to the next room, check the name, sprint again, until I slam into that asshole Tristan exiting a suite. We both stumble back.

Fuck.

Greer is written on the board behind him, and I can hear beeping, Kendall's moan, and Evie talking as the door closes.

"I need to get in there," I growl, trying to get past him.

But the pissed look on his face matches mine, and his arms cross over his chest. "Absolutely not."

I size him up. We're about evenly matched in height and weight and stand toe to toe, glare to glare. I'm considering pushing him aside when he rears back his fist and punches me.

FUCK.

"What the hell was that for?" Staggering away from him, I jam my palm against my smarting cheek. While I want to hit him back, the last thing I need is to end up in a brawl right before Kendall delivers and get kicked out. Thank God no one saw.

"Is Kendall all right?"

"Yes. Fucker. No thanks to you." He stands between me and her door. "Wanna tell me why my best friend is in tears over you? Yes, she's about to push out two humans, but she's heartbroken over you."

He jams his finger into my chest.

Panic seizes me, overriding the need to punch this asshole in the face. Overriding the desire to shout that *I'm* her best friend. That I'd never hurt her intentionally.

Because it's starting to settle in.

I might not be allowed into the delivery room.

"I can explain—"

"About what? That you're having orgies at your house while she's pregnant with your kids?" His voice is a sneer. "She's had enough of your lies, Merritt."

"What orgies? What lies?"

A concerned nurse and a security guard hustle up to us. "You gentlemen need to leave—"

"My girlfriend is in there," I snarl.

"Leave. Now. Take it outside." She points to the reception.

"Fine," we both say.

He and I walk down the hallway while the security guard follows close behind. When we get to the small lobby, I pull Tristan into a side hallway that has some privacy.

"How could you do that to her?" he hisses. "How long has it been going on, Merritt?"

While I hate this guy, there's nothing to lose with sincerity. I look him straight in the eye. "There is absolutely *nothing* in my life except Kendall and those babies."

Then I tell him everything.

Once I've spilled my guts to Kendall's partner and I'm so desperate to get in her room I'm ready to sign away my trust fund to a security guard to make it happen, Tristan finally relents.

"You have some shit luck, man," he says with a frown.

But I'm done with the inquisition. It's my turn to ask questions.

"What about you? Are you done making a play for Kendall?"

The asshole stares at me blankly and then laughs in my face. "We're not like that. Kendall's like a sister."

I growl, and he snickers again before he pats me on the back. Lowering his voice, he says, "Actually, when Evie called me and asked me to come to the hospital, I was at Frankie's house."

My head jerks up. "My Frankie?" His nostrils flare, and it's my turn to laugh. "You mean my assistant?"

He shrugs and looks away. "Maybe."

It finally sinks in.

Tristan's not into my girlfriend and conspiring behind my back. He has a thing for the Frank-meister.

It's my turn to be the protective brother. "You treat her right or next time I'll be kicking *your* ass."

"Yeah, yeah. Go find your girlfriend and help her deliver your babies, Merritt."

My babies. My girlfriend.

Without another word, I spin on my heel and race back down the hallway, my pulse throbbing in my ears.

Please, God, let my family be okay.

40

DREW

*W*hen I peek my head into her room, Kendall is strapped to a hospital bed with various monitors surrounding her. Evie sits next to her while Josh stands by the window.

"Hey," I say quietly. "Do you mind if I talk to Kendall?"

The pain in Kendall's eyes slashes through my heart. "Get. Out."

"Please. I need to talk with you."

A tear trickles down her cheek. "Drew, you have to go. I don't want you here." Her lower lip quivers.

"KK, I can't go another second without explaining what happened tonight."

She wipes a tear with the back of her hand, and Evie hands her a Kleenex. "You aren't going to leave me, are you?"

Evie and Josh glance at each other, and Josh nods and leaves, giving me a pat on the shoulder and an understanding half-smile as he walks past.

The fact that he doesn't second-guess me right now means more than he'll ever know.

I gesture to Evie as I lock eyes on KK. "Evie can be here, if it makes you more comfortable. Anyone can hear what I have to say, especially our friends. I have nothing to hide. But I need to talk to you before our misunderstandings get any worse."

Kendall's tear-filled eyes look to Evie with such agony my chest feels like it's going to cave in. "Can you come back in a few minutes?"

Evie nods and exits, leaving me and Kendall with the beep of her monitors and her tortured breathing.

"Are you in pain?" I ask.

She grits her teeth. "The contractions hurt like a mother, but I'm hardly dilated. I'm supposed to get some meds to speed things along."

Then I better talk fast. I sit in Evie's chair, pulling it right beside Kendall so I can see her eyes. "I love you, Kendall Greer. I'm sorry I haven't said it until now."

Her breath hitches, and tears stream down her face.

"Shh, babe. Shh." I wipe her cheeks with a tissue, trying to be gentle. "I fucking love you so much. I've been scared to tell you, because I thought you didn't feel the same way about me."

She opens her mouth to say something, but I stop her.

"I had the best day with you at the shower today. Having babies with you is the highlight of my life. But the shit at my house?" I look into her eyes, hoping and praying she sees I'm being one hundred percent honest. "I was on the patio for so long, I didn't know how crazy things had gotten. Didn't realize how many people had come over."

Sniffling, she wipes her tears again, and hiccups.

I grab her hand. "I promise you, I'd never throw a party like that intentionally. In fact, when I went home to check, I thought it was only a few friends, and"—I shrug—"I was so fucking happy about the shower and being a dad and got caught up in celebrating. But I wasn't drinking. Someone handed me a glass, and I held it but I didn't take a sip. I didn't use any drugs. After you left, after I saw what was going down, I kicked everyone out, but God, I'm so fucking gutted you saw that, and it made you doubt me."

She's quiet, so quiet, and I can barely breathe knowing she might tell me to go to hell.

But she lets me keep hold of her hand, which has to be good, right?

"What about that girl?" Kendall whispers. "The one who wrapped her arms around you and kissed you?"

Another round of tears well in her eyes. Fuck, she's breaking my heart right now.

When Tristan accosted me outside and told me Kendall thought I was possibly cheating on her, I'd never felt more devastated in my life.

"KK, she kissed me on the cheek to congratulate me. She's dating Mark, who was standing right there. I can call him if you want to hear for yourself."

I pull out my cell phone, about to offer it to her so she can call my friends and clear this up, when a contraction hits.

She scrunches her eyes, holds her belly, and groans. The monitors beep faster. My gut churns.

I can't stand to see her in this much pain.

"You got this, babe. Like they said in class. Deep yoga breaths."

"Fuck yoga breaths. They do jack shit." She grunts, sweat beading on her forehead.

I smile, loving that she's fierce. That will be her next T-shirt. #FierceAF.

She's trying not to scream, and I'm blown away by her strength. When the wave passes, she closes her eyes.

There's so much more I need to say, but dumping everything on her in the middle of labor seems wrong. That's about me, and this needs to be about her.

But she clears her throat, and I look up to see her tired blue eyes studying me. Her raspy voice cuts through the silence. "So there haven't been any other women? You've been leaving in the middle of the night."

Christ. I hate that I made her doubt my fidelity.

"There are *no* other women. There's only you." I squeeze her hand gently. *Some days my name should be Dumbass dot com.* "I, uh, I made the mistake of reading about sex and pregnancy with twins on the internet, and it freaked me the fuck out."

A lump the size of Montana lodges in my throat when I think of all the shit I read. "I didn't want to jeopardize anything, and you were exhausted. There was no way I wanted to hurt you or the babies if we got too, you know, excited." I magically fuck up everything, and I didn't want to fuck up this. "It seemed the best way to keep you safe was to avoid sticking my dick D into your spaces A, B, or C until our children were out and breathing on their own."

Thankfully, the tension around her eyes softens. "Why didn't you just ask the doctor?" Her voice is gentle. Curious. Understanding. "You asked her ten thousand sex questions at our first appointment."

"I almost did. Every appointment. But then—" Shaking my head, I ignore the fear that grips me when I remember what I saw on the internet. "It's one thing to look up the worst-case scenarios. It's another thing entirely to speak them out loud. To voice those concerns. To test fate or the gods or whatever."

I feel like a tool saying all of this, but she has to understand I'm not sneaking around behind her back and never would.

Never, until this moment, did I ever realize I was superstitious.

But yeah, I'd fucking die if anything happened to Kendall and my babies.

Her eyes glance away a moment before they return to me, a

regretful slant to her lips. "I think I know something about worst-case scenarios." The sigh that leaves her weighs a thousand pounds and savages my heart. "I just...I wish you would've said something. I thought it was me. I thought—well—that you weren't attracted to me anymore."

Fucking hell.

I lean down to kiss her. "Being attracted to you has never, *never* been the problem. Do you hear me? It was impossible to sleep right next to your sexy, gorgeous self when you were forbidden fruit." I laugh awkwardly. "So I'd go home alone and beat off."

She gives me a watery smile. "You did?"

Of course my girlfriend thinks it's cute I ran off to jerk it. "Sad but true."

"I was afraid you were leaving to go be with someone else. Someone thin and not pregnant." She nibbles her bottom lip. "Maybe someone like Frankie."

"Baby, no." I wrap both of her hands in mine. Is this how she feels when I give her grief about Tristan? "Frankie's like my nutty little sister. Trust me, there is no other woman for me. You make me a better man. Why would I want to go elsewhere when I have the most precious, beautiful, amazing woman right here?"

Kendall opens her mouth to speak again, but a nurse enters the room. She notes down some numbers and adjusts Kendall's blankets. On her way out, the nurse says, "The anesthesiologist will be in here for an epidural shortly."

"Thank God," Kendall grunts as another contraction overpowers her.

Once the nurse is out of the room and Kendall isn't wracked with pain, she lets go of my hand and brushes away a wisp of her hair.

"I thought you were ashamed of me," she says quietly. "That

you didn't want to be with me. Didn't want to tell your parents or friends about me."

Shit. I'm an asshole. *That's* what she's been worried about? Something so easy to explain?

"I'm fucking ashamed of *them*. You saw them today. I wanted to shield *you* from *them*. And my parents?" I shudder. "I told them about us, about the twins, but they were awful. Said horrible, hateful things. And they wanted all this shit. Wanted you to take a paternity test and sign a prenup." Merely saying those words makes me seethe. "You've had a hard enough pregnancy as it is. You don't need their shit. Fuck them."

Tilting her head, she stares up at me. "I'd sign off on a paternity test." She opens her mouth. Closes it. "Or a prenup." Her eyes widen with understanding. "Would that mean..."

"Yeah. It means..."

My heart beats in my ears.

This moment.

It's the giant slalom at the Olympics, the chance I've been waiting for my whole life but never knew it.

For once, don't fuck up, my head chants.

I stand up and dig in my back pocket with a fumbling hand, pulling out my wallet. Yes, the Ninja Turtle one Bee gave me. I open it up and dig out something hidden in the flap.

A ring.

The one I've been carrying around for months.

Kendall gasps, and I hope it's not with a contraction.

"I bought this for you a while back, but I didn't think you wanted to get married."

"What? You did?"

I'm trying to read her expression here, to figure out what she thinks, but I realize I have to get this off my chest. Tell her how I feel.

It's now or never.

"When we told your parents about the twins, I got the impression you were totally opposed to getting married. You're so strong and independent. That's one of the things I love about you, and I didn't want to hamper your ambitions or cramp your style. I didn't think you wanted to get married, but I have to tell you how I feel because if I don't, I'm afraid I might lose the best thing that's ever happened to me."

I get down on one knee.

"Kendall, I adore you. And I want to spend the rest of my life with you—loving you, arguing with you, making up with you. You are the fiercest, most beautiful, most amazing woman I've ever known. And I love you with all my heart. Baby, will you marry me?"

41

KENDALL

"*W*ill *you marry me?*"

A million emotions rush through me. Relief that Drew's here. That he's apologized. That the story of what went down at his apartment makes sense.

Although I'm still seriously irked it happened, I get it.

Even his ridiculous reasons for going home in the middle of the night make sense. I've read how fathers sometimes get wigged out by pregnancy. By the worst-case scenarios.

And I've noticed how cautious Drew's been with me. How he treats me like I'm precious. Like my cargo is precious.

It all makes sense.

Tears pour down my face because I'm fucking hormonal and still moderately homicidal despite his assurances. I can't turn off these feelings pummeling through me while my children try to kick their way out of my body.

"I was never opposed to marrying you. I'm so sorry you thought that." I hiccup and drag my arm across my face. "I just didn't want us to do it for the wrong reasons. Because you thought you *had* to propose."

His eyes get glassy as he takes my hand. "It would be my

greatest honor to have you as my wife. Nothing about this moment is about obligation. I'm here, on my knee, because I love you like I've never loved anyone before in my life. Let's do this. Be a family. Be my family. Be mine."

I swallow the lump in my throat.

"I'm already yours."

A bright smile stretches across his mouth. "Is that a yes?"

"That's a yes."

He lets out a loud whoop and jumps up to pull me into a gentle hug. We're both laughing because, seriously, drama.

But I guess Drew's my kind of drama.

People come rushing into my room, probably drawn by Drew's howl.

"Are you okay?" a concerned nurse asks as she rushes toward me. Behind her, Josh, Evie, and Tristan hover in the doorway.

"We're fine." When I release Drew's hand, I realize he's placed a gargantuan diamond on my left ring finger. I hold it up to our friends. "More than fine, actually."

They cheer and clap, drowning out the nurse who reminds us this is the maternity ward and we need to keep it down.

But then the monitor beeps, signaling another contraction, and it hits me so hard, I put Drew's arm in a death grip while I curse and growl.

Vaguely, I register his soothing words. His concern. The way he brushes gentle fingers over my brow to wipe away the sweat.

Despite the pain, so much pain I can barely see straight when it's over, I realize I'm not afraid the way I was when I arrived.

Because Drew's here, and he's not going anywhere.

Then the room is empty again, except for Drew.

He kisses my forehead. Presses another gentle kiss to my lips.

"I'll sign your prenup," I whisper again. "I don't want your money or for your family to think I'm in this for any kind of monetary gain. I just want you."

"We're not getting a prenup. What's mine is yours. Ours." He laces our hands together. "And I don't give a fuck what my parents think. You're the only one who matters."

Aww, Drew.

His green eyes bore into me, full of love and sincerity. "I'm so sorry I made you doubt me. I promise I'll be more open moving forward. You're the love of my life. You're the only woman strong enough to handle me at my worst, even though I've been trying to give you my best."

"You have—"

"But being partners is sharing equally in the good—and the bad."

Oh, *Drew.*

"I'm gonna let that be my guiding principle. Trusting you with everything. No matter what."

"I promise to trust you, too. To communicate better. I know I've been wrapped up in work, and I'm sorry I didn't make you a bigger priority. Because you are so important to me."

He kisses my forehead.

"I hate that all this honesty means telling you about my awful parents."

"I can handle it."

"Just know that I don't give a shit what they think about us or what we do."

I don't care what they think. Too much.

I squeeze his hand. "Maybe don't mention that we're having butt babies." He stares at me a long moment, probably trying to understand what I mean. "You know, the cabin? Not having a condom. Going backdoor and everything."

His head tilts back, and he barks out a laugh. "Jesus. I

fucking love you and our butt babies. Can I make little onesies that say Butt Baby? I bet I could sell a million of those."

I smack his shoulder. "No, weirdo. You can't announce to the world we got pregnant after having anal sex."

Hours later, when a tiny but gorgeous Evelyn Beatrice Merritt gets placed in my fiancé's arms, and a rambunctious but handsome Andrew Thomas Merritt gets placed in mine, I know, without a doubt, that getting snowed in with Drew last winter was the best thing that's ever happened to me.

Even if I didn't realize it at the time.

42

KENDALL

a few days later, we carry our delicate bundles out of the hospital, and as I watch Drew strap baby Evie into the car seat he had Josh install yesterday, my heart is overwhelmed with love and happiness.

The babies were early, but healthy, thankfully. Every time I lost my lunch or gained a pound or stretch mark was worth it for my precious darlings.

"She looks so tiny. How is this right?" Drew tugs on the seatbelt to make it tighter.

I rub my son's back as I wait in the wheelchair. Hospital protocol means I can't walk to the parking lot. Fine by me. "Don't forget the head support wrap thingy."

"I used it. There's still space. What if we have to stop suddenly?"

"That's why they're facing backwards. And why you have three mirrors in the back, so you can see them."

He wipes his face, clearly distressed. "I'm driving five miles an hour. Not one mile faster."

I chuckle. "No arguments here."

It takes us another half hour to get Andy in his seat, all the while Drew curses under his breath and sweats.

He wasn't kidding about driving five miles an hour.

I'd tease him about it, but I understand the paranoia.

When we get closer to his condo, I'm quiet for a whole different reason, though.

As I step into the elevator, my heart starts to knock in my chest. We each hold a car seat in our arms as we stand side by side and watch the numbers light up.

We agreed we'd make do with a few things at his place until we could move all of the baby stuff from my apartment. That's not what's making me anxious, though.

It's hard not to think about the last time I was here. How heartbroken I felt.

"Hey." Drew switches Evie's car seat handle to his other hand and then drapes his arm over my shoulders, tugging me close. "Everything's different now. We're doing this. Full throttle."

I smile. "Full throttle?"

"Yeah. Like, balls to the wall. You and me. Go hard or go home. The full monty."

"You know that means full-frontal nudity, right?"

"Stop trying to turn me on."

A laugh spills from my lips. "Actually, yeah, it means the whole enchilada."

"Do you want my whole enchilada?"

Arching onto my tiptoes, I kiss him. "I'd love your whole enchilada. As soon as my kit and caboodle can take it."

Whispering into my ear, he says, "Been dreaming about your kit and caboodle." Then he groans and tucks his head to the crook of my neck. "How long do we have to wait again?"

I run my hand through his hair. "Four to six weeks. But we can do other things. My hands and mouth are perfectly healthy and eager to service you."

"God, don't say that in public." The elevator for our floor

dings, and he arranges himself with a smirk. "I'm obviously down for being serviced."

Just like that, my dirty sex fiend is back.

Although I'm sure we'll make due for the next few weeks, I'm eager to go no-holds-barred. The thought of being intimate with Drew again makes my whole body light up, even the sore parts.

When he opens the door to his condo, I freeze. "Oh, Drew." Twinkle lights drape all across the ceiling of his living room like a canvas of stars. In the corner are two bassinets and baby blankets and stuffed animals. On the wall is a giant framed photo of our babies, a shot he must've taken at the hospital.

On either side are smaller photos of us. From the cabin. Photos I'd forgotten he'd taken. Of us laughing. Of us falling in love. Of our beginning.

The place is spotless and smells like a fresh breeze has cleansed it. Drew must have paid his housekeeper overtime to make his home—our home—shine.

Tears leak down my face as he leads me down the hall and opens the door to the spare room.

Which is now a nursery.

I gasp, my eyes wide. "When did you do this? It's beautiful." I can't take in the room fast enough. Two gorgeous white cribs. A rocking chair. Bookshelves with baby books and toys. The beautiful sage-green walls. Plush blankets and more twinkle lights.

After we set the babies down in their car seats, I throw myself into Drew's arms.

"Shh. Baby. Don't cry." His palm strokes my back. "Been wanting to surprise you with this for a while. Been wanting to beg you to move in with me."

Leaning back, I look around one more time, realizing nothing in here is from the shower.

Drew. I've been so wrong about him. So many times.

My heart can't take it, and I sob in his arms.

When I calm down, I take his face in my hands. "I love you so much. I'm sorry I ever doubted you."

He hugs me close. "I'm not perfect."

"You're perfect for me."

That night, when he's lying in our bed with Evie snuggled on his bare chest and Andy in his other arm, grinning from ear to ear, I pull out my phone to take a few pictures. I've already taken ten million, but seriously, I can't get enough of this sexy daddy with our littles.

If only his parents could see how fantastic he is with our babies.

And that gives me an idea.

EPILOGUE

DREW

A month and a half later

"*D*on't get too attached, little nugget," I mock-scold Andy as he opens his toothless mouth to latch onto Kendall's boob. "Those titties may be for your sustenance, but they're mine to play with when you're done. God*damn* they're lush."

Shit, I said that last part out loud.

Kendall chuckles from her pretzel-like position on the couch as our baby boy closes his eyes and begins to nurse while she proofs a press release on her iPad propped up on a pillow.

With drinks and diapers and papers and blankets strewn everywhere, we're a mess. But it all seems to work out, even if we're constantly juggling kids and stuff.

I hand KK a tall drink of ice water with lemon—her favorite—and snag Eves from her bouncy chair, planting a smooch on the top of her silky-smooth baby head. Water's my drink of choice these days, too. I haven't come this far in sobriety to fuck it up.

Kendall closes her eyes and takes a sip, then focuses on her iPad again. "You're distracting me. I'm almost done."

"It is my solemn duty to be your distraction," I say.

She might be laser-beamed on the words in front of her, but her lips pull up. The truth is, if I actually left my woman alone, she'd wonder what's wrong.

This press release notwithstanding, Kendall's finally taking a break for real from the office. She talks to Tristan daily and video-conferences with her staff often to make sure the transition runs smoothly, but she's let go of the need to be there physically every day.

To his credit, Tristan's not uttered a word of complaint about the extra work. Maybe I misjudged the guy. Whatever. We get along now, so the likelihood of future fistfights decreases daily.

KK and I have talked out her plan for going back to work—three days in the office and two from home. Neither one of us wants a nanny, and Kendall's mom is dying to watch them, so she'll be helping on Kendall's days in the office. KK doesn't have any idea I've tricked out the space next door to her office as a nursery and playroom for when they get older. Can't wait to surprise her.

I'm also on parental leave because it's not fair to ask my fiancée to take time off while I jaunt off to the office. Plus, I really fucking like being with my kids.

"How's Tristan managing without you today?"

"Splitting his infinitives," she mutters, typing with her thumbs.

"I'd like to split your infinitives, baby." I waggle my eyebrows like a dork.

She bursts out laughing. "I can't believe you just made a press release dirty." Andy frowns at his mama for the outburst but returns to her nipple with fervor.

"Like the way we *errand*. We errand so hard."

The appreciative smile Kendall gives me makes my nerve endings tingle. Gazing at her, I'm yet again blown away that she's mine. While we've had plenty of days in sweats and pajamas, today she's dressed in heather-gray leggings that show off her legs and a navy blue off-the-shoulder sweater accentuating her smooth skin. She's piled her auburn hair on top of her head in a messy knot that my fingers itch to undo, and every time she flashes me her boob, I get a little turned on.

Chill, dude.

Seems my entire body realizes we now have doctor clearance for naked exercise. Not that we haven't, ahem, gotten *creative* a few times.

Cradling Eves on my forearm and against my chest, I stride over to the changing table, where I carefully place her on her back. She kicks in a rhythm all her own, and her arms go up and down like Miley Cyrus is playing her song.

With the baby gazing up at me, I begin my repertoire of silly faces. While it's too early for babies to laugh, that doesn't mean I'm not gonna practice. My personal goal is to be the first one to make them giggle.

After receiving a raspberry or two on her little belly, Eves sports a jaunty fresh diaper—it only took a few hundred changes for me to get the hang of the procedure—and I've tucked her tiny, flailing arms into a clean, fresh baby suit. Once Andy has his meal, if we're lucky, they'll take a nap.

If we're *really* lucky, I've got plans with Kendall while they sleep.

And they don't involve clothes.

Hopefully.

Not thinking of how long it's been. Only thinking about how good it's gonna be.

Still, it's been a fucking adventure being parents. Looking

back at when we first brought the babies home, Kendall and I are both so much more confident now.

To be honest, the first two weeks at home with the kids were a blur. I'm not entirely sure what we did. Survived. Ordered in. Slept at random times. Day turned into night. Night had as much activity as day.

But now we're starting to get the hang of it. Most days, at least.

With Kendall in my—no, *our*—bed every night, I'm not sure how we ever slept apart. She completes me in a way I've never experienced. I just like holding her. Being next to her. Kissing her. Waking up with her in my arms.

We take turns getting up in the middle of the night, although sometimes a hungry little soul wants to feed from mama rather than a bottle. Still, I try to double up on diaper duty when that happens.

After some tough nights, we've managed to put the kids on a schedule, which makes it easier for all of us. In fact, we're even doing well enough that Kendall and Evie Senior are talking about having a girls' night out with Frankie. KK could really use a break, and I like that she's open to friendship with the Franka-roni. I'll just have Josh over for diabetic-friendly salad and breast milk.

To be clear, the second one is for the babies, not us. Not that I've thought about trying it.

With Evelyn ready, I position her on my chest to get cozy, but my phone rings. Kendall smirks at my ringtone—*I Love It When You Call Me Big Papa.* Hey, Biggie knows what he's talking about.

When I see who's calling, my eyebrows knit together. "It's my mother."

"It's okay to answer it," Kendall says with a shrug, switching Andy to the other boob.

I try not to drool at the nip slip, but the thought of speaking to my mother is like a bucket of cold water all over my nutsack.

"Andrew." My mother's voice comes through the line in a slightly gentler tone than usual. "Your father and I are in the neighborhood. Would it be all right with you and Kendall if we stopped by?"

What the what?

I blink slowly.

I told her we had the kids, the names of the kids, and their birthday, but she hasn't made a move to meet them, and I haven't made a move to invite them. I figured I'd do it sometime.

Maybe.

If they wanted.

"They want to come over," I mouth to Kendall.

Her eyes tell me a million things.

That she's happy they've called. That it's okay for them to stop by. That she wants me to try.

"Uh, fine," I say into the phone. "I'll tell the doorman to let you in."

We hang up.

Still walking around with Evelyn, I turn to Kendall. "So, my parents aren't—well, I mean... Don't expect..."

The warmth in her expression floods me with all the feels. This is what it's like to have support. "I'm just glad they want to meet their grandkids. Most people tend to be fond of them."

It's true. When people meet the babies, they don't want to let them go. My Bumble Bee practically had them both singing songs by the time she left, and Kendall's parents come over every other day. Even Brooke, Kendall's sister, has fallen for the babies, and Ken's niece says she can't wait until they're older so she can play with them. Hard to believe we created something so small and precious.

Two somethings.

Kendall's barely finished feeding Andy and set herself to rights when my parents arrive. I answer the door with a baby in each arm and nerves in my belly.

"Hey," I say, scrutinizing their faces for an agenda.

As usual, my mom's dressed in a straight skirt, heels, and a silk blouse, my dad in slacks and a button-down shirt. Not exactly get-on-the-floor-and-play-with-babies wear.

But my mom's face breaks into a light smile and her voice lowers to an awed hush. "Are these our grandchildren?" She holds out her arms to take one. "May I?"

"Yeah, but they just ate, so it's possible they'll spit up." I hand her Evie and reach for a burp cloth.

I have to give credit to my mom. While I figured she'd hold the babies gingerly, she's not. She's a little stiff, and I can tell she doesn't want to get her clothes dirty, but the coos she's giving little Evie are those of a grandma, not those of my mother, and the hug is real.

She heads toward the couch, where Kendall is waiting, and introduces herself.

"Oh, my dear, you're beautiful," she gushes to Kendall. "Thank you for inviting us over."

My eyes widen at Kendall. *I'll tell you later*, she responds with a look.

"Congratulations, son," my father says, shaking my hand as he steps in. I shuffle Andy into the other arm. He eyes the baby. "Strong little ones you've made."

"And good-looking, too," my mom pipes up. "Evelyn and Andrew are nice names. I think Evelyn takes after you, son. And Andrew has his mother's eyes."

My parents want to start a relationship with their grandkids.

Hell has frozen over.

My dad ambles over to the couch and sits across from us.

"And you must be Kendall," he says. "It's a pleasure to finally make your acquaintance."

He emphasizes the *finally*, but his voice is less asshole than usual.

"Mr. and Mrs. Merritt. It's nice to meet you both." Kendall shakes his hand firmly, and I can see that he's impressed. But I shouldn't be surprised that he and my mother are immediately charmed by Ken.

My parents don't stay that long, but they each hold both babies and get a tour of the nursery. I can see my mom holding her tongue about some of my décor, but she's actually nice to Kendall.

I let out a breath I'd unconsciously been holding.

As they get set to leave, my mother says to KK, "If you'd like help with planning the wedding, please give me a call. I know several wonderful caterers and florists."

"That would be lovely," Kendall says graciously. "Thank you for the offer."

My mom doesn't seem to want to let the babies go, but I finally get Evie back and Kendall cuddles Andy. My dad shuttles my mom out the door, then turns and addresses me, gesturing to Kendall. "This woman is the best thing that's ever happened to you." My dad adopts the warning tone he's good at. "Don't screw it up."

I smirk. "I don't plan on it."

But I'm so grateful he sees what I see.

When they leave, I stare at the door, unsure of what just happened, but happy that it did.

"I have a confession," Kendall says, holding a yawning Andy. "I invited your parents over. I've been sending your mom photos and videos of you and the kids."

My eyebrows shoot up. "Say what now?"

While I take a million pictures and videos of the kids, I don't share them. With anyone.

Maybe I'm paranoid, but I don't want their images floating around the web. Not with my social media following.

I had to be practical, though, and needed to stave off the hangry internet. Frankly, I wanted to stop this Portland's biggest bachelor-slash-douchebag shit. So Kendall and I brainstormed, resulting in me posting exactly two non-work pictures. One of my hand threaded through Kendall's that shows her ring. I kept the caption simple: "She said yes." #ImALuckyPhucker

And the other, a snap of me wearing a #phuckifino shirt, holding an infant in each arm. You can't see the babies beyond their two tiny plaid skull caps, but you can see my grin. The caption: #MyPrideAndJoy.

Mischief managed.

Still, given all our conversations about sharing pictures, I'd never expected Kendall to be sending some to my parents.

The concern and caring on her face is genuine. "I didn't want to upset you if they didn't warm up to the idea. But you've changed, and I wanted them to see that first hand."

"That's...um... I'm stunned. They wanted to see me."

"I hope it's okay with you that I did that." She cringes a little. "I hated keeping it from you, but I thought if we could find some common ground—"

"Of course it's okay." I kiss her, overwhelmed by gratitude. I'd never in a million years expect my parents to come around like this. And it's all because of her. "Thank you."

I stare at her, wondering how I ever got so lucky.

We smile at each other as we head toward the nursery. Maybe this is a good time to see how she feels about another reunion.

"Speaking of mending fences, Ian texted me that he's going to be in town next week—"

Kendall freezes.

"I know, I know," I say, putting up my free hand in surrender. "Actually, he wants to take us out to dinner to apologize. I think he wants Fernando and those guys to come too. Everyone wants to meet you officially. They feel terrible about the last time you saw them and promise to use silverware and not pee on the sidewalk."

She laughs. A good sign.

Ian understands he's losing a testicle if he so much as looks at her sideways. Pretty sure he's planning to behave.

"I might make Ian work for it, but I'm not going to hold a grudge." Her eyes soften as she stares up at me. "I've been wanting to meet your friends. Even if they still need to be housebroken."

A smile bursts out of me. Fuck, I love her. "Yet another reason why I love you. You give people a chance to change."

"One person in particular."

"Yep. Me." I give her a kiss.

Andy's getting fussy and Evie's practically asleep. Kendall and I tiptoe to their room and settle them into their bassinets. I turn on the baby monitor.

"How are you feeling?" I ask my wife-to-be, looming over her in the hall.

She runs a finger up my chest. "I have to say, seeing my sexy fiancé handle babies like a boss gets me all hot and bothered."

"Yeah?"

The heat behind her eyes tells me she's serious. "The crooked smile helps too. And the promise of what that mouth can do," she whispers.

I lean down and kiss her hard. Not a light smooch. This kiss says, *I want you. I need you. I love you.*

I need to fuck you.

She opens her mouth, inviting in my tongue, and I take her

up on the offer. But a deep, wet kiss in the hallway makes me want to turn up the pace.

Now.

Still kissing her, I palm her ass cheeks, then hoist her up. She wraps her legs around my waist.

"I seem to remember, when I carried you through the snow up on Mount Hood, that I held you on my back," I say between kisses, as I carry her to our bedroom. "Only I wanted you facing this way. So I could see you. Kiss you. Be inside you."

"Yes," is all she says.

When we get to our bed, I lay her down gently. I'm antsy, but I gotta go slow. No reason to delay nudity, though. I tear off her sweater, and yank down her leggings and undies at the same time.

Her beautiful body greets me. All of her yoga and healthy habits during her pregnancy and after have kept her a goddess. Side effect? Because of her cooking, my glucose readings rock.

I thought she was hotness embodied before. But now? With those luscious tits and fuller hips? Fucking perfection.

I do a double-take.

"Wait. You waxed," I say. I toss my T-shirt, and catch her looking at my chest.

"I bit the bullet and made an appointment yesterday. It didn't hurt as bad as I thought it would. The fuzz drove me crazy while I was pregnant."

Running a finger along her smooth mound, I murmur, "You drive me crazy now." Who has the hottest fiancée on the planet? I do.

I kiss my way up the inside of her legs to the apex.

Leaving a love bite on her inner thigh, I get up close and personal with her freshly-groomed pussy.

It's glorious. I dart out my tongue to taste, and I groan. "Fuck,

I've been dying to do this all day." With my shoulders, I spread her legs wider for access. Her calves dangle over my arms.

As my tongue starts swirling and making broad strokes, her hips rise, and she starts to writhe.

"Nuh-uh-uh. Hold still," I order, and go back to giving all of my attention to her.

I want her to understand how much I worship her.

How I would do anything for her.

How I want her to feel good.

Everything has changed, but as we do this, it's like we're clicking back in place.

How long has it been since we've had sex?

Too fucking long.

When I slide a finger into her, she gives me a louder moan. And when I gently insert two and start stroking in a come-hither move?

Fuck. I almost jizz my pants.

"Come on my face, babe. I love when you do that. Let go."

After more licking, more stroking, more loving, more swirling, I feel her legs tense up, and her abs clench.

Then, with a delicious rush, she comes, her body shuddering and quaking, her nails scratching on the sheets.

Yes.

In no time, I shuck off the rest of my clothes and give myself a few tugs. Her eyes widen in appreciation. I settle on top of her, trying to hold my weight off of her body, but wanting skin-to-skin contact nevertheless.

Weaving my fingers through hers with one hand, and using my other to guide myself in, I enter her.

My eyes lock on hers, and I pause to make sure she's still feeling good. I don't want to rush anything if she's not up to it yet. Even though the doctor gave us the go-ahead since KK didn't have any tears and was in great shape physically, I don't think I can be too cautious.

Judging by her fingers that dig into my ass and yank me closer, we're good to go.

We have liftoff, Houston.

Flush against her, I squeeze my eyes shut. Because her pussy feels sublime wrapped around me.

"You're glorious," I mutter as I sink in deeper. "You feel so good."

Her hips rock up to meet mine, and I start thrusting. Slowly at first, then faster and faster. Her boobs shake against me, and because I really am a kinky asshole, I suck on a taut nipple until sweetness floods my mouth and then aim the base of my cock so it rubs her clit.

"Oh my God, Drew." Her back arches beneath me while she clutches me closer. "Yes."

And I hold her hand the entire time.

Because I am her man.

Her somewhat deviant, highly irreverent, always unconventional but absolutely-ass-over-head-in-love-with-her man.

As we kiss, it feels like this is where we belong. Joined to one another. Warm skin touching, breaths joining, bodies moving, hearts thumping.

What I feel for Kendall is more than sex, but with sex I renew my vows to her.

I will take care of you.

I will be there for you.

I will love you.

Always.

Even as the words rush through me, when I look into her eyes, she's saying those very things back to me.

Neither one of us lasts long. Kendall's muscles tighten again, and she comes, which sets off my orgasm. And I come so long and so hard, I wonder if she can feel it in her body.

Lacing my other hand through hers, I push myself up on my elbows and gaze down at her.

"I love you, Kendall Greer."

"I love you too, Drew Merritt."

When I roll off of her, I pull her to my side.

We lay next to each other, breathing and enjoying the intimacy of touching. My fingers journey along her arm. Hers mess with my hair. And we hold each other.

Out of nowhere, our cat comes skidding into the bedroom, fur akimbo like he's been spooked, yowls a meow, and tears off down the hall.

Typical random feline behavior.

We snicker.

"He lives up to his name. Shazam," I say, doing jazz hands, then shake my head. "What a nut." I tug KK closer and breathe in her irresistible scent. "Got any plans for Thanksgiving? It's a few months away, but I hear Mount Hood has some great holiday rentals. Maybe we can even find a place with hot water."

She bursts out laughing. "I'd love to go up there with you and the babies."

"Good thing. 'Cause I already rented the perfect place. Can't wait for you to see it. It even has electricity. And more than one bedroom."

"Sounds perfect."

A smile spreads on my face and then hers.

One that doesn't even dim when our young 'un cries a few minutes later.

Because life with Kendall—with our babies and crazy cat and so much fucking love I don't know what to do with myself?

This is perfect.

TO OUR READERS

Thank you for reading SURPRISE, BABY! If you could leave a quick review on Goodreads and the vendor where you purchased it, we'd love to hear what you thought! And be sure to check out Evie and Josh's book, ALL ABOUT THE D. You can read the first chapter on our website, www.lexandleslie.com.

ACKNOWLEDGMENTS

A huge thanks to our fabulous husbands. Without their love and support, we'd never have the time to write.

We're so grateful to Najla Qamber, our designer, and Cory Stierley, our photographer, for our beautiful cover. To RJ Locksley for editing; and Jerica MacMillian, Keri Roth, and Amanda Maria for proofreading. To Kimberly Brower, Lex's fantastic agent, for always going the extra mile for us.

Lex thanks her awesome beta readers for their insight and encouragement: Serena McDonald, Whitney Barbetti, KL Grayson, Kristi White Bivens, Amy Vox Libris, Bella Love, Becky Grover, and Elizabeth Clinton.

Hugs and ass smacks to Lex's Facebook group, Wildcats, for all of their support and book love, and extra smacks to Serena McDonald for helping Lex keep her shit together.

Leslie thanks her tireless team of Kristy Lin Billuni, Heather Roberts, Mary Carr, Katy Cuthbertson, Deb Markanton, Stacey Read, Lacey Taylor, Monica Marti, Lucy Rhodes, Erin Remaley, Phala Theng, and Julia Heudorf for support and feedback. She's also grateful for the support of her darlings in Southwinds Coffee, her Facebook group, and her patient family and friends.

Special thanks to makeup artist Leah Robledo, the daughter of Leslie's good friend Theresa Robledo, who did the makeup for our lovely models, Lela Hazary and Nate Peterson.

To all of the bloggers who've shared our posts and pimped us out, you are the best! We are so grateful for your help!

And to our readers, thanks for picking up our books! We hope you enjoyed Drew and Kendall's story as much as we enjoyed writing it.

Licks and kisses,
Lex & Leslie

ALL ABOUT THE D SYNOPSIS

Temptation has never come in a hotter package.

You know how people say you can never believe what you read on the interwebs? That a hot guy online is probably a creeper with a beer gut and a shoe fetish, not the sexy beast he pretends to be?

So I had no clue that the anonymous blogger who contacted my law firm about his naughty website would be droolworthy in real life. Not that I'm interested in him in that way.

Attorneys can't go around sleeping with their clients. Not even if he is the most beautiful man I've ever met and so ridiculously smart he makes my nerdy-girl heart sigh.

Besides, he has too much on the line to risk taking a chance on the insane chemistry building between us. We both do.

I've always followed the rules. Too bad he makes me want to break each and every one of them.

∾

All About the D is a romantic comedy and a full-length stand-alone. Head over to our website, www.lexandleslie.com, if you'd like to read the first chapter.

OTHER BOOKS BY LEX MARTIN

Dark Texas Nights Series

Shameless (USA Today bestseller)
Harley-riding tattoo artist Brady Shepherd isn't at all prepared to inherit a lavender farm or a baby. So he turns to a family friend, the sexy-nerdy babysitter Kat, for help. She can't resist falling for the handsome brooder, except he's supposed to sell the farm and move back to Boston. Will he break her heart or can she convince him to stay in Texas?

Reckless (USA Today bestseller)
The last thing Ethan Carter needs is a hot nanny strutting around his ranch while he deals with a hellish divorce. His priorities are his kids and business, not the little vixen sleeping across the hall. Tori Duran is the one woman he can't have and shouldn't want, no matter how much he craves her.

The Dearest Series

Dearest Clementine (bestselling romantic comedy)
When Clementine Avery swore off men, she had no idea she'd need real life experience for that romance writing class she accidentally signed up for last spring. Fortunately, sexy RA Gavin Murphy offers to help her find a little inspiration... in the name of academics, of course.

Finding Dandelion (#1 sports fiction and bestselling sports romance)

Hooking up with that hot guy at the club should've been an easy item to check off Dani Hart's bucket list. But when Dani realizes the hottie is her snarky new roommate's brother, what should've been uncomplicated suddenly isn't.

Kissing Madeline (#1 sports fiction and bestselling sports romance)

Maddie McDermott is confident no one will stand in her way of becoming a broadcast reporter, not even the subject of her new segments—her hot new neighbor Daren Sloan, the NFL's latest "it boy." Daren doesn't seem to care that Maddie can't stand him. In fact, he'd love nothing more than to show her that being friends has its benefits.

OTHER BOOKS BY LESLIE MCADAM

The Giving You Series

The Sun and the Moon (A 2015 Watty winner, featured in Cosmopolitan.com)

After a heartbreaking tragedy, successful attorney Amelia Crowley has numbed herself to the pleasures of life, clinging to a specific set of rules, finding strength in order and organization. When she meets easy going surfer Ryan Fielding, that organized life is turned upside down by a sea of washboard abs and sun-kissed hair. Sexy and charismatic, Ryan looks for pleasure however he can find it in an effort to silence his own inner demons. Until Amelia crashed into his life the only thing he chased. Can Amelia let Ryan take the lead or will she cling to her rules and wipe out their chance at love?

The Stars in the Sky (#1 in Western Erotic Romance and a bestseller)

When foul-mouthed, tattooed, vegan Marie Diaz-Austin accepted a summer internship on a ranch north of Santa Barbara to work with underprivileged and special needs kids she was expecting hard work. She wasn't expecting the gorgeous, but conservative rancher, Will Thrash who wants nothing to do with left-wing hippies like her. Although they hate each other's politics, they can't deny their immediate and growing attraction to each other. But when they're forced to make a choice, what will give? Their principles or themselves?

All the Waters of the Earth (International bestseller)

Romance novelist Lucy Figueroa lives a life of the imagination. While her stories are filled with fictional alpha male heroes, her real life is filled with nothing but Mr. Wrongs. Lucy's sexy new neighbor, Jake Slausen, looks like one of her characters come to life. While he fits the heartthrob part, he doesn't act it, too distracted by his cell phone and his job for any relationship. First drawn together by chemistry, then by a fierce need to protect each other even from themselves, will Jake and Lucy learn to accept their pasts or will they convince themselves that happily ever afters only exist in romance novels?

The Ground Beneath Our Feet

Jessica, a curvy, driven, neat freak lawyer, is ecstatic when she finally gets her dream job—even though it's taking her away from her hometown. When she meets over-the-top, man-mountain Mikey, a fitness buff and veterinarian with a messy life in all senses of the word, she thinks she just walked into the second-most exciting adventure of her life. If they give into their undeniable attraction, is it just a train wreck waiting to happen? Or will their desire fuel a chance at real love?

Love In Translation Series

Sol

After a stolen kiss, Trent left his best friend's sister to join the army. Now he must deliver heartbreaking news to Dani, a teacher in Spain. Once the truth is out, will she be able to forgive him?

Sombra

Kim steps off the plane in Madrid and meets Tavo, with his warm eyes, crooked smile, and devastating charm. Worse, he's courteous. Honorable. Sensuous. Impossibly attractive. Tavo awakens her desires—her body—without even touching it. But she doesn't want to be attracted to him. She's made her promises, and her future has already been determined. After all, she's wearing someone else's ring.

Standalone novella

Lumbersexual (winner, Ist place in Romance, Summer Indie Book Awards 2016)

Maggie Washington has always been the fling or the friend. Court Thompson is a gorgeous (and bearded) forest ranger with a love-em and leave-em reputation. When he shows interest in her, she's torn. Even though she's flattered by his attention, she doubts his sincerity—and her ability to get out of the friend-zone. Will Court be able to coax Maggie into trusting him that he's for real? Or after a summer of s'mores and skinny dipping, will he let her down like everybody else?

STAY IN TOUCH!

We love hearing from readers!
The best way to stay in touch with us is to subscribe to our newsletters, which you can do if you stop by our website.
Email: info@lexandleslie.com
Website: www.lexandleslie.com

Stalk Lex:
Email: lex@lexmartinwrites.com
Website: www.lexmartinwrites.com
Facebook Group: Lex Martin's Wildcats
Facebook | Instagram | Twitter | Goodreads
BookBub | Book + Main

Stalk Leslie:
Email: info@lesliemcadamauthor.com
Website: www.lesliemcadamauthor.com
Facebook Group: Southwinds Coffee
Facebook | Instagram | Twitter | Goodreads
BookBub | Book + Main